"I should go," Addy said, not moving an inch.

He ran a finger along her jaw. "You should stay."

"I don't want to ha—"

"—have sex with you, Cade," he finished for her. She smiled, but it wouldn't hold. "I mean it. There's more to tell, and sex will make things . . . messy."

"Sex does that all right." Cade touched her crazy ragged hair. Amazingly soft. Then he reached behind her to turn off the lamp beside the chair. The room went into half light, some of it slanting through the open door of the bedroom. "I still think you should stay." He ran a finger around the curve of her ear. "First, because you have a story to finish, and second, because I don't want you to go."

The second reason was the critical one, the truest one, the one that would, in the end, cause the most trouble.

He took her hand, led her to his bedroom.

Novels by E.C. Sheedy

PERFECT EVIL

ROOM 33

Novella by E.C. Sheedy

"PURE GINGER" in
BAD BOYS NEXT EXIT

KILLING BLISS

E.C. Sheedy

ZEBRA BOOKS
KENSINGTON PUBLISHING CORP.

ZEBRA BOOKS are published by

Kensington Publishing Corp.
850 Third Avenue
New York, NY 10022

ISBN 0-7394-4845-5

Printed in the United States of America

For Tim . . . always.
Not a word would be written without him.

For my Red Door friends. You know who you are . . .
Not a word would be sent in without them.

Chapter 1

The tall, Hollywood-handsome man stuffed his SCI-Smithfield Prison T-shirt into the overflowing washroom garbage can and shrugged into a new checkered shirt. Not first-class, but it would do. For now.

He walked into a stall, locked the door behind him, and took his first private piss in seven years. When he was back in his jeans, he stepped out of the stall, washed his hands, and studied himself in the cracked mirror over the sink.

Looking good, looking damn good! He lifted his chin, ran a hand over the double shave he'd given himself this morning before they rolled him out.

The first thing I'm gonna do is find myself a nice, soft bed with a not-so-nice, even softer woman lying in it—with her legs open.

He forked his fingers through his dark blond hair and slicked it back, Valentino-style, then turned his head from side to side for one final check.

And that's all you'll have to do, sweet cheeks, just lie there, because Frankie boy will take it from there. Be the quickest fuck and the easiest buck you ever did see.

He picked up his duffel bag and rummaged through it for the aftershave he'd bought in the bus station gift shop. Figured he'd give himself another shot. His fingers closed around his envelope, and he pulled it out. There wasn't an ex-con from here to California who didn't leave the pen carrying a goddamn manila envelope, the official walking papers. According to his dumb-ass counselor, over sixty percent of them walked back in within three years.

Dumb fucks!

Shaking his head, he tore the envelope in half, then quarters, and crammed it in the garbage along with the T-shirt.

Where he was going, he wouldn't need either one.

Because after he'd dried out the first whore, he knew where to find the second one.

Three years he'd waited, three miserable years he'd tracked the bitch.

His nerves jumped at the thought of her. Crazy kid back then, tight as hell . . . *Oh, yeah.*

He splashed on the musky scent, then, smiling into the mirror, he checked his straight teeth. Liking what he saw, he lifted his chin again to admire its cleft, then adjusted his cock more comfortably in his jeans.

Seven years in the Smithfield prison gym had given him rock-hard biceps and a six-pack gut—the best body he'd had in years.

Hell, maybe Miss Hot-Stuff herself would *come,* explode under him like a goddamn bomb. He straightened his collar.

And if she didn't? Who the hell cared?

He walked out of the washroom whistling. One good thing about prison, with a few bucks and a couple of solid connections, you could find out anything about anybody. Put the Internet to shame.

He was a free man with information, and for the first time in his life, he had a plan.

He knew what he wanted—and he knew who was going to give it to him.

And he knew exactly what he'd do to her to get it.

Addy Michaels shoveled the last of the topsoil into the wheelbarrow and straightened to backhand wipe the sweat from her forehead, adding more grime to the smear she'd made earlier.

The final load after a long day.

When the soil was spread and raked, and after she did some paperwork—she groaned inwardly—she'd head for the lake and have a swim. This great weather wouldn't last forever, and she planned to enjoy every minute of it. If she got in before the tall cedars at the far end of the lake blocked the sun's rays, she'd be swimming in golden water. Star Lake might be more giant pond than lake, but the water was as sweet as a mountain spring—and right now darn near as cold.

She went to work. Spreading the topsoil loosely, she formed the base of the flower bed around Cabin Four. A half hour later, she stretched, hitched up the straps on her overalls, and headed for the motel office that sat on the top of a gentle slope near the entrance to the property.

She'd plant the tulip bulbs sometime in the next couple of days.

"Hi, Addy," Toby called from the doorstep of Cabin Three. "Warm one today, huh?"

"Uh-huh. Some kind of record for this time of year, according to the weather guy."

"Late October, and it still feels like summer," he said, shaking his gray head.

Addy nodded, smiled, and dropped the thread of her and Toby's daily weather conversation.

Toby was a regular, a crony of Lund's who came every year in the fall for a month, and had ever since Addy arrived. Her guess was he and Lund shared a past of the criminal kind, but she never asked. The way she saw it, you ask a question, someone asked one right back.

"I have some iced tea in the fridge, Toby," she said. "How about I give you a call when I've cleaned up, and you can come up to the house and have some?"

"That'd be dandy, sweetums." Toby smiled.

She waved at him, opened the office door, and stepped inside. As she lifted the hinged section of the counter separating what Lund always called the "back office" from reception, she glanced at the pile of mail sitting at the far end of the counter and grimaced. So far, she'd done a fine job of ignoring it, which would be a whole lot easier if the motel office didn't form the front of her house.

Her house. Her motel. Her lake.

Her life was so perfect, she owed whoever was in charge up there a thank-you note and giant box of chocolates.

It had been six months now, and Addy still couldn't believe the Star Lake Resort was hers, all hers. Maybe she had almost paid it off before Lund passed on, and for sure all the years of work without pay had to count for something, but in her wildest dreams she hadn't expected him to forgive the balance in his will and deed the place to her. Likely he figured he had to do something, and she'd been handy—like that ancient wheelbarrow of his she'd stowed in the maintenance shed minutes ago.

She smiled now, thinking about him, how he'd hated it when she poked at his delusions of grandeur by calling the place a motel.

"It's a resort, girl," he'd growl. "Can't you get that through your mule-stubborn head?" Cranky as usual.

"Resort, my skinny butt, Lund Baylor," she'd say. "It's a crappy old motel on a pockmarked bypass road, and you darn well know it." Then she'd watch him mutter and stomp off to tackle some project he'd been fussing over for years and never finished. Never would finish.

He may have been cranky and as chilly as an Alaskan sleigh ride, but darned if he hadn't come through in the end and done the right thing. For that she'd be forever grateful.

Star Lake was all hers.

She took off her dirty sneakers and sport socks on the tile she'd installed inside the house door and walked barefoot across her new carpet. Pale pecan, the saleswoman called it. Addy called it builder's beige, but whatever color it was, it didn't matter. It was fresh, it was new, it was her choice, and when she walked on it, she felt as if she were a princess walking on mink. Before she left the carpet's soft nap for the scarred hardwood floor of her bedroom, she wiggled her toes in it and rolled her head to ease the tension in her neck in a most unprincess-like way.

Another six months, if business stayed okay, she'd have this place looking like the resort Lund Baylor claimed it was. She'd already spruced up the office and some of the cabins, and if the new sign she'd put up on Kite Road near the highway brought in more business—maybe some of the skiers heading for Mount Baker—she'd soon have the money she needed. Then all it would take was hard work, and she was no stranger to that.

A few minutes later, she stepped into the shower. She soaped herself, quickly shampooed, then let the water course over her back and between her sweaty breasts. Heaven!

Out of the shower, she toweled off and dragged a comb through her short brown hair, glad she'd taken the time to lop more of it off yesterday. A bit ragged maybe, but it was easy, and she sure as heck didn't have the time to fuss with it. There was that mess of paperwork to do. Then some accounting.

Her stomach seized up, always did when she had a problem and not a solution in sight.

She went to her bureau, opened a drawer, and rifled for some underwear. What she found was a thought.

Toby could lend a hand!

He used to help Lund, she remembered. She brightened. Maybe he'd do the books the whole month he was here, and she'd give him a break on his cabin rate.

The knot slipped loose in her stomach, and she hastily finished dressing, donning clean jeans and a yellow T-shirt.

With the idea of Toby doing the book work afloat in her mind, it was as if the New York Public Library had been hoisted off her back. Hungry, she went into the kitchen, planning to eat a horse— or maybe a small herd of them.

She studied the packaged dinner she pulled from the freezer. What the hell was a Salisbury steak, anyway? Didn't matter. It was edible, and it was fast. She tossed it in the microwave.

With dinner in progress, she walked to the kitchen window. Across the lake, the autumn sun was settling contentedly into evening, its brilliance turning the placid lake a deep sapphire, the gold yet to come.

It was too beautiful.

Life was beautiful . . .

Addy Michaels had been given more than she deserved. Her eyes watered, and she brushed at them with the back of her hands and smiled.

She always was a sap for sunsets.

It didn't get any better than this—the sun going down all lazy and slow, the spicy smell of cedar and freshly cut grass drifting in with the breezy evening air.

Star Lake. Her world, her safe harbor . . .

Addy's heart fluttered, then expanded to fill her chest with ease and gratitude.

So much more than she deserved . . .

If she had one wish, it would be to hold this feeling in her heart forever.

Chapter 2

Cade Harding pulled his Cherokee to a stop, looked out the driver's side window, then up. Way up.

Susan Moore's house, with its three stories and expansive footprint, was massive.

Odd, though, it had seemed larger still when he'd come here as a boy. But then, when you're a kid, everything is on a grand scale—houses, monsters . . . passions.

He let his truck idle, and one memory surged back, made him wince—his mother towing him along to visit his Aunt Susan, the woman she privately referred to as her "rich-bitch cousin," her hand out for yet another "small loan." "Begging trips" he'd come to call them, until he'd put his sneaker-clad, ten-year-old foot down and refused to go.

He'd loved his mother, but she hadn't made it easy.

been dead fifteen months. *Plus one week and two days.* About as long as it took her to die. The cancer took its time and its loathsome measure of pain.

Susan reached across the sofa between them, touched his shoulder. "I wanted to attend the service, but I was out of the country at the time. I regret that."

"I understand. Not a problem." He shifted his position on the sofa, rested an ankle on his knee, and laid a hand on it. He hated, but was accustomed to, these awkward moments.

"You don't like to talk about it." She nodded. "God knows I understand . . . grief. I was just trying to find a—"

"She was trying to find a place to start." Stan reentered the sunroom, carrying a full tray. "The woman's having trouble getting to the point." He set the tray down, moved a couple of the rosebushes out of the way, and poured three strong coffees before taking a seat opposite them.

"And you're a lot more than her gofer." Cade took a coffee, eased back in his seat. Stan Brenton provided a welcome detour around further talk about Dana.

Stan pulled out his wallet, flipped it open, and passed it to Cade.

"A private investigator. The plot thickens," Cade said, returning his wallet.

Stan shoved it back in his pocket, shot Susan an encouraging look. "Just ask, dear. All he can do is say no."

"That's what I'm afraid of."

"Susan." A hint of admonishment colored his tone.

She let out a breath. "Cade, I assume your mother told you what happened to Mariah, my daughter?"

"Yes." He didn't repeat the details, or his sense that his mother had somehow relished the tragedy as some kind of overdue bad luck for the cousin she envied so much. "I was in college at the time." His memories of Mariah were sketchy at best. He'd met her during the begging trips, of course, but her being older—and cooler—required that she treat him as a lower life-form.

"It was a drug overdose. She was twenty-five." She met his gaze and, although the tragedy was long past, it bloomed in her eyes—a drug-death memory, dripping in residual pain.

"I'm sorry, Susan." The standard words. How often he'd heard them. So little to appease so much, but all there was.

"Yes." She looked away as if to gather up her lost poise, then added, "So long ago, yet it feels like yesterday."

Cade thought of Dana, his thinking going gray. He said nothing.

"Mariah and I were . . . estranged when she died," Susan went on. "She'd been gone, out of touch, for years." She rose from her seat, walked around the table of delicate roses, and stood beside a tall bench hosting a dozen orchids. Leaning against it, she looked down at him. "I tried to help her, but when she kept going back to the drugs, I . . . let her go. Which I will regret forever." She closed her eyes briefly. When she looked at him again, her face was etched with sadness and regret. "I quit on her. I gave up too soon."

He shifted on the sofa, uncomfortable. If she

was waiting for a reply, either of castigation or dis-approval, he sure as hell wasn't the one to give it.

"Odd, isn't it? How it's the things you don't do in life, the sins of omission, that bring the most re-gret, the most pain."

Cade wasn't sure he agreed, but he hadn't come here to debate what kind of sin did the most dam-age. Hell, he didn't know why he'd come.

Susan, who'd gone silent for a time, seemed to force herself out of her painful reverie. "No mat-ter. My mistake is irrevocable. I have to live with it, but I don't have to repeat it. All that matters now is finding my lost grandson. His name is Josh. Or so I was told."

Cade had his coffee cup close to his mouth. He set it down. "Grandson?" This was news to him.

"If I may?" Stan said, looking at Susan.

"Yes, Stan, please." She looked relieved. "I'm sure Cade will appreciate a more orderly presenta-tion of the facts."

Stan fixed pale gray eyes on him. "Mariah had a son some months before she died. Father unknown. She never told her mother she was pregnant, nor did she inform her of his birth. I've confirmed she was clean when she had him and for a time after he was born. She went back on drugs when the man she was living with—not the father of the child—took off." He glanced at Susan, his eyes question-ing.

"Go on," she said. "Tell him. All of it."

He didn't look as if he relished the task. "Mariah was squatting in a condemned building when she overdosed. She was dead two or three days before they found her. Josh was a toddler, sixteen months old. He was . . ." He shifted in his seat. "Let's say the boy was lucky to be alive."

Cade got the picture.

Stan went on. "With no one to contact, the state scooped him up, gave him what medical attention he needed, then put him into an interim care foster home. It took over two weeks before they linked Mariah to Susan."

"And?" Cade urged.

"It was too late." He paused. "Josh disappeared from the foster home within hours of being placed there."

Cade looked at Susan, then at Stan. "Disappeared?"

"The boy was taken to the home in the afternoon. Two o'clock, according to the social worker's records. There were three other foster kids there at the time. A boy and two girls. Ages ranging from thirteen to seventeen.

"That same night, the foster mother, a Mrs. Belle Bliss, was murdered. Four bullets in the head. She was not, by all accounts, an attractive corpse. By the time the police arrived, the house was empty except for one of Belle's sons, Frank. He had called the police. Her other son, Brett, was staying the night at a friend's place. All of which checked out. Frank's statement named the three foster kids as responsible for the murder. He said the boy pulled the trigger while the girls stood by, egging him on."

"The gun?"

"Never found."

"And the kids?"

"As gone as they could get. Probably disappeared into the streets. Pretty easy for kids, then and now. Especially ones as savvy as those three."

"And the child? What did Bliss say about him?"

"Nothing. Said after they shot his mother, they turned the gun on him, and when it didn't fire— out of bullets, I guess—they jumped him, beat the crap out of him, and knocked him cold. When he woke up, the boy was gone."

Susan spoke up. "The police did look for Josh, but after a few months, with nothing turning up to keep them going . . ." She lifted a shoulder, dropped it. "They said one possibility was that the kids had taken him—for God knows what reason—then, when he became too much trouble, abandoned him."

"There are other possibilities, Susan," Cade said, careful to keep his tone mild.

"That they killed him? Disposed of the body?" Her words were hurried, and she glanced away for a moment. When she turned back, her face was tight. "Possible, yes. But possibilities prove nothing. I need to *know*."

Cade saw it then, in the depths of her eyes, the same look he'd seen so often in Dana's, unyielding and impermeable: the light of hope, the endless, lingering hope that rushed to fill the void after a disappearance. While no one longed for a funeral, he'd come to believe it infinitely preferable to its alternative, living with the ache of never knowing whether the one you loved—or hoped to love— would be in your arms again. Hope had failed Dana; it would probably fail Susan Moore.

"And you want me to find him, or at least find out what happened," Cade said, figuring it was time to cut to the chase.

"Yes, that's exactly what I want."

Cade drained the last of his coffee, cold now, like the leads in this case. Colder yet was his desire to begin a fruitless search for another missing child, risk another failure.

"I'm sorry." He stood. "I can't help you. Besides," he gestured to Stan, "it looks as if you already have the best man for the job." His skeptical side knew there was a chance Stan had been freeloading off Susan's guilt and grief these many years, but watching him with her, his gut told him no. "If he's come up empty, I'd probably do the same."

Stan rose, towered over him, giving him that weird small-man feeling he'd experienced earlier. "I've been on this case for what seems like forever, Harding. Took over after the third guy Susan hired got himself hit by a truck—and, yes, you can take that literally," he said, lifting a believe-it-or-not brow. "Since then, I've run down more blind alleys than I can count. Only one good thing has come out of it." He nodded at Susan. "Meeting this fine lady. But I'm tapped out. Plus, Susan thinks it's time for a different approach, and she believes you're it. You being into all that, uh, psychological stuff."

Cade knew he meant criminal profiling, the cross between art and science with the dubious reputation. Airy-fairy crap, his first sergeant called it. Maybe so, but it had taken him eight years to get that stuff in his head, and an equal number putting it in the heads of hundreds of listless students.

Stan added, "Susie here, she wants one last kick at the can, before she calls it quits. Me? I want what she wants." Stan gave him a hard stare, intimating he should feel the same way.

He didn't. He wanted to be left alone. He had a house in Pullman to move out of and a condo in downtown Seattle to move into. He had a new life to get started on.

A life without Dana . . .

"I'm a teacher, not a cop, Brenton," he said. "Definitely on the sidelines. There's a thousand guys with better qualifications."

Stan pulled out his wallet again, withdrew a folded piece of paper. "Professor of Criminalistics, specializing in juvenile behavior. Two-year sabbatical to work hands-on with Seattle problem youth at request of the mayor's office. Chair, federal committee on youth crime. Successful negotiator in high-profile kidnapping case involving missing teen—"

"You did your homework," Cade said.

"Some."

"All that was a while back." And the successes paled when compared to his singular, very personal, failure.

"And you were a cop. For three years." Stan put the paper he'd been citing back in his wallet, his hands on his hips. "Susan's asking you to take a look, give an opinion. That's all."

Cade looked at the two aging lovers—and he'd decided they were definitely lovers. Susan's eyes were wide, expectant. Stan's were judgmental and pissed off.

Cade turned to Susan, genuinely puzzled. "Why now?" he asked. "After all these years, why ask me now?"

"Mainly because I didn't know, until your mother's funeral, that you *could* help. It was your wife who told me what you did, how successful you were. She was very proud of you, you know." She paused. "As for your mother? Whenever I asked about you, she said very little, other than you'd 'taken off' and left her alone, just like your father."

Cade might have protested, except for the glint of understanding in Susan's eyes, an understanding that no doubt came from years of lending her cousin money. He didn't bother defending himself, say how he'd kept in touch with his mother until she died and sent a regular monthly check. His business.

"That it?" he asked, wanting to end the conversation.

"No. The big reason is Frank Bliss is being paroled after serving seven years for manslaughter."

Stan interjected. "Go back a bit, Susie."

She pursed her lips. "A few months after the murder, I met with Frank Bliss. I'd hoped to learn something the police hadn't—stupid, I know—but . . ." She took a few steps, then turned back to face him, her expression defiant. "Ever since, I've felt that boy knew more than he'd told."

"You 'felt'?" Even though Cade's career centered on building a whole loaf from discarded chaff, he'd learned to distrust the *I felt* phrase—so often too close to its sister phrase, *I wish*, to be worthwhile.

"I figured you'd glom on to that word, but regardless, I'll stand by it. Frank Bliss was either lying or not telling everything he knew."

"If you consider his mother was brutally murdered—literally before his eyes—why would he lie? What do you think he'd gain from it?"

"I have no idea," she said. "But ever since the murder, Frank Bliss has been in jail more than he's been out. I suspect he lies for all kinds of reasons."

"And his brother?"

Stan answered. "Dead. Knifed in an alley after a fight in some club. About three years after the murder."

"Unlucky family," Cade said. "A good psychologist might say it was his mother's murder that turned Frank bad in the first place."

"He'd be wrong," Susan said, "because Frank didn't like his mother."

"He told you that?"

"He didn't have to. It was in his face, in his eyes. I think he was happy she was dead."

"Even if you're right, it still doesn't prove—"

She stopped him with a raised hand, her eyes coal hard and direct. "If he didn't care about his mother, he certainly wouldn't care about a sixteen-month-old baby. Whatever his reasons, I think he lied." She waved her hand in a frustrated action, her voice rose. "Maybe he killed his mother, maybe the lies were to protect himself, or his kid brother—"

"That's a lot of maybes, Susan." Cade said quietly. "Besides, you said the police checked Brett's alibi."

"They could be wrong. It wouldn't be the first time."

The room went quiet, and Stan arched a brow and looked at Cade, his expression bordering on sympathetic. "Susie hasn't let this case go since she found out about Josh. She's not about to stop now," he said.

Maybe not, but Cade knew they'd stepped hip

deep into the realm of conjecture and wishful thinking on a murder that occurred fifteen years ago. "It's a waste of time. Mine and yours," Cade said. He hadn't left WSU to get mired in someone else's problem, someone else's grief—or to work a case with a serious case of freezer burn. He'd walked this walk before. Swampland in a fog. "I'm sorry," he said again, more firmly this time. "I can't help you."

Again the room fell to silence, broken finally by Susan's heavy sigh.

"I didn't want to do this," she said. "But you leave me no choice." She met his eyes, her gaze unwavering. "You do this for me, Cade, and I'll forget what your mother owed me, which over the years came to over sixty-five thousand dollars."

She might as well have hit him in the gut with a two-by-four. His breath swooshed out, then he shook his head, muttered, "Son-of-a-bitch."

"No," Susan stated in a clear, measured tone. "I'm the mother of a dead daughter who's missing her grandson. Sons-of-bitches don't even come close."

Chapter 3

Cade plumped the pillow behind his head and settled his gaze on the ceiling. The house was a minefield of boxes, some for the movers, some for the local thrift shop, and some for the trash. Most for the trash.

The thrift shop cartons were his killing field. Dana's things.

She'd been gone for months, but her clothes, hanging in the closet, still carried her scent. Dust grayed the garment shoulders like cremation ash. He'd let it lie, breathing it in as he crammed everything she'd owned into cardboard boxes, scrawling "THRIFT" across them with a harsh felt pen.

He wanted them gone.

He wanted her back.

He put a forearm over his eyes to shut out the early sun blasting through the window, but it wasn't the sun making his eyes water.

Redge wandered in and nuzzled his other hand,

the one hanging corpselike off the edge of the bed. When Redge licked his palm and whimpered, Cade turned on his side to look at him.

"Life's a bitch, Redgie boy. For the last month or so, I've been making it. There were at least a couple of hours a day when I didn't think of her. But now"—he waved at the boxes—"I feel like . . . Hell, I don't know what I feel like."

He closed his eyes against the goddamn tears. Who the hell said men don't cry? After Dana died, he'd wept an ocean, and here he was starting all over again.

Shit!

Redge whimpered again, and Cade swung his feet to the floor, sitting a moment on the edge of the bed before getting to his feet.

"Come on, boy, you can give me a hand with these boxes. The truck will be here in an hour, and Dana would hate it if we weren't ready for it." He smiled and roughed up the dog's neck, his reward a wildly wagging tail.

"That's the spirit." He hefted the first box. "And when this is done, we'll head for Seattle, settle in to the new place. Get started on that new life I've been promising you."

But first I have a debt to pay and a missing boy to track down. Everything's changed and nothing has changed.

By eight that night, Cade's condo possessed a semblance of order, and he and Redge were on their new deck looking down into the bustle of Seattle's crowded streets, Cade with a cold beer in his hand, Redge with a bone the size of a brick between his teeth.

"So, what do you think?" Cade asked Redge, gesturing with his beer to the city skyline. "This acceptable?"

Redge glanced up from his bone and offered up two tail thumps. Cade took it as a yes.

He turned from the view and walked the few steps to his new desk. Over the next couple of years, what he did at this desk would make or break him. The advance on his first book wasn't the greatest, but with that, some okay royalties, and his savings, he had enough to live on for at least two years.

After that it was up to Zero, his crime-fighting street kid, to put food on the table.

He couldn't wait to start making it happen. What with closing out the house, organizing the last of his classes and files, he hadn't written a word in weeks.

A stack of paper sat on his desk—notes, manila folders with elastic bands around them, and a box of newspaper clippings. Stan Brenton was nothing if not thorough.

He took a swig of beer and frowned.

Damn it, he resented the hell out of having to deal with Susan's problem, but as she'd not hesitated to point out, he owed her. Or his mother owed her. Same difference. And no doubt that sixty-five grand had put more than one slice of bread on his table through the years.

Yeah, he owed her, all right. Another swig of beer and he sat down, shuffled the mess on his desk.

He'd planned to begin with Bliss himself, get a

firsthand account of what happened that night, but according to his parole officer, the guy was already AWOL. He'd been released from the State Correctional Institute at Smithfield in Pennsylvania just days ago, but chances were he was already out of the state.

Cade needed a new place to start.

He opened one of the files Stan had given him to the first page and ran his index finger down the list of names, the key players in the long-past tragedy.

Gus Vanelleto, seventeen, the boy Bliss accused of shooting his mother.

Dianna Lintz, sixteen, aka "Beauty," the daughter of a south Seattle prostitute who'd been running with Vanelleto for over a year before the murder.

Addilene Wartenski, aka "the Wart," a thirteen-year-old runaway. Mother dead, father unknown.

God only knew what names they were using now.

Under the heading "Department of Social and Health Services (DSHS)," he stopped his finger on the name Wayne Grover, the social worker of record at the time for the three foster kids in the house that night—and the guy who'd placed Josh there the day of the murders.

He read Stan's notes on Grover: "Very cooperative. Still feels responsible for what happened to Josh. Still checks in with Susan regularly. Only on the job a couple of years or so before this happened. Helpful guy. Will give you a good overview."

"Okay, Grover," he muttered. "You've drawn the lucky number."

* * *

Frank Bliss walked out of the classy San Francisco menswear store a new man. Hugo Boss did that for a guy, and it helped that his waist was two inches smaller than when he went into the joint.

He settled his Ray-Bans and lifted his face to the late morning sun. Not too hot, but seriously bright. Man, he loved California. When this shit was over, he might settle down here.

Spotting a phone booth, he headed for it, then pulled a piece of paper from his jacket pocket. It hadn't taken more than ten minutes to get this number. Now, if she'd oblige by being home, he'd get things started. Couldn't wait.

He dialed.

"Hello."

The voice was low and velvety, exactly as he remembered. His heart raced at the sound of it and damned if his mouth wasn't dry. "Is this Fallon West?"

"Yes."

"My name is Ches McQuade. I'm in town for the next few days, and if you have some time available, I'd like to meet you."

"Meet me, Mr. McQuade?" There was a smile in her voice. "Now why would you want to do that?"

Her low tone and the hint of a tease rumbled around his groin and stiffened his cock. "Because I've heard you're beautiful, you keep good company, and I need an . . . escort. For a couple of days." He was pleased with his cool. Hell, he was as good as he ever was. And what hooker would turn down a two-day gig?

"And you think it's that easy?"

"No." He lowered his voice, enjoying himself. "From what I'm told, there's nothing easy about you. Which is why I'm intrigued."

She laughed. "Good answer," she said then added, "Are you local, Mr. McQuade?"

"No, I'm here on business, from Pennsylvania. And it's Ches. Short for Cheswin. As you can guess, my mother didn't like me very much." Which was the first truth out of his mouth.

She laughed again, smooth as silk panties. "I take it you have references?"

"I do. When can we meet to make the necessary arrangements?"

He heard paper rustle. "Where are you staying?"

"The Calista." He was shooting the last of his wad doing it, but a guy had to make the right impression.

"Very nice. It has a wonderful bar. How about tomorrow? Say six-thirty?"

Damn, he'd hoped for tonight. He choked back his irritation, his impatience. "Perfect. I'll look forward to it."

"And, Ches"—her tone firmed up, all business now—"be prepared to talk about those references of yours. I'm a cautious woman."

Not cautious enough, Beauty, baby. He grinned and hung up.

Fallon West clicked off the phone, tapped a scarlet-tipped fingernail on the display screen of the pearl-gray receiver, and glanced at the clock. Almost noon. Indecision—and unexpected guilt—

rattled around in her blond head and collided with a growing clump of pure fear.

The fear had nothing to do with the jerk she'd just spoken to. Nothing to fear there except the depressing truth that business was booming, which meant an unending supply of men with needy dipsticks on the other end of her phone.

No, the fear was wrapped around Burke Holland—the very rich Burke Holland. He should have called by now. Two days it had been since she heard from him. Two days!

She told herself not to panic.

He hadn't called, so it was business as usual, and that meant Ches McQuade, but not tonight. Tonight was her night off. Nothing changed that. All she'd do for Ches was decide what to wear.

She headed for her closet, scanned the over-full but orderly racks without enthusiasm. The thought of having to stroke another paying customer's bloated ego for two freakin' days made her bones ache with weariness. She hoped he was at least decent to look at and not some tired old paper-clip salesman from Podunk, and he'd sure as hell better make it worth her while.

If Burke had called, she'd have blown this Pennsylvania john off without a thought.

The sick truth was, if Burke didn't come through with the marriage proposal, she'd be servicing fuck-jocks into the next millennium.

She thought about calling him, but knew it would be a mistake, a sign of anxiety, and she'd slit her wrists before she admitted to desperation.

Burke Holland, age sixty-nine, rich as goddamn Croesus—whoever the hell he was—was her gold-plated passport out of The Trade. She was thirty-one and she'd seen enough dicks at full attention to last her lifetime.

One thing was certain, if good old Burke did come through on the marriage deal he'd been hinting at—for damn near four years now—her first act as a bride would be to dump his goddamn Viagra down the toilet.

One night of bliss to cement the relationship was all he'd get from her.

In the meantime, it was back to business and deciding what to wear for Ches Whoever from Pennsylvania. She rifled the white section of her closet.

"Hey, missy."

Beauty turned, hanger in hand. "Hey, Lisa, what's happening?" She opened a lingerie drawer, poked around. "I hope I didn't leave too much of a mess for you."

"You always leave a mess." The young girl chided with a smile, showing a broken tooth, a gift from her pimp.

Lisa was sixteen and the best in a string of girls Beauty had taken in over the past few years. Beauty liked having her around and, temporarily at least, off the street. Lisa was talking about going back to school, and Beauty was toying with the idea of helping her, making their living arrangement permanent.

No one knew better than Beauty what happened to girls taken in by sadistic jerks who used them as walking profit centers. She was no do-gooder, but it didn't cost her much to give the girls a break—a few bucks earned standing on their feet instead of lying on their backs—and she welcomed the help. Other than with her working clothes—those she organized with the precision of a SWAT team leader—she was a born slob, a fact Lisa reminded her of regularly.

"A call came for you this morning when you were getting your hair done," Lisa said.

Beauty stopped the lingerie search and looked at her. "You didn't tell me."

"You weren't here to tell, and I had a counselor meeting, so I left the message on the hall table." She held out a yellow sticky note and made a tight face. "Are you mad?"

"You know I don't get mad." She took the note, smiled away her nerves. "I get even."

"Yeah, right," Lisa scoffed, unconcerned. "Want some coffee?"

"Love some." Another of Lisa's talents: she made great coffee.

Lisa looked at the brimming closet and offered up a prayerful sigh. "Jesus. Whoever said sex doesn't pay?"

"Nobody. Sex pays just fine. Trouble is there's all those icky customers to deal with. The over-head"—she lightly rapped her skull—"is too damn high."

Lisa nodded, obviously remembering one or two "icky" customers of her own. "At least your customers are high-class."

"A high-class dick is still a dick," she reminded her.

Lisa laughed. "You gonna marry that guy?" She gestured with her chin toward the note.

"See Fallon run—to the altar in a New York minute." She wiggled a brow. "Now, how about that coffee?" She took another glance at the note. "And maybe a movie later?"

"Cool."

When Lisa left, Beauty walked to the window of her condo. The day was clear, and the sun entered the sixteenth floor unobstructed. The message was from Burke all right, and the news wasn't good. He was going out of town to visit his grandchildren in Montana. He'd call when he got back, he said, and make it up to her, buy her something pretty.

"Shit!" She crumpled the note, seriously frustrated.

She went back to the closet. Burke might not be a sure thing, but Ches McQuade was, so she'd best get her act together.

"Shit," she said again, softer this time, and leaned her forehead against the door jamb. She wondered how many more McQuades she could handle before she split into a zillion ruined pieces.

If that "something pretty" Burke mentioned wasn't a diamond the size of the Astrodome, she'd . . . she'd . . .

Hell, she had no idea what she'd do.

Cade's call to Wayne Grover paid off, and Stan Brenton's assessment of the man was right-on. He was affable and accommodating, and they agreed to meet for lunch at a seafood place near Pike's Market.

Cade arrived first, Grover a few minutes later, looking rushed and complete with the stock sorry-I'm-late intro.

When they'd taken their seats, Cade prodded

himself to record his first impressions, something he'd learned never to disregard. Update, perhaps. Disregard, no.

Wayne Grover was maybe five-ten, overweight in a soft-bellied kind of way, and pale. Not an outdoorsman, and not a workout king, Cade concluded. He was balding, but probably by most accounts a reasonably attractive male. Eyes blue, mouth narrow, jaw soft. Eye contact direct, expression open, handshake firm. Clothes? Exactly what you'd expect a government employee to wear, but these days seldom did: a suit, neat, clean, and not expensive. Overall? Basically one of those harassed-looking everyman types indistinguishable in a crowd. Late forties according to Stan, but he looked older, exhausted.

"I appreciate your coming on such short notice," Cade said as the waiter filled their water glasses.

Grover pulled his chair closer to the table, laced his fingers and locked his hands, leaving them to rest on the table. "Anytime anyone wants to do anything about the Bliss murder and that child's disappearance, I'll be there. I think about Josh Moore all the time. If I hadn't—"

"You couldn't have known. No one could."

He sighed. "That's what I keep telling myself," he said, adding, "Still no luck finding Bliss?"

"No. I talked to his parole officer again, and it looks as if he's skipped. There's already a warrant out on him."

"Not surprised. All looks and no brains, that boy. The other one, Brett, he was okay, but Frank . . ." He shook his head. "Anyway, I've brought the files on the kids. Thought they might help." He patted the briefcase he'd put on the chair next to him.

Cade arched a brow, surprised.

"Yes, I know I'm not supposed to, but Stan filled me in. I know your credentials, Harding, and I know how important this is to Susan—who I consider a friend, by the way—so . . ." He patted his case again. "Here they are."

Cade gestured toward the briefcase. "That could cost you your job. Those are state documents."

"Yes, but as I see it, the state missed the boat on this one," he said. "As did the police. They all gave up on Josh much too soon." He sat back in his chair, looked tired. "That said, after all these years I'm not sure anything I can say, or give you, will be much help."

"Everything will help. Thanks." But Cade knew Bliss was the real key, that not talking to the main witness was going to cost him. Time, if nothing else. Chances were Grover's ancient files would be interesting but not much else. Still, they were a place to start.

Grover studied him avidly. "Do you have an angle?"

"If you call starting at the beginning an angle, yes."

"And your definition of the beginning is?"

"The kids, Dianna Lintz, Addilene Wartenski, and Gus Vanelleto." He paused. "And whatever you can tell me about the missing Bliss."

"I can't help you much there. Not the brightest kid on the block, as I recall, but other than doing the usual teenage stuff, worrying his mother by driving too fast and drinking a bit too much, pretty much okay." He scratched his chin. "I was surprised he ended up in so much trouble. Mother's death probably." He looked into the distance, shook his head. "What he saw that night, I can't imagine."

"How old was he at the time?"

"Sixteen."

"How much do you remember about the others?"

"Everything. They were picked up on University Avenue, generally called The Ave. Back then, the street was pretty rough. Drug dealers. Prostitutes. Drunks. The usual suspects. It's cleaned up quite a bit now, but then? A real bad-news kind of place." He picked up his water glass and took a drink. "The three of them were living in some kind of squat house with a bunch of other kids, but they stuck to each other as if they'd been joined at birth." He stopped. "So I bent the rules and put them where they'd be together, the Bliss place. As it turned out, that was a big mistake." He inhaled deeply, ran an index finger along his eyebrow, the gesture frustrated, nervous.

Cade took advantage of the pause to ask, "You were their caseworker, before and after the murder?"

"The girls, yes. Vanelleto didn't have a caseworker, because he wasn't in the system and never had been. I kind of inherited him along with the girls when they were picked up," he said. "The three of them were only supposed to be with Belle Bliss a few days. She was a widow, always good about taking kids in on an emergency basis. I thought it would give me a chance to sort things out."

"Sort things out?"

"For the girls, it meant getting in touch with their existing foster parents, trying to get them back there. With the boy, I was starting from scratch, trying to locate his parents or relatives. If none of that worked, given the kids' ages, they'd probably end up in a group home." He looked away, his expression grim. "Where they'd take off from, so we could start all over again."

"Fun job." Cade said, knowing it was anything but. In his opinion, people working on the front line with lost, confused, and lonely kids deserved medals of valor, and Grover obviously cared about his job. He must—he'd been doing it for over twenty years.

"Yes." He smiled slightly, and Cade realized it was the first one he'd seen on the man's face since he'd taken his seat. "But with those three," Grover went on, "things happened so fast I didn't get a chance to do anything. If only I'd moved those kids . . ." He let the sentence fade out, as if too weary to finish it.

The waiter interrupted to take their order.

When that was done, and before Cade managed his next question, Grover asked, "Are you open to a suggestion?"

"Absolutely."

"Why don't you read the files? Everything is a copy, so you have all the time in the world. And when you're done, give me a call. I'll be happy to fill in any blanks."

"Sounds good." Cade nodded, then leveled his gaze to meet Grover's. "But I'd still appreciate you giving me a thumbnail on the kids."

"Sure." He paused as if to gather his thoughts. "Dianna Lintz was a looker, a teenage Lolita. She'd run away from her mother, a low-rent prostitute on the south side, a couple of years earlier. Addilene Wartenski was the youngest, thirteen at the time of the murder, and an orphan. She'd been living with an aunt, described by her as Mrs. Clean on supercharge"—he half-smiled again—"I've never forgotten that. The aunt was a bit strange, but seemed okay, but no way would Addy stay there—"

"Addy?"

"Or Wart, which was what her friends called her. Dianna was known as Beauty."

"Beauty and the Wart," he repeated. "Has a ring to it. Did the boy have a nickname?"

"No. He was just Gus." He laced his fingers together again in that tight knot he'd made earlier. "Anyway, when Addilene was picked up with Gus and Dianna that last time, the aunt wanted no part of her. That was fine with Addy who said if I sent her back there, she'd be out the back door before the front was closed. Tough little nut, that one. Had the mouth of a merchant sailor and a will as hard as the sidewalk she slept on. But a good kid, I thought. I liked her." He frowned. "Shows you how wrong a person can be."

"And Gus. What about him?"

Grover's mouth tightened. "Bad news. Very bad news." He appeared to chew on his thoughts a bit. "Street-smart and also, according to what I found out from other kids who knew him, a kid who knew how to work people to get what he wanted.

"From what I learned, he'd been living on sidewalks forever. One of the patrolmen on The Ave told me he was pimping for the two girls, although neither of the girls would admit to it, of course. Street loyalty? Fear? I don't know, but I do know Vanelleto had a reputation for a TNT temper with anyone who crossed him. Funny thing was he had no juvenile record." Grover lifted a shoulder. "No records at all, in fact. When I confronted him about it, tried to uncover some background on him, he laughed, said the spaceship that dropped him off didn't go in for record keeping."

Cade tilted his head. Interesting. "Go on."

"He made a habit of changing his name, and he kept his mouth shut. If he did have living parents, he made sure DSHS never found them. I've met a lot of kids in my time, but I've never met one as . . . disengaged as Gus Vanelleto. That boy could have survived on the top of Everest wearing shorts and a muscle shirt. Cold, sure of himself, and leather-tough." Tired, tight lines furrowed around Grover's mouth. "It was Vanelleto's prints they found in Josh's blood on the kitchen counter and on his crib. But I guess you know that."

Cold sliced along Cade's spine. "No. I didn't." He worked to hide his irritation that neither Stan nor Susan had bothered to give him this vital piece of information. Probably because they knew damn well if Cade started believing the child was dead, he'd be less aggressive in his investigation. *Damn!*

"I know Susan won't let go, and I admire her for that, but"—Grover lowered his chin, massaged it— "I hate thinking about that blood. What it might mean." He seemed to drift away, blinked a couple of times as if to bring himself back, then he interlaced his fingers, meshed them so tight that his knuckles whitened. The guy was way overdue for stress leave.

Not that Cade wasn't feeling stress of his own. They should have told him about the blood, the fingerprints.

Angry or not, Cade had to ask the six-million-dollar question of the only man, other than Bliss, who had personal knowledge of the three teenagers. He raised his voice a notch to snag Grover's obviously wandering attention. "Given what you know, Grover, do you think those kids were capable of murder, of kidnapping—possibly killing—a child?"

"Vanelleto, definitely."

"And the girls?"

He met Cade's gaze, his expression gloomy, beaten, as if in surrender after a long, losing battle with the uglier side of human nature. "That boy owned those girls, Harding. He was their version of God. They'd have done anything he told them to do, and smiled while they did it."

"Anything?" Cade tilted his head, a thousand hideous images marching through it. "Even murder?"

"Even murder." Grover confirmed.

Chapter 4

Frank Bliss sat at the back of the bar, the corner dark and secluded, the table lit by a single candle in a red votive holder.

He'd downed one Jack Daniel's but was nursing the second. No way did he intend to have blurred vision when Beauty walked into his line of sight. He was revved, his blood coursing through his veins like a rain-high river over a weak dam. He wondered if she'd recognize him right away or if it would take a while.

What if she didn't recognize him at all? Jesus, that would be fun. He'd play her long enough to get her pants off—like he had years before. Fifteen years ago . . .

When I'd loved her, like the skinny-butted fool I was. When I'd have done anything for her, and all she ever did was laugh at me.

She wouldn't laugh now. He smoothed his hair back, irritated when his hand shook.

He looked up and saw her standing at the entrance to the bar. When she glanced around the room, obviously looking for someone, a waiter stopped and pointed to Frank; she started toward him.

Frank didn't want the moment to end. He wanted to rerun it in slow motion forever.

She looked like a goddamn goddess, even better than the Beauty he remembered. Way better. A mile-high kind of better. He took a drink to calm down. Shit, he was hard as a prison bar. He shifted back until his face was in shadow.

"Ches?" She stood over him now, smiling.

"Yes." He stood, careful to stay out of the light. "And you must be Fallon West." He gave her a slow once-over, figured she'd expect that. "You're more beautiful than I was told." His knees might be shaking, but he sounded cool enough. Nothing mattered more to him right now than keeping his cool, which made him a fuckin' idiot for wanting to impress her—when the past was just a memory away.

She tilted her head, glanced at the empty seat beside him. "May I sit down?"

"Of course." He pulled the chair out for her, and she sat, stowing a large tote beside her chair. Dressed in white, her long pale-blond hair coiled at the back of her head, she looked more like an angel than a high-class hooker.

Bliss settled back in his chair, wishing this moment would last forever, that he could start over with her, make her his woman, but that wasn't in the cards and he knew it. What was in the cards was sex, and money—lots of money—and if he got real lucky, a taste of revenge. "What can I get you?" He leaned forward, flagged the waiter.

"Water. I don't drink when I'm working." She gave him her full attention then, her smile turning to a frown. "Have we met before?"

"Am I familiar to you?"

"I'm not sure. There's something . . ." Her frown deepened, and she scanned his face this time with intense concentration.

He leaned into the candlelight, raised a brow.

"Jesus Christ! Frank Bliss." Even in the dimly lit bar, he saw her face drain of color.

Lifting his glass in salute, he said, "I'm disappointed. I'd hoped you'd be a bit slower on the uptake."

When she started to get up, he shot out a hand and pulled her back to her seat. "Don't be in such a hurry, baby. We've got some catching up to do, and a public scene won't do either of us any good."

She tried to wrestle her arm free. "You . . . slimy bastard."

He held her without effort, until the waiter arrived. He ordered another JD for himself and a water for her.

He squeezed her arm until she winced. "Will you be a good girl if I let you go . . . *Fallon?* Pretty name, by the way, but I think the cops will like Dianna Lintz better. Me, I'll stick to Beauty."

The look she shot him was lethal, but she seemed calm enough, so he let her go. She didn't move, but she didn't speak, either. Her face was as white as the clothes she wore.

"I take it you're not happy to see me."

She turned her head, refused to look at him.

"I'm happy to see you." He put his hand on her knee, ran it under her short skirt, up her thigh. Squeezed. God, how did a woman manage it, to be lean, firm, and soft all at the same time? She didn't move, not a tic of a muscle. "You like this, baby." He touched her crotch, stroked the silk of her panties, his own breath quickening.

She went absolutely still, turned to stare at him across the table, her lip curled. "You're a pig, Bliss." She said. "You were a pig then. You're a pig now. There isn't anything about you I like. Now take your fucking hand off me."

He laughed and pulled his hand back, ran his finger under his nose. "Exotic."

"And too good for you. Always was. Always will be." She took a drink of her water—and her damned hand didn't even shake.

His gut started to simmer. This wasn't going how he planned it. After the shock, there was supposed to be fear. He'd counted on it, looked forward to it. Back then, there'd been plenty of fear. God, how she'd bucked and screamed.

The simmer rose to a boil, the heat of it ringing his throat.

Who the hell did she think she was, talking to him like that? Sitting there like she was the goddamn queen of the world. She was nothing but a two-bit hooker; he could have a dozen like her for a hundred bucks.

"Why are you here? And what do you want?" She looked at her watch, then at him, nothing but impatience registering on her perfect face.

The rage in his gut bubbled like deep-core lava. "Got a john waiting?"

"Thousands of them. I repeat. What do you want?"

He put his face inches from her. "I want you, whore—whenever and however I decide to take you." He ran a finger along her tight jaw. "And I want Vanelleto and Wartenski."

Now the color in her face heightened, and her back went straight as a steel beam. He smelled fear . . . finally.

"And did I forget to say," he added. "I also want money. Lots and lots of money."

Wayne Grover tidied his desk and glanced at the clock. Well after six. He cursed. The sudden rain would slow traffic, and Sandra detested his being late. At the thought of her, his head started aching again, and he chugged down a couple more pills. God, he was tired. Too tired for Sandra's harangues, the usual games.

"How about a beer, Grover? A few of us are going to Holly's Tavern. Are you in?"

At the sound of the voice, he tensed uncomfortably. Lifting his head, he met the eyes of Linda Curl, a coworker and the closest person he had to a friend in the whole department. Everyone else had given up asking him out years ago, and he had no doubt Linda would soon do the same, leaving him with no one. The bleakness in his soul intensified.

Linda would understand. I could talk to her. . . . No!

He pulled back, did busy work tidying his desk. Those kinds of thoughts were dangerous. He was just overly anxious today. It had been hard talking about Josh Moore, reliving the tragedy that changed his life forever.

"Not tonight, Linda. Thanks," he said, the words automatic, his expression carefully impassive. He stuffed some files in his case. Tonight, with luck, Sandra would allow him to work. He needed to work, needed to keep his mind off what Harding was digging into, because he wasn't sure he could go through it again.

Through the years, he'd pushed thoughts of what happened to Belle Bliss, those teenagers, as far back in his mind as they'd go, and they'd stayed there—most of the time.

He never forgot Josh.

His job was to protect the little ones, keep them safe, not put them in a place of blood and danger. He'd never forgive himself for Josh. Never. But he'd had no choice but to move on, continue with his work, because without it, without the kids, he'd have nothing. Now, thanks to Susan Moore and Cade Harding, that brutal night would be dredged up again. He liked Susan, respected her dedication, but he wished she weren't so stubborn, wished she'd accept that the odds of finding Josh alive were less than zero. Her tenacity could cost Wayne everything. Another shaft of pain severed his head, strong enough to make him grimace.

Rubbing hard at his temple, he looked up from his desk, surprised to see Linda still there. Damn! The mist surrounding his headaches were getting heavier, confusing him, making him forgetful, too easily distracted. He blinked.

"You okay?" Linda asked.

"Fine."

"Then come for a drink."

He shook his head. "Not tonight," he repeated.

She slanted him a bold, curious gaze. "Not to-night. Not last night. Not last week. What gives, Grover? You think I'm after that hard body of yours?" she teased.

Linda was no looker, or fashion plate. She wore a series of colorless, rumpled suits and badly tied scarves, but she had a quirky, often blue, sense of humor, and she was a damn good social worker, really cared about the kids. Wayne liked that. Wayne liked her, which was a huge waste of emotional invest-ment—and frightening. If Sandra got suspicious . . .

He thought of Sandra at home, waiting for him, china dinner plates just so on the white linen-draped table, knives and forks in perfect alignment, the layout and structure as rigid as the routine that supported their useless lives. He sucked back a sigh. Pointless. Everything was pointless.

His eyes met Linda's and his stomach clenched. God help him, he wanted to reach out to her; the urge was so strong it frightened him. But he wouldn't do it. He patted his ample and too-soft gut, formed a lame joke. "If this is hard, you need glasses."

"I'll bet with a little tug and pull, there's a part of you that would get hard enough to make up for it." She twisted her lips and raised a brow.

His dick twitched. *My God!* "You'll never know." He raised his left hand—leaden with regret—and touched the finger circled with the gold band.

"That's a ring, Grover, not a noose. I asked you for a beer, not a orgy." She stopped, tapped her chin. "Although an orgy's not out of the question."

Wayne forced himself to smile, then stood and shrugged into his suit jacket. He picked up his briefcase. "I'm hardly the orgy type."

"So what type are you? Give me something to go on." Her expression turned speculative.

"I'm the married-man type." He tried to sound forceful, lace the words with an integrity he was far from feeling.

She shook her head. "At least you didn't say happily married man, which gives you points for honesty."

He didn't have a response for that, so he said nothing.

After another long look at him, Curl picked up her own briefcase, which she'd propped up on one of his guest chairs, walked up to him, and looped her arm in his. "Come on, Saint Wayne, I'll ride the elevator with you." She smiled up at him. She was a tiny thing, all flyaway hair and sharp eyes. "And I promise I won't attack you." She wiggled a brow.

He managed another smile and patted her soft hand, fought the urge to bring it to his mouth.

Too bad Sandra wouldn't promise the same.

Beauty stared into her makeup mirror and slowly creamed the makeup from her face. Stopping abruptly, she tossed the cotton pad she'd been using onto her dressing table. Damn stupid face! It's what caused all this trouble in the first place, it and what men insisted on calling her "made-for-sex" body.

She stood and started to pace, tugging the front of her filmy thigh-skimming wrap closed as if it were thrift shop flannel instead of a satin and lace ensemble worth hundreds of dollars.

Frank Bliss! The thought of him chilled her blood, froze her brain. Paralyzed her. How could she have been so stupid!

Her mind again went to that day three years ago.

She'd remembered spotting the TV crew, and it had crossed her mind to walk away when they approached Burke. But she hadn't. Oh no, scatter-brained and vain as ever, she'd hung on Burke's arm and smiled at the press like the idiot she was.

And Bliss had sat on his prison cot watching her.

She cursed and swung around in the empty room, feeling caged and . . . terrorized.

She knew Burke Holland had a high profile, but she'd thought the operative word was *had*. For God's sake, he was virtually a recluse! By anyone's standards, old news. What she'd forgotten was that he was also old money—warehouses of old money— and the Holland family had a history in San Francisco that rivaled the Hearsts. Still, who'd have thought a quiet dinner in an out-of-the-way restaurant would have attracted a damn news team?

Now, because of it, Bliss was on her doorstep and everything was at risk.

She could sure as hell kiss any plans to marry out of The Life goodbye. Burke might walk down the aisle with a discreet high-class call girl—who he introduced as a model—but she doubted he was in the market for a murderer . . . or accomplice to murder, to be more exact.

Damn Bliss to hell! If anyone deserved to be murdered, it was that creepy no-good shit. Christ, knowing he was out there gave her the shakes. Not that he'd ever see them.

Thank God, she was in a secure building. It would take an armed unit to get past the electronics, let alone Geordie G on the lobby security desk. The man was sharp, and she'd been smart enough to slip him a few bucks to keep him that way.

A sound from the kitchen brought her to an abrupt halt. Lisa was out, there was no one but her in the three-thousand-square-foot condo. Her lungs tightened, the air in them suddenly iced and heavy. She stood still as stone.

"Meow . . ."

Her breath fled her lungs. "Spike! You mad thing. Come here." She squatted and reached out her hands. Her trembling hands . . .

The fiercely arrogant tomcat ambled over, and she scooped him up, both to cuddle him and steady her nerves. Holding him close, she wished he were the tiger he thought he was.

Wished he'd tear Bliss to bloody shreds.

When he leaped from her arms to escape her too-tight embrace, she sat on the delicate chintz settee near the window, poured herself a glass of wine, and tried desperately to think.

Bliss was a disaster waiting to happen, a dirty, massive mud slide that would ruin everything in its path.

In the two hours since she'd left him, her mind hadn't stopped racing. Trying to pull a plan out of the blur was impossible, not that planning had ever been her strong suit. On the road she'd traveled, looks and sex were the only currency needed. She shuddered.

With Bliss, sex was not an option. She'd cut her wrists first. She would!

If it were only money, she'd handle it. She hadn't been lying on her back for the best and brightest in San Francisco for years without hoarding some serious cash.

But Bliss wanted more than money; he wanted Gus and Addy, and she knew why. Revenge.

He wanted her so he could, as he'd said, "fuck her brains out"—anytime he wanted.

Never!

Whatever it took, she had to get rid of him.

If only she could talk to Gus, he'd know what to do, but she hadn't seen him since the . . . murder. Gus. The thought of him filled her, warmed her.

Oh, Gus, why didn't you take me with you?

Her heart stammered and stilled.

The lurking fear that she knew the answer to her own question froze her very bones. Abruptly, she downed the last of the wine in her glass and poured herself another.

Denial fit perfectly in a wineglass.

She forced herself back to the problem at hand. Bliss. Reminded herself this wasn't just about her.

Addy! She'd call Addy.

Maybe Beauty wasn't much as a problem solver, but the Wart was so smart it was scary. She'd come up with something.

And maybe, just maybe, she knew where Gus was.

She pulled herself together, went to the antique desk in the corner of her bedroom, and searched out the number for Star Lake.

Drawing in a calming breath, she picked up the phone.

* * *

Addy was getting milk from the fridge when the phone rang.

"Star Lake Resort," she said brightly, grabbing the milk container, then swinging the fridge door closed with her hip.

"Addy?"

One word. In a voice barely above a whisper.

"Mary Mother of Christ! Beauty."

"The latter," Beauty said, her tone lifting a notch. "And nothing at all like the former." A pause. "How are you, Wart?"

Her mind still a shocked whiteout, she mumbled, "I'm good." She set the milk carton on the countertop and pressed a palm against the fridge to steady herself. "Damn it. I can't believe it's you."

"I guess it has been a while."

"Yeah. Like fourteen years."

"That long?"

"Close to." Addy took her hand from the counter and rubbed her stomach. Something slithered there, a wary tension, settling, coiling itself into place. "Where have you been all these years? Even Lund couldn't find you."

"You mean he actually roused himself to give a damn? Amazing." She laughed, and when she did, if there'd been any doubt it was Beauty, that low, smoky laugh of hers put it to rest. "How is the old geezer anyway?"

"Dead. A few months ago."

"Oh." After a moment of silence, she added, "I'm sorry to hear that. Lund was okay."

"Yes, he was." *And better to us than we deserved.* "You should have called, let him know you were all

right. He would have appreciated it. So would I.
God, Beauty, we thought you were dead, figured—"
She didn't finish, didn't want to show that her
trust in Beauty ran so deep she'd actually thought
she had to be dead not to call, that she'd been
dumb enough to buy into the sisters-forever routine Beauty had promised so many years ago.
Lund had given up on her long before Addy did.

"As you can hear, I'm very much alive." She
stopped again. "And I'm coming up to see you."

"Up? Where's down?" The slithering sensation
intensified. She tamped down the surge of excitement that came with the idea of seeing Beauty
again. It was for sure if she did show up after all
this time, trouble would follow.

"San Francisco."

Addy's lips twisted, not quite a smile, not quite a
sneer. "Let me guess. You married a ton of money,
and you're living on Nob Hill." She might be jok-
ing, but she wouldn't be surprised, either.

"I'm working on that, but no. I followed in my
good mama's footsteps. I'm a prostitute. One of
the expensive ones." She said it as calmly as if
she'd announced she was a teacher of third grade.

"Oh, Beauty. You idiot!"

"Maybe, but an idiot who's made a buck or two,
and she's coming to see her sister."

"Quit with the sister stuff, would you?" Addy
snapped. "Sisters don't run off with the milkman,
then not call for half a lifetime." God, the amazing
thing was, hearing her voice now, it was as if all
those missing years had the weight of a Kodak moment.

"He wasn't a milkman, sweetie," she said. "He

was a long-haul driver with a thick wallet and a generous hand, and I didn't call because I had nothing to say."

"And you do now?"

"I do. And it's important." Beauty paused, and Addy heard her inhale long and deep. "Have you ever heard from our mutual friend?"

Addy knew Beauty meant Gus. It was her turn to inhale, hesitate. "No." Her heart boomed in her chest, and she coughed to clear her throat. It wasn't as if she were telling a lie, exactly. "And, Beauty—"

"Uh-huh?"

"About your coming here. I don't think it's a good idea. Maybe even . . . dangerous."

"You're probably right, but I'm coming anyway." This time the pause was longer, and when she spoke her voice was shaky, her tone low. "Because it's even more dangerous if I don't come. There's a big bad wolf out there, Addy, and unless we do something, he's going to huff, and he's going to puff, and he's going to blow my house down." She stopped again. "Then he'll come after yours."

"What are you talking about?" The hair on the back of Addy's neck stood up and screamed. Screams that vibrated down the cords of her memory.

"Put some fresh sheets on a bed, Wart. I plan to drive—safer, I think. I'll be there as soon as I can." She hung up.

Addy replaced the receiver on its wall cradle and stood staring at it, dread clawing at her ribs in long gouging scrapes, her breath refusing to settle in her lungs.

She pulled out a chair from the kitchen table,

ignored the late dinner she'd hungered for, and sat down heavily. She was still there when the sinking sun disappeared behind the cedars, still there when the warm October day cooled into evening.

It couldn't be about that night. It just couldn't.

But in a deep, long, unlit part of her soul, she knew it was.

Chapter 5

Wayne Grover arrived home by seven-thirty. He tried to close the door quietly, but even the soft click of the lock was enough. Sandra immediately came to meet him, her face pale and tight. "You're late. Again. I told you dinner would be on the table at seven-fifteen."

He turned his back to her, hung up his coat, and stowed his briefcase in the closet. "Traffic," he said, not adding further explanation, knowing more words made a bigger net for her to catch him in.

She snorted. "Get in there, then. I don't want to be doing dishes all night because you don't know how to press down on the pedal."

She waited until he passed her. "You had some calls. One of them was a man named Cade Harding."

He turned to face her, his expression carefully blank. "Yes."

"Well?"

"Well, what?"

She pursed her lips, adding, "I don't know the name. You know I like to be apprised of all your colleagues."

He walked the few steps to the dining room, took his seat, and surveyed the perfectly placed cutlery. He thought about Linda Curl, her froth of unruly hair, her smart mouth, her plump, willing body. "He's not exactly a colleague, Sandra."

"What then?" she said, her tone sharpening.

"He's a man looking into a file of mine." Wayne sighed, rubbed his forehead. "Can we just eat? It's been a long day. I'm hungry." There was no food in evidence, but Wayne knew it was in the kitchen, each portion aligned perfectly on pure white plates, enough to feed at least a pair of robins, with no chance for seconds, because Sandra was watching his weight.

Thank God for lunch.

"What file?" she demanded.

He laced his fingers, placed his hands in front of him on the orderly table, knowing now there'd be no escaping her interrogation. "The Perkins file," he lied.

She frowned. "The Perkins file? I've never heard of it. You haven't told me."

"It's new. A missing girl. Harding's been hired by the family to find her. She was in the system for a few weeks. He came into the office today, thought I could help him find her. I told him I couldn't. He probably had a last minute question." He waited to see how the lie played.

"You're not telling me everything."

"No, I'm not. Because I don't know everything."

He realized too late his reply was edgy. He ignored the headache belching fire into his skull, and took her hand in his, stroked it in an effort to calm her. Unlike Linda's hand, Sandra's was narrow, and the bones made high ridges under her pale skin.

"You're lying, Wayne. You always lie."

"Sandra, please."

She yanked her hand from his. "Someone else called today," she said, her voice ominously low, her eyes hot and unblinking.

"Who?"

"Frank Bliss."

The name entered him like a blunt, jagged knife, and along with Sandra's vicious grin, twisted and jerked in his chest. He struggled to catch his next breath. Frank Bliss. Dear God! Seven years he'd been in prison, and the minute he was out, he was on Wayne's back like a voracious, creeping fungus, his promise never to call Sandra again lost in his bottomless greed.

"What did he say?" He kept his tone mild the way she liked it.

"Nothing. He asked for you, and when I said you weren't home, he hung up in my ear."

Wayne nodded, swallowed the clot of nerves in his throat, tried to think.

Sandra set her gaze on him. Leaning over him, her face so close to his he had to blink to bring it in focus, she said, "If you'd dealt with him, Wayne, when you should have, if you'd acted like a real man, he wouldn't be troubling us, would he?"

He didn't answer, couldn't deny her accusation.

"*Answer me!*" She screamed and slapped the

table. The cutlery on the table jumped—as did his heart.

He tightened the knot of his hands. "No, Sandra, he wouldn't. It's my fault. All my fault. I'll take care of it. I promise." If he only knew how. If only he had the power to make Bliss go away. Forever.

Her laugh was sharp, derisive. " 'I'll take care of it, Sandra,' " she parroted, her voice rising. "That's what you said then, you stupid, stupid fool. We could have lost everything, your job, this house. But you did nothing. Nothing!" Her voice turned shrill. "You're useless." The look she gave him was filled with disgust and loathing. "You were useless then, and you're useless now." Her expression shifted, darkened. "You deserve to be punished for your weakness."

"No, Sandra . . ."

She ignored him. "But you like that, don't you, Wayne, being punished. Because you're not a real man. If you were, you wouldn't like the things . . . you like. The things only I can give you."

No! Wayne's pulse quickened, a mixture of fear and arousal. "Don't, please," he pleaded. "This time I'll do it. I'll take care of Bliss. He won't bother us again. Let's just have dinner. Please, Sandra."

"Oh, yes, Wayne, you'll take care of it, all right, because I'll make sure you do."

Her hand came suddenly, as if from nowhere, slapped his cheek, palm open, taut, and mean with intent. Again. Then again. His head snapped and swiveled under each blow.

"Get up, you dumb, ignorant beast!" She hissed, putting her mouth to his ear, filling it with heat and spit. "Go to bed. There's no dinner for you tonight."

Wayne took in a breath, drowning in his shame. Shame for his lies, his failures, his growing erection. More than anything, shame for his sinful abiding rage. He thought longingly of his office, his files, the work he could bury himself in. He should leave, walk out the door, and never come back.

He should run . . .

"I said get up!" she ordered, her voice shrill, feral.

He stood, which put him eye-to-eye with the dark-haired woman whose brilliant, burning gaze poured into his worthless soul like boiling tar, whose mouth frothed with fury—and whose hand now curled, knuckles white, around a steak knife.

She put the knife to his chin and prodded; blood trickled down his neck. "Did that feel good, lover?"

He did what she expected—what he'd always done—and nodded obediently, his mouth slack, his eyes wide and dry.

She dropped the knife in disgust. "Go upstairs, you piece of filth. I know what you like, what you want, and I'm happy to oblige. You know what to do. Wait for me."

He lowered his gaze, placed his napkin on the table, and walked out of the room, his impotent rage no match for the depravity that ruled his rotting soul.

He was an evil man, the devil's own tool.

Grover went up to the bedroom, removed his clothes, dropped to his knees, and said the same prayer he'd intoned for years, tonight more desperately than ever, his need grown terrifyingly critical as if his brain were fissured, threatening to fragment into a million jagged, violent pieces.

Any time now.

Any moment.

His mind a fog of pain and blinding fear, a blizzard of despair, he prayed again and again . . .

"Dear God, I beg you to make me strong. Give me peace. And, please, please stop me from killing my wife."

Addy stooped, picked up an empty cola can, and walked to the back of the house to put it in the garbage bin. Lord, people were messy. Most days, she accepted litter pickup as part of the job, but since Beauty's call her nerves were so fierce and jangled every task seemed like a mile-long broad jump.

One part of her longed to see her friend again, another part dreaded it. Her being here would raise the dead, force an unwanted trip down mortuary lane. But damn that "big bad wolf" comment of hers. Irritated and confused, Addy took a deep breath, looked up at the bright sky, and reminded herself calmly how Beauty always did have a flair for the dramatic, and she shouldn't put too much store in it. She'd get to the bottom of things soon enough when Beauty got here. Until then, the smart thing to do was forget about it and go to work.

She spotted another can as Toby, coming out of the office, spotted her.

"Hey, pretty lady, I was looking for you." He gave the cola can in her hand a broad disapproving look. "Weren't you made for better things than picking up garbage?"

She straightened. "That's what I keep telling myself, but our litter-challenged guests don't see it that way." She managed a smile. Her troubles weren't Toby's, and she didn't intend them to be. "How are you doing with the books?" She grimaced, waiting for his answer. He was probably hating every minute he spent with them and was past ready to dump them back on her.

"I'm doing good. Pretty much got them whipped into shape." He rubbed at his chin, gave her a quizzical look. "I'm thinking you and I should get ourselves a computer."

"A computer? You and I?" she echoed.

Toby laughed. "I didn't ask you to marry me, sweetums, just spring for a box and some accounting software."

"Now what would I do with a computer?" Even the idea of a computer gave her hives. All those telephone-book-sized manuals. Ugh!

"You? Nothing. Me? I'll make the baby dance."

"And after you've gone?"

He tugged his earlobe and looked oddly nervous. "Well, now that's it, isn't it? I was thinking I'd stay on, kind of permanent, part-time. Help out around here." His gaze narrowed. "But only in the office, mind. The physical stuff is all yours. I'm too old to be hefting paving stones or pushing a wheelbarrow."

When she didn't say anything—because she couldn't think what it would be—he coughed, went on, "Thing is, I like it here. No real need for me to go back to Seattle. Except maybe to pick up some stuff and give some notice to my fleabag landlord. And I figure with my pension and a nice cut on my cabin rate, things should work out just fine."

"You're serious!"

"Damn right." He looked nervous again, as if he weren't sure what to expect.

She saw him straighten his bent shoulders as he waited for her answer. God, he expected her to say no. Did he think she was crazy? "Toby! That would be great," she said, relief drowning her worries. *You can do all the paperwork. Take care of the bills, the mail. And I'll be free to finish the cabins.*

"We got ourselves a deal then?"

"Deal." She put out her hand. Toby took it and pulled her into a bear hug. She pulled back as soon as she could, uneasy, as always, with physical contact. In that respect, she and the remote, sober Lund were soul mates. "I think you being around all year will be terrific," she added, smiling broadly to mask her awkwardness.

"Good. Now, about that computer . . ." he added and stuck his chin out.

"What do you know about computers anyway?"

"Enough to get started," the old man said, aligning his seventy-year-old shoulders. "And what I don't know, I'll learn. There isn't anything a person can't learn if he puts his mind to it."

Addy wished she had half his confidence—even though she didn't believe what he said was true. "Okay, but all those bits and bytes will be your business. I want no part of it."

"Like I said, you take care of the buildings. I'll take care of the books. Never was one for having a woman look over my shoulder anyway." He started to walk away, then turned back, his wrinkled face beaming a smile. "Be nice to work with you, sweet-ums. You're a damn clever girl, and you've done wonders for this place." He shook his head. "Lund Baylor was my friend, but he never did appreciate you, no sir. But you and me? We'll make this old motel a real going concern. Yes, we will."

She watched him go, caught off guard by a wash of tears filling her eyes. She brushed them away, wondered why she always cried when she was happy and never when she was sad. Toby was wrong about her being clever, but she wished with all her heart he wasn't wrong about the future success of the motel.

Star Lake was her home, her safe place—or so she'd thought until she'd heard Beauty's voice again. The miserable, tight hand of worry grabbed at her chest again.

If someone had found them . . .

The thought of leaving, of running again, weak-ened her knees, made her heart weep in her chest.

Then don't run this time, Addy. No matter what, don't run!

A brave vow, but in a couple of months she'd turn twenty-nine—make that a hundred if you counted the street years—and if she knew one thing, it was that there were times when running was the only option, the only way to survive.

For now, she had to believe this wasn't one of them; that whatever their problem was, it could be fixed with some smart thinking and a good idea.

She bent to pick up an empty potato chip bag,

tucked it into the trash, and looked across the lake. Her lake.

Positive thoughts aside, she couldn't shake the dreary sense her time was up, that maybe that special Someone Upstairs had looked down on Star Lake and decided Addilene Wartenski had been safe long enough—that it was past time she pay for what she had done.

Or hadn't done.

Frank was pleased with himself, and with Beauty. At first, when he'd seen her load her suitcase into that fancy Lexus convertible of hers, he'd been mad as hell. Then he'd thought on it a bit, decided on a wait-and-see attitude.

Chances were good she was sneaking off to see the Wart—maybe even Vanelleto.

The thought of Vanelleto made his guts churn and his mouth go hate dry. That vicious bastard deserved to die, one bullet at a time.

Bliss slid his hand under the newspaper on the passenger side of the car, stroked the cold steel of his newly acquired Glock. If he got lucky, and Beauty headed where he thought she was heading, he'd get his chance to provide those bullets.

For now, he'd wait, play it cool.

Revenge was good, but it didn't pay shit.

His mouth twisted into a thin smile. Wouldn't it be sweet, Vanelleto, Beauty, and the Wart all under one convenient roof?

Three chickens to pluck, two to fuck, and one to kill.

Warmed by the thought, he settled back into

the seat of his rented Chrysler and watched the expensive red car switch deftly into the fast lane—but stick carefully to the speed limit.

He nearly laughed aloud. That's what made his plan so damn perfect: the woman driving the car had no more interest in attracting a cop's attention than he did.

Which made him and his Glock safe as babes in a stroller.

Cade mentally gave the DSHS, and Wayne Grover specifically, an A+ for record keeping. There was much more to go on in his files than the police report he'd borrowed from the SPD, Seattle's finest. Being a one-time criminalistics prof had its perks.

He shoved the Vanelleto and Lintz files aside and again opened Wartenski's.

It was thicker than the other two, more detailed, and he'd already committed most of it to memory. The child that was Addilene Wartenski now filled his mind and poked at his imagination. There were two pictures in the file, one of the girl at age seven or eight locked in the embrace of her mother, the other a stark portrait taken when she was eleven, the year she went permanently under the state's wing.

Cade wondered about the family photo. It was unusual to find a happy picture of a mother and daughter in the cold confines of an overworked caseworker's file. There was a sticky note on the back—in Grover's handwriting—*return to Addilene at Belle's.*

Obviously, he'd forgotten to do so, or the murders and her running away precluded it.

There was no record anywhere of the father, and her birth certificate, like Dianna's, stated "father unknown." But even that scant information was more than there was for Vanelleto. There was zero documentation on his background, his birth, or his school time. Nothing. How he'd managed to stay in the cracks as long as he did was astounding, and it made profiling him impossible—and the worst place to start.

Addilene had at least attended school, albeit intermittently, until she hit the streets, although her grades were brutal and her attendance even worse.

According to her file, her mother, Marylee Wartenski, died when the child was nine, and Addilene was taken in by Marylee's sister, Gloria. Neither Marylee nor Gloria had married, and according to Grover's files, there were no other relatives. At least none he ever found. And from what Cade could see, the man had knocked himself out trying to find some.

He picked up the case photo and studied the likeness. The girl looked pale, glum, and plain. Blue eyes, long dark hair, apparently unbrushed when the photo was taken, and lips that were either knife thin or tightly compressed. Hard to tell.

There were no birthmarks listed in the description, but it was noted she had a thin scar under her chin—probably invisible by now—acquired as a toddler when she fell from her tricycle.

While there was considerably more about Addilene's background than either Dianna or Vanelleto's, when it came to the murder of Belle Bliss, her name carried the least weight in both the police reports and in Grover's file.

Because of her age, Cade guessed. She would have been thirteen when the murder occurred and the youngest of the three. She'd been in the system for only two years and on the streets for most of that, after running away from Aunt Gloria for the third time.

With no home, no real family, no roots, Addilene would have been sweet pickings for a hustler like Vanelleto. Cade could easily imagine it, a smile, a few smooth promises . . .

Acquiring a virginal twelve-year-old would have been a gold mine for a guy like that. A guy who, according to Grover's notes, was in the process of earning his stripes in the girl-selling business. At seventeen, two other girls had already named him as their pimp and crack dealer. But before anything came of their charges, they disappeared, the case along with them.

Cade wasn't surprised.

Life on the streets had the stability of jelly in the sun. One day you had a witness, the next day you had a missing person. And so it went.

Cade tossed the photo on the file and pushed away from his desk. When he stood, Redge stood with him, eyes alert, tail waving hopefully. "Good idea, boy. Let's walk. It'll clear my head. Force it to focus." At the door, he snapped the leash onto the dog's collar.

In minutes they were outside the building, and while Cade drew in some of the early evening air, Redge lacquered the nearest parking meter.

They headed for the small park around the corner, Redge's brain dedicated to cataloging the neighborhood smells, Cade's preoccupied with Addilene. A murder. A missing child.

Dana wanted a child so badly . . . her child.

He killed that thought. Suddenly weary, all he wanted to do was walk away from the whole damn mess, disappear into the fictional world of Zero. A world where he could make everything turn out right. Where no one died unless they deserved to die, and he was judge, jury, and executioner.

He told himself he didn't owe Susan Moore squat, the debt was his mother's. But it didn't hold up. What was his mother's debt was his debt.

And there was Addilene, aka the Wart, who was fast getting a hold in his brain.

He never had developed skin tough enough to block out the damaged, lonely Addys in the world, which is why he made a better teacher than he did a cop, but it was the cop part of him that made one fact clear.

Of all three kids, Wartenski was the only one with a reasonably documented life before DSHS scooped her off the streets, which gave him some chance of getting to know her and come up with a profile that might give him a place to start.

Back in his apartment, Cade looked down at his cluttered desk, hit a key on his sleeping laptop, and woke up his screen.

With a few clicks, and an ounce of patience, he located Addilene's aunt, Gloria Wartenski, her phone number, and her current address. He considered the quick find, and the fact she lived less than an hour's drive from his apartment, an omen. It helped that Gloria was an upstanding citizen. The Internet unearthed the innocent faster than those with something to hide.

So Addilene Wartenski it was. If he were lucky,

she'd lead him to the others—and to what happened to Josh Moore.

Addy sat bolt upright, her heart pounding.

The phone. It rang again, striking the quiet of her room like a lightning bolt.

She swallowed the shock that came with being roused at—she looked at the clock—three-fifteen in the morning and picked up the phone.

"Hello?" She shoved her short hair out of her eyes, then pressed her hand to her chest.

"Addy, it's Fallo— Beauty."

Fully awake now, Addy said, "I thought you'd be here by now." And because she was late, Addy had operated in submerged panic mode all day. "Where are you?"

"Bakersfield." She stopped.

"Bakersfield?" Addy didn't get it. "You're driving south, not north."

"Tell me something I don't know," she said dryly. She sounded tired. "I've been driving in circles since I left San Francisco. Trying to figure out what to do."

"I don't understand. What's happening?" Addy clutched her throat to still the wild pulse at the base of it.

Silence.

"Beauty! Tell me."

A labored sigh drifted down the telephone line. "That big bad wolf I mentioned?"

"Yes." She held her breath.

"It's Bliss, Addy. Frank Bliss."

"Oh, God . . ." The hand she held to her throat

fell away like a dead thing. She couldn't breathe. Her eyes went to her bedroom door as if expecting to see him lurking there . . . or to mark her way out, her escape.

"He got out of prison a couple of weeks ago. He saw me on TV—"

"You were on TV! Are you crazy?"

"No, I'm not crazy," she snapped. "And quit with the exclamation points, would you? It was dumb. I didn't intend it to happen, but it fucking did. So here we are."

"Oh, Beauty . . ."

"Anyway, none of that matters now. The thing is he saw me. He found me—" She stopped. Addy could hear her drag on a cigarette. "And he's following me."

"God!" Addy's mind raced, hunting and pecking for a solution, as it always did when confronted with a problem. And Frank Bliss was definitely a problem.

Frank Bliss was a catastrophe.

"I'm scared, Addy," she said, her words a rush. "I haven't felt so damn scared in years."

Strangely, Beauty's fear calmed her own. "I know. I'm scared, too."

"He raped me," she whispered. "And the son-of-a-bitch says he's going to do it again." Fifteen cold years swept in on the smallness of her voice, the lost innocence of it.

"I remember . . ."

The past rested between them, sour and deadly, a tangle of terror, mindless flight, and horrifying—unforgivable—mistakes.

"I hate him. You can't know how much I hate

him. What he did to me . . ." Her voice, still low, firmed, laced with a rage only she could own.

Addy's heart thumped heavily in her breast, a beat for a death march. But she wouldn't go there, wouldn't let Beauty go there. Not now. There wasn't time. "Don't think about it. Listen to me. You have to lose him. For the moment you're safe. My guess is he's following you because he thinks you're going to lead him to Gus." Saying that name, after all these years, chilled her to the bone, constricted her lungs.

For a moment there was silence, another drag on the cigarette.

"That's what I think," she said, sounding stronger. "If that wasn't his plan, he'd have grabbed me by now."

"You have to keep moving, keep going around in those circles, until I figure something out."

"Or he figures out what I'm doing. Which he will sooner or later."

"Just lose him and get here, Beauty. You can do it." Addy scrambled to her feet, rummaged through her bedside table for a pen. "Have you got a cell with you?"

"Uh-huh."

"Give me the number."

"Four—Jesus! I've got to go. I'll call when I can." The click was loud and final, followed by a heavy, aching silence.

She was gone.

Chapter 6

Gloria Wartenski was what was commonly referred to as a real piece of work. She was short, square-jawed, obese almost to the point of immobility, and nasty as a starved snake.

She didn't want any part of Cade or his questions. But by overworking both what charm he possessed and his flattery factory, he eventually made it in the door.

"You're wasting your time and mine looking for that useless, murdering girl," she said when she finally let him in.

She gestured toward a door down the hall, turned her back to him, and headed toward it. "Kids. Trouble. Nothing but trouble. Which is exactly what I told Marylee, but of course she wouldn't listen. Then she had the nerve to die and drop the brat on me."

She didn't seem to expect a response, so he didn't offer one.

When she trundled through the door to what was her kitchen, he followed her in.

The place was surgically clean, with stainless steel counters and appliances and an array of gleaming utensils hanging from a ceiling-mounted pot rack above the stove. The floor was white, as was—so far as Cade could see—anything else in the room that wasn't glinting metal. With a bright but chilly fall sun coming in the window, the place scorched the eyes.

She went to a drawer, took out a dish towel, and draped it over the seat of one of the chairs arranged around a rectangular table. She pointed to it. "Sit," she instructed.

Hygienically obsessive? More than a bit, he guessed, taking the seat he'd been instructed to take. Gloria Wartenski sat at the head of the table and eyed him as if she were considering hosing him down. "So, what is it—after all these years—you want to know?" she said, her face a crisscross of bad humor and what looked to be reluctant curiosity.

"I want you to tell me about your sister, Miss Wartenski. And more specifically, Addilene."

"Stupid sister, even dumber kid." She sat back in the chair.

"Why stupid? Why dumb?" He hid his shock at her cold, blunt assessment.

"Stupid sister because she got herself pregnant in the first place. She was diabetic, you know. Damn near died having that baby. All kinds of complications. It was diabetes that killed her in the end. Did you know that?"

He nodded. "And Addilene."

"Sassy, ungrateful, and sloth lazy. Which her

mother encouraged, I should add. When Marylee
was alive, most days you couldn't tell the difference between the adult and the child. All they did
was play, play, play. The girl didn't go to school
half the time, let alone do her chores."

"Your sister never married. That must have . . .
bothered you." He might not get a rapport with
this woman, but he'd make his questions as open-
ended as possible.

She snorted. "Hell, that was the only smart
thing she ever did. You think a kid's trouble, try
having a man around."

He ignored the slam against his sex. "Did you
know Addilene's father?"

She shook her head. "Some drifter, I guess.
Marylee was always"—she made quote marks with
her pudgy fingers, lifted a brow—"looking for love
in all the wrong places." She gave him a direct look
and what might have passed for a smile, had her
upper lip not carried such a mean edge. "And she
was pretty enough. Not that a man cares much.
When the lights go out, he'd stick it in a rat hole if
the mood's on him. Marylee? She could have screwed
every male from here to Siberia for all I know."

Cade gritted his teeth and pushed on. "I assume
from what you're saying, you and your sister weren't
close."

"You assume right. Marylee Addilene Wartenski
was the silliest creature on God's green earth. Kept
a house like a pigsty and only came around when
she needed something, which was too damned often
after that girl was born." She shook her head. "Going
on about how maybe her baby would make us
closer." She snorted again. "All she did was moon

over that kid." She said the last as if mother love was akin to contracting the Ebola virus.

But Cade had heard something he'd never heard before. "Your sister's name was Addilene, too?"

"Our mother's name, our grandmother's name. From the second she was pregnant, she started rambling on about passing it on to her daughter. Said she knew right away she was having a girl. Ordained, she said." She looked away for a moment and her mouth pursed. "Name should have been mine. I was the oldest."

"It must have been difficult, given your feelings about your sister"—or lack of them—"taking her child in after her mother died."

"Didn't have much choice." She shrugged. "I've got bad legs. The girl was nine or so. I figured once she got over grieving for her mother, she'd be some help around the house. Floors, dishes, maybe some laundry . . . that kind of thing. It didn't happen. Only thing she was good at was crying."

"A bit young for work that heavy, I'd think." Cade looked at the shining steel, gleaming pots, and thought of a grieving child thrust into this moonscape environment. Hell, he'd cry a few buckets himself.

"Never too young to start earning your keep." She gave him a combative look as if she sensed his disapproval. "You done?"

He was done all right. Who the hell in their right mind would spend more than five minutes in this bitter woman's company? But he did have one more question. He asked it as he stood to go. "I understand that before Addilene was taken in by DSHS, she ran away several times."

She hefted herself to her feet. "That's right. Her and me didn't get along. When I was finally rid of her for good, I hired a proper cleaning woman." Impatience shot through her features. "Hired a stream of the miserable creatures. Not one of them any damn good, but every one of them better than that shiftless, good-for-nothing girl."

Cade nearly swallowed his tongue in his attempt to hold it. "When Addilene ran away, where did she usually go?"

She half-laughed as she trudged back to the front door. "That's easy. She went to visit her 'mommy.' Graveyard's about twelve blocks from here. Found her there every time." She opened the door for him. "Like I said, a stupid girl."

Cade got in his truck, turned the motor on to activate the air-conditioning, and put his head on the headrest. He closed his eyes and let what he'd learned from Gloria Wartenski free-float in his mind. A powerful mother/daughter bond. A strong-willed, grieving child. A family name. Tears. More tears. A gravesite.

He opened his eyes and reached for the pad he had ready on the seat beside him, jotted down his impressions.

Wherever Addilene Wartenski is, it isn't far, he wrote. And he'd bet his last buck she'd kept her first name in some form or another. There was a chance—small, but there—that she'd visited her mother's grave in the last few years, when she started to feel safe. Maybe someone had seen her.

Not enough. He needed another connection.

No one to ask. No more family. No aunts, brothers, cousins . . . *sisters*.

Dianna Lintz. Hadn't Grover said the girls were like sisters?

He decided to take a shot in the murky and chaotic world of the street hooker, the world of Dianna's mother.

Anything was better than a cemetery stakeout, stalking the dead and capitalizing on their grief.

Cade drove away, trying to believe his own righteous thinking, and knowing damn well that he just didn't want to see another graveyard.

Beauty looked in the rearview mirror and cursed. She took a hand off the wheel to rub her forehead and shove her hair behind her shoulder. A thin layer of perspiration coated her neck and shoulders.

She'd been sure she'd lost him, but the sleek dark Chrysler had shown up again, a couple of cars behind her. Over an hour ago now, and it had stuck like a burr. Her gut, seldom wrong, told her it was Bliss.

The I-5 was jammed, a chain of diamond lights behind and rubies ahead. It was getting late, she'd been driving for hours, and she desperately needed sleep. She spotted a sign for a town called Kenner thirty-six miles down the road. It had to have some kind of motel, and she had to risk staying there. The alternative was pulling over and sleeping in her locked car, but the thought of waking up to Bliss on the other side of the window made her stomach lurch.

It had to be a motel. She hoped Addy was right, that he was following her to find the others. If he was, she was safe—for now. If he wasn't . . .

She leaned to reach the glove box, opened it, and ran her hand toward the back.

"Thank you, Burke," she whispered, and pulled the small ivory-handled revolver onto her lap. When she glanced down at it, her mouth went desert dry, and a slurry of fear and apprehension congealed in her chest. She didn't like guns.

Beauty had fucked more than her share of men, but she'd never killed one—didn't know if she could. But one thing was certain, Frank Bliss was never going to touch her again, and if she had to kill anyone, he was a deserving candidate.

Her breathing quickened, and she could smell the wet hay in the shed, feel the prickle of it against her naked back.

The ropes . . . "If you don't spread them, baby, I'll do it myself." *The screams* . . . "Shut up, whore! You let Vanelleto in, you let me in. You got that?" *The pain* . . . "Now who'd have thought it, a fuckin' virgin! Looks like I beat Vanelleto to it after all." *The laughter* . . . "Might as well really break you in, have myself some real fun. Got all the time in the world to do it."

The blood, the terror, the endless run . . .

On some level, she'd been running ever since.

Beauty dropped her hand from the wheel, stroked the short, sleek barrel of the gun that rested on her thigh, and experienced a sudden, acute surge of power—and conviction.

If I'd had you back then, baby . . .

Again, she glanced in the rearview mirror. The

Chrysler was still there. Ignoring the shiver in her spine, she caressed the revolver and set it carefully on the empty passenger seat.

Her new companion, her lethal new friend.

"You're a dead man, Bliss, you just don't know it yet," she spoke the words into the rearview mirror, her mouth twisted into a cold smile. "And you're not getting within five hundred miles of Addy or Gus."

Her heart settled into a steady, easy beat, and her fear lifted, leaving her feeling loose, eerily relaxed.

She was no longer afraid, no longer the hunted.

She'd become the hunter.

She was going to kill Frank Bliss—commit a cold-blooded murder. But before doing that, she'd lead him as far away as possible. She'd choose her moment—like he'd done years ago when he'd lured her into that filthy shed—and she'd do it in her own time. Slowly.

And she knew exactly where she'd fire the first bullet.

Roxanne Lintz was surprisingly easy to find.

Mainly because she was dying.

When Hep C had brought on a failing liver, she'd been taken in by a small charity-run hospice in Tacoma, a short drive south of Seattle.

Cade found her in an upstairs room, sitting by the window in a clutter of books and magazines. A TV sat unused at the foot of her unmade bed. The furniture was old and battered, but the place was clean, and a fistful of fresh flowers sat in a painted can on the windowsill. A magazine rested forgotten on her lap as she stared out the window.

"Mrs. Lintz?"

She looked up him, her expression mild and questioning. "Yes?"

Even ill and well past fifty, her skin a sickly yellow, she was beautiful; her features were fine, her hair—well below her shoulders—still shadowed with the dark auburn of yesterday. It didn't take much imagination to visualize the younger, vibrant Roxanne Lintz. "I'm Cade Harding. I called."

She set the magazine aside but didn't get up. "Yes. You said you wanted to talk about my girl." She gestured to the bed, the only other place to sit in the small room.

When he'd taken a seat, she went on, "I have no idea where she is, you know." She smoothed her hair back behind her ears, her hands painfully frail and weak. "And if I did know, I wouldn't tell you."

"Actually, I'm not looking for your daughter. I'm looking for a friend of hers, Addilene Wartenski."

She shook her head. "Don't know her. But then I didn't know any of Dianna's friends—except that boy she ran off with." She frowned. "Can't remember his name. Lived down the hall for a time. Good-looking boy"—she grimaced and shook her head—"but then they always are, aren't they?"

"Excuse me?"

She looked away. "The ones who cause all the trouble. Tall, handsome, full of dreams. Their mouths dripping in sugar and promises. Like they say, 'every woman's dream, every mother's nightmare.' "

Cade let her be, waited.

"Add to that, Dianna didn't like my line of work."

"You fought?"

She shook her head. "Dianna didn't bother with the fighting part. She just came to me one night—when I was working—and said she was leaving." She looked away, then back. "Said she didn't want a whore for a mother. She was thirteen. I saw her once after that. Downtown . . . can't remember where. When she saw me she took off, and I let her go." She stroked her thigh with a too-thin, long-fingered hand. "A woman like me, in the trade? Never should have had a kid. But when she came, I thought—" She stopped abruptly. "It doesn't matter what I thought."

"You loved her."

"Yeah, I loved her. But it didn't stop me from screwing up. Big-time. But when Lund—" She stopped again, looked out the window.

"Lund?" he prodded.

"Lund Baylor. A client, and an okay guy. Didn't say much. I almost married him. Maybe if I had, things would have been different. He wanted me to quit the trade, put a white fence around me." She sighed softly, then shrugged. "But I was making good money. Looked a lot better then than I do now"—her smile was quick and proud—"and I wanted to hang on for a while, get a stake . . . The upshot was, Lund took off. Dianna and him had kind of hit it off, you know. And when he left, she left."

She pushed herself out of the chair and took the two or three steps to the window. It seemed to take all her strength. "Lund bought himself some kind of resort or something, north somewhere, up near the Canadian border—a place called Star Lake. Dianna went to him after that awful murder business. He called me to let me know she was okay. I was thinking I'd go up there, but she didn't stay long, took off with some truck driver, Lund said. Never heard a word after that." A sad twist of a smile altered her face from wistful to cynical. "Like mother, like daughter."

"She never called you?"

She shook her head slowly. "Haven't heard her voice or set eyes on her for over sixteen years."

"Did you tell the police—about Lund? Her going there?"

She snorted derisively and sat down again as if the effort of standing by the window had drained her. "I'm a hooker, remember? Hookers don't talk to cops, and even if I did, Lund wouldn't have. He didn't like cops any more than I did. Spent a few years behind bars somewhere along the line. Never said what for." She paused. "I probably shouldn't be talking to you, either. I don't want to give my girl any more trouble. She had me for a mother. That was enough for any kid."

"She got herself involved in a bad situation."

"Maybe, but that's life, isn't it? One long line of 'bad situations.' She didn't kill anyone. No way. She wouldn't know how."

Cade wasn't going to argue with a mother's heart, even if it hadn't cared enough when it damn well should have. "Probably not, probably just afraid. And like I said, I'm not looking for your daughter, Mrs. Lintz, I'm looking for Addilene Wartenski. She was with Dianna in the house that night. There's a chance they ran away together." He stood. "If you could tell me where I can find Baylor, he may know something."

"If he did, he'd have a hard time telling you." She raised her eyes to his, looking tired and empty. "Lund's dead." She opened a drawer in her bed-side stand and pulled out a jeweler's box, offered it to him.

Cade opened it. Inside there was a gold bracelet inscribed *All my love, Lund.* And a note.

> *You'll get this when I pass on, Rox, because I want you to know you were always the one for me. Too bad about us, but it was your choice. But I never did stop thinking about you. This here bracelet proves that.*

There was a P.S.

> *Don't you worry about your Dianna. Or about what people say. She'll be okay. She's a strong one, and her and her friend are good girls. I did the best I could for her while she was here.*

Cade held out the note and box to return it and, for a moment, it linked them. Love lost. Cade knew all about that. "Lund Baylor," he said gently, "One of your regrets, Roxanne?"

She sealed her lips into a tight line, took the box from his hand, and put it back in the drawer. She fingered the note a moment before lifting des-olate eyes to meet his. "The biggest in a life filled with them." She turned away. "Good-bye, Harding."

When he reached the door and had his hand on the doorknob, she spoke again, quietly. "Harding?"

"Uh-huh?"

Silence.

"If you find my girl, hear anything about her, would you let me know? Before I . . . go, it would be nice to know she made it somehow."

He turned. She was facing the window and didn't look back at him. "Count on it," he said.

Outside, he didn't immediately get in his car. Instead, he walked across the street to a seedy half-block neighborhood park. The grass was brown and dry, and what was left of a children's play area rusted forlornly in the far corner: two broken swings and a lumpy slide that would do a hell of a job of tearing a kid's pants.

He sat on a wooden bench, feeling bleak—and angry. In an odd way, Roxanne Lintz reminded him of Susan Moore. Both had used the same expression, "I let her go." One, because she didn't believe she could do any more for a self-destructing, drug-addicted girl, the other because the call of the trade, money, meant more to her than providing a decent life for her daughter.

I let her go. . . .

Dana had used those same words. "I let him go, Cade. You have to find him, you have to!"

He clasped his hands between his knees and dropped his head. *I didn't find him for you, love. I tried. God, how I tried. . . .*

"Fuck!" He stood, straight and abruptly.

He was going home, he was going to have a beer, and he was going to find Star Lake. A dead end? Probably. But it was a place to go—and he was sick and tired of talking to himself.

He had a child to find, then a life to try and live.

Maybe Baylor was gone, and no doubt the Wartenski girl split years ago, but there was a chance someone in that small town might remember something.

Anything.

Chapter 7

"Addy! You're not going to believe this." Toby was close to hopping down the path to Cabin One, where Addy was putting the last paint strokes on the door trim.

"What?" she said, not taking her eyes off the bright blue ready to drip from the edge of her brush. She'd been a workaholic ever since her last call from Beauty—two days ago. And because she jumped every time the phone rang, she'd been happy enough to leave the office to Toby and keep herself busy with the maintenance.

"That last call"—he gestured with his head toward the office—"it was someone called Mrs. Jesse Nordham. She says her daughter's getting married in the spring, and there are a lot of guests coming from out of town. She says she drives by our place on her way to work, and she's noticed how much work's been done."

"And?" Addy made the last stroke, stood back and studied her work.

"And . . . she thinks this'd be a perfect spot for her guests." He paused, puffed up his chest. "All twelve cabins! In early March. Can you believe that?"

Addy's first thought was *will I still be here in March?* But she shoved it aside, determined to act as normal as she could, considering Frank Bliss stood at the edge of her life like some not-so-jolly green giant. *One day at a time, Addilene, one day at a time. And today is a good day.* "That's great, Toby. What dates exactly?" She rested her brush on the edge of the can, poured some paint thinner on her blue hands—she was a thorough, but messy painter—and rubbed at them with a rag.

"Well, now, that's the next part," he said. "She wants to come by and see the inside of the cabins, make sure the place isn't all show on the outside and crappy on the inside."

"She said that? The crappy bit?"

"No, not in those words, but I got her meaning." He smiled.

She smiled back. "Most of them are crappy . . . but by spring they'll be, if not chic, at least cute." She thought a moment. "If she comes, I can show Four, Six, and Eight. That'll give her an idea. The others"—she waved the paint rag in a circle—"she'll have to trust me on."

"That's what I figured. Anyway, I told her to come by next week sometime. That okay?"

"Okay," she said. "Thanks, Toby." Despite the black fog of worry she'd been in for the last two days, Addy couldn't help the surge of satisfaction warming her breast—Star Lake being noticed by someone driving by and looking good enough for her to call was a big turning point.

Toby was halfway up the hill to the office when he yelled back. "I meant to tell you, there was another call—someone named Beauty. She said she'd call later. Told me to tell you to stop worrying, that she has everything under control. She said you'd know what she meant."

"Toby!"

At the office door, he turned back.

"I told you to come and get me if she called—no matter what."

"She said not to, that her battery was running down—or something like that. She said just give you the message, and she'd call back later." He went into the office, no doubt to boot up his new computer. He hadn't been off the thing since she'd brought it in yesterday.

Damn!

What was Beauty doing? Addy's skin prickled thinking about her. She hoped she wouldn't do anything foolish. God knew Beauty was capable of some huge leaps of logic. That, coupled with her impulsive nature, could mean trouble. Surely she wouldn't try to play games with Frank Bliss.

She picked up her paint gear, straightened, and let her gaze drift over the lake. Ruffled by the wind, it was a blanket of rippling diamonds in the afternoon sun. She swiveled, her gaze feasting on the tiny property: the cabins, ten of them sporting new paint jobs and looking proud and pretty, the fresh gravel she'd laid in the driveway, and the new sign in amusing fifties-style lettering she'd had done for over the office door. All of it her work, her dream, her safety net.

She'd hated it when she'd arrived, and detested the cold, cranky Lund Baylor—a man who never seemed to care if she came or went. But over time, Star Lake became her home, and Lund became a friend. She shook her head, smiled faintly. For all the words exchanged between them over the years, she might as well have befriended that old oak down by the lake. But like that oak, Lund was always there—like Star Lake was here now.

The idea of running again, of leaving her home made her soul ache, but if that's what it took to protect Beauty and Gus, that's what she'd do.

She sucked in a breath, told herself to stop worrying. There was nothing she could do—at least not today. For now, she'd accept that Beauty told the truth, that things were under control, which she took to mean she'd lost Bliss somewhere on route. If she was wrong, she'd find out soon enough.

She headed for the maintenance shed, but hadn't taken more than three steps before she heard a car turn off the highway and scrunch its way along her new gravel.

She looked over her shoulder to see a Cherokee—maybe three or four years old—pull up to the office steps. A man and a dog—probably the same age as the truck—got out. Knowing Toby would handle them, Addy continued on to the shed and stowed her supplies neatly on the shelves.

The man was coming out of the office as she approached. The big yellow dog, who'd been sitting outside the door, got up, wagging its tail and wiggling its rear end as if he'd been abandoned for a month rather than the few minutes it had taken for his owner to check in.

There were three steps up to the office door. From the bottom one, she said, "Friendly?" And nodded at the dog.

The man smiled and patted the dog's head. "A teddy bear, especially if there's food around."

"Does he have a name?" She ran a hand along the silky fur on his back. She really should get a dog . . . if she stayed.

"Redge." He shifted his gaze from the dog and met hers. "What about you?"

Her nerves jangled, and she tucked her hands in the pockets of her overalls. "Me?" she said, sounding confused and stupid and knowing she was neither.

"Name. Do you have one?"

She pulled her hands from her pockets, stuck one out straight as a lance, and said, "Addy Michaels. I'm the owner of Star Lake."

She wasn't sure, but she thought she saw him blink a couple of times, his eyes sharpen. He definitely hesitated before taking her hand, then smiled as if he was obliged to, kind of cool and polite. "Addy. I'm Cade Harding. Nice to meet you."

"Likewise. I take it you'll be staying with us?" She dropped to one knee to pet the dog, and get out from under his eyes, which suddenly seemed a bit too intense.

"A couple of days at least." He hesitated. "Maybe more."

She got to her feet, risked looking up at him. He resembled Gus a little, or how she imagined

Gus would look with a few years on him. Dark hair, dark eyes, a bit of stubble around the chin, body on the lean side. Gus's face would be harder though, colder, not so . . . bookish or calm. And his eyes were a strange amber brown, nothing at all like Cade Harding's, which were a green color that reminded Addy of cedar boughs. "You sound like a man without a destination."

He didn't smile this time, but he did tilt his head a bit. Her nerves skittered again. She didn't like it.

"I've got a destination, all right," he said. "The end of a book. It's in my car. I'm a writer looking for a quiet place to get some work done." He glanced around. "From the road, Star Lake looked perfect."

Addy started up the stairs to the office. "What cabin did Toby put you in?"

He dangled his key. "Number Two."

She shook her head. "Wait here." She went into the office and grabbed the key for the newly renovated Cabin Six.

Outside she handed it to him. "Six faces the lake. If quiet is what you want, it's the best one." Their hands brushed when they exchanged keys.

"Thanks," he said, and continued to look at her in that funny, concentrated way he had.

She studied him, a tickle of nerves playing along her nape. "Do I remind you of someone?"

"Why do you ask?"

"You stare. Quite a lot, actually."

He averted his eyes a second, then swung them back to meet hers directly. "I didn't expect—I'm surprised, I guess. Resort owners aren't usually so young . . . so pretty."

Addy's jaw slackened. She had paint on her pants, probably her face, and she was certain her hair was a fright wig with blue highlights. The man was mad! If her nerves had jangled before, something was plucking them wild now. She had no idea how to respond. Getting a compliment was a whole new experience.

It turned out she didn't have to. The man tossed his key, let it fall back into his palm, and closed his hand around it. "Cabin Six. Thanks, Addy Michaels." Then he walked away, Redge hard on his heel.

She stood there like a dope and watched him and his dog get in his car and drive down to his cabin. He waved from the door before going inside.

Addy stepped into the office and peered out the window. Her nerves weren't rattling anymore. They were sensitized and on full alert.

She remembered the feeling from being on the streets—a weird tickle across her shoulders, like a dozen spiders playing hopscotch on her nape. Experience had taught her to heed that tickle, because more times than she could count it meant trouble ahead.

"Seems like a nice enough fellow."

She started. She'd forgotten entirely that Toby was in the office, lurking behind his new computer screen. "Yeah," she said, turning away from the window. "Where's he from?"

Toby peered around the screen. "Seattle, he says. And he isn't married."

"Huh?"

Toby wiggled his eyebrows. "I thought you might be interested, the way you were staring out that window."

"Toby, if you start the matchmaking thing, that computer goes back in the box—and you along with it."

Undaunted, he waved his index finger. "You were watching him . . . I saw you." The last three words were singsong.

"Oh . . . go multiply something. Preferably our profits." She rounded the counter and made a straight line for her apartment behind the office and firmly closed the door.

Toby was right, she was watching him, but not for the usual you-Tarzan-me-Jane reasons.

And I'll continue to watch you, Cade Harding. Those hopscotching spiders haven't been wrong yet.

Cade couldn't believe it. If that wasn't Addilene Wartenski, he'd get down on all fours and eat Redge's dinner.

Same age, same coloring . . . and that name. Addy. Too close to be a coincidence. It had to be her, had to.

Which meant she'd been here all along. The whole fifteen years since the murder and kidnapping. How the hell had the cops missed finding her? Then . . . considering Roxanne's relationship with the law, how could they? No way would she tell them Dianna and her friend had a safe haven with an old client.

If Cade had a million questions before, now he had another million. His slim hope in coming to Star Lake centered on finding a fresh lead, and he'd thought that chance remote. He sure as hell hadn't expected to come face-to-face with Addilene

Wartenski, wearing torn overalls, covered in blue paint, with a hairdo that looked as if she'd done it herself with dull shears during a sleepwalk—and the brightest, shrewdest eyes he'd ever seen in a woman.

Standing in the sightline of those eyes was god-damn life-threatening.

He was so shocked upon finding her here, he was paralyzed, had no idea what his next move should be—which meant the smart move was to do nothing at all.

He walked to the cabin window and looked across the small, pristine lake to the stands of trees that hid the farmland he knew was on the other side, and the mountains behind that. Near the dock, which had a half dozen or so canoes and rowboats tethered to it, a weeping willow rested its branches on the water.

Cade focused on the gently swaying branches, ran a hand through his hair, and told himself to ease down, think.

Information. He needed information. Which meant taking it slow and easy. He didn't want to scare her off, set her running. He reminded himself he was dealing with a woman who had an out-standing arrest warrant. She might have been a kid at the time, but when murder and kidnapping were the charges, the case was never deep-sixed.

He tried to think of the woman he'd just met as an accomplice to murder, as a kidnapper. But while he couldn't make the image stick, he told himself not to forget the police reports, Frank Bliss's damning statement.

He looked at the phone, thought about calling

Susan and Stan, but decided to wait. To be on the safe side, he'd drive into Lynden, at least a half hour back on the road he'd come in on, and call from there. Tomorrow. Not that he knew what in hell he was going to say.

All he knew was he had to be careful. He didn't want Susan Moore driving up here in a state of panicked excitement, demanding answers, maybe bringing in the police.

Redge whined from the door, anxious to explore his new territory.

"You're going to get your chance, boy, because we're definitely going to be here a while." At least he'd been quick enough to set up a reason to hang around.

He tossed his bag on the bed, unzipped it, and pulled out some running shorts and a black T-shirt.

The old guy at the desk said there was a good path circling the lake. He decided to try it. He needed to calm his mind, and running would let him zone out for a time. Exactly what he needed. After that, he'd do what he wasn't doing now. Think clearly.

He stripped, donned the shorts and top, and headed for the door. With the cloud cover and a slight breeze, the weather was perfect.

He set off, Redge at his heel.

Bliss was pissed off.

Either Beauty had no idea where she was going—possible, considering how many fuckin' gas stations she went into and pulled out that map of hers—or she was yanking his chain. Trying to make an ass of him.

And the whore never slept. Last night, she'd driven until almost two, pulled into a fleabag motel for maybe four hours, then hit the road again.

He watched her now, through the diner window, munching on a burger as if she didn't have a care in the world.

Him? He'd slept in the car, dreamt about her naked and alone in that swaybacked bed. Thought about how he could fix the "alone" part of the equation real fast—made his dick hard enough to shatter.

Now he was parked beside a gas station, across the street, while she gorged on a burger. His back was killing him, his stomach felt like it was filled with ditch water, and his head was a drum. All of it, her fault.

Plus the fact he was broke, which was beginning to worry him. He hadn't budgeted for this damn road tour he was on. He had one ace up his sleeve— Wayne Grover—if he could get hold of him. He was beginning to think that stupid bitch of a wife of his was lying when he called. Trouble with Grover was, he was small change. Handy, but not worth much.

He flicked on the radio, found some serious rock, and cranked it up. If Beauty was playing him, she'd answer for it. He'd make sure of it. For now, he'd wait it out, play the hand he'd planned.

Messing with her now might seriously cut into his profits, ruin any chance of meeting up with Vanelleto and Wartenski. Bliss couldn't decide what he wanted more—a wad of cash, to fuck Beauty stupid, or make Vanelleto pay for what he'd done. The good thing was, right now it was looking like he'd get all three.

Of course, she could be heading to Wart, which only doubled his chances. A little pressure, and one or the other of them would rat Vanelleto out, and applying pressure to Wartenski and Beauty would be the first genuine fun he'd had in seven years.

He straightened. Beauty was coming out of the diner. He slunk down into the seat, but kept her in view.

She got into her car and pulled out of the parking lot onto the highway.

Yes! She was heading the same way she was going yesterday.

It looked as if she finally knew where she was going.

This time when Addy's phone rang at one A.M., it didn't wake her up. She picked up on the first ring, her chest thick with worry. "Hello? Is it you?"

"Yes, it's me. I called earlier, but you weren't around."

"I know. Are you okay?"

"Better than I was yesterday."

"Did you lose him? Tell me you've lost him." She could barely draw a breath as she waited for an answer.

"Actually, I'm looking at him right now, from my motel window. He's parked across the street," she said, sounding calm. Then she laughed as if pleased with herself. "Exactly where I want him."

Addy went cold. "Beauty. What are you doing? Please, please, don't do anything stupid."

"Wouldn't be the first time, Wart."

Oh, God . . . Addy pressed a hand to her chest. "You are still coming here, aren't you?"

"That's why I'm phoning. I don't think so. Like you said, it would be dangerous." There was a pause. "I'll handle Bliss my way and the less you know, the better. You got dragged into enough dirt fifteen years ago. You don't need any more." Her voice trailed off, low, weary. "Seeing Bliss again, thinking about—"

"Don't!" Addy said. "Don't go there. You've got to stick to the plan. Try and forget . . ." She closed her eyes. *Stupid, stupid words. As if any of them could ever forget that day, that brutal night, and Beauty had more to forget than any of them, except maybe Gus—or that baby, if he'd been old enough to remember.*

Addy shoved her chair away from the cabin plans she'd been working on. Outside the halo of light provided by her desk lamp, she stood, carried the phone to the window. She forced her heart to quiet, her brain to still. "Tell me what I can do, Beauty. I love you. I want to help."

A drift of quiet came down the line.

"How can you say that, Wart? I walked away from you, from Lund. I never looked back."

"I don't care about that. We all had to get some kind of life going. I was mad, sure. And hurt, but none of it mattered. You were there for me when no one else gave a damn." Addy choked up, the confusions and loneliness of a thirteen-year-old girl heavy in her mind, weighted in her soul.

"Gus was there, too. Don't forget that." Beauty said, her tone soft, drifting to the past. "Do you ever wonder about him, Addy? Where he went? What he's doing?"

Addy swallowed. "Where he is, or what he's doing, doesn't matter now. You're the one who matters." She brushed back her hair, left her hand tight on her nape. She couldn't talk about Gus, couldn't think about him without her brain hurting. She'd never understood him, what his . . . power was, and she was as confused as ever about her own feelings for him. Back then, it was like she was hypnotized by him, because he knew all the answers, or she'd thought he did until that night. But Beauty's fascination for him—back then she'd called him her one pure love—always scared her. To think it might still be there made her weak in the knees. "Tell me what you're planning," she said. "I'll help you." *Talk you out of it.*

"What I'm going to do is between me, Bliss, and whoever up there gives a damn."

Addy gripped the phone, her hands cold, her grip painfully tight. "You're not going to lose him, are you."

"I'll lose him all right. Permanently."

"Don't say that!"

"Why? What difference does it make. I'm already wanted for one murder. I might as well up the count and get some satisfaction while I'm at it."

"Beauty, listen to me." Addy knew there was desperation in her voice, but it was nothing compared to the fear simmering low in her belly. "What happened back then . . . to you, to Belle Bliss, it was bad. Horrible. We made a terrible mistake. We didn't think things through. Maybe because of how we felt about Belle, or because we listened to Gus—"

"Gus saved our asses, Addy. Don't you forget that!"

"Maybe you're right, but so many times I've wondered how it would have turned out if we stayed." She rubbed at the knot in her stomach. "If we'd done the right thing, instead of running like scared rabbits."

"We had no choice. What cop would have listened to three kids fresh from The Ave, while the local crime techies were mopping up Saint Teresa's blood?"

"Belle Bliss was a long way from being Saint Teresa."

"You know that, I know that, but no one else did. Sure as hell Washington State's child protection unit—or whatever they called themselves—didn't."

"Frank did."

"Yeah, but it wasn't in his interests to tell anyone. Frank Bliss was a lying, brutal, raping pig. He still is. He deserves to die." Her voice was higher now, slightly breathless.

"Maybe he does." Addy worked to stay calm, but it wasn't easy. She'd never discussed committing murder with anyone before. Last time, it had just . . . happened. "But it's not your job to choose the time and place." She lowered her voice to a soothing level. "Listen to me, Beauty. Get in your car, point it north, and come here. So what if Bliss follows? We'll handle him—together."

"Addilene Wartenski, always the problem solver," she said, her voice low and disinterested.

"And there's another thing."

"Uh-huh," she sounded bored.

"You don't have it in you to kill, Beauty. Not Frank Bliss or anyone else. There's another way. All we have to do is think it through."

"And I think this problem's way beyond you, Wart. So I'm going to hang up now. I'll call you when it's over."

"Beauty! Don't hang up." She put her free hand to her face, clenched her eyelids tight, and prepared to say the only words she knew for certain would buy time—but not at all certain they'd do anything to save Bliss's miserable life. "I'll call Gus."

Chapter 8

Addy heard Beauty gasp. "You know where Gus is? You said you hadn't heard from him."

"I lied."

For a long time, the line between Beauty and Addy was filled with silence.

Beauty finally broke it. "Why, Addy, why did you lie?"

"Gus asked me to. Made me promise if you ever did come back to Star Lake not to—"

"Not to tell me where he was."

"Yes."

More silence, then a hissing breath Addy knew came with a shake of the head, and a crushing hurt. "That son of a bitch," she murmured, the words completely lacking in malice.

"It was Lund who found him, not long after you left. He thought there was a chance you were with him. He never said as much, but he missed you, and he worried." She stopped. "Anyway, those old jailbird pals of his had friends in the right places. They had no luck finding you, but they found Gus—can't remember what name he was using— in less than two weeks. I guess it was easier for them to find a booster in San Diego than a seventeen-year-old girl in the cab of a long hauler." She went back to her chair, weary suddenly. "Lund said I should be the one to call Gus, so I did. When he heard my voice, he got mad. Real mad. He said it was dangerous for us to talk, always would be, and that I could blow everything. He said never to call him again, and that when our call ended he'd cancel the telephone number."

"Same old Gus, still giving orders," Beauty interjected, that predictable and dangerous trace of awe in her voice.

"Yeah." Addy smiled weakly. "Gus was good at that. When I finally got him to listen, I told him about you leaving, that we had no idea where you were, and asked could he help."

"What did he say?"

"He went quiet for a long time, then he said he had no idea where you were, and that you and I weren't his business anymore."

"And he told you not to tell me you'd found him. You're sure."

"I think he was afraid you'd call him, want to see him."

"Where is he, Wart?"

"I don't know."

"But you said—"

"I know what I said, but I don't know where he is. It's not like I have him in my address book. And I never called him again." She stopped. "The odd thing is he called me a few times after that. Never said much, asked if you'd turned up, if we'd heard anything. Never said a word about . . . that night, what he was doing, where he was. Nothing. His last call was a few months ago, just before Lund died." She hesitated. "On that call, he either forgot to block the call display feature on his phone or assumed I didn't have it. I do, and I wrote down the number."

"Give it to me."

"No." It was the only hand Addy had, and she intended to play it close. "But if that number is still good, I'll find him, and I'll tell him to come here. That's the best I can do." With Gus as a lure, she had a good chance of keeping her friend alive, and she wasn't above using it. In a calm and certain voice that didn't come close to reflecting her own fears, she added, "Here's the deal. You forget this stupid idea you have of killing Bliss, and I'll do everything I can to find Gus. He'll know what to do." Which was exactly what she was afraid of. "I think that's a good trade-off, don't you?"

A wash of tense silence claimed the line. Addy waited.

"You've turned into a sly little bitch," she said, sounding more impressed than angry. "You know damn well I'll wait forever if there's a chance of seeing Gus again." She stopped. "And you're right, he'll know what to do. Hell, if I'm lucky, he'll kill Bliss for me. Finish what he started in that shed." She stopped and Addy could hear her heavy breathing. "Find him, Addy. Please. I'll check in tomorrow night." She hung up.

Addy sagged against the windowsill, clicked the

off button, and did some deep breathing of her own. Beauty was right. Gus would kill Frank Bliss. In a heartbeat.

What have I done?

Probably made the biggest mistake of your life, Addilene Wartenski.

After all these years, Gus's hold on Beauty still lay coiled within her—an unbreakable bond as strong, and as dangerous, as ever—and Addy had used it to put herself, Beauty, Gus, and Bliss on a collision course.

Like that hellish night fifteen years ago.

Her stomach an aching knot, she looked up at the black, star-studded sky outside her window. "Don't like unfinished business, do you?"

The question begged an answer, but it didn't come from the starry sky. It came from her uneasy heart. "I started this, I'll finish it somehow," she vowed. She had to stop Bliss—or Beauty—from spilling more blood.

So much blood . . . She closed her eyes.

Beauty was rash, unpredictable, and Gus had the soul of a gravestone, but they'd looked out for her when no one else did, and now it was her turn. She owed them, because she'd never have made it without Beauty's brash optimism or Gus's endless pool of strength.

But that was then and this was now. She closed her eyes. She wasn't that thirteen-year-old girl anymore, and she didn't need anyone to take care of her.

Addy yearned to know the truth about that night, the whole truth. But all she had were sounds, pieces of a puzzle that wouldn't fit. A dark night, a baby screaming, a gun firing over and over. Gus's shout to *get out*. Stumbling through the black fields behind Beauty.

Then the years of questions with no answers. In the year before Beauty left Star Lake, she'd never talked about it, and when she'd ventured to ask Gus about it during one of his rare calls, he'd cut her off, said he didn't want to "go there with her."

She pulled the shutters closed on that barren part of her brain, squashed the simmer of disloyalty that made her stomach turn, and tried to concentrate on the job at hand—saving Beauty from herself.

She'd bought some time, now all she had to do was find Gus Vanelleto.

She lowered her gaze, looked out in time to see Cabin Six's lights go on. She looked at her watch. Nearly two.

It looked as if she weren't the only one not sleeping tonight.

Cade worked until six o'clock, showered, and headed for Lynden. He ate breakfast at a bright, surprisingly busy diner for such an early hour, and to kill more time, and give his and Redge's legs a stretch, he walked the small town's main street. If he were in tourist mode instead of edgy mode, he'd have spent more time enjoying the Dutch-themed farming town.

But edgy won out, and he stopped at a gas station pay phone.

Susan picked up on the third ring. "Hello?"

"Susan, it's Cade."

Briefly, without embellishment or specifics, he told her about finding one of the girls.

"Which one?" she asked, her voice sharp with excitement.

"Right now, I'd rather not say. There's always the chance I'm wrong."

She ignored his evasion. "I can't believe it. After all this time, finally a break." She sounded as rocked as he'd been yesterday, when he'd first looked into Wartenski's crystal blue—very wary—eyes. "Where exactly are you?" she asked.

He imagined her reaching for a pen, jotting down the address, her and Stan jumping into that big Mercedes of hers, and arriving within hours. Screwing everything. "I'd rather not say that, either."

The line went quiet a moment. "In other words, keep your distance, Susan Moore, or you'll mess things up?"

"In a word, yes." He was damn sure Susan not getting what she wanted, when she wanted, was a unique experience for her. "For now I want you—and Stan—to leave it to me. Finding the girl was more dumb luck than anything else, and if she gets suspicious, that luck will run out. She'll be gone, and anything she knows about Josh will go with her. In a few days, when I know more, I'll call."

Silence bled down the line, then a deep inhalation. "Very well. I'll leave it in your hands—for now. You've got your few days. But I'd like a daily report—and your cell number."

"Don't have one, but I said I'd call and I will. Not every day, but often enough to keep you in the loop."

He was about to hang up when he heard, "Cade."

"Uh-huh."

"Find Josh. Please find Josh." Every trace of demand had left her voice.

"I'll do my best." He put the receiver in its cradle, left his hand on it—not sure his best was good enough.

When he got back to Star Lake, it was close to ten. He spotted Addy rolling a wheelbarrow of dirt toward Cabin Five. He watched her for a time—the deftness of her movements, her intense concentration, the easy strength in her slim body.

Yesterday, after his initial shock at finding her, he'd been surprised at how pretty she was, how different from the tight-lipped, sullen young girl in the DSHS photo. He'd started out looking for a girl—her image strong in his mind—and he'd found a woman, an attractive woman with a direct gaze and a strong handshake. Both of which caught him off guard, as an investigator—and as a man.

Curious feeling . . . dozens of women must have crossed his path since Dana died, and he hadn't looked at any of them twice.

But he was looking at Addilene Wartenski now and liking what he saw—a hell of a lot more than he should, given what he was here to do, which was get to know her, figure her out, and gain her trust. Whatever it took to find a missing boy.

He got out of his truck and opened the back door to let Redge out. He immediately ran to visit Addy, and Cade followed him. Thank God for dogs. They made one hell of an icebreaker.

"That"—he gestured at the overloaded barrow—"looks like a good alternative to the gym."

She grunted in response, tipped the wheelbarrow, and shook the last of the soil onto the pile. That done, she wiped her forehead with the back of her hand, which gave him a good look at a strong, finely muscled, tanned arm. She didn't waste any time picking up the shovel and digging into the hill of dirt. "You were up and out early," she said, not looking at him. "Lots of energy for a man whose light was on all night."

"You have a curfew around here?"

"No. I don't sleep much. And I like to keep an eye on the place. We've had occasional trouble with town kids coming through." She stopped long enough to point toward the dock. "They like midnight canoe rides."

He followed her gesture and looked out over the jewel-like lake, its surface silvered under the autumn sun, its dock home to a dozen or so canoes and rowboats. "So do I, with the right person." It occurred to him that Dana would love this place.

When he looked back, Addy was leaning on her shovel, studying him. "And who would that be? Your wife, girlfriend, or what's that other term, 'significant other'?"

He let the wife reference drift through him, and the usual void opened up. He forced himself up and out. It was easier than usual, and he wasn't sure how he felt about that. "At the moment, none of the above," he said, adding, "the only 'significant' woman in my life right now is standing in front of me." He looked toward the lake. "You interested in a canoe ride?"

She didn't blink. "Are you . . . flirting with me?" She looked at him as if he were six years old and had said his first curse word.

"Taking a stab at it." He rubbed his chin as he felt a grin take shape on his mouth, not the usual good-for-all-occasions twist, but a real smile.

"You're wasting your time. I'm unflirtable," she said matter-of-factly and went back to work, spreading a shovelful of dirt as if it were a tablespoon of cereal.

"There are men who'd take that as a challenge."

She looked up sharply, warily. "Are you one of them?"

"How about I leave you wondering about that and go back to work?" He glanced down. Redge was scraping lightly at the soil, preparing himself for a deeper, more serious excavation. "Before my dog destroys all sign of your work in progress."

He collared the dog and headed for his cabin.

"Mr. Harding?"

He turned back. "Obviously when it comes to flirting, I forgot rule number one—get on a first-name basis. The name's Cade, remember?"

She nodded but looked uncomfortable. "Cade, what do you do, exactly?"

"I thought I mentioned it. I write."

"Yes, but what do you write?"

"Right now? A series. What they call young adult. Targeted to teens, mostly."

She frowned. "You write teenage stuff?"

She didn't look impressed, and he didn't expect her to be. He wasn't so sure he was, either. "I wrote a book about a character called Zero a couple of years back, a street kid turned crime buster. It worked, and the publisher wants more."

Her frown turned skeptical. "What do you know about kids, especially ones who spend time on the streets?"

"I write fiction. I don't have to know. I make it up as I go along." Old joke, but usually enough to satisfy a nonwriter's curiosity, and he had no idea how she'd react to the rest of his résumé. He'd have to think about that. "And the streets hold a lot of stories, especially for kids. And a fascination."

She cupped her hands over the top of the shovel, rested her chin on it, and looked thoughtful. "You make it sound easy. But I think it would be hard to make a book sound . . . true enough for kids. They can spot bu—what isn't real from a mile off."

"You're right, which is why I avoid the B.S. Talk about life on the streets as it really is, hard and dangerous." *As you very well know.*

Her lip twisted upward into the slightest of sneers. "And this Zero character of yours comes along to save the day for all those dumb street kids?"

"Street kids aren't dumb—at least not many of them. Most of them wouldn't be on the walk if someone threw them a lifeline. They're more confused than anything. All those surging hormones, alien feelings, peer pressures. Maybe some bad breaks tossed in the mix. Add to that a lot of them got the booby prize in the parent contest." He stopped, knew he sounded too much like the prof he once was. Hell, next thing you know he'd be citing stats. "It's tough being a kid. Always has been. Even harder now, I think."

She'd had those blue crystal eyes of hers locked to his like twin lasers, her expression growing more intense as he spoke. "You like kids, don't you?" Her words were shaded with amazement.

"Yeah, I do. Especially teens. They're fun, wide open to life, and they all think they're going to live forever. What's not to like?"

Her expression still thoughtful, a smile briefly softened her sober expression. "You must write very good books, Cade Harding."

He walked the few steps back to where she stood. Time to change the subject, time to remember why he was here, time for him to stop talking and her to start. When he got closer, she straightened. "And you've given me a compliment, Addy Michaels. And I, being a male who comes with the standard, overly developed ego, officially take it as a return flirt." He lowered his head until their eyes met. "So how about one of those midnight boat rides the local teens are so keen on? I'll bore you with my literary aspirations—the amazing adventures of Zero Nash—and you can tell me all about you."

She went stone still. "There's noth—"

"Nothing to tell? Definitely a cliché. And definitely not allowed."

She took a step back. "You're weird."

"But in a good way?" He lifted a brow.

"I'm not sure yet."

"If you let me buy you dinner, you can get 'sure.' "

"I don't go out for dinner." She started to dig.

"But you do eat."

"Straight out of the microwave, every third Thursday in May." She kept on digging. "You could try again then."

As brush-offs went, it left him little recourse. Addy Michaels, aka the Wart, intended to keep to herself.

He did have one ace up his sleeve though, and tonight he'd pull it out.

Bliss watched Beauty pull up to the parking area for registration at the best hotel in Sacramento, get out of her red Lexus, and walk in. A few minutes after that, a bellman came out with her keys, opened her trunk, and took out her baggage.

He guessed she'd tired of the roach motel circuit.

When the bellman disappeared inside, bags in hand, Beauty came out. She covered her eyes to look into the setting sun and scanned the street both ways. He hunkered down in his seat, but not far enough that he couldn't see her say something to the doorman before crossing the check-in lanes and heading to—

What the hell . . .

He dropped below sightline.

The next thing he knew, she was knocking on his window.

Fuck! She'd made him. Found him cowering in his cheap rental car like some kind of two-bit Peeping Tom.

She rapped again. Bliss gathered up some brain cells—and some cool—and hit the down button. She put both hands on the door.

"Don't even think of getting out." She pointed toward the doorman, who was standing by a marble pillar watching them closely. "I told him you were an ex-boyfriend, that you were stalking me, and that if you got out of the car, he was to call the police immediately." She tilted her head. "You got that?"

He laughed. "The cops don't bother me, baby, but they'll sure as hell bother you." And send him back to prison for more years than he cared to count for skipping the state while under parole, but no need to tell her that.

"Yeah, well, if the cops don't bother you, you sick creep, this damn well should." She turned sideways, slid a compact piece out of her tote. Pearl handle and all, a nice little girly gun. Making it no less lethal.

"Now that's cute. You planning to gun me down while that guy in the long coat over there"—he lifted his chin toward the hotel entrance, the watching doorman—"plays witness and takes notes?"

"No. As a matter of fact, I want you alive, Bliss. Very much alive. What I'm doing is taking control of the game. And this," she lifted the gun slightly, "is my good luck charm. You? You lay a hand on me and I'll blow your dick off—piece by piece."

"Oh, I'm so scared." He really didn't like the look in her eyes. "And, baby? This isn't all about that honey-dipped pussy of yours, it's about money. Remember." He lifted his hand, rubbed his thumb and index finger together. Out of the corner of his eye, he saw the doorman straighten. He pulled his hand back, gripped the lower part of the steering wheel.

"You'll get your money." She stood now, took a step back from the window, fixed her eyes on him. "Gus is bringing it. I told him we needed a quarter of a million dollars and you'd be out of our lives for good. Matter of fact, we'll throw in an airline ticket—to Antarctica."

Vanelleto! He was right, she did get in touch with him. Fantastic! He tried to stem the rush of adrenaline. "Vanelleto giving me money? Gotta love that." He shook his head and smiled. "Bastard would rather put a bullet in my head."

"Who the hell wouldn't?" She gave him a cold smile.

"But now that I think about it, moving doesn't come cheap." He met her gaze, his own as cool as he could make it. If Vanelleto offered a quarter of a million, there was probably plenty left in the strongbox. "A half mil, in cash, and I'm history."

"That's a lot of money."

He looked at her crotch, made a loud smacking kiss. "If your boyfriend, Gus, wants me to stop dreamin' about *that* every night, he'll pay."

"You know, after you, Bliss, I could never look at another man without remembering how truly tiny your penis was. Smallest one I've ever seen. And I've seen a lot."

"Bitch!"

"Now I'm going into that fancy hotel—with its nice secure rooms—and take a bath, wash you away. Then I'll make some calls. Gus isn't easy to find. It'll take a while." She spun on her heel.

"Don't you want to know where to find me?"

She gave him a filthy look. "You want your money, you'll stay right where you are. Chasing my tail—like always." With that, she walked away and didn't look back.

"How long?" he yelled out the window.

She kept on walking.

Bliss slammed his palm against the steering wheel—pissed off, hard as a rail, and pulsing with excitement. He needed to figure things out. Half a mil! Shit. Hell, he should have said a million. Still, this was turning out better than he planned.

Through the windshield, he watched Beauty go into the hotel, say something to the doorman, and slip him some cash. He checked his watch, almost four P.M.

He turned the key in the ignition, slammed the car into gear, and headed out of the parking lot.

The way he figured it, while she took her bath and made her calls, he'd make one of his own. This thing was taking longer than he thought. He needed a few bucks to tide him over.

Thank God for Grover. No half million there, but a convenient piggy bank all the same.

Chapter 9

Grover parked his car on the street and walked up the driveway to Susan Moore's posh house, his hands sweating, his nerves jumping.

In his job, most of his days were spent visiting rat holes on the lower south side where his kids lived—off and on—with parents who couldn't see past the whiskey level in the bottle on the kitchen table, or the needle full of poison they planned to ram into their arms.

Grover hated them all. Useless junkies. The world would do itself a favor if it tossed them, and their addictions, behind a chain-link fence. Let them rot there with a mountain of heroin or crack just out of reach as added torture. Maybe that way they'd quit ruining their kids' lives and self-destruct.

Like he should have . . .

Again he looked at the beautiful home, the wealth and safety it represented.

If he hadn't placed Josh Moore with Belle that

day, the boy would have grown up here, been loved and cared for, had nothing but the best.

Grover's chest deflated, and he stifled the urge to turn tail and run. Like it or not, he was no better than the junkie parents he reviled. His sin was no lighter than theirs, because as he'd learned to his unending sorrow, there was no addiction baser than the passions of love.

He rang the doorbell, heard the rich chime of the bell inside the house. He swallowed the nerves tingling in his throat and pulled in his gut. Much as he enjoyed this beautiful home and the woman in it, he didn't want to be here, start the pretense all over again, but he had to keep his eye on things, especially Harding. If he connected with Bliss . . .

He swallowed again when he remembered the message on his business voicemail.

"Hey, Wayne. Guess who? I'm out—but I'm guessing Sandra already told you that bit of news." He chuckled, sounded pleased with the threat his call to Sandra implied. "But I'm short on cash, so I'd appreciate you floating me a loan. Right now I'm checking up on a mutual friend of ours, which puts me on the road for a time, but I'll call to set something up. Western Union maybe." Then a pause, the prod of a white hot poker. "Had a nice chat with the little woman, by the way. Didn't quite get to going over old times, but there's always next time. And the job, Grover, how's the job going? Talk to you soon, buddy."

He'd expected the call, the reference to his work, had even got some cash together for his blood money, but the "mutual friend" reference troubled him. He hoped it didn't mean what he thought it did.

Between hearing Bliss on his voicemail and being unable to reach Cade Harding, Grover was wrecked. Bliss was trouble enough, but Harding, with his probing eyes and endless questions, was a dangerously loose cannon. Who knew what he'd turn up?

Which was why he was here, he reminded himself, to get a line on that cannon, and get what information he could. No way would Harding find anything incriminating in the files he'd given him, and thank God Bliss had skipped before Cade could talk to him, but it made sense, considering what was at stake, to be extra careful.

Stan opened the door, his smile warm and immediate. "Grover, how are you? Come in, come in. Susan and I were about to have lunch. You can join us. She'll be so pleased to see you."

"I don't want to intrude." Lunch. His stomach leaped at the thought of food. Sandra had given him half a grapefruit and black coffee, and he hadn't had time to so much as grab a donut since. He'd been too busy tearing a malnourished four-year-old from the arms of her crackhead mother.

Stan stepped aside, waved him in. "No intrusion at all. And your timing is perfect. We've had some good news."

"Good news?" His every nerve jumping to alert, he stepped into the entry.

"Very good news. At least we think so." He gestured to the hall, which Wayne knew led to the kitchen.

Years ago, he'd spent many hours at this house, consoling Susan, offering his help. His endless, soothing lies. They'd become friends. And know-

ing her stubborn dedication to finding her grandson, he'd made sure to nurture that friendship,
dropping in occasionally to touch base, keep abreast
of things. Wayne followed Stan through the short
hall. "You're sure my timing isn't inconvenient,"
he said.

"Not at all. You know you're welcome in this house
anytime. God knows, Susan is grateful for all you
tried to do."

"Unsuccessfully," he muttered, as always uncomfortable with Susan's gratitude, his endless duplic-
ity. He hated to think about what he done, what he
hadn't done, and what fate had befallen Susan's
grandson because of it.

"You worked harder to find that boy than any
detective in Seattle." He put a hand on Grover's
shoulder. "Now, come and eat with us. If our gratitude isn't enough, maybe I can tempt you further
by telling you Susan has made a pasta salad big
enough for a not-so-small army. And . . . a peach
pie."

Grover rubbed his belly. "That's the closer, Stan.
Lead on."

Stan chuckled, and Grover followed him down
the hall to find Susan in the kitchen. It always surprised him that, with her money, she did her own
cooking. Years ago, he'd remarked on it, and she'd
told him the kitchen was the only place she relaxed—there and with her tiny roses. One winter,
she'd given him a rosebush to take home to
Sandra, its pink buds just breaking into flower.

For the rest of the evening, he'd answered questions about Susan Moore: how much money did
she have, how old was she, was he having an affair

with her. When she was done with the questions, she took scissors to the vibrant little bush and cut it to bits. Then she'd turned on him. He'd never taken her a gift since. Too risky.

"Wayne, what a pleasant surprise," Susan said when she spotted him. She came to him and hugged him hard, the dish towel in her hand swinging across his back. "It's been too long."

It had been too long since he'd been warmed by a woman, taken in the comfort of their soft, magical bodies. He returned the hug, drew her affection in deep where he could savor it later, then let go. He held her from him. "You're looking wonderful. This man treating you right?" he said, forcing a smile and glancing at Stan, who loomed over them like a giant oak.

"Yes, he's treating me fine." She smiled, wiped her hands on the dish towel, and set it on the counter. "Sit down, both of you," she commanded, gesturing at the table. "I'll get the sandwiches and salad."

When they were all seated, she said, "Has Stan told you?"

"He mentioned some good news." Afraid Susan's good news would ruin his appetite, he took a bite of his sandwich—simple ham and cheese, loaded with mayo, perfect.

"We've heard from Cade," she said.

The bread lodged in his throat, and he took a swig of water, shifted back in his chair. "Where is Cade? I've called him a couple of times to see how he's doing and don't get either an answer or voicemail."

She rolled her eyes. "Doesn't have voicemail, or a cell phone. The man's a Luddite."

Stan laughed, dug for more salad. "Hardly. He simply likes to control who he talks to and when. Nothing wrong with that."

"Anyway"—she waved a hand—"it doesn't matter what he is or what he does. He's found one of the girls."

Grover's heart seized up and his breath ballooned in his throat. A faint layer of sweat oozed out of the pores on his forehead. He dabbed at it with his napkin. "Which one? And where is she?" He knew he'd asked the question too quickly, too panicky. He had to cool down.

But Christ, finding one of the kids from that night was his worst goddamn fear in living color.

Wayne's brain, already fevered by Bliss's message, couldn't process it. He prayed his anxiety passed as pleased excitement.

"That's just it. He won't tell us. He says he wants to be absolutely sure before he does anything. Apparently he's afraid Stan and I, if we knew too much, would scare her off." She sniffed, looked angry, but it didn't last long. "Can you believe it, Wayne? After all this time, a chance, a real chance to find out about Josh." She stopped. "I should be there. I really should. If I could talk to her, woman to woman, I know it would help—that she'd help."

Grover reached across the table and took her hand. "This is wonderful news, Susan, but Cade's right. It's best you sit back and let him finish the job. If he wants more time, give it to him, because if he's gone this far, this fast, the man knows what he's doing." *Damn him to hell!*

"I second that." Stan tossed his napkin on the

table. "But the PI in me is damned keen to hear how he pulled it off."

"Me, too. I put years in looking for those kids, and it was as if they'd all disappeared down a rabbit hole." He covered the lie with a shake of his head and forced the fear down, tried to get himself into a more useful frame of mind. "Did he at least say how he found her?"

"Not really," Susan said. "I know he was starting to interview everyone associated with the case, but in the end he said it was mostly 'dumb luck.' "

Grover took another bite of his sandwich, gave himself something to chew on, so he wouldn't be expected to speak and would have time to think. His terror mounted. Dumb luck wasn't easy to duplicate—and luck of any kind in his life had always been in short supply.

Stan added, "Dumb luck, my butt. I know he talked to some people. My guess is he found something in those early interviews that no one else did. Hate to admit it, but maybe there is something to that profiling stuff after all."

Wayne nodded. "Must be." He wiped his mouth with his napkin, reached across and patted Susan's hand. "And I hope for your sake it leads to something concrete, and soon."

"Cade said he needed a few days," she said. "So we've no choice but to wait."

A few days . . .

"Good idea, I think," Wayne said. "Like I said, give the man some time." He looked at his watch, got to his feet. "I didn't realize it was so late. I've got a foster parent review in less than an hour." He bent and kissed Susan on the cheek. "I really am pleased for you." He wagged a finger and gave her a mock frown. "But you will call me, keep me informed of any new developments, won't you?"

"You know I will, Wayne. The minute I hear anything." She stood and faced him, her expression grave. "And even if what we learn about what happened to Josh isn't . . . what we want to hear, at least we'll have the truth. The whole truth."

The whole truth . . .

Wayne didn't want to think about what that would do to him, to Sandra. To his work.

His thoughts were a random, insane mess until well after he'd cleared Susan's elegant circular driveway, but in the end only one thing made any kind of sense. Odds were Bliss and Harding were onto the same girl, that "mutual friend," Bliss had bragged about on the phone.

A few blocks from Susan Moore's house, he pulled off to the side of the road to think, to plan.

No way could he find Harding, but Bliss would be contacting him again. His need and greed would ensure that.

Grover pressed his fingers against the sudden flash of pain in his head. One thing was certain.

It wouldn't be Western Union delivering the cash.

After six o'clock, Addy tried Gus's number again—or at least what she hoped was still his number. The area code put him in Florida, but remembering the nomadic Gus, he could have moved a dozen times in the year and a half since she'd picked up his number off the call display.

Damn! Voicemail—again.

What worried her was that it wasn't Gus's voice on the recording. It was a generic message confirming the telephone number, asking her to leave a message, and nothing else.

She'd called off and on all day, and each time her nerves arced and spiked through her like a summer lightning storm. The difference this time was she'd left a message—about an hour ago. *Call Wart ASAP. It's urgent.* She hoped it was cryptic enough and made him angry enough to return her call.

Now all she could do was wait, and hope Beauty would do the same.

She stood and stretched. God! Every bone and muscle in her body ached from the day's work. And she was starving.

She remembered Cade Harding's invitation to dinner. If she'd accepted, she'd be tucking into a good meal right now—a meal cooked on a real stove, by a real person who used herbs and spices, wore an apron, and wielded wooden spoons with the skill of a master.

Too bad that would have meant playing nice with Cade. She was too exhausted for that, too keyed up. What she really wanted to do was scream and run naked into the lake.

Neither of which was an option she could exercise without sending every guest at Star Lake running for the exit road. Not that there were many at this time of year.

She stretched again, planted her hands on the small of her back, and massaged deeply. The microwave beckoned. She did have a new rice thing, not too appealing, but it would have to do.

When the phone rang, her heart landed in her mouth, and she rushed to pick up the receiver.

"Addy?"

"Beauty, are you okay?" She closed her eyes, said a silent prayer that her old friend hadn't done anything stupid in the last twenty-four hours. With Beauty, you never could be sure.

Her question was met with a languorous and very noisy sigh. "Better than okay. I'm in a four-star hotel in a bathtub so deep I could drown in it. I have a glass of perfectly chilled chardonnay at my fingertips and room service on the way."

Addy heard her drag deep on a cigarette and a shaft of furious and totally irrational envy poked her chest like a sharp nail. She shoved it aside and got to the matter at hand. "What are you doing?"

"Taking a night off from Frank Bliss." She laughed, and Addy suspected she was drunk. "You know, I'd forgotten how incredibly stupid he is, and when I—oops, dropped my wine in the tub."

"Beauty, what did you do? Tell me." *You crazy fool! If you were here, I'd wring your long, beautiful neck.*

"I had a chat with him. Told him we'd pay him a half million dollars to get lost." She giggled. "Of course, he accepted."

The air departed Addy's lungs in a loud exhale. "A half mill—" She couldn't even say it. "Where are we going to get that kind of money?"

"We're not, my foolish friend, but that slime bucket doesn't know that. And by the time he figures it out, Gus will be here."

Addy's stomach dropped. She should have known, now that Beauty had Gus on her brain, she wouldn't think about anything else.

Beauty picked up on her silence. "Did you reach him yet?" She took a drag or drink or whatever, but Addy knew she was waiting for her answer.

"No," she said. "Not yet. And Beauty?"

"Uh-huh?"

"I want you to stay in that hotel until you hear from me. Do you understand that?" She didn't bother to add that there was always the chance—a good one—that Gus would blow her off and want nothing to do with them or Bliss. That was way too much reality for a woman in a bubble bath drinking chardonnay.

"Yes, ma'am!" She giggled again. "But you can stop worrying, little sister, because I've got everything under control. For the next couple of days, you can consider Frank Bliss officially on ice. Call you tomorrow. Ta ta."

"Beauty!" Too late. All she could do was stare at the dead phone in her hand. Except . . . she picked up the number from call display and dialed.

"Carlton Towers, how may I help you?"

"Sorry, wrong number. But can you tell me what town I've dialed?"

"Sacramento, California."

"Thanks." She hung up, walked to her beat-up sofa, and slumped into it like one of those sacks of cement she'd had delivered yesterday. There was nothing more she could do. At least she knew where Beauty was, knew she was safe—for the time being.

She rested her head on the back of the sofa, bone weary, and closed her eyes. Her brain wanted to shut down, while on another plane entirely, her stomach wondered what Beauty had ordered from room service.

A rapping on her back door brought her head up.

She groaned. What she didn't need right now was a cranky customer complaining about "crisp" toilet paper or a lack of towels.

When she looked up and saw who was on the other side of the door, her senses went on red alert.

It was Cade Harding, his face grayed by the mesh in the outer door. She went to the door, opened it, but left the screen door closed. She braced one hand on either side of it and stared up at him.

He stared back. The sun, settling somewhere behind him, made it difficult to see his expression.

It wasn't difficult to make out the smell.

He lifted a giant bag, waved it in front of her as if it were an incense burner.

Chinese! She loved Chinese. The man was evil.

"I said I didn't eat." The last thing she needed right now was Cade Harding and his easygoing, not-a-care-in-the-world attitude and silver-green eyes that spent too much time looking too deeply into hers. She'd get rid of him.

He waved the bag again. "It's either you or Redge. I bought enough for two."

She smelled the scents of the Orient—or at least what passed for the Orient in northern Washington—and her resolve was burned away by the thought of American-style chow mein, deep-fried pork, and sweet and sour sauce. "You don't play fair."

"Nope."

She opened the screen and grabbed for the bag.

"Uh-uh." He pulled it back. "This bag and I come as a set."

"Come in then, but don't be surprised if I fall asleep with a chopstick in my mouth. I'm not up for conversation."

"Fair enough."

Cade stepped in and looked around. "Nice." When he looked at the carpet, he shucked out of his sneakers.

She liked that. Truth was, she liked Cade. Which of course was stunning timing, considering what was playing out in the background of her life. She reached for the bag again, and this time he gave it up. "This way." She headed for the kitchen, which wasn't far. Only a tiled bar—she'd done it herself—separated it from the living room. "And you can tell Redge if he's a really, really good dog, he can lick the bags."

"I'll do that." He smiled, watched while she took plates from the cupboard.

"Where is he, by the way?" she asked.

"Left him home playing guard dog."

"He's welcome here. I like dogs."

When she went for some glasses, he reached over her shoulder and plucked a couple from the shelf. "These?"

"Uh-huh. And you'll find milk in the fridge."

"You drink milk with Chinese?" He said it as if the idea was akin to swilling pickle juice with a good steak.

She set the dishes, along with the glasses, on the counter, and flexed her biceps, à la Popeye. "I eat spinach, too." She risked a quick smile. What could it hurt? He'd be gone in a few days, and in the meantime, it was smart to act as normal as possible. But she spotted her lie right away. She wasn't being smart, she was looking for a diversion, and as diversions went, Cade Harding beat another wheelbarrow full of dirt hands down.

And he'd brought food.

Of course, his idea of a diversion would have more to do with sex than hers did, but she'd deal with that problem as she always did.

When she started to dish out the food, he stopped her. "Sit down. I'll do the honors." He glanced around, nodded toward the sofa she'd been sitting on when he came. "How about we eat in there?"

When they were both seated and their plates were full—hers twice as high as his—she took her first mouthful, then her second. "M-m-m . . . this is good." She gave him a sideways glance. "Did I say thank you?"

"No, but you eating that piece of pork and looking as if you'd tasted heaven will do." He winked at her and went back to demolishing his own plate, wielding his chopsticks like a pro.

She stuffed some noodles in her mouth, swallowed, and said, "If my source of food is a microwave, I'd say yours is takeout."

"You'd be right. Since I moved to Seattle—a couple of weeks ago now—I haven't turned on the stove." He put down his plate, wiped his mouth with a red napkin spotted with dragons, and looked at her. "I actually like to cook, just not every day."

"I hate it." She crunched into an egg roll. "Nuking is my life." She tackled the chow mein.

He laughed. "I don't think so. I think this resort—"

"—motel. It's a motel." What was it with men? They always wanted things to be more than they were.

"Motel," he corrected himself. "I think this motel is your life. And I'm guessing the physical work you do around here leaves you too tired to cook."

"Some days, that's for sure."

"And on the others?"

She glanced out the window. "I'd rather watch the sunset, take a swim, or—"

The phone rang. Addy's heart jumped, and she barely managed to put her plate on the coffee table without dumping it in her lap. "Excuse me. I'm, uh, waiting for a special call." She bolted toward the phone.

Chapter 10

Cade watched her hurry, almost run, to the telephone on a desk near a makeshift drafting table at the other end of the room. Before she picked it up, she turned her back to him, then she hunched over the receiver to muffle whatever conversation she was expecting to have.

Her greeting was barely a whisper, then she straightened and turned back to face him. She gave whoever was on the other end of the phone a list of rates and some information about fishing in the lake, then hung up. Walking back to him, she rubbed her forehead, looking both relieved and disappointed—and frustrated.

It was obvious she'd been expecting a call, and the one she'd answered wasn't it.

With those amazing eyes and lithe, strong body, Cade guessed she expected a lot of calls—all of them male.

He waited until she was again sitting beside him. "I guess those calls never stop."

She finished chewing on the piece of pork she'd put in her mouth and said, "Sure hope not."

When she didn't say more, he picked up the thread of their broken conversation. "So when you're not nuking, swimming, or sunset-watching, what fills your time?"

She tilted her head, leveled her gaze to his. "Why are you so interested in what I do?"

"You're an interesting woman. Why wouldn't I be?"

She studied him a long time, then burst out laughing. "Interesting? Me? A woman who runs a third-string motel miles from the highway or nearest town? You must not get out much, Cade Harding." She rose from the sofa. "Thanks for the food, but I'm beat."

As a dismissal, it didn't leave much room for maneuvering.

Cade didn't stand. Instead, he leaned back into the sofa and spread his arms across the backrest. She hadn't pulled her punches, nor would he. "You don't like questions much, do you?" He let his eyes wander over her. Not hard. "Is there a reason for that?"

The laughter in her eyes died a sudden death, but she didn't answer him right away, seemed instead to take some time to gather her resources and plan her next move. She picked up their dishes and headed for the counter. "Does someone need a reason to be a private person?" she asked, setting down their plates.

He stood. "Ah, the classic answer-a-question-with-

a-question ruse. But I'd say yes, they generally do."
He walked toward her.

She took a step back, her eyes darkly wary. "Then
you'd be wrong."

He backed her against the tiled counter, looked
into her dangerous eyes, caught the scent of her,
soap and lemon. When she was within arm's reach,
she straightened, gave him an I-dare-you-to-come-
closer gaze. His heart thumped heavily in his chest
and his groin tightened. Both reactions confused
him, stilled him. Hell, he was acting like a goddamn caveman—and he damn well felt like one.

An image of Dana flowing into his arms drifted
across what was fast becoming a one-track mind.
He could never love another woman the way he
loved Dana, he knew that, accepted it. No one
would be as good, as honest, or as openhearted.

But Dana was gone, dead for months, the living
dead for months before that. She'd loved and
trusted him, given him all of herself—and he'd
failed her.

Addy would never trust him, would give him
nothing, but for the first time after what seemed
like an eternity of grief, he wanted . . .

Hell, he wanted sex. A feeling so amazingly normal, he hardly recognized it. And so powerful, it
made mincemeat of his common sense. This was
the last woman on the planet he should sleep
with . . . and he didn't give a damn.

When he placed a hand on either side of her on
the cool tiled counter, he had her trapped. Her
eyes blazed, then narrowed threateningly. She
quickly shifted position, put her knee between his
legs—damn close to his groin—and folded her

arms tight across her breasts. He didn't expect her to panic, and she didn't disappoint.

"You're pushing your luck, Harding," she said, her tone as lethal as her gaze.

Cade didn't ease back, but he didn't advance, either; that knee of hers could do some damage.

Checkmate.

She looked up at him, half smiled, half taunted him. "I'd do it, you know. It wouldn't be the first time." She lifted her knee, nudged his genitals, and brought it down again. "Must hurt like hell."

His groin quickened at the rub of her touch. "It does. As any guy who's ever played football without a cup will testify."

"Then why don't you back off? It's the smart thing to do."

She was dead right. He wasn't here to seduce Addilene Wartenski, he was here to get her help in finding a lost boy. Instead, he spread his legs to give her a clear shot, and took her face in his hands. "The thing is"—he lowered his mouth to within an inch of hers—"I don't feel very smart at the moment. What I feel is . . . interested."

He brushed his mouth across hers, softly and without threat. His breath stopped deep in his throat. Her scent slammed into him, woman, lemon, Chinese food. With effort, he lifted his mouth from hers, studied her amazing eyes, and saw surprise, mixed with hot blue and a trace of a confusion. He stroked her lower lip with his thumb. "And the truth is, I haven't been interested in much of anything for a very long time."

He kissed her again, another brush of his lips over hers, a warm mingling of breaths. God, he wanted more, wanted to crush and take, but he held himself back.

She inhaled sharply, and he lifted his head, looked down at her in time to see her eyelids open slowly, the light color of her eyes darker now, her pupils dilated. In the quiet of the room, he heard her breathe, saw her breasts rise and fall under the red cotton T-shirt.

Shaking her head, she said, "If there was an award for lousy timing, Harding, that bit of business would win hands down." She placed her hands on his chest. "And now that it's out of your system, I'd like you to step back."

He stepped back. "It's not out of my system." He was raw, hard, and sexually hungry. Add a triple shot of fascination to the mix, and it was a serious call of the wild. She was right about one thing: definitely lousy timing, which didn't stop him from adding, "And I don't think it's out of yours."

She walked around the counter, surprised him by not starting to fuss with the dishes in a busy attempt to ignore him. Instead, she sat on a stool, put her elbows on the counter, and cupped her face in her palms to look up at him, her eyes sharp and speculative. "Assuming you're looking for some quick, uncomplicated sex, you should know I don't do sex with strangers." She frowned, briefly looked away, before again looking him in the eyes. "Actually, I don't do sex at all."

"Excuse me?"

"You heard me. I tried it a couple of times." She dropped her hands to the counter and flattened her palms there. "And I didn't like it much. I'm what you call frigid, I guess. No fun in bed at all.

The first guy I slept with said I was a minus ten on his 'hot-babe scale.' And the second said—let me see if I remember right—oh, yeah, you'll have to pardon my French. He said 'fucking me was like putting his dick in a bucket of ice.' " Not for a second did she take her eyes from his face when she added calmly, "So you're wasting your time."

"I see," he said, seeing nothing but a beautiful woman who was as matter-of-fact discussing her libido as she was dumping soil from her wheelbarrow. True or not, it was a hell of a successful road-closed sign.

"Good." She picked up the Chinese food cartons sitting on the counter and headed for the trash. When she turned to look at him again, she appeared surprised he was still standing there.

So was he, but he was busy rummaging around his so-called educated brain looking for a string of words that made some sense. *Nada.*

"I embarrassed you," she said.

"Astounded me, more like it."

"Yes. My news flash tends to do that."

"I'll bet it does." He looked down at her, her placid expression, her too-wide eyes. Her too-clever eyes. Something inside him gave way, shifted from astounded to suspicious.

Addy walked to the door and picked up his sneakers, held them out for him. "I'm glad we had this talk, cleared the air. I hope it doesn't affect the rest of your stay at Star Lake."

He moved toward her, his sport-sock-clad feet soundless on the plush carpet. When he was directly in front of her, he took his shoes from her with one hand and used the other to grasp her chin, pull her face to his. "An ice bucket, huh? That's not the way you feel to me." He kissed her again, quick and hard, swallowing her surprised gasp, tamping down his need for more. "I'd say you went to bed with the wrong men."

"And you're the right one, I suppose." Her tone dripped sarcasm.

He looked at her a long time, until her defiant gaze slid sideways. "I think I am," he said quietly before he walked out.

Outside, he rammed his feet into his shoes and headed for his cabin. Along the way, he took some deep breaths of fresh air and inhaled some reality.

He'd damn near made a big mistake back there, the normal result when a man did his thinking from behind his zipper. Hell, the woman was wanted as an accomplice to murder and as a possible kidnapper—a couple of grisly facts he'd be wise to keep front and center from here on.

What mattered was Josh Moore, not his own back-from-the-dead dick.

But, Christ, she felt good . . .

Not that it mattered, because from here on, he planned to stay as far away from touching her as Star Lake allowed. He'd play the necessary part, gain her trust, and see where it took him. He couldn't hold Stan and Susan off forever, and if they showed up on the scene, Addy would be gone in sixty seconds.

He did not want that to happen—even if his reasons for it had muddied since he'd kissed her.

*   *   *

Addy watched Cade stride to his cabin, disappear inside. He came right back out with Redge at his heels and headed for the path around the lake.

She let the curtain drop and slumped against the windowsill, her body white-hot, her brain on fire.

Cade's lips on hers were like . . . it was like some kind of crazy magic potion thrown on a smoldering fire, making it wild and sky high.

Her stomach, a storm-tossed ocean, wouldn't settle.

And she needed to settle, because she had more to think about than Cade Harding's mouth touching hers.

She touched her lips, closed her eyes, and for a second drew back the taste of him, the sharp, clean scent of him—the sensations she couldn't afford to feel, to risk.

Not that it was worth thinking about.

She opened her eyes, and shoved her adolescent emotions aside to get to her brain, and her current problem. She needed to think about Beauty, about Gus, about Frank Bliss—not the possibility of sex that actually felt like something for the first time in her life.

She hadn't lied to Cade—maybe laid it on thick, but not lied. She'd never come close to enjoying sex, and she had given up on it. She'd tried it because her body told her to, but her mind set itself against the whole crazy idea. All it did was whir and beep inside her skull like some kind of whirligig of worry, sounding alarms and ringing warning bells.

Mostly she'd felt like she wanted to leap off the

bed and run for her sanity. It made no sense until she thought it through, came to an understanding of herself.

Hot sex—and, God forbid, any kind of long-term commitment—didn't pair up well with an outstanding arrest warrant and the lies and evasions that came with it. Pretty impossible to relax in bed when you had one eye on the emergency exit and an ear cocked for the sound of a police siren. And none of that had changed, or would, no matter how many times Cade Harding kissed her.

Getting stars in her eyes back then was risky enough. If she let it happen now, it would be beyond stupid.

And she had Beauty to worry about.

She walked away from the window, her eyes again drawn to the phone.

Call me, Gus! You and I have to stop Beauty from killing someone. I need you, because I can't do it alone.

"Hey, Wayne, how's it going?"

Grover swallowed, shoved the file he'd been working on to the side of his desk, and tightened his grip on the phone. "Frank?" Stupid response; he knew exactly who it was. Let the game begin.

"The one and only. I've been trying to reach you, but keep ending up in voicemail hell."

"Sorry about that," Wayne uttered, his blood running through his veins like skim milk. "I'm not in the office all that much."

"Yeah."

Wayne coughed. "What can I do for you?"

"Like I said, I find myself a little short in the

pocket, what with getting out of prison and all, and I was hoping you—or maybe Sandra?—would help me out."

Grover rested a hand on the pad of his stomach, told himself he wasn't going to be sick. He was smarter than Frank Bliss. He could handle him. Had to handle him. "I'd appreciate it if you'd leave my wife out of this." Grover glanced through the glass wall of his office toward the sea of people and cubicles on the other side. He'd been given the office five years ago. In lieu of a promotion, Sandra said, but Wayne didn't care how he got it. He loved this tiny space. Within these walls, he was somebody. He did good things, had control. He would not allow Bliss to spoil that.

"That's the idea, isn't it? To leave savage Sandra out of it." He chuckled. "Shit, quit worrying, will you? I can't tell Sandra anything that she doesn't already know. Now that boss of yours, that's another thing."

Wayne blanked his mind, swiveled in his chair, and lifted his face to the warm sun filtering through his window. "How much do you want?"

"Ten thousand ought to handle things. For now."

Ten thousand!

When Wayne found his tongue, he said, "You know I don't have that kind of money." Not even close.

"I know you'll get it."

Wayne cut in. "I'll need some time."

Silence.

"Okay," he said. "I can give you a couple of days."

"But, Frank," Wayne added, holding his breath a moment before going on, keeping to the putridly obsequious tone he used in all his dealings with Bliss, "I don't think it's safe to use Western Union. I'll bring it to you. In cash . . . if that will work for you."

"Suit yourself. Give me your cell number."

Wayne gave it to him.

"I'll call you," he said. "When I do, you better have the money and be prepared to move that fat butt of yours and make tracks. You got that?"

"Yes, I understand. You don't need to worry," he said, then took a deep breath. "May I ask who is included in that 'we' you mentioned?" Grover asked, his chest thick with dread.

"I figured you'd be curious about that." Bliss laughed, went silent for a bit as if considering whether to answer, then said, "What the hell. How about this for a clue? It's the bitch I pumped, while you were pumping dear old Mom." He stopped, added in a hard voice. "Get the money, Grover."

He hung up.

Grover had no idea which girl he was talking about.

During his lunch hour, Wayne worked through the errand list Sandra had given him; make arrangements to have the gutters cleaned, pick up the dry cleaning, go to the hardware store to buy those special bulbs for the dining room chandelier. The routine was welcomed and worked to regulate his increasingly bizarre thoughts.

When his chores were done, he went to the

bank and withdrew the funds from his secret account. He walked out of the bank into an unseasonably hot day, the sun a glare in the western sky. He ignored it until he got to his Honda, parked a block away.

The car was warm and stuffy. He didn't have air-conditioning, so he rolled the windows down and sat for a time, waiting for the heat to dissipate.

He rifled through the glove department for some Tums. His gastrointestinal tract felt as if someone were hosing it down with lit kerosene—and another headache loomed. After gobbling some tablets, he put his head back on the headrest, weary, but grateful he had a few minutes to let his mind clear.

In seconds, his thoughts turned to Sandra.

She'd gone too far these past months. Way too far. He made fists of his hands and felt again the first lashes of the cane slapping languidly at his buttocks, the early prickles of titillation, the powerful pull of his sick desire.

Then the pain, Sandra's foul angry words. The beating.

He deserved it, she said, all of it, because he was bad. He was evil.

And she was right.

Excitement knifed through him and anticipation filled his lungs until his breath labored for release.

God, she was good . . . Oh, how he hated her.

The sun pierced the windshield, and he clenched his eyelids closed. On the screen behind them the image came, blood running between his thighs after last night's beating, then pinking to run down the shower drain.

He had to leave her. Had to.

His muscles knotted, and his breathing shallowed.

But that would mean leaving DSHS, the only place he was safe, the only place he did some good. The only place he was a whole man. Because of Bliss, Sandra knew everything. She'd ruin him. Never let him be.

Never, never, never!

Thinking about her exhausted him, and he switched to Frank Bliss. Damn him to hell for stirring things up.

If it weren't for him, Belle would still be alive, and Wayne wouldn't have a damn hole in his life the size of Mount Everest. If anyone could have given him the courage to leave Sandra, it was Belle. No one understood him like Belle had.

His heart withered in his chest, tears welled, until holding them back hurt his eyes. In the end, he'd understood why her sons hated her so, but it was too late. He loved her, mindlessly and without reservation, and with a dark passion that all but destroyed him.

Belle. Oh, Belle . . .

Belle's image gave way to the present, to Linda Curl. She'd asked him out again this morning, and he liked that, liked how she took the lead, the way Belle had from the very first when he'd called on her to assess her home as an interim foster-care facility. She was so strong, so sure of herself . . . of him. He'd have done anything for Belle, and proved it by putting all those lies in the system, approving her, taking all those chances with his placements.

There hadn't been anyone like her until now, until Linda.

His chest constricted. Maybe that feral nose of Sandra's had picked up the scent of his need for another woman. Maybe that was why the beatings were growing so intense.

Sandra didn't trust him, hadn't since Belle. Everything would have been okay if Frank hadn't called her, told her everything.

Then he'd threatened to call DSHS, tell them about the sham placements. He could still hear him.

"You're going down, Wayne old man, unless you come up with some cash. Brett and I need to get out of this burg and you're our ticket. No way is that DSH or whatever the hell it's called gonna be happy to hear you're sending money old Belle's way, putting little kids with a woman who whores on the side—and dipping your own dick while you're at it."

Whores on the side . . .

His neck burned, his throat seized up.

Belle Bliss. She'd made him feel like a man—a real man—not the "sad excuse for his sex" Sandra said he was. He'd thought she'd opened her heart to love him, but it had been only her bag of tricks she'd opened to con him.

Now Frank was back, demanding money and putting everything, his job, what passed for a life, and all his good work in peril.

And the ten thousand dollars? It wouldn't be enough. There'd never be enough for Bliss. When his stomach recoiled at the thought of what he had to do, he did some deep breathing, told himself to calm down, get rational.

He had no choice . . . no choice.

He had to burrow under Bliss's skin, then finish him once and for all.

Weariness crept over him like a fog, and he rested his head on the velour headrest and let the heat in the car swaddle him, ease his nerves. He must have dozed off.

A harsh rap on his half-open window snapped his eyes open, and he stared blearily at a man standing outside his car door.

"Sorry, man, but this is a parking lot, not a park bench. Are you planning to leave anytime soon?"

Grover nodded and turned the key in the ignition. "Sorry. Headache," he mumbled, then pulled out of the spot and out of the lot, back to the office, back to his dark, painful thoughts.

Back to formulating his plan, how to get close to Bliss, and how to kill him.

Addy didn't dare leave the phone, so she'd asked Toby to take the old Ford Ranger truck into town for some supplies. She was on her own at the desk when an elderly couple came into the office, checked on the Star Lake rates, then registered for an overnight stay.

Because they were probably quiet, she put them in the cabin next to Cade's. She hadn't seen him since last night, although she did see his light go on at four.

She smiled at the woman and handed her the keys. "Enjoy your stay at Star Lake, and if you need anything, be sure and let me know."

"Everything looks lovely, dear. Thank you."

As she went out the door, Cade came in—and the phone rang.

He nodded at her to go ahead, not that a herd of thundering elephants could have stopped her. Not only might it be Gus, it was a chance to get out from under those sharp eyes of his. Eyes she hadn't looked into since the Chinese food fiasco.

The phone call wasn't Gus—again—and while Addy got edgier by the minute, Beauty, now an impatient prisoner in her four-hundred-dollar-a-day suite, was getting bored, and she was drinking. Either one was a dangerous condition, together they were a recipe for disaster—or murder.

Their call last night had been an arduous hour and a half of Addy attempting to calm Beauty down, insisting she wait until she could talk to Gus, assuring her she would—when she was no closer to it than she was when she started. If Gus didn't call soon, she didn't know what she'd do.

She talked briefly to the woman on the phone, who was determined to sell her a vending machine, then hung up. She turned to Cade, who was idly scanning the tourist pamphlets in the rack on the counter.

"Hey," he said, when he looked up to see her attention finally fixed on him.

"Hey back." She stacked some loose papers on the counter, but forced herself to meet his steady gaze. "Is there something I can do for you?" she asked in her best motel-owner's voice.

"Yes." He dropped a pamphlet back in its slot. "You can stop avoiding me, which will give me a chance to apologize."

"Done. Apology accepted. Anything else? Extra pillows, towels . . ."

"Did I actually kiss that smart mouth?"

"Yes, you did, and I didn't like it one bit."

He studied her. "Liar." Then he shook his head. "But if that's how you want it, that's okay with me. I was out of line, and I'm sorry."

"You already said that."

"And I don't plan on saying it again." He lifted the hand that was below the counter. "I brought you this." He held out a book.

Addy pursed her lips, looked at the book. It had a picture of a teenage boy on the cover. He was sitting on a blanket on the sidewalk, his back against a concrete building. She stared at it, her stomach tightening. She didn't take it. "I don't read . . . much." For the first time, she added the last word reluctantly. She glanced up at him, and as she did so, saw his expression flatten to a blank.

He pulled the book back. "Fair enough."

He was at the door when she said, "Cade."

He turned back, his face still unreadable.

"The thing is, I, uh, don't read at all."

"That's okay. Not a problem." His expression didn't change, and he opened the door and walked out.

She thought of calling him back, explaining, but she couldn't say it again. It was too mortifying. She hadn't even told Toby yet. She watched Cade go, her stomach sinking.

He was halfway to his cabin when he stopped abruptly and called Redge who was running ahead of him. Making an abrupt about-face, he headed back to office and confronted her. "You mean you can't read . . . at all?"

Chapter 11

Addy swallowed, feeling outed against her will, and promptly kicked herself for trying to save his feelings by exposing her awful secret. "That pretty much nails it."

Silence.

"Pretty much?" he queried, tilting his head and studying her as if she were a new life-form.

She busied herself with the guest register, which of course, given her admission of illiteracy, was the ultimate in stupidity. She slammed it closed. "I didn't do well in school. Okay?" She sharpened her tone, wished she could cut her tongue out. "I can read some. I'm not stupid." Addy knew the "some" wasn't nearly enough, and hated herself for sounding defensive. She certainly didn't owe Cade Harding excuses. Smart enough to get by this far—harder since Lund's death—she'd continue to cope. No problem. For one thing, she used her ears. If a person listened hard enough, she discovered, it was amazing how much they could learn and keep filed away. The rest, like getting someone to read for you if you were completely stuck, just took creativity.

"Obviously," he said, his tone matter of fact. "If you were stupid, you wouldn't be running this resort—"

"—motel," she corrected automatically, wishing with all her heart he'd go away and take this uneasy conversation with him. He still held the book in his hand, and she looked down at it, adding, "Now why don't you go back to putting more words on paper for people who can appreciate them and leave me alone?"

"Why did you tell me?"

She shrugged, not about to say she hadn't wanted to hurt his feelings.

When she didn't answer, he said, "If you like, I can teach you to read."

She fixed her eyes on him, couldn't help herself. She laughed, hollowly and without humor, but for some reason she couldn't come up with her usual quick response.

"What's so funny?"

"The idea of you being teacher instead of lecher."

"Ouch." He inhaled sharply. "You may not read, but you're sure as hell not deficient in the vocabulary department." He took a step closer to the counter. "But, for your information, I *am* a teacher"— he glanced away briefly—"of sorts. Until a few weeks ago, I was head of the criminalistics department at Washington State."

It was as if a frigid wind had raced through the door. She froze. "You're a cop?"

"Ex-cop, and that was years ago. When I figured

out I preferred the classroom to the streets, I went back to school." He settled his green eyes on her. "I taught at WSU until a couple of months ago."

Was she imagining it or was he staring into her soul? Whether he was or wasn't, Addy was so stunned at the idea of her standing there talking to a cop, she couldn't think of a thing to say.

"That bother you?"

"What?" she mumbled.

"That I wore a blue suit for a while?"

"No, why should it?"

"Good." He put the book on the table. "Take this. It's called *Zero Intolerance*. See what you can do with it. The offer to teach stands—right alongside a promise not to 'lech.' You know where to find me."

He walked out the door, and Addy was left with a book, a slack jaw, and a spike of terror up her spine as sharp and rigid as a fire poker.

Cade let himself into his cabin, unsure whether he'd made the stupidest decision of his life, been fiendishly clever, or simply capitalized on someone's weakness. He was no expert in illiteracy, but he knew the stats: up to 50 million adults in the U.S. suffered from either not being able to read at all, or they read only at the most rudimentary level.

It didn't surprise him that Addilene Wartenski, who'd barely attended elementary school, then hit the streets at thirteen, would be among them.

He rubbed his throat, massaged the knot lodged there. God, as intelligent and ambitious as she was, she must hate not being able to read.

Not his problem, he told himself, and went back to the fiendishly clever scenario.

If Addy took the bait, it would give him the chance he needed to get close to her—get down to the business of finding out what happened to Josh. Enough time, enough of a comfort level, and she'd slip up; he was certain of it.

What then, smart-ass? You turn her in, make her pay for being thirteen, alone in bad company, and scared out of her mind?

He mulled on that a bit, then decided to cross that bridge when he came to it.

Right now he had two goals. One of them was to keep his hands off Addy Michaels, alias the Wart, and the second was to get a line on Josh Moore.

When the phone rang after midnight, Addy picked up on the first ring.

"What the hell do you think you're doing, calling me? And where did you get my number?"

God, it was like the sun coming out after a hundred days of rain. "Gus . . . finally." The tension seeped out of her body as if it were syrup going through mesh. The easy feeling lasted approximately three seconds.

"Make it good. Damn good," he snarled. "And make it fast."

She could see his black eyes, shiny and hard, and her insides shivered. In a matter of days, her life had shifted from happily organized to a state of emotional chaos. First Beauty's low, teasing voice on the phone, now Gus's, harsh, sharp, and commanding. The clock dial spun in reverse, and she was twelve again, a chronic jumble of confusion and fear, desperation scratching at her insides like a cat in a box. She was on the street again, hungry and tired—until Gus had taken her in. Taken care of her.

Until she'd learned to take care of herself.

"Shit, Wart, I didn't call to hear you breathe. What do you want?"

His tone yanked her to the present, reminded her she wasn't that little girl anymore. "Same old Gus," she snapped. "Still bossing people around."

"Yeah, same old Gus." He said, his voice tight with anger. "And if you don't like it, here's a flash. Don't call."

She shoved her feet into the mules beside her bed, and said as calmly as she could, "I wouldn't have called—if I'd had any other choice. If you don't know that by now, you're more arrogant and miserable than I remember."

Silence. She heard him blow out some air, suck in more. "It's about Beauty then."

"Yes, it's about Beauty."

"She's not my business, Wart. Neither are you. Not anymore."

Addy stood, stared out the window toward the lights of Cade's cabin. She wished she were looking into his calm, quiet eyes instead of listening to the distaste and violence in Gus's cold voice. But that was impossible. Gus was her only hope, which didn't mean for a moment she liked what she was about to do. Knowing his deep hatred of Frank Bliss, she couldn't shake the worry that involving him would only make things more dangerous, more unpredictable.

But Bliss had to be stopped, not shot, and her hope was that if Gus could stop Beauty from killing him, she could stop Gus. And vain though it may be, it was the only plan she had. If she failed she'd be an accessory to murder . . . again.

She sucked up some courage and put her play in motion. "Beauty's about to make us your business, Gus, because she's decided to kill an old friend of ours."

"What the hell are you talking about?"

"Beauty is planning to kill Frank Bliss."

His curse was blue and descriptive, and immediately followed by another when she filled him in on the details. Then the questions came, Gus-style, precise and terse.

"When did he start following her?"

"A few days ago. He saw her on TV—"

"TV!" He cursed again.

"Yeah, that's what I said." She rubbed her forehead. "But you know Beauty."

"Yeah. Where are they now?"

"I won't tell you that."

Silence.

"Don't play me, Wart. You'll lose."

"Maybe so, but I'm not telling you where she is. You'll have to come here."

"There? Are you fuckin' nuts?"

"Here," she said, forcing the word to a firm stand, "or I let Beauty do what Belle stopped you from doing fifteen years ago." She held her breath deep.

"And we all know how that turned out." He sounded disgusted. "Tell me this. Is she safe right now?"

"I'd say yes." She hesitated. "She told Bliss you were going to give him money to make him go away. She's sure he won't do anything until he gets it."

"How much money?"

"Half a million dollars."

More expletives.

"That's why you've got to come here, to Star Lake," she urged. "When Bliss finds out she's lying, he'll kill her in a heartbeat. Telling her you're coming is the only way I can get her here, keep her from doing something stupid."

"I don't see anything stupid about killing Bliss."

"Do you honestly believe that? You'd take the risk of Beauty being wanted for another murder?"

This time the silence was so long, Addy thought he'd hung up. Then he said, "Tell her to keep it together and start heading to your place, but not to get there before I do. No way do I want that son-of-a-bitch lying in wait for me. Make that clear—she is not to arrive at Star Lake before I do."

"Which will be when?"

"When I get there."

"Something more definite would be good."

"That's the best I can do."

"Fine," she clipped her answer, knew that was all she was going to get out of him anyway. And ask why? Forget it. Gus didn't give reasons—for anything.

"And tell her—" he started, then stopped abruptly. Addy knew his too-fast brain was going in scheme-mode overdrive. "Tell her I can't wait to see her again . . ."

Liar! You deserted her like you deserted me, but while

I only cried for a lost friend, Beauty's tears were from a broken heart. But the sentiment was manipulation at its best, and Addy knew she'd repeat his exact words to Beauty.

". . . but she's got to stay in control, and she has to bring Bliss to me. Make her understand that."

It was exactly the reaction she'd expected, and it made her sick to her stomach, raising old pain and even older questions. "Gus, I don't think—"

"Save it. As of now, Bliss isn't your problem. I'll take care of him, like I should have done when he—" She heard him draw in a breath. "Better I do it than Beauty."

Addy's blood chilled. "I don't think he killed anyone that night, Gus," she said, her voice the barest of whispers.

"You know that for sure, do you?" he asked, his voice hard, his tone derisive.

"I'm not sure of anything." *Because I didn't see anything!*

The line went numb—or was that her soul?

"And if you're smart, you'll keep it that way," he said, his voice losing some of its edge. "When I hang up, this number will be canceled. I'll be there"— he hesitated—"as soon as I can. As for you, Wart, you do nothing other than make sure I have a cabin. Got that?"

"Yeah, I've got it," she said, knowing that argument or more questions would be a waste of her time. Now, like then, Gus had taken charge.

"Good." He hung up.

Addy put the phone down, sat on the edge of her bed, and took her head between her trembling hands. "Oh, God, what have I done?"

You bought time. A small bit of time—before either Gus or Beauty kills Frank Bliss.

And you fixed it so his blood will run on your doorstep and seep like sewage into Star Lake.

She lifted her head, shook it until it hurt. No! She would handle this. She didn't know exactly how right now, but she'd come up with something, because one thing was certain.

Addy Michaels wasn't in the business of taking orders—even from Gus. Those days were past. She carried enough guilt and confusion about that long-ago night in Belle's house. She would not add to it, nor would she stand by and let her friends make things worse by killing Bliss. She'd do anything to stop that. Anything.

No one would die at Star Lake.

Better they all go to prison for a murder they didn't commit than for one they did.

Never once, in all these years, had her belief in her friends' innocence wavered. They had nothing to do with the murder of Belle Bliss or the boy's disappearance—she was sure of it.

She stood, paced a few circles on her carpet.

So maybe it was time to put that faith to the test, trust her instincts enough to do something about it.

With a hand that felt as if it were encased in a lead glove, she picked up the phone to call her friend. She had no doubt that Beauty would obey Gus's instructions to the letter.

Something the Wart didn't intend to do.

Chapter 12

"Toby," Abby said, handing him a hot coffee. "Can you do something for me?"

He took the coffee, but didn't lift his gaze from the computer screen that had fascinated him for days now. "Sure," he muttered.

Eyes still glued to the screen, he sipped the cream-laden coffee. Today he was wearing an eye-popping Hawaiian shirt, lots of yellows and blues, and he'd had his hair cut. Even in her fog of worry, she registered how much Toby had changed since taking over the office. He looked good, he'd said when she'd commented on it, because he felt good about being useful again.

She sat down in the chair next to him, not sure where to start and even less sure if she was doing the right thing.

"You know the man in Cabin Six?"

"Uh-huh. Harding. Nice guy. Great dog." He tapped some keys, frowned.

When she didn't say anything in response, he turned his head to look at her. "You got some trouble with him?"

She shook her head. "Not trouble exactly. But I was wondering . . ."

He cocked his gray head. "This going to take all day? I'm getting ready for month end."

"I'd like to, uh, check up on him."

His beetle-bright eyes sharpened. "Why's that?"

This was what she was afraid of—questions. Questions she couldn't answer. "Can we drop the 'whys' for the time being?"

There was no hesitation when he answered. "Done. Now what do you want, sweetums?"

"He told me he was a teacher, and an ex-cop . . ."

His eyebrows went up, then his gaze narrowed. Addy guessed anyone who'd plied his trade on the other side of the law for a time would have the same reaction, and she knew from Lund that Toby had spent enough time behind bars to have no love for the police. She knew exactly what he'd say if she confided her idea to him. He'd think she was nuts and tell her so, and maybe he was right.

"The magic word is 'ex,' Toby." She tucked her lower lip under her teeth. "Or so he says."

"And you want me to confirm that? Check him out?"

"Yes. I know you helped Lund find . . . another friend a few years back, that you know people."

"Some I'd rather not." He pushed his roller chair back. "But yeah, I 'know people.' What do you want to know?"

"Everything you can find. Where he lives, what he does, that he actually was a teacher like he said he was, but especially if he's lying about that 'ex' he put in front of cop."

"I'll make some calls. Shouldn't take long, him being an upstanding citizen and all. Consider it done."

Stepping out of character, but unable to stop herself, she leaned in to kiss his freshly shaved cheek. "Thanks. Don't know what I'd do without you."

"Me neither, especially with you having that reading problem of yours. You should get on that, you know. Time's a-wastin'."

Addy's mouth dropped. She obviously wasn't as clever as she thought she was, considering her embarrassing secret had been outed twice in two days. "How did you know about the reading thing?"

"Lund told me, and even if he hadn't, it would've taken me about five minutes to figure it out for myself." He shrugged. "Can't blame a girl brought up by a billy goat like Baylor, of course."

"It wasn't his fault. When I came here, I was so far behind, going back to school was pointless." And dangerous. Within days of her and Beauty's arrival, Lund had a story. Told anyone curious enough to ask about her—and who didn't mind getting their heads bitten off—that she was sixteen, had quit school, and was working for him. No embellishment, no excuses. His dour face stopped any further questions about his recently acquired "niece" who'd come to live with him after his sister's death. As a cover, it worked.

He didn't have to say much of anything about Beauty, who at sixteen looked at least four years older. Staff, he'd said in his abrupt way, and that was the end of it. Within a month of being under his wing, their new names were on shiny new birth certificates and the questions stopped for good.

"Didn't you get schooling before?"

"Not much. My mother didn't, uh, worry much about things like school." *And my darling aunt had other things on her mind, like surgically clean floors, bacteria-free linen, and miteless mattresses.* "I can read . . . some, just not very good." And, since taking over the motel, she'd agonized over her failing more and more.

She had to do something about it, and soon, she knew that, and the prospect both intrigued and terrified her, because along with her pride of ownership in Star Lake had come her decision to renovate and rebuild. She'd fallen madly in love with construction and decorating magazines. She worked from the pictures well enough, but the words . . . the words were like prayers she couldn't say.

"Never too late, sweets. Never too late."

He was right, but—

An idea sprung loose.

Cade had offered to teach her how to read! It was perfect. If he passed Toby's check, she could use her disability—or whatever the heck it was—to get to know him better. Trusting anyone was a terrible risk, but she had to trust someone, and better an ex-cop than one on the job—who'd be bound to turn them all in, ask questions later. The thing was, if her friends wouldn't listen to reason, she'd need backup, and she didn't have a lake full of choices.

You really want something from a guy, Wart? Sleep with him. It's foolproof. A guy will do anything if sex is the payoff.

Addy felt her face heat, her body chill. Beauty's words came at her like a sudden hot gust of wind, making her weak-kneed and dizzy. She pushed them back. That was Beauty's style, not hers. Addy didn't have a style, couldn't believe she'd even remembered the comment.

"You okay?" Toby eyed her, waited.

"Yeah, fine. I was just thinking about the reading thing. You're right. It's never too late."

Toby stared at her, didn't say anything for a long moment. "You sure you're not in some kind of trouble, Addy girl, maybe with that Harding fellow?"

"Nothing I can't handle." She rubbed her hands down her thighs and forced a smile. "Just do the background check, will you, Toby?"

He pinched his mouth, appeared to think on it. "Okay, but if you need me, you know where to find me."

She nodded. "I'm going to start work on Cabin Twelve now." She couldn't wait to start pounding nails and slapping paint around. She always thought more clearly when she was doing something physical, and she had lots to think about, considering she might be about to take the biggest risk of her life. "Let me know what you find out about Harding as soon as you get any info, okay?"

"Okay." He turned back to his computer as if their strange conversation had never happened. Addy wondered if prison was some kind of permanent cure for curiosity.

She hoped she—or Beauty and Gus—would never have to find out.

* * *

Stan Brenton entered Susan Moore's bedroom, and said, "Damn, but I'm clever."

She looked up from her newspaper and over the top of her reading glasses. "What?"

He threw back the quilt and got in the bed beside her, the smile on his face Grand-Canyon wide. "You remember when you first came up with the idea of contacting Cade? You asked me to find him?"

"Uh-huh."

Stan shook his head. "I figured that girl had a thing for your nephew."

Susan flattened the paper across her lap, gave him an impatient look. "Is there a middle and an end to this story, or merely a beginning?"

Stan chuckled and patted her knee. Leaving his hand covering it, he gave it a squeeze. "When I tracked him down at WSU, I checked him out, ended up talking to one of his colleagues, very helpful at the time, a woman named Justine Clark—"

"You never told me you went to the university. I asked you to find him, Stan, not investigate him. He's family, for heaven's sake!"

"Exactly, and that made you vulnerable, likely to take one of those risky leaps of faith with nothing to back it up. I didn't want that." His expression not in the least apologetic, he added, "You, my dear, are a rich widow and ripe for the picking."

"And more than capable of making my own judgments, thank you very much. I'd say you overstepped the boundaries of our agreement."

He patted the narrow strip of bed between them. "I'd say my 'overstepping' is what got us to where we are today." He grinned. "That and my amazing sexual prowess, of course."

"Not to mention your overripe ego." Her lips twisted to contain a smile.

Stan laughed outright, plumped the pillow behind his head.

"So? What about this Justine . . . whoever?" Susan asked.

"She works in faculty admin or some such, which I take involves the care, feeding, and endless paperwork generated by the teaching staff in the criminalistics department—which of course, until a few weeks ago, Cade headed up." He paused.

Susan shook out her paper, took her reading glasses off, and gave him her full attention.

"Apparently someone is poking around WSU asking questions about him," Stan said.

Susan's brows knitted to worry. "Who could that be?"

"No idea, but she wants me to tell Cade about it, or better yet have him call her. She's called his place in Seattle several times, but he hasn't returned her calls. She called me because she knew my connection to his family—that being you."

"What do you think it means?"

"My guess? He's getting close to something or someone that isn't good for his health."

"God, don't say that! I never intended to put him in danger."

"I'm sure you didn't, my darling. You're always so focused on finding Josh." Stan's look was knowing and thoughtful. "You tend to forget the murder, a murder Cade has to walk through to find your boy. Danger is a given."

"I didn't think—"

He took her hand in his. "But Cade did. You can

be sure of that, so don't worry. He knows what he's doing."

"If only he'd left a number, told us where he could be reached, we could warn him."

Stan leaned over her, kissed her forehead, and turned out her reading light. "I'll call him tomorrow, let him know."

The light was immediately flicked back on. "You know where he is? And you didn't tell me?" Her expression was irate and incredulous in equal measure.

"I knew where he was within three hours of his call."

"How?"

Stan again reached over her to turn off the lamp. "I had a computer search done on his credit card. And to answer your next question, no, I'm not going to tell you where he is. For now, we'll do it Cade's way."

Silence, a wall of it.

Stan smiled in the dark. "From that tomblike response, I assume any attempt to activate my vaunted sexual prowess would be wasted tonight?"

"Good night, Stan."

"Good night, my love."

The next morning, shortly after nine, Cade hung up the phone, more impressed than angry. Brenton was good, and he found it vaguely surprising that after his years on the case, he'd never come up with a substantive lead on Josh Moore.

He sure as hell had no trouble finding Cade!

Cade had spent the last three years getting himself up to scratch on the increasing role the Internet played in crime solving—yet the technology, and the abilities of the people who used it, continued to leapfrog over his current store of information. Not that a computer search on credit cards was new, but the ease with which a hacker could pull it off these days was daunting.

He shook his head, his mind turning to the substance of Stan Brenton's call. Cade had a pretty good idea who was checking up on him, and he took it for a good sign. Fortunately, he hadn't burdened himself with more lies than he could handle.

The knock on his cabin door surprised him. Redge went into bark mode, and he quieted him on his way to the door.

Addy was on the other side, a pugnacious expression settled on her clean, unmade-up face. Her hair, catching some shine from the morning sun, was its usual tornado of spikes and curls. Wearing jeans and a pale blue denim shirt, she managed to look ordinary and remarkable at the same time.

She stuck out a hand. It held *Zero Intolerance,* his book. "I've decided to take you up on your teaching offer. It's pretty slow right now, probably will be for a few days." She walked into his cabin as if she owned it, which of course she did.

"A few days?" Cade's amazement at her casual demand overtook his surprise at her being here. "Not enough, Addy."

"It's all I have." She looked around the room, and her expression changed to one of surprise. "You're really neat."

"Most of the time."

"You should see some of the cabins when people move out." She gave him a disgusted look. "A sty of pigs would be cleaner."

"I'll bet." He put out his hand, and she put the book in it. "What made you change your mind?" he asked.

"Didn't change it. Made it up." She moved around the room as if she were on an inspection tour—or jumpy as hell.

"Okay." He decided not to go into the business of splitting hairs, or thinking how good that argumentative mouth of hers looked. "But tell me this. Was it before or after you checked up on me?"

Her eyes shot to his, but she didn't look in the least chastened. "How'd you know?"

"A friend . . . at WSU." Again, not exactly a lie, considering it was Justine who called Stan.

"Are you mad?" If she cared, it didn't show.

"No. Surprised maybe. An offer to tutor for a few hours usually isn't reason enough to call in the FBI."

"I'm careful, what can I say?" She stopped in the middle of the room, stuck her hands in her jeans' back pockets. "You want to teach me or not?"

I want to teach you all right, but I'm not sure it's anything you want to learn.

He killed the thought. "Yes, I want to teach you—whatever the hell I can in 'two or three days.' Let's go."

"Go?"

"It's a great day, we might as well make use of it—and one of those rowboats of yours. There's no law saying you can't learn outside." He expected an argument. Instead, she looked relieved, like a caged bird faced with an open door.

"Good idea. I'll get the boat ready." She looked at his feet. "While you get your shoes on." At the door, she looked back, gestured to his book. "Let's start with that, okay?" For the first time, she looked ill at ease. "I actually managed a few words of it last night." She met his gaze, gave him a quick lop-sided smile. "It was really . . . interesting."

"Okay, we'll start with Zero," he said, not that he had much choice. He hadn't come to Star Lake equipped to run an early reading program.

Addy left, and he pulled on his Nikes, shook off the feeling his book had been anointed by God with those two innocuous words—"really interest-ing." Damned stupid of him, considering they'd come from a woman who'd never read a book in her life.

He put it down to writer idiocy—or ego—grabbed the quilt from his bed, and headed for the dock.

Cade planned to row to the other side of the lake and get settled under a large chestnut tree he'd spotted on his runs. Addy had other ideas.

"I'll row, you read," she said.

"That's not what I had in mind."

"Cut me some slack, will you? I'm not in a hurry to show off my stupidity."

Standing on the dock, he looked down at her. She was more nervous than she let on. "Your not reading has nothing to do with stupidity, Addy."

"Maybe not, but if you don't mind, I'd like to ease into the embarrassing phase of this experi-ment, Professor Harding. That handle is kind of intimidating, you know."

"Fair enough. Head for that tree." He pointed to the chestnut. "We can work there."

"Start on page twelve," she instructed, when they'd settled in the boat, her on the rowing seat, him in the aft. "That's where I left off last night." Using an oar, she pushed off from the dock.

"Are you always so damned take-charge or am I getting special treatment?"

She glanced at him, tilted her head. "Will you *please* start on page twelve, Professor?"

Half irritated, half amused, he said, "Drop the professor tag, okay?"

"Now who's giving orders?"

Cade caught the smile she tried to hide by looking over her shoulder and decided he was in a no-win situation, which meant it was time to shut up. The lady liked to be on top. He'd remember that. On that pleasant thought, he settled back in the seat of the sturdy rowboat and opened *Zero* to page twelve. "Take us away, Captain," he ordered before starting to read.

Cade read his way across the lake, at first vaguely uncomfortable about using his own words as hooks into Addy's trust, but when he glanced at her from time to time over the spine of the book and saw her avid interest in the story, his unease dissipated—then he realized she was rowing in circles.

He'd put a stop to that. He read:

Zero stood in front of the new girl, his heart banging in his skinny chest.

He couldn't take his eyes off the knife in Slam's hand. Long and serrated, it glowed wickedly under the dim light of the lamp above the alley door of Harper's Deli.

"Take off, Slam," he said, sounding harder and tougher than he felt. "Leave her alone."
Slam laughed, lifted the knife, and—

Cade closed the book and put it beside him on the seat.

"Hey, you can't stop there."

"Just did." He gestured with his head toward the chestnut tree, raised a brow.

She stopped rowing and eyed him. "I'll bet your students called you names behind your back."

"No doubt."

She eyed the book, made a couple of dips with the left oar, and redirected the tiny craft to the shore near the tree.

When they were sitting on the quilt, him with his back against the tree trunk, Addy in a semi-relaxed lotus position, he pulled out *Zero Intolerance,* held it out to her. "You said you'd made it through to page twelve, so how about rereading it for me?"

"Okay." She took the book. "But I'm warning you, it took me all night to get that far." She looked seriously edgy now, and he saw her swallow.

"I'm in no hurry. Read what you can and skip the rest."

She turned the book over, opened it up, then slammed it closed again. "Toby says a person can learn anything if they set their minds to it. You agree with that?"

"Uh-huh. Just takes practice and courage."

"Courage?"

"To look stupid, take the knocks, fail, and keep going anyway. That takes guts." He leaned toward her, put a hand on her knee. "So, unless you're short on same, I suggest"—he nodded at the book now in her lap—"you get on with it."

She nodded, straightened her shoulders as if he'd ordered her to lead a frontline artillery charge without ammunition, took a deep breath, and opened to the first page.

Chapter 13

Addy stumbled through the first six pages before stopping abruptly. She felt like an idiot. If this reading business took practice and courage, she was in trouble, because all she had was frustration and embarrassment.

She wanted to bash something, and what really ticked her off was she'd read these same pages last night and done okay. But today, with Cade watching her from under those lowered lids of his, every stumble felt like a face planted on cement. Add to that the warm autumn sun, the shade of the chestnut tree, and the light of Cade's undivided attention, and she'd completely forgotten she wasn't here to learn to read, she was hear to pick Cade's ex-cop-professor-of-criminology brain and decide if he could be useful.

"Why'd you stop?" he asked.

"Because I'm hurtling toward thirty years old, and I read like . . . like a windup toy with a broken spring." She didn't add she was tense as a drum, either because of her strained effort to read or her inability to forget the worry circling her mind like a robot sentry armed to the teeth.

Cade's thoughtful expression gave way to a smile that so warmed his face she couldn't help but smile back. He said, "You were doing great. To be honest, I expected worse. Taking a totally unscientific guess, I'd say you're reading at a fairly decent grade-three level. Another guess? With some serious practice, you could be reading smoothly—well beyond that level—in a few weeks."

Reading smoothly in a few weeks . . .

The idea excited her mind, engaged her normally optimistic nature, even, momentarily at least, immobilized her robot sentry—but not for long. When the muscles in her stomach quivered, and her thinking darkened, she tightened her grip on *Zero,* and entered reality therapy.

In a few weeks, if she didn't stop Gus and Beauty from killing Frank Bliss, she'd be reading *Run, Spot, Run* under the gray light of a jail cell—and they'd be right beside her. "And you'll help?" she added lamely, forced to keep up the pretense until she could be sure she trusted him enough to help her save Frank Bliss's miserable excuse for a life.

"Sure, why not?" He reached over and took the book from her hand, tucked the cover flap inside, and closed it. "But for now, let's give it a rest, soak up some of this sunshine." He tossed the book to his side. "Then tonight, we'll drive into town and I'll buy you dinner." He put his head back against the tree trunk and closed his eyes, looking as bonelessly at ease as Lund's old bloodhound did when he passed out on the couch.

She fixated on his breathing, watched his chest rise and fall with the flow of oxygen in and out of his lungs, then studied his mouth, the relaxed, easy line of it above his firm jaw. When her own breath became untrustworthy, she swallowed and turned away.

"What's with you and the food thing?" she asked, sounding unreasonably irritated. She shifted to claim part of the tree trunk for her own tense back.

He smiled with his eyes still closed. "I generally use the 'food thing' to lure attractive women into compromising situations." He peered down at her. "As a starter, it's generally foolproof." He paused, closed his eyes again, and rested his head back against the tree trunk. "Except with diehard nukers like you, of course."

Addy's lips twitched, and she couldn't think of a comeback, so she opted to match his position, head against the tree with eyes closed.

She could count on one hand the number of times she'd eaten out or even been off the Star Lake property for other than the necessary trips into Lynden for supplies. And since she'd turned seventeen, the once-a-year visit to her mother's grave that was such a nerve-racking experience, she couldn't sleep for days before going.

From the day she and Beauty arrived, Lund told them to stay out of town, keep to themselves. Beauty, tired of being "stifled," she said, ran off when she couldn't take it anymore. But Addy was okay with playing it safe. Now, away from here—her home, the calm waters of her lake—she was jumpy and ill-at-ease. But not here, now, with Cade beside her.

"Cade?" she said, suddenly curious about something.

"Uh-huh." He didn't move.

"Have you traveled much? Like to Europe, maybe Italy?" If he said he'd been to Venice, she'd be green with envy.

He didn't speak for a time. "Yes, my . . . wife and I went for several weeks. Spent a month in Siena."

She sensed his mood lowering, her curiosity rising. "I thought you weren't married." She was disappointed, and it shocked her. Dear God, given the situation she was in, whether Cade Harding was married or single was a piece of news that should rank up there with the report of a clogged drain in Cabin One. Her illogical reaction scared her, reminded her how emotional her thinking was these days, and when you had a problem as big as hers, emotional thinking was worse than useless—it was dangerous.

"Was married. For six years," he added, then paused. "She died . . . over a year ago now."

"Oh." Death again. Death everywhere. But not at Star Lake. Not yet. "I'm sorry. That must have been tough."

"Beyond tough." He opened his eyes, stared straight ahead. "I miss her."

Addy knew about missing people you loved, knew the raw soreness of it, and couldn't think of a thing to say.

"She was a lawyer. A good one," he added.

"Any kids?"

The silence lasted so long Addy grew uncomfortable. She'd asked more questions in the last five minutes than in the past five years, and they were all the wrong ones.

"No, no kids. When Dana miscarried a second time, the doctors said trying again wouldn't be smart—or safe."

She said nothing, decided to firmly reel in her curiosity before Cade developed some of his own.

He shifted away from the tree, looped his arms around his knees, and looked across the lake. The position put her slightly behind him, and she could see the tension in his neck, the rigid set of his shoulders. "Dana had a child, though. She told me about him after her second miscarriage."

A breeze, warm and mellow, suddenly ruffled the calm water, lifted to chatter among the leaves above their heads. When it blew at Cade's dark hair and set it across his forehead, he left it there, seemingly transfixed by either the lake or what was going on in his head. Addy waited.

"She was a kid when she had him, barely seventeen, so her parents, and Dana—she never did blame anyone but herself—thought it best he be adopted."

"A boy then?" Addy was riveted, and somewhat stunned he was letting go of something so personal.

He nodded. "William. She didn't tell me about him until after the second miscarriage. He would have been fourteen then." Cade picked up a leaf from the grass beside the quilt, rubbed it between his thumb and index finger. "After that, she was determined to find him." The leaf tore apart in his hand, but he didn't appear to notice. "She only wanted to see him, she said, not make trouble for him."

"What happened?"

"We located the adoptive parents easily enough, but we were too late. The boy was gone." He tossed the damaged leaf and turned to look at her. "Turns out he'd run off eight months before—and it wasn't the first time—and it didn't look as if mom and dad had put a hell of a lot of effort into finding him. According to them, he'd been nothing but trouble, and they were leaving him to the 'proper authorities.' " He shook his head. "I never did understand what they meant by that, or who exactly the 'proper' authorities were. Not that it mattered. The bottom line was they'd written him off."

"I guess adoptive parents don't come with any guarantees." Or foster parents.

"Dana was sick with guilt," he went on. "Said she should never have given him up, should have told me sooner." He shook his head. "Should have, should have . . . the most overworked words in the English language."

Addy agreed with that; her whole life was one long should-have.

"I promised her I'd find her son, that we'd make things right for him." He leaned back against the tree, but this time he didn't look relaxed. His jaw was hard-set, his mouth a thin seam. "Hell, it's what I did . . . find people."

"And did you? Find him?"

"Yeah. Two years later. A month before Dana's diagnosis—and two weeks after he'd died from head injuries sustained in a car crash. His blood alcohol level was off the charts. He was barely sixteen. If I'd have known what she was faced with—the cancer—I'd never have told her. I'd have—"

"Let her go on hoping?"

"That hope might have kept her alive."

"Did she see it that way? Blame you?"

"No. When she was diagnosed, she said maybe there was some kind of cosmic plan after all, because now that she knew William was on the other side, she had something to look forward to."

"She sounds very . . . cool, and smart."

He slanted her a gaze. "She was both those things, and losing her damn near killed me."

"But it didn't." Addy remembered her mom, the black aching hole her death punctured in her nine-year-old heart. "And you did the right thing. She trusted you, you had to tell her the truth."

He met her gaze, his own switching from brooding to speculative, but he didn't say anything, which made her nerves jump.

He probably saw right through her. After all, who the hell was she to talk about truth when her whole life was a lie? A lie designed to keep her safe, keep her from answering for her spinelessness that long-ago night. Gus said run, so she'd ran, then she'd erected an I-was-only-following-orders excuse to survive the guilt. She'd told herself she'd had no choice; she had to run to protect Gus and Beauty. She'd made a terrible mistake, been as ignorant of right and wrong as she was about words in a book.

"Are those things important to you, Addy. Trust? Truth?" He asked the question so quietly, it was almost a whisper.

She opened her mouth, closed it, unable to form an answer to a question she'd slammed into as if she were a semi with bad brakes. It would help if he quit looking at her with those policeman eyes of his, eyes that so easily pierced the fog of denial she'd hidden behind for years.

"Yes," she finally said, feeling dizzy, scared, and determined all at once, and knowing she couldn't lie anymore—didn't want to lie. Her secret, like a caged lion, was suddenly wild at the gate of her mind. She added, "They didn't used to be, but they are now."

Beauty made her decision—Diva jeans, the new sneakers she'd bought in the local Wal-Mart, and a big white shirt, perfect for driving. Pulling her hair back, she scrunched it together with a clip, then moved closer to the mirror to smooth the deep red lipstick away from the corners of her mouth. That done, she stood back.

God, she looked more like Dianna Lintz than she had in years. She studied herself, tried to find that vain, silly, so-very-young girl, with her big dreams and even bigger bra size.

"Too many men, idiot girl. Way too many men."

She sighed noisily, making the sound more a snort than a murmur of nostalgia, because she knew damn well what had happened to that girl. She'd grown into a silly, vain woman with no dreams—and with an even bigger bra size.

Would Gus notice the change? Would he be disappointed in her . . . what she hadn't done with her life?

Would he hate her for being a hooker? Like her mother, a mother she hadn't called in years because she was too ashamed of what she'd said back then, and of what she was now.

Damn, thinking of her mom always made her cry. What a snot she'd been . . .

She brushed away the tears, her thoughts going back to Gus. Always Gus. And what would happen when they saw each other again.

She shuddered and clenched her eyes tightly closed.

He'd take her face in his hands, scrutinize it, see every three-hundred-dollar trick she'd ever laid drawn there as if by a permanent black felt pen— and she was powerless to erase them. For better or worse, she was what she was, and there was no turning back the clock.

She wondered how he'd changed, what time had taken from him, or given. Would the heat between them still burn, be as raw and wild now as it was then?

His mouth blistering hers, his fingers clutching fistfuls of her hair, his breath blowing over her neck like a wild, hot wind . . .

Of all the men she'd been with, most of them rich and powerful, many potently attractive, none had made her heart stop, ignited her body the way Gus did.

She closed her eyes, rolled her head to ease the tightness binding at the base of her neck. Back then she'd been so smart-mouthed, so ridiculously sure of the power in her face and body—and so damned scared. Gus didn't know what being scared meant. At seventeen, darkly handsome, he had the mesmerizing charm and unshakable confidence of a warrior god.

"Crap!" She stalked away from the mirror.

Christ, if this was the kind of thinking inspired

by wearing jeans and sneakers, she'd best get back
to silks and satins ASAP.

She shook her head. Hell, by now Gus was probably as bald as a fridge door, had a matched set of
love handles, and a criminal record of biblical pro-
portions.

Maybe he had told Addy "he couldn't wait to see
her again," but that didn't mean squat. He might
have been a warrior god, but he'd still walked out
on her. A smart woman would remember that, remind herself he wouldn't be coming to see her
now if it weren't for Bliss.

She took some calming breaths and went back
to the bed to finish packing her bag.

She'd decided to head for Seattle, wait for Gus
there, and thanks to her original erratic efforts to
lose Bliss, she had a lot of time to make up.

Now, losing him was the last thing she wanted to
do. But she had no doubt he'd pick up her tail the
minute she got in her car.

She scanned the luxurious suite one more time,
closed her bag, looped her tote over her shoulder,
and headed for the door.

When she opened it, Bliss was on the other side.

The hotel hall was deserted.

And her gun wasn't in her hand.

"Hey, baby," he said, shoving her back into the
room and closing the door. He looked at her bag.
"We going somewhere?"

Cold, hot, her heart banging a fear drum in her
chest, she stepped back, away from him. "How did
you—"

"Get in here?" he finished for her, while he
glanced around the posh room. "No sweat. Just

waited for the right moment. There's always a right moment." He set his sharp, cold eyes on her. "I kept thinking about you all alone"—he jerked his head—"in that king-sized bed you got there. Thought you could use some company."

"That'd be a half-million-dollar fuck, Bliss." She forced her gaze to his, willed herself to "keep it together" like Gus wanted her to, and casually put her tote at hand level on the gilded oval table against the wall in the entryway, then leaned against it and crossed her arms. Her voice was dead level when she said, "Because you touch me and Gus hears about it, instead of rich man, you'll be a dead man. And that sticky dick of yours will be maggot food within a week."

He sneered, turned his back to her, and walked across the room to look out the window, giving her the moment she needed. "Relax, Mizz Fallon West." He exaggerated the false name, turned to face her, and dropped the smile. "Even your pussy isn't sweet enough for me to risk the meet with my old buddy Gus. That motherfucker—or should I say mother-killer—and I have a score to settle."

"Gus didn't kill anyone."

He snorted. "True blue to the end, huh? Gus's very own whore." He curled his lip. "Like you know shit about Gus Vanelleto." He strode toward her, surveyed her boldly, and suddenly grabbed her breast. "And why the hell would I pay for something I already had for nothing?" He gave her breast a painful twist, looked down at her, and abruptly the expression in his eyes, until then snide and purposeful, shifted to a darker, deeper emotion, his breath quickened.

Beauty knew the signs . . .

"Then again . . ." He grabbed her by the back of the neck, pulled her face to his.

She tasted the bile of her own vomit in her mouth, swallowed it—and rammed her gun hard against his ribs.

He let go of her, lifted his hands in the air. "Easy, baby. Take it easy. You know you're not going to shoot that thing." He dropped his hands, stuffed them in the pockets of his slacks.

"That a risk you want to take?" she said, "Get back, and stay back."

"Sure. Anything you say."

"If that was true, Bliss, I'd tell you to drop dead and my troubles would be over."

He laughed, stepped away from her, and sat on the edge of the bed. "I didn't come here to fuck you, baby. I came to make a deal."

"Yeah? It didn't look that way to me." With five or six feet between them, Beauty breathed easier even as she tightened her grip on the gun. "And we've already made our deal. You get money. You leave—preferably this planet. Never to be seen again, like you promised." If he thought for a second she believed that last part, he deserved the most-brain-dead-of-the-century award.

He rubbed behind his ear, relaxed as hell. "And I intend to do that, but I figure it'd be easier if we meet where we're going to end up. Much as I admire your tight ass, following it down the highway is a waste of my time. Plus I've got a guy to meet. So, you name the place, I meet you there." He shrugged. "No more traffic tag, and you can stop checking the rearview mirror hoping I've been taken out by a bus. How about it?"

Beauty's mind raced. She could take off. Disappear like she had fifteen years ago. Hell, she'd done it once. She could do it again. Then when things were clear, safe, she'd call Addy and force her to tell her where Gus was.

And Bliss would walk, get the chance to live out his miserable existence. Is that what you want?

Her mind at warp speed, her stomach a stew of emotion, she settled her expression to a careful blank. If he even thought she'd bolt . . .

"I hope you're not dumb enough to think this new arrangement is your ticket to pass Go and collect two hundred dollars." He tugged an earlobe, and for the first time Beauty noticed he wore a gold hoop. He turned it, adding with one of his smarmy smiles, "Because you should know, I've already connected with that roommate of yours. Lisa, isn't it? Nice little piece. Be some real fun if things don't work out with us—or you try to screw me over. I'd go in deep with her, that's for sure, really take my time." His eyes narrowed. "Not that I'd let her live to tell the tale." He gave her a cold look. "Made that mistake with you. I won't make it again."

"Jesus, she's a kid! Barely sixteen. She has nothing to do with any of this."

"She's a two-bit hooker. No great loss."

Beauty's mind went into sharp focus. "Just when I think you can't get any lower, any slimier, you surprise me." She lifted the gun. "I should kill you now and be done with it."

"Probably should. Probably would, if we were in a nice dark alley where you could make a run for it. But here"—he waved a hand around the posh suite and shook his head—"I don't think so. Wouldn't be smart. Once I was past the dragon at the gate, I made sure a few people saw me coming in here. Even scheduled room service and promised a big tip for prompt delivery." He stopped, looked at his watch. "Should be arriving any time now."

Beauty gaped at him; it wasn't just her face that was blank, it was her useless brain.

Hell, she could hear a cart coming down the hall!

The hand holding the gun shook with a white-hot anger and frustration. He'd set her up.

She stuffed the gun in her tote, picked up her bag, and opened the door. Any thoughts of running, of leaving Frank Bliss alive for any longer than she had to, were gone. "Enjoy your meal, Bliss. I only wish it was your last. I'll see you at the Evenwood in Seattle."

"Seattle," he repeated. "I should have guessed."

"Room service?" The server said brightly.

"Only if you're the fumigation crew," she said as she strode out.

Two seconds later, she punched the elevator button, her mind definitely made up. No more confusion. She couldn't wait to hit the road.

The day after tomorrow, if she put in some long driving hours, she'd be in Seattle, less than three hours from Star Lake. When she got there, she'd call Addy, then settle in to wait for Gus—to come and take care of Bliss.

But this time she wasn't going to be left out of the action. This time she'd watch Gus kill the son of the bitch.

She came near to smiling at her apt turn of

phrase, but couldn't dredge one up. Instead, she walked grimly out the front door of the hotel.

God, she needed a drink!

Bliss sauntered out of the hotel, his stomach full, his head clear, and a plan in place. Hell, he'd even managed to catch a Mariner's game before he left. He spit out the toothpick he'd lodged in the corner of his mouth, and walked down the street, on top of the goddamn world.

He had Beauty exactly where he wanted her; he had them all where he wanted them.

And a half-million on the come.

Whistling, he stepped into a phone booth, placed the call collect.

"Hello."

"Wayne?" He knew Grover was shitting his pants hearing his voice on his home phone. He heard a quick intake of breath.

"You really should call the office, *Jimmy.*"

"Gotta hand it to you, Wayne baby, you're cool as glass when you have to be." He paused, enjoying himself. "Is savage Sandra hanging around?"

He got his answer when Grover, his tone business-formal, said, "What can I do for you, Jim?"

"I've got some instructions for you," he said. "First, get me an airline ticket on the next flight out of Sacramento and into Sea-Tac. Pick me up at the airport and bring the money. When everything's set, call me at this number." He lifted the matchbook he'd taken from his motel to the streetlight and reeled off the number. "Don't fuck up, Grover."

Before Grover got started on the questions, or

the poor-me whines, or about how he didn't have any money—blah, blah, blah—Bliss hung up. He didn't have time for that crap.

He walked the last block to his rental car. Christ, Wayne Grover was a stupid mush-for-balls bastard.

But handy. He smiled, opened the car door.

Kind of like having your very own ATM.

Chapter 14

Addy circled her living room. Again and again. Her own words, what she'd said to Cade earlier today—about trust and truth—sticking in her brain like a pair of those long, old-fashioned hatpins.

After saying them, she'd barely opened her mouth again, because she couldn't come up with anything better to say, or shake the feeling that if she did the wrong thing again, ignored those words, she'd . . . die, at least inside, no matter how hard she tried to stay safe in her cozy and contained world.

She had to tell the truth. Had to! Which meant trusting someone. Her instincts shouted it should be Cade. Trouble was, she wasn't sure which instincts were yelling loudest, the ones she'd honed in the fine art of character assessment or the ones he'd managed to drench in hormones. About to take the biggest risk of her life, she hated to think her decision was based more on her simmering sex drive—and a pair of sexy green eyes—rather than cold, clear logic.

So she'd chewed on it all afternoon, thought things through—and painted the whole interior of Cabin Eight while she did it—and her mind always returned to Cade, that warm feeling in her chest when she thought about him.

It had to be him.

He was smart, he'd been a cop once, and he was . . . calm.

And she was going out to dinner with him, which would change her life forever.

You could end up in jail, Addilene Wartenski—you, Beauty, and Gus! You gotta understand that, be prepared for it.

She nodded in agreement with her own thoughts, tugged distractedly at the top button on her best shirt, and tried to ignore the dread tangled into all that truth and trust she was so high on. She told herself it didn't matter.

She had it straight, finally. Right was right, and she'd hold that thought until it was proven otherwise. She coughed out a lump of air clotted in her throat and breathed, if not easier, at least more surely.

Her stomach tight, she walked to the window in time to see Cade say good-bye to Redge before heading toward her house.

To take her out to dinner.

It was kind of funny, if you squeezed a bit of humor into all the worry. Here he was, buying her dinner in the hope he'd get her into bed, while sex was the last thing on her mind.

Almost . . .

Cade rapped on the door, and as she walked toward it, she noticed her bedroom door was open. Her suitcase, packed but still open, sat on her bed. She quickly backtracked and closed the door.

Well, Professor Harding, I hope you're half the man I think you are, because I'm about to put my friends' lives—and mine—in your hands. Let me down, make one wrong move, and it's a midnight border crossing for me.

"You always so quiet?" Cade asked, ten minutes into the drive to town. He slanted her a glance, saw the tense lines around her mouth, how she held her head high, her eyes straight ahead on the road in front of them.

"I'm thinking. I don't talk when I think."

"Then you must do a lot of thinking." They passed a stand of trees and turned into the setting sun. It tore through the windshield, nearly blinding them both. He flipped the visors down. "You're also very sneaky."

Her eyes shot to his, annoyed. "I am not."

"You managed to get me reading *Zero* all the way back across the lake." He lifted a brow. "As I remember, you said your brain was hurting."

"It was," she said, not giving an inch. "When you're not used to them, words are hard. Like eating nuts without any teeth."

"You do have a way of putting things." He laughed.

Fifteen minutes later, he pulled into a parking spot a few feet from the café, the same one where he'd had breakfast the first day he'd been in town. "Here we are."

She looked out the car window, tucked her lower lip under her teeth, then said, "We could go back to my place." She looked at him, her expression hopeful and . . . scared. "Maybe get some Chinese. Like last time?"

He got out of the car, went around, and opened her door. "We go back to your place, and I can pretty much guarantee I'll try to kiss you again. And we both know how happy that makes you." Hell, he'd had trouble enough under that tree today, watching her struggle to form his words with that beautiful mouth of hers. He'd been a saint so far, but he wouldn't take any bets on how long it would last. This stubborn, workaholic, uptight brunette stirred salsa into his testosterone. Dinner out, a table between them, was the safest option.

"Maybe I'd like it this time." She widened her eyes, as if to convince him she meant it.

He eyed her. "You're being sneaky again. But if you're so wild to kiss me all of a sudden, we'll fit it in later." He shook his head, irritated at how tempted he was. "Now get out of the car, would you? All that reading made me hungry."

Flounced was the word to describe her royal descent from his Cherokee and her walk to their table at the back of the tiny restaurant. When they'd taken their seats, the waitress, a middle-aged dynamo with a down-home smile, filled their water glasses and dropped off two menus.

"Sorry, no specials tonight," she said. "Cook's hurt his toe."

The cause and effect between a sore toe and the lack of a special might be shaky, but Cade let it go and turned to Addy. "Do you like red or white?"

"Pardon?" she said distractedly, continuing her careful scan of the small café.

"Wine. Red or white?"

She sat, ramrod straight in her chair, her eyes barely connecting with his when she said, "You choose. Either's okay."

When he'd ordered them a decent red, the waitress moved on. Cade picked up his menu but didn't look at it, because he was too fascinated by Addy. She looked like a gazelle on the lookout for a hungry lion, ready to bolt on cue.

He relaxed back into his chair, studied her: tight mouth, darting eyes, hands locked together on the top of the table. "You're scared," he finally said, not masking his surprise. Hell, this cozy café in the heart of farm country was anything but threatening.

"I am not scared."

"Liar."

The word, meant as a tease, seemed to upset her. "I'm not a liar . . . not anymore. I hate lies." She looked away from him and sighed. "My mom said every lie you tell puts a scar on your soul." Her eyes were wide when they met his again, and strangely innocent.

The waitress arrived with the wine and poured. When she was gone, Cade raised his glass, mainly to hide his shock at her mention of family. "To your mother, obviously a very smart woman." Talk about lies. Hell, he was in a box made of the damn things, and it grew smaller by the second, but he saw an opening and took it. "Are you and your mother close?"

"Were. She died when I was nine." She said the

words quickly, as if the speed of delivery would pull her past the pain of grief. Like running in the rain, Cade knew it wouldn't work.

"Tough." He wanted to reach across the table, take her hand. Instead, he drank some wine.

"Uh-huh." Her gaze slipped away from his. "She was the best."

"Then what?"

"Then?"

"After she died? Then what?"

She hesitated, but only for a moment, then she swallowed. "I went to live with my aunt." She raised her eyes, met his directly. "Gloria Wartenski." She looked ashen, but when she lifted her chin, her gaze was determined, even reckless. "That's my name, too. My real name. Addilene Wartenski."

Jesus! Cade's heart started to pound.

He wanted to bolt, suddenly scared shitless about what she might tell him, the risk she was taking, and what he'd be ethically bound to do with the information.

There'd been a murder, he reminded himself, and a boy was kidnapped—or worse. Addy might not have had anything to do with either crime, but someone had, and it was his job to find out who. Which didn't stop him from feeling like the worst goddamn cur on planet Earth. He drummed up a response, couched it in neutral tones. "What prompted the change?"

"Ready to order?" The waitress came up behind Addy and she nearly leaped from her chair.

Her eyes, wide and bright, and looking fevered, locked on Cade's. "Can we go?" she pleaded. "Right now. I, uh, don't feel well."

He started to say . . . God knows what, stopped and pulled out his wallet. Tossing enough cash on the table to cover the wine and a generous tip, he said to the waitress, "We'll be leaving, thanks."

"No problem, honey. Ya'll come back when the missus is feeling better."

He went around the table, took Addy's arm, and helped her to her feet. She was so passive, he thought she was going to faint.

When they were outside, he stopped, turned her to face him. "Breathe," he said. "Nice and deep."

She closed her eyes and did what she was told.

"Better?" He bent his head so he could see her face, brushed some spikes of hair off her forehead.

She nodded. "Much, thanks."

"Come on, I'll get you home." He put his arm around her and she let him, not saying a word until they got to the truck.

"I'm sorry about what happened in there."

He opened the door. "Forget it." Truth was, he was relieved she'd stopped talking when she did, because it would give him time to think or procrastinate. Hell, even with what she'd already told him, he should call in the police. Addilene Wartenski's name was on an outstanding arrest warrant as an accomplice to murder, for God's sake. But it was one of those *shoulds*, for right now at least, he decided to ignore.

A few miles up the road, he heard her sigh long enough and hard enough to expel every trace of oxygen from her lungs. "Cade?" she said, keeping her face toward the passenger-side window.

"Uh-huh."

"When we get home, I want to tell you a story. And I want you to listen—to all of it. Will you handle it?"

He kept his eyes on the road, his mind off her odd turn of phrase. Even so, he sensed when she turned her head and set those blue-gray eyes of hers to bore into him. "Sure." He spared her a quick glance. "If that's what you want to do."

"It's what I have to do," she said, her voice barely a whisper. They drove the last few miles without words, as if both of them knew her story would change everything, and neither of them were happy about it.

He pulled into the Star Lake driveway, and she immediately said, "Your place, okay?"

His cabin was dark, so he switched on the lamp beside the chair he'd been reading in earlier. He got them both a bottle of water from the fridge, then gestured with his chin to the chair. He sat on the edge of the plaid sofa. They were face-to-face, about five feet apart.

The cabin was cool, shadowy, and silent as a crypt.

"This is hard," she said, both hands clasping the bottled water. "Really hard. I wish I had your way with words. It would make it easier."

"It's your story. Use any words you want to."

"That's the problem. I don't have any—words. I've never talked about . . . *it* before."

"Try this," he said and smiled, "Once upon a time . . . It works for me."

"And Zero." She looked curious but didn't smile back.

"Uh-huh."

"Once upon a time," she repeated as if testing the phrase on her tongue. She got up and went to the window overlooking the lake, stared out a long time. "Once upon a time, on a day long ago, there were three friends, Gus, Beauty, and . . . the Wart. They met on a mean street—" She looked over her shoulder at him. "That's the right term, isn't it? For a street people live on, hungry, cold most of the year, and wet for the rest?"

"I'd say that covers it."

She went on. "The Wart met Gus and Beauty when she was twelve." She stopped, her mind seeming to wander. "It was outside Bertrand's Diner. Bertie was an okay guy, used to put his leftovers out in the alley after closing. Most places tossed them, but he always set his out in a couple of big steel pots for whoever wanted it. Sometimes there wasn't much, but there was always a crowd. Everybody was supposed to wait their turn; seems there was some kind of special pecking order." She shrugged. "The Wart— hungry as usual—didn't know that, so she sort of pushed her way in, which really pissed off the big guy who'd thought up the pecking order, which meant he got his dibs on the food first. He really let her have it—"

"What did he do to you—I mean, to Wart?"

"He gave her a fistful of knuckles. Knocked her flat." A brief sad smile played over her lips. "She had a great shiner, though. Showed it off for days."

Cade's stomach twisted, but he kept his mouth shut.

"Anyway, Beauty helped her up, started to curse Big Guy out good, which made him go after her. Big mistake, because nobody messed with Beauty when Gus was around. Gus laid that guy right out. Broke his nose, it looked like, because there was blood all over the place. After that, Gus and Beauty adopted the Wart, and nobody messed with her, either. The power of three, Gus called them." A wistful look played across her face. "He said he was the Sun, Beauty was the Moon, and Wart was the Earth. Wart didn't know about all the planet stuff, but she knew they were . . . family. Good family, the kind who looked out for each other."

"How long were they together?"

"Until one awful night." Addy left the window and went back to sit in the chair. "About a year after the fight in the alley, the family was picked up on The Ave and slammed into the system. Until the *system* could figure out what to do with them, they put them in the home of a woman called Belle Bliss, the original Wicked Witch of the North. The wicked witch had two sons, Brett, who was harmless enough, and Frank, who . . . wasn't harmless. More like mean, sly, and vicious."

Cade didn't know much about Bliss, but what she said tied in with his criminal record.

"A man called Wayne Grover took us to Belle's place, kind of a run down farmhouse outside of Seattle." She got up again and went back to the window, set her bottom on the low ledge and crossed her arms. "He was my caseworker, Beauty's too, as it turned out." She rubbed her forehead, looked tired suddenly, as if she were running out of energy. "He said he'd put us somewhere safe." The last was a murmur, a note to herself. "What he did was put us in hell . . ."

Chapter 15

Damn! Cade coped better with story-telling mode, and it looked as though Addy did as well. The second she made it personal, she'd taken on the air of that lost kid she'd been years before.

He forced himself to a professional stillness he didn't feel, resisted the urge to take her in his arms, tell her everything would be okay. He needed to hear this and, more than that, she needed to get it out. "You mentioned an 'awful night,'" he said. "Tell me about it."

She surprised him by pushing away from the window ledge and coming to sit beside him. "Turn more lights on," she said. "I need to see your face."

"Why?"

"So I can decide if, after I've told you the whole story, I need to hop the next train out of town before you call the men in blue." Gone was her wistful expression, the look of melancholy; she was all business now, sharp-eyed and focused. "I don't usually trust people much. Especially ones who were cops." She stopped, rubbed her palms together. She looked edgy again, afraid. "But this time, I have to. Trust someone, I mean."

"That makes me what? Your only choice?" He turned on the light.

She nodded, looked frustrated.

"Then do it." In order to meet her eyes directly, he altered his position on the sofa, resting one knee on it and leaving one foot on the floor. "Tell me the whole story. Get it out, and we'll see where we go from there. Okay?"

For a time all she did was breathe. The sound of it filled the quiet room. Then she mirrored his position on the sofa, settled in as if to ground herself, prepare for the words she was about to say. "When I was a teenager," she said. "I was . . . involved in a murder." The last four words came out so fast it was as if they'd burned her tongue.

"Whose murder?" he asked, hating himself for having to ask a lying question, and grateful she didn't register his lack of shock.

"My foster mother's, Belle Bliss."

He kept his face impassive. "Go on."

"We'd been at the Bliss place about a month when Frank raped Beauty in the barn. More of a shed, really. Dirty place, leaky, full of moldy hay. He kept her there for a long time. He had a knife . . ." She closed her eyes, looked as though she were struggling to sort through the ugliness. "When he let her go, she was a mess, hurting something awful, had a cut here"—she ran a hand over her collarbone area—"but Belle didn't care, wouldn't get a doctor." She stopped, and her forehead crinkled as if she'd remembered something long forgotten. "You know what she did? She hit Frank with a rolled up newspaper, across the back, like he was a dog who'd messed on the carpet. Then she went into the kitchen and got a bottle of whiskey—or something." She shook her head. "She said getting a doctor involved would mean police and police meant trouble. Frank was 'just havin' some fun,' she said, and Beauty better get used to it, because 'Frankie' wouldn't be the last man to 'dip his wick.' " Her expression hot and sick, she added, "I've never forgotten those words."

"No, I guess not."

She took a deep breath, went on, "Gus wasn't there when it happened. Some social worker had come, taken him downtown"—she shook her head, looked confused—"something about finding out who he was . . . I can't remember. But I know Frank wouldn't have done it if Gus had been around to stop him. Anyway, when Gus got back and found out what happened, he went after Frank. Nearly killed him before Belle broke things up—"

"How did she do that?"

"Not with a rolled up paper." Addy winced. "This time, she used a poker. Really tore Gus up." She touched her face fleetingly.

"That'd do it."

"After that, she locked us all in our room— Beauty's and mine—on the third floor, more of an attic really. She told me to 'fix up my stupid friends' and keep my mouth shut." She glanced away in disgust. "I remember her—and Frank— shoving Gus into the room, him stumbling to his knees, and Belle kicking him in the back so he fell facedown." She moistened her lips.

"You were scared," Cade said, his gut knotted with fury.

"Terrified. Belle was a horror, and Frank—" She let out a breath. "Anyway, after they left, when Beauty wasn't sobbing into—or pounding on— her pillow, she banged on the door, screaming how she was going to kill Frank—and Belle—the first chance she got. She was crazy, wild crazy. Gus tried to calm her down, but he wasn't in such good shape himself, could hardly see because of all the blood in his eyes. And his face . . ." She swallowed. "It looked like the poker had torn away part of his cheek. Beauty stopped yelling when he promised he'd take care of the Blisses 'for good' when the time was right. I told him he was as crazy as her, that nobody wanted to kill anyone, that we all had to keep it together, think things through." Her eyes looked into his, fervent and questioning. "Gus didn't really mean it, just said it to make Beauty stop crying."

"What time was this?" He ignored her defense of Vanelleto, wanted to forge through the ugly scene she described, merge it with Grover's more objective account, Frank Bliss's statement to the police.

"I'm not sure. Midafternoon sometime? I knew I needed to get to the bathroom, find some towels for Beauty and especially for Gus. He was bleeding so bad. . . . Anyway, I took the hinges off the door and sneaked down. The bathroom was on the second floor."

Impressed as hell by a thirteen-year-old girl with enough wit and know-how not to be held back by a locked door, Cade nodded, said, "What about Frank?"

"After he walked out that bedroom door with Belle, I never saw him again. And never want to." She shuddered and massaged the knee she had propped on the sofa. "Not long after my trip to the bathroom, I saw Wayne Grover's car pull up outside."

"You must have called from the window. Didn't he hear you?" The question was a throwaway, because he knew they hadn't connected with Grover. If they had, things would have turned out differently.

She gave him an odd look. "We didn't call."

He frowned. "I don't get it."

"Belle Bliss was a prostitute, Cade. Men came to the house at all hours of the day and night. Grover came oftener than most."

He hoped the shock pummeling his brain didn't show. "You sure about that?"

"Sure enough. Belle wasn't the kind to be quiet about things, and Gus saw—Well, he saw enough to prove it."

"Which was?"

"You're not going to let this go, are you?" She sounded annoyed, as if he were shoving her down a path she'd rather avoid.

"I'm having a hard time accepting that an experienced social worker like Grover placed kids with a practicing hooker."

Her eyes narrowed. "Who said he was 'experienced'?"

"If he was your and Beauty's caseworker, he had a track record of some kind—had to have. They generally don't hand runaway teens to the new kid in the department." *Nice rally, Harding.*

She eyed him a moment, then shrugged. "Maybe not, but I'm telling you Belle was a prostitute, and she had the whips and chains to prove it."

"Come on."

"I'm not kidding. She called them her 'tools of the trade,' showed them to Gus—she was always coming on to him—asked if he was interested in a demo. He told her to fu—He blew her off."

"And you think Grover was a customer."

"Do I know for sure? No. But why else would he put kids with her? Because we certainly weren't the first. It had to be some kind of payoff. Maybe she gave him free . . . whatever, in exchange for a monthly government check." She bunched her shoulders. "That's what Gus figured. Anyway, we weren't about to take any chances on the guy who'd put us with Belle in the first place. That would have been stupid. What we planned to do was run, get out of there. Go as far and as fast as we could." She drained the last of the water from her bottle, set the empty on the maple coffee table. "All Grover did was complicate things."

"How so?" Cade asked, but only half listened. His mind raced, struggled to morph the harassed but helpful social worker he'd met over lunch into a man who used the DSHS to fund his sexcapades. God knew, anything was possible when it came to sexual appetites—and the ways people appeased them.

"When he got out of the car, he was carrying a baby—maybe a year or two old. The idiot was bringing Belle another foster child."

At the mention of Josh Moore, Cade's heart slowed. Again, Addy had his full attention.

"A little boy," she said, then went dead quiet.

Tension snapped around the room like an invisible lightning storm. Addy got up from the bed and paced the cabin before coming back to stand in front of him.

"I never heard his name, never even saw him," she added. "He was gone when—" She stopped abruptly, rubbed her hands down her denim-covered thighs. "Grover didn't stay long, because a few minutes later his car pulled out of the driveway. Belle, with the baby in her arms, was smiling and waving at him like"—she frowned as if the image needed weight—"like one of those homemaker types in a fifties magazine ad, like it was any old normal day, and there weren't two kids upstairs, one bleeding all over the room, beaten half to death by her, and the other raped by her sicko son."

"Seems to me there were three kids up there— one who'd seen more than any thirteen-year-old should have."

"Me? I was fine. Scared, but fine." She looked at him, her eyes bright and sad. "And I was lucky. At least I was all in one piece. Beauty patched up okay, but Gus . . ."

One piece? Cade didn't see it that way, but didn't argue. What he saw was that the events of the afternoon of the murder had provided plenty of motivation for Vanelleto and Beauty, aka Dianna Lintz, to kill Belle Bliss—and try to kill her son.

"And the boy, what about him?" he asked.

Her expression bleak, she said, "He never stopped

crying from the second Grover left. Belle did her usual thing, shoved him into her room—there was a beat-up crib in there—and ignored him. Her bedroom was off the living room at the bottom of the stairs, and the stairway hall magnified every cry. I heard her yelling at him, telling him to 'shut up, or she'd do it for him.' "

She shook her head. "Can you imagine? Yelling at a baby. He must have been hungry and awfully frightened. All alone like that." She closed her eyes a moment. "I wanted to go downstairs, do something, but Gus wouldn't let me. He said he was afraid I'd run into Frank, that he'd do to me what he'd done to Beauty. He said he'd take care of the boy on our way out.

"We were going to take off that night the first clear chance we got, but things went wrong." She tugged an earlobe. "Belle and Frank were drinking. A lot. The baby was crying. The TV was blaring. Brett came home, turned on the stereo, and right away started to fight with Frank, I think about Beauty. Brett kind of liked Beauty, I think. When Frank laughed, shouted something about 'doing me' next, Brett must have gone for him. We heard stuff breaking, lots of cursing, and Belle screaming—shrieking really—at both of them. It got crazy down there. I think Brett left, because I heard the door bang a couple of times." She cupped her hands over her ears as if to mute the din from that long-ago night, then dropped them to her sides and clenched them into fists. "But that didn't stop Belle and Frank. They kept right on yelling at one another, over the stereo, the TV, the crying baby. Then Gus said it was 'now or never,' that while there was so much noise, and they were busy hollering at each other, they'd never miss us. He wanted us to wait upstairs while he went down to check things out. I think he meant to get Belle's keys, take her car. I'm not sure." She shrugged. "Beauty, of course, wouldn't let him go without her."

"And you?"

"Gus told me to stay behind, pack some of our stuff. He said he'd call me when it was safe. By the time he did—"

"Belle Bliss was dead," He finished with his own assumption, then asked the question he was loath to put into words. "Did you see it happen? Did you see who killed the woman?" He forced himself to stay seated, resisted the urge to go to her.

Silence, dark and heavy, shrouded the air between them. "No. At first I wasn't even sure the shots I heard were real. Thought they might be from the TV—there was so much going on down there. But, no, I didn't see anything. Gus called up the stairs, and I came down. By then, it was all over . . . except for the bleeding. Belle was on the floor—" She shuddered.

"What about Gus? Beauty?"

"Beauty told me later they'd been hiding in Belle's room, that while they were there she'd calmed the baby down. She said she didn't see anything, either."

"When Gus went downstairs, did he have a gun?" She looked stunned by the question. "No!"

"Logical question," he said calmly.

"We might have been street kids, but that doesn't mean we were armed and dangerous."

"Then what?" he asked, shifting away from the

gun talk—and not so sure about the armed and dangerous part, considering what he'd heard about Vanelleto.

She glared at him a while longer, then said, "Gus yanked me into the bedroom, then nearly threw me out the window. Beauty was already gone. He said he'd be right behind us, but he never came. We waited—a long time—then we took off together, stuck together, too, for over a year before she moved on. Actually, coming to Star Lake was her idea. Gus? He disappeared like smoke. He was good at that."

"And the boy? What happened to him?"

"I don't know." She shook her head, the gesture weary. "I didn't even see him. Gus got me out the window so fast . . . All I know is he wasn't crying anymore."

"Beauty was in the room with him for a while with Gus. What did she say?"

She hesitated, then again rubbed her forehead. "She said he was sleeping in the middle of Belle's bed, which was probably why I didn't see him."

Cade's logic denied the sleeping scenario. Through the sound of gunshots? All that racket? Damned unlikely.

Bliss's police statement reared up in his brain. *Gus did the killing; the girls egged him on . . .*

Someone was lying: Addy to protect her friends, or Frank Bliss to protect himself. The thought unsettled him, and he reminded himself—again—he wasn't here to solve a murder. But no matter how much he denied it, the murder and Josh's disappearance were a sealed unit—Josh, a box within a box—with the odds of finding him alive lessening with every word Addy said.

Damn! He shouldn't believe a goddamn word out of her mouth. He wasn't sure she believed herself when it came to what happened to the boy. He shouldn't care about a young girl who'd found herself in the wrong place at the wrong time, whose loyalties were probably skewed by too many nights sleeping on a cement mattress.

He should be the hard-nosed skeptical cop.

But then, he'd always been a lousy cop.

Addy stared morosely out the cabin window, as if lost in the pain and horror of that long-ago night, as if talking about it had emptied her.

He stood, walked to her. "You miss your friends," he said, lifting her chin, and deciding to, if not change the subject, change the course of it.

She pulled back, but not right away. "Yes. We took care of each other. We were family, you know. Loved each other. Like you and your . . . wife."

I don't have a wife, not anymore. The pain in his chest was sudden and sharp, but not a dagger this time, more like the thorn on a rose. "That I know," he said.

She raised a hand to her face, brushed at what he expected was a tear. "You know those should-haves we talked about? That little boy is one of mine. Always will be. I shouldn't have listened to Gus. I should have gone downstairs when I wanted to, took that baby, and put him somewhere safe. Then at least I'd know for sure I'd done something." She turned back to face the lake, added. "Other than run away."

"You were a scared kid."

"Yeah, I was that all right."

The silence in the room grew, and he sensed

the woman in front of him, looking out over Star Lake, was emotionally drained. He knew the feeling. He also knew the past was an unstable place, the disconnect between then and now irrevocable, only as clear as drifts of memory allowed. And when the past was shaped by fear and violence, as Addy's was, the effort to retrieve something of value from the confusion, denial, might-have-beens, and endless should-haves was exhausting. And it hurt like a son of a bitch.

He touched her nape, gripped her shoulders. Tension, transformed into knotted sinew and compacted muscle, ridged hard and high along her shoulders. When she tried to pull away, he held her tighter. "Don't," he said, pressing his thumbs into the base of her neck under her short hair, kneading gently. "You don't have to say any more. Not right now, at least."

"I should—"

"—do nothing except relax," he whispered close to her ear.

A dark silence filled the room, and Addy stood quietly, and very, very still, the tension in her shoulders unyielding under his massaging fingers. It was like trying to make an oak tree bend in a breeze. He leaned close to her ear. "I'm not going to hurt you."

Her answer, after a long pause, was a nod, then a long bone-loosening shudder. Feeling her soften under his hands, her muscles mellow under his thumbs, was a gift. A gift he'd won with a lie—because he knew in the end he would hurt her, and the thought of it settled on his brain like a burr.

"I don't want to have sex with you, Harding,"

she murmured, letting her head fall forward so he could run his fingers up to her hairline.

"I know. You've made that sadly clear." He bent to kiss her neck, and she sighed. "And believe it or not, I'm okay with it."

"Good thinking. Smart men avoid sex with women wanted as accomplices to murder."

He spun her around, lifted her chin, and forced her to look at him. "Did you kill anyone, Addy?"

Her expression darkened, moisture gathered in her eyes. "No, but I should have done something for that little boy, and . . ."

"And?"

"I wanted to kill someone." The words came in a low halting rush.

"Who?"

"Frank Bliss, for what he did to Beauty. Belle Bliss, for what she did to Gus."

"I wanted to kill the dry cleaner who ruined my graduation suit, but I didn't."

She surprised him by leaning into him and wrapping her arms around his waist. "Yeah, I get your point. There's a world of innocence between the wanting and the doing." She recited the last with the resignation of a child forced to repeat the instructions of an overbearing parent.

"Someone tell you that?"

"Lund Baylor—when I first came to the lake." She raised her eyes to his, her expression open and stark. "You asked if I killed anyone, and because I'm going to ask you for your help, I'll say it again. No. I did not kill anyone—and I didn't help anyone else kill anyone, either. And it's important to me that you believe that." She looked up at him, her gaze fearless, but slightly baffled, as if she couldn't believe what she'd said.

He touched her chin with his knuckles. "I do believe you," he answered, and despite it going against all his logic and experience, his years of training, and the cynicism he'd nurtured as a cop, he meant it—which made him as baffled as she was.

Her gaze settled on his mouth, and he recognized the longing that misted her eyes, felt the same way. "I should go," she said, not moving an inch.

He ran a finger along her jaw. "You should stay."

"I don't want to ha—"

"—have sex with you, Cade," he finished for her.

She smiled, but it wouldn't hold. "I mean it. There's more to tell, and sex will make things . . . messy."

"Sex does that all right." He touched her crazy ragged hair. Amazingly soft. Then he reached behind her to turn off the lamp beside the chair. The room went into half light, some of it slanting through the open door of the bedroom. "I still think you should stay." He ran a finger around the curve of her ear. "First, because you have a story to finish, and second, because I don't want you to go."

The second reason was the critical one, the truest one, the one that would, in the end, cause the most trouble.

He took her hand, led her to his bedroom.

Chapter 16

Addy let him lead her to the side of his bed, but once there she stopped, scanned its even surface with an expression part curiosity, part terror. "I wasn't kidding, you know. Sex really isn't my thing."

"Sex is everybody's thing, but not tonight." He turned on the bedside lamp, tossed the quilt back, and looked over his shoulder to where Addy stood, rigid as a steel girder.

She looked at him, looked at the bed, looked at him again. The light from the lamp, casting downward, showed the polish of the maple cabinet it sat on, but did little to illuminate her face.

He sat on the edge of the bed, offered his hand. "Come here."

She took his hand, and he pulled her down to sit beside him. "That wasn't so tough, was it?" He smoothed some hair back behind her ear. When it sprung free again, he repeated the move, stroking her soft cheek with the back of his hand on his way back.

When she closed her eyes, he eased her back onto the bed, stretched out beside her, and pulled her into his arms. She was tense, but she didn't protest. After a few moments, she shifted closer to him, and he kissed her hair, careful to hold her loosely.

Neither of them spoke, until Addy broke the silence. "I guess you're pretty good at it, huh?"

"At what?"

"The sex thing."

"Okay . . . given the necessary inspiration." He kissed her hair again, and she nuzzled under his chin. Her breath, breezing hot and low across his neck, currently provided all the inspiration he needed. He kept that flash to himself.

"I bet."

No response required, so he didn't give one, and the silence deepened.

"Can I ask you something?"

"Uh-huh."

"Do you think there's something wrong with me?" she asked, her voice low and serious. "I mean, because I don't, uh, want it."

"No."

She pulled from his arms and sat up lotus-style on the bed to look down at him, her expression intense, deeply curious. "Then why don't I? Want it, I mean?"

He put one arm under his head. "Probably because you've got a damned skewed idea of what it's all about. I'm sure life on the street and Beauty's rape didn't help. Add in a couple of unsuccessful trial runs with summer tenants you probably didn't care about, and from your point of view, what's to like?" He reached out his hand, tugged her earlobe. "That kind of experience makes a wheelbarrow full of dirt and a good day's work beat sex hands down."

"What made you so damn smart, anyway?"

"That's not smart, it's common sense." He shifted his head to look at her more directly. "Which doesn't stop me from wanting you, by the way."

She picked at the sheet, did a bit of lip chewing, then said, "Even if I'm a loser in bed."

"Even if." He propped himself up on one elbow. "Though I seriously doubt—if you had the right partner—you'd be a loser. In anything."

She rested her elbows on her thighs, cupped her face in her hands, and stared at him. Whatever her thoughts were, she kept them to herself. And whatever they were, they didn't make her happy. She looked edgy and annoyed.

He patted the bed beside him. "Don't overthink it. Let it go."

"I don't think I want to. Let it go, I mean." She took her hands from her face and clasped them loosely between her knees. "When I finish what I started tonight, when you know all I know about Belle Bliss's murder, it's going to change everything. You might not feel . . . what you're feeling now. I mean about wanting me." She sighed. "Which means I might never have this chance again." She looked at him then, with her own delicious mix of innocence and courage. "I think we should make love, Cade. Because"—she faltered—"because I trust you. And because you make me feel like . . . like an ice-cream sandwich under a hot sun."

When Cade located a working part of his brain, he reached for her hands, took them in his. "You sure about this?"

"I'm sure, but"—she swallowed—"you'll have to do all the work."

He kissed her palm. "Sweetheart, making love to you will be about as far from 'work' as I can imagine." Although there was a problem. Addy was virtually a virgin, and he hadn't made love since before Dana died, which could be a challenge to his long-ignored libido.

Handle it, Harding. You're thirty-eight years old, long past the Neanderthal age. His next thought was protection. He didn't have any, and the chance of Addy being on the pill was less than zero. He must have frowned, because she pulled her hand back and straightened away from him.

"You're thinking about your wife, aren't you?" She looked hesitant. "That maybe this isn't a good idea."

He pushed himself up. "Yes, and no." He undid the top few buttons on her shirt, ran a finger from her neck to the top of her cleavage, then took her by the shoulders, and pulled her toward him. If he didn't taste her mouth—now!—he'd damn well implode. Condom or no condom, tonight he'd make love to her. He'd just have to be creative. Leaving him with one caveat to put on the table— or bed, as the case may be.

He brushed his mouth across hers, felt the purr of her breath across his cheek when he pulled back. Hard and too damn ready, he looked her in the eyes. "I'm going to go as slow as I can, but it's been a very long time for me. You understand what that means, don't you?"

Her expression book-learnin' serious, she nodded. "It means you'll want to go inside in a big rush." It didn't look as if the idea pleased her. "I guess that'll be okay."

"No, it won't be okay. That's never okay, unless a woman wants it that way."

"Do they ever?" She looked skeptical.

Definitely virginal. He smiled. "Yeah, sometimes they do." He cocked his head. "Now, come here, and let me undress you. I want to see you. All of you."

Her hands flew to her buttons. "I'll do it."

"Uh-uh. That's my job."

She dropped her hands, swallowed. "Okay."

He undid the last few buttons on her white shirt and pushed it off her shoulders, exposing a cotton bra with a front closure. He opened its clasp, and his breath, already ragged, stopped in his throat.

Hell, he didn't know why she even bothered with the bra. Her breasts were high, full, and perfect. "You're beautiful." And the night ahead, the control required, was beginning to look more like work every minute. He lifted his eyes to look at her face.

She had her eyelids clenched tight.

Okay, the lady's nervous, maybe even scared.

He knew his way around that.

He traced one plump breast with his index finger, chose a nipple, and rolled it gently between his thumb and forefinger. When it hardened into a tight, willing nub, he leaned forward and licked it, determinedly ignoring the clamor behind his own zipper. Time enough for that, and the longer his cock stayed behind metal, the better. Even the thought of its release, the jut of it rubbing against soft flesh after so long, made his blood pound. He gripped Addy at the waist, licked her other nipple and drew it fully into his mouth, used his tongue to lash, taste, and savor.

"Oh, God!" She plunged her fingers into his hair, and pulled him closer.

He suckled her, deeply, lightly, deeply again, then took the nipple between his teeth to nibble and tease. His own blood crashing in his ears, he lifted his head. This time their gazes met and locked. "You taste like heaven."

"Then there's no oxygen there, because I, uh, can't breathe."

"You don't have to breathe." He popped the top button on her jeans, unzipped her. "Lie back," he instructed. She did what he asked, and he pulled off the denim, then her plain cotton panties. When he went to work on his own shirt buttons, she watched his every move.

When he didn't do a damn thing about removing his jeans, she reached for his zipper. "Later," he said, and leaned over her. "Right now, all I want to do is kiss you. All over. Starting here." He took her mouth, and she gave it willingly.

A loser in bed? No way.

He kissed her deeply, and their tongues circled and searched, tasted each other, instantly demanded more. He slid down, nuzzled her nipple, the tight bud of it sweet and hard against his lips, came back up to her mouth.

Addy moaned, her body jerking as if she didn't know what to do with it, her hands scrabbling over his back, one moment uncertain, then sliding surely inside his jeans to claw at his bare buttocks.

A sheen of perspiration bonded their bodies like shimmering glue, and Cade pulled back, desperate to fill his lungs with air, with control. "You're killing me. This is killing me," he murmured. "You're too hot. Too soon."

"I, uh . . . am." She spoke as if she didn't believe her own words.

He looked at her wide, shocked eyes, the mad spiked hair, then down to where moisture gilded her pubis, and shook his head, tried to rattle some willpower into place.

He knelt between her legs, braced himself over her, and kissed her mouth, her neck, her shoulders, each breast in turn, her navel . . .

Aroused to insanity, he moved his head lower, crazed by the scent of her, the wildness that simmered under her skin, the soft moans now coming from over his head.

He cupped her boldly, opened her to stroke her clitoris, play in the wet, sweet rush that his probing caused. She was wonderful. And he was dying. Hard to the point of breaking, so focused, he couldn't think past the open, willing body under him.

"Spread your legs." His voice sounded husky, ragged in his ears.

She did what he asked.

"Wider, sweetheart, wider." When she complied, he bent his head to her pubis, took the engorged nub deep, and caressed her with his tongue.

Every muscle in his body taut to restrain his own

release, he gave her a long deep stroke, another . . . until she squirmed under his tongue. Lifted toward his mouth.

"That's it," he murmured into her flesh. "Let it go. It's beautiful. Let it go." She bucked high, and he held her to him.

He heard a long aching moan, and a prayer. "Oh, God. Oh, God."

She collapsed back onto his bed, her breathing a series of gusts and gasps. His own breath the same, he raised himself, took his weight on his forearms and looked down at her, wanting to see her eyes, what was in them.

But before she opened them, she moaned again.

"Are you okay?" he asked.

Her eyes opened, all shadowy and sated. She touched his face. "I'm way beyond okay. That was like . . . like being a kite in a hurricane." She stretched then, a movement that brought her lower body into close contact with his penis, which in its current state was hard enough to cut diamonds.

He rolled himself to her side and focused on the unlit overhead light fixture. As a distraction, it was a bust. Damn, he hurt.

She sat up immediately. "You didn't . . . I mean you're still—"

"Ready, willing, and able? Yeah." He covered his eyes with an arm, tried some deep breathing.

"I don't get it."

"No condoms. And I didn't figure you'd be on the pill." He had to grind the words out, because the breathing thing wasn't going too well.

"I'm not."

He closed his eyes, nodded from under his arm.

"It's all right." He felt the bed move, but ignored it, kept his eyes closed. For sure, opening them to see a naked Addy wouldn't be a good idea.

But they popped open real quick when his zipper went down. "Jesus, what are you doing?"

She put her hand inside his pants, felt him through his shorts. He groaned, sucked in his gut.

"What do you think I'm doing?" She bent her head, kissed him slowly and rubbed his hard, aching cock. When she raised her head, she smiled down at him. It wasn't the smile of a reticent girl, it was the seductive, teasing smile of a woman with sex on her mind and in her eyes.

"I don't think—"

She put a finger across his lips and shook her head.

Cade shut up.

She tugged at his jeans and briefs. Not with a lot of finesse, he noted, but those strong arms of hers were efficient.

When she circled him with her fingers, his head fell back against the pillow as if he'd been slugged. His body thrummed, ached to go with the flow, let Addy give him—

Too much, too soon.

He rallied himself, covered her hand with his. "Addy," he ground out, "you don't know what you're doing."

"Did I hurt you, hold too tight?"

"No, it's not that, but making a man come . . . like that is a bit . . . advanced."

"Well then, Professor Harding, you'll be glad to know I'm a graduate of late-night TV."

* * *

Addy woke to a blaze of morning sun, Cade's leanly muscled body pressed to her back, his arm resting across her waist. She closed her eyes against the light, and snuggled deeper into the pillow.

Last night played in her mind like a badly edited movie, all shaky camera shots, stops and starts, blur and focus—a crazy mind-bending swirl of hot images and even hotter bodies. She'd never have believed she'd do what she'd done, take what she'd taken, give what she'd given. And, with Cade, she'd do it all again—and again—in a heartbeat.

She pulled his hand to her naked tummy, held it there, and wiggled her behind into his groin. He hardened against her buttocks. She grinned. The man had to be on autopilot, because he didn't wake up, just pulled her closer and slept on. His breath ruffled her hair, sending a sultry breeze through the sensual fog she'd woken in. Eyes still tightly closed against the morning, she worked herself closer to his long, hard body, now so relaxed against her own. It hadn't been relaxed last night!

He was like her lake, she thought, wildly frenzied by a sudden wind, then growing calm and warm under a lazy-making sun.

A smile, one she couldn't have stopped if she tried, played across her mouth. Her body hummed in a kind of peace, all languid and honeylike. She was happy.

Happy. Happy. Happy!

More herself than she'd been in days. She'd heard about sexual afterglow, but she'd never ex-

perienced it. Never experienced fore-glow either—
she smiled wider—until Cade.

*Thank you, thank you, whoever up there is in charge
of the Department of Earthly Delights.*

Yes, they'd handed her a sexual master! If she
could, she'd tie him to the bed, lock him in Cabin
Six, and keep him forever—just for fun and games.
And every day after they'd had wild and crazy sex,
he'd teach her to read.

She stretched, opened her eyes.

A shadow moved across the carpet, and she
watched it idly, until her chest constricted on an
indrawn breath.

No.

She didn't want to think, didn't want to move
from the cocoon of warmth and denial she'd been
in since last night. Since Cade took her body and
made it reach and fly.

And he'd listened to her, so intently, those calm
eyes of his remaining level and without judgment.
He'd believed her—or at least said he did. But
when he knew what she wanted from him, what
then?

Oh, yeah, Addy the problem solver, what then?

She had no idea.

What she knew for certain was that if Gus and
Beauty refused to listen to reason, she needed
something stronger, a serious threat.

Cade was that threat.

Not that he was a sure thing. If he refused to go
along with her plan, insisted on calling the police
immediately . . .

Fear snaked up her throat; she swallowed it. She
couldn't afford fear. She had one goal, to keep

Beauty and Gus safe—which meant stopping them from killing Bliss.

The shadow crept relentlessly across the floor, darkened the base of the fridge at the far end of the room, edged upward to dim the shine on the maple cupboards above the sink, then slowly spread the weight of its gloom over the lightness in her heart.

Behind her, she heard a grumbled moan, and the hand she'd taken to her midriff moved up to cup a breast, toy with her nipple. "M-m-m. Nice."

Her breath caught and the sensual fog drifted, fell like a cloak over her worries, her dread.

He'd give her more, do to her what he'd done last night. Touch her in that way he did. Take her away. His hand slid across her tummy, down, until his fingers combed through her curls, stroked her, caressed her. She closed her eyes, began to dance to the magic in his hands.

"No!"

Brain engaged, she stumbled out of bed, eyes wide and dry, chest heaving, body tight and hungry. She ignored it all. She stared down at Cade; his heavy dark hair looked as if she'd cut it herself, all rumpled and spiky. His eyes fixed on her, confused and not quite awake. The sheet covering his lower body didn't cover what she'd just said no to.

"We have to talk," she blurted, feeling the flush of their morning encounter on her face, like a hot, damp, very red towel. Half crazy with wanting sex and wanting safety for her friends, she said, "I have things to say. Things that need to be said, before . . . before anything."

"Good morning to you, too." He finger-combed

his hair and leaned back against the headboard. "Talk wasn't how I planned to start the day, but what the hell." He sat up and set those terrible, beautiful eyes of his on her as if she were sin and he were a devil in training. Her stomach did a drop and roll. Did another when his gaze traveled lazily over her naked body, from bed-head to unpainted toenails.

Oh, lord, this is so wrong.

A woman needed to be on her toes if she were to hold her own under those damn green eyes of his. And there wasn't much chance of getting the upper hand when the scent of sex in the room was so strong it was as if it had been sprayed—for about an hour!—out of one of those atomizer things.

"I'm going to take a shower," she said, deciding on a mini-retreat to get her act together. But when she bent to gather up her clothes, he grabbed her wrist and tugged her to the rumpled bed.

"Not before I do this." He kissed her forehead, her face, under her ear, ran a hand down her back and over her naked butt in a long possessive caress. "Thank you, Addy," he murmured close to her ear. "Last night was spectacular." He let her go.

"Ditto," she said, and jumped to her feet before she weakened—or did that tying-him-to-the-bed routine.

"Ditto?" he echoed. He raised his brows, a smile and a frown dueling across his morning-stubbled face. "That's it? Ditto?"

"It was good . . . okay? But until we finish what we started last night—"

"I thought we finished damn well."

"You know what I mean." She pulled her mouth into a serious line, ignored the heated blush searing up from her collarbone.

He looked as though he were going to argue, nodded instead, his face tightening to acceptance and at the same time reluctant. "Yes, I know what you mean." He gestured toward the bathroom. "Go take your shower." He got up and slid into his jeans—no briefs. "I'll give Redge a quick morning bathroom break, then I'll have mine." He pulled a shirt on, called Redge from his corner behind the kitchen counter, and headed for the door. "Then, Mizz Wartenski, we can talk all you like."

He walked out without another word.

Chapter 17

Fifteen minutes later, Addy, showered, dressed, and hot coffee in hand, watched him come up the cabin path, and her stomach instantly filled with butterflies and leftover desire. Her heart felt like a rose pressed in a Bible. That scared her more than anything. This wasn't the time for hearts or flowers.

Dear God, tell me I'm not stupid enough to fall for the first man who gives me an orgasm.

God must have been busy, because he didn't answer. She blew out a noisy breath, took a long swig of too-hot coffee, and walked away from the window to sit at the table.

Cade came in, Redge at his heels. "Hey," he said, and smiled.

He did that a lot, she noticed, and his smiles always had that just-for-you quality that made the hair on the back of her neck ruffle. "Hey back," she said, and drank some coffee to douse the stars she knew were in her eyes. "I made coffee."

"My kind of woman, but I'll have that shower first. Keep it hot."

Five minutes later, he stepped into the room toweling his dark hair. He wore jeans, a blue shirt, unbuttoned, and he hadn't shaved. He made Addy's mouth water, but didn't take her off course.

He poured himself a cup of coffee, sat across the table from her, and calmly leveled those unnervingly intelligent eyes on her. "Chapter Two. Let's hear it," he said.

"I think, if it's okay with you, I'll start with the favor I want from you. Work back from there."

"Fair enough."

"I have some, uh, friends coming to Star Lake. They'll be here in a day or so."

"Uh-huh."

She took a breath, ignored the boulder of conscience rolling through the thickness in her chest. "It's Beauty and Gus."

Cade's brows shot up, and he set his coffee on the table. Frowning, he said, "Let me get this straight. Last night you told me you hadn't seen either Gus or Beauty since the murder, and now they're dropping in for a summer vacation?"

"Not a vacation, exactly. And not exactly dropping in." She took a deep breath, reached across the table and took his hand, gripped it tight. "They're coming here to kill Frank Bliss, and I want you—need you—to help me stop them."

At Sea-Tac, Grover waited nervously for Bliss near the bookstore on the main concourse, not sure he'd recognize him after the years he'd spent in jail.

Everything that had gone wrong in his life was this man's fault. Everything. If Frank Bliss hadn't called Sandra that day, told her Grover was "humping his prostitute mother and had the state paying for it," things would be different. Belle might still be alive, and Josh would be in the loving care of his grandmother.

Grover tried to forget, control the twisted needs that had once made him betray everything he believed in, but Bliss wouldn't let him.

The weight of him, what he knew, circled Grover's neck like a mile of spiked iron chains. Having Bliss in your life was like dying slowly, a drop of blood at a time.

Dear Jesus! He had Sandra. Wasn't she enough of a burden for any man?

His jaw trembled, and his mouth went dry. He'd suffered enough. He would suffer no more, no matter what he had to do. He would stop Bliss. Forever.

First he had to calm down, get information— about the girl. He licked his lips, forced himself to focus while he still could. At the moment, no headache drilled into his thoughts, and other than the terror that bunched at the base of his skull like stones, his thinking was clear.

Bliss thought him weak and spineless. All true enough, but years with Sandra had instilled a useful slyness and the talent to deceive. He hoped they would serve him now. Bliss always called him Groveling Grover or good-old-Wayne. He would expect him to be diffident and ingratiating; he wouldn't disappoint.

"Hey, Wayne-man, how the hell are ya?"

A hand slapped his back, then clapped on

Grover's shoulder and squeezed. He looked up and into the blue eyes of the man he planned to kill.

"Frank. Nice to see you again." The words cut his tongue on the way out.

Bliss snorted his disbelief, his underlying disapproval, then smoothed a lapel. "Yeah, sure it is, Grover."

On a closer look, his revulsion at Bliss's touch was replaced by a sharp stab of envy. Frank had his mother's good looks, he noted, tall, golden-haired, and leanly muscled, handsome by any standard. Wayne had never come close to physical beauty— as Sandra, and his mother before her, reminded him at every opportunity.

"You look well," he added, remembering Frank's vanity and not above playing to it. But the truth was, he did look fit and very strong, which troubled him.

Bliss laughed. "Yeah, like you care how the fuck I look." He patted his flat stomach. "Doesn't hurt to spend seven years in the gym, though." He poked Wayne's soft belly. "You ought to try it sometime, Grover. That gut of yours could use some trimming."

Wayne ignored the slur, nodded. "Yes, I suppose you're right. Now where can I take you?"

"Got the money?"

Wayne nodded.

Bliss put out his hand. Wayne clasped it as though it were intended as a handshake and leaned forward. "Considering the amount of security in the airport, both in uniform and out, I don't think it's wise to exchange the funds here." He shook Bliss's hand and let it go.

Bliss glanced around, then looked back at Grover, his expression speculative. "Getting some smarts in your old age, huh?" He picked up the bag he'd put at his feet, held it out for Wayne to carry. "Let's hit the nearest bar then. I could use a drink." He clapped a hand on Wayne's back. "And you can fill me in on all the exciting things that go on in the life of the underpaid social worker."

"This way." Wayne took his bag, tamped down his jittery nerves. He didn't need a drink, he needed a chilled brain and icy nerves, so he wouldn't tremble when he pulled the trigger.

A half hour later, they were in the back booth of a place called Jaeke's, a tavern a few miles north of Sea-Tac.

Bliss ordered a beer, a double burger, a side of deep-fried onion rings, and dug in. "You know, I haven't been able to get enough real food since Smithfield. Christ, that place had the worst goddamn cook ever to ladle slop in a prison kitchen." He swigged back some beer and tossed a glance at Wayne. "So, how's things going anyway?"

The question was half-civil, and Wayne replied, "Could be better."

"Now why doesn't that surprise me?" He took another bite of his burger and cocked his head. "Where you getting your rocks off these days anyway, Grover? You still into getting your lily-white ass whipped?" He pulled a disgusted face. "Weird, that crap. You wouldn't catch me letting a woman beat on me. No fuckin' way."

Wayne's stomach curled into a hard ball, and

his face flamed. Thank God the bar was dark
enough that the piece of dirt sitting across from
him couldn't see it. He said nothing.

"You must have hated losing Ma like that. Brett
and I could vouch for the fact the bitch was good
at doling out the pain. Must have been one long
boner for your kind. But a stroke of luck the way
things turned out." He shook his head, lifted his
lip in a half smile. "Mama bought the farm, and
Brett and me inherited it. Funny, huh? Hell of a
lot like having your cake and eating it, too." He
laughed, obviously pleased at his own joke.

"Your mother wasn't all bad, Frank." Wayne re-
verted to counselor mode, gripping the table edge
to the point of pain, terrified his rage—or fear—
would burst like an abscess, and he'd leap across
the table and strangle him. No, that wouldn't do.
He needed information, needed to know the
name of the girl, needed to know if Harding was
on her tail. Needed to protect himself, now more
than ever.

"You know, Grover, you're right. Old Belle definitely had her moments, taking in all those needy
kids like she did." Bliss snorted softly. "Matter of
fact, she's the reason I'm about to pocket a half
mil—maybe more, if I play it right."

"How's that?"

"Because a certain high-toned hooker who currently goes by the name of Fallon West, but was
once known as Dianna Lintz, is about to lead me
to the end of the rainbow."

"The pretty one," Grover said softly, another
piece of the puzzle slipping into place. He tried
not to look anxious.

"Uh-huh. Beauty herself."

"Where did you find her?" *Stay calm, Grover, stay calm.*

"San Francisco. Vain little bitch was stupid enough to show up on TV a couple of years ago on the arm of some rich geriatric type. I had a few friends on the outside, so it wasn't hard to track her down. And when I found out she was a hooker"—he gloated—"hell, nothing's easier to find than a working gal, them being creatures of habit, after all."

Grover's blood iced in his veins.

Bliss and Harding hadn't found the same girl!

Susan said the girl Harding found was "right in her backyard." And if Beauty were coming here, to Seattle, she had to be meeting Addilene somewhere. His head throbbed, and he closed his eyes, rubbed at his temple. Behind his eyelids was only blood.

No . . .

A voice from somewhere in the depths of his building headache murmured that the girls should live, go on with their secret lives . . .

But the risk!

His stomach contracted in fear and his head thrummed.

Bliss, busy ogling a young girl wearing only enough to avoid imprisonment, turned away. "You know who else is gonna be at the end of that rainbow?" He turned back to Grover, smirking.

Grover, busy worrying about the girls, how he'd kill them, if he could kill them, didn't quite hear him. So he shook his head, took a drink of beer. He hated beer, and this early in the day, it made him nauseous.

"A badass we all know and love. Our very own Gussy-baby—the last person on earth you want to clap eyes on."

Vanelleto! Grover's mind went sand blank, and his blood jellied in his veins. If Bliss found him, no doubt Harding would, too. And Gus Vanelleto was the biggest threat of all.

Frantic, his heart cartwheeled in his chest, and his gut cramped painfully.

Get a hold of yourself, Grover. Breathe.

He took his own advice and brought himself down. Everything was okay. For now, all he had to do was keep on top of things, maybe let Bliss live a little longer—until he led him to Vanelleto, at least. Yes, that would work. And to make him do that, he needed to gain his confidence. But how? All he wanted to do was run.

When his hand trembled, he secured it around his beer glass. "You'd better be careful, Frank," he said, when he'd leveled off enough to speak. "You remember how, uh, *tricky* Gus was." Read that cunning—and dangerous.

Bliss put down his burger, took a napkin from its metal holder and dragged it across his mouth. "Yeah, like you give a rat's ass what happens to me. Give me a break."

"I don't wish you any harm, surely by now you know that." He twirled his beer glass, tried to don a sincere expression. A thought came to him, lightning fast. So fast he had no time to think it through. "And I have tried to help you through these past years." He stammered it out, his brain racing ahead. He blessed the God who gave Bliss an inflated ego and a soft brain.

"Help? Are you nuts?" Bliss said. "I've been fuckin' blackmailing you, Grover."

"Yes, I knew you saw it that way, and that was all right. But I never resisted you, did I?" He paused to let that fact, as true as his own fear, take on a new spin. "The truth was, I wanted to help. I always kind of thought I owed it to Belle—you know, for what I'd done and all. The trouble I caused."

Bliss frowned and looked at him as if he were the village idiot on dumb pills. "You get saved or somethin'?"

"No." Grover soldiered on, prayed he wouldn't choke on his own lies. "But I did get too involved. And I did put those kids in your home, and in the end, that's what caused her death. If I hadn't done either of those things, you and your brother's lives might have turned out differently."

"Jesus, Grover, what're you trying to pull? You were looking out for number one—just like everybody else. Like me when I called that vicious bitch you live with, told her about you and Ma."

Grover lowered his head, ignored the sweat building up on his brow. "Back then, yes, I wanted to protect myself, didn't want the disgrace of losing my job, my standing—"

Bliss snorted again, stuffed an onion ring in his mouth.

"But believe it or not, I did feel guilty, and you coming at me for money like you did helped me ease that guilt. Somewhat, anyway." Grover faltered, formed his risky lie, and forced himself to meet Bliss's cynical gaze. "The thing is, I'm dying, Frank. I have a few months at most, so I won't be able to help you much anymore. This"—he shoved an envelope with ten thousand dollars in it across the table—"is the last of it. I've already organized my affairs to take care of Sandra, and as to your calling my employer, telling him about Belle and me, what I did . . ." He lifted a shoulder. "It doesn't matter now."

Frank's brow furrowed. "You're full of shit."

"I wish I was. I really do, but what I'm full of is . . . disease." He'd leave what disease to the idiot's imagination.

"Christ!" Bliss actually moved back in his seat as if germs were coursing in antlike masses across the wooden tabletop.

"So you see, I'm glad you'll be doing all right— that you've found your, uh, rainbow." Grover folded and refolded his napkin, but didn't look down at it. "Not that I'm surprised, you always were incredibly bright and capable." He choked out the last lie, and took another drink of his beer.

Bliss still looked suspicious, but Wayne finally had his full attention. "Like you noticed my brain power while you were humping mother dearest?" Still cynical, his voice had an edge of wistfulness, as if he were setting out on a flattery-fishing expedition.

Wayne nodded. "Hard to miss, Frank," he said, leaving a silence before adding, "But it is strange, isn't it? How things turn out? After all these years, you'll finally get some justice for what those kids did to you. In a way they owe you—maybe even more than I do."

"Damn straight." He shoved his burger plate aside. "You know, Grover, you're not half bad." He stopped, and his face went into neutral. Grover knew the look; every teenage boy he'd ever dealt with had it down pat. It was a you-can't-get-to-me look, used like white-out over the emotions, to accent how tough they were. It was usually accompanied by a curled lip. Bliss skipped the curled lip, but he had the blankness nailed, when he said, "You know, back then, when you were doing the dirty with Belle, you were pretty okay with Brett and me. Better than most of her johns."

"Thank you, Frank." Grover, his lie exhausting him, kept his face sober, avoided trudging deeper into Bliss's emotional landscape.

Bliss drank the last of his beer, nodded toward his glass, hesitated, then asked, "How about another? You being on your last legs and all, a man shouldn't deny himself."

Grover's smile was weak—and sincere. "So true." He nodded at Bliss's vest pocket, where sat half his retirement savings. "But you're buying."

Frank laughed. "Sure, Grover, why the hell not?"

"And about your plan, son"—he thought the word *son* a nice touch—"there is one problem you should know about."

Bliss was flagging the server. "Uh-huh," he said distractedly.

"Someone has found the other girl."

His head swung back as though whiplashed. "What are you talking about? Who?"

"A private investigator, by the name of Cade Harding, hired by the grandmother of the missing boy."

"Grandmother?" He frowned. "Shit, I forgot about her. Susan something. She came nosing around with questions a couple of times. Way back." He stopped.

"She's still looking after all this time? Hiring PIs? Must have more money than brains." His face was flat, thoughtful.

"She never stopped looking."

"Waste of time and cash. Damn little screamer. She'll never find him now." He looked away.

Wayne swallowed his repugnance at Bliss's casual disregard for the life of an innocent child.

He should die. He deserves to die.

His hands stopped shaking, and his heart found a steady rhythm for the first time since he'd sat down with Bliss. He felt right suddenly . . . convinced the world would be a better place without Bliss in it. "Maybe not, but Harding has turned up one of the girls, and based on what you've told me, it has to be Addilene Wartenski—"

"She was a kid. Doesn't know nothing."

"Maybe not, but if she leads him to Gus before you get to him . . ." He shrugged and let the suggestion carry its own weight. "It could cause you some trouble."

"Shit!"

Grover left him to stew in silence before adding, "If you like, we could keep in touch for the next while. If you keep me informed of your whereabouts, I'll keep you informed of Harding's. That way, you'll have no unwelcome surprises."

He was immediately suspicious again. "And for that you'll want what? Half?"

"This isn't about money." Wayne shook his head, sadly he hoped. "I won't live long enough to spend it."

"What then? Everybody wants something."

"I just want what you want, Frank," he said, then

to allay his suspicions, added, "And the promise you'll leave my wife in peace after I'm gone."

"Ah, the little woman again." He stuck out his hand, looked relieved that Grover had asked for something in return. "Sure, Grover, why the hell not? Besides, leavin' that bitch of yours alone would be about the easiest thing I ever had to do."

After a serious round of pacing, cursing, and flat out avoidance, Cade picked up the phone. He was lucky; the person he wanted to answer did.

"Brenton, this is Cade. We've got a problem, and I think backup is in order. I assume you carry?" Cade was licensed, but he'd gotten rid of his artillery years before. By now, he'd probably have trouble nailing a soda pop can from a foot away. But he wasn't going into this drama unprepared. Addy had no idea what wheels she'd set in motion, what to expect. She'd admitted as much.

She wanted him in; he was in—his way. It was for damn sure the cast of characters he'd be dealing with would be armed to their back molars.

"Not as a matter of course," Stan said, in his easy way. "Generally keep it in mothballs."

"Well, get it out of mothballs and bring it here. Do the traveling salesman routine and check in. I'll watch for you. When you get here, I'll fill in the details. But for God's sake, leave Susan behind." One more person to look out for might prove one too many. If he could work things out with Addy, there was a chance of avoiding bloodshed—and finding Josh—but if he showed his hand too soon, she'd warn the others, then bolt herself. He'd bet on that. If that happened, he'd lose any possible lead to Josh—and Addy would be out of his life.

Neither thought was palatable.

"I'll do what I can. Care to tell me what's going on?"

"Like I said, I'll fill you in when you get here. For now, it's enough that you know I've verified my original suspicion. I've found Addilene Wartenski." *And she's going to break both my legs when she finds out I've called you.* But while that made him feel like a rat, her safety came first.

"You sure it's Wartenski?" Brenton said. "Absolutely sure?"

"It's her. And she's told me most of what happened the night Belle Bliss was killed."

"Hell!" he said. "You're good, Harding. Maybe you and I should partner up."

"Not in this lifetime, Brenton. I'll take my thrills from plotlines and carefully edited mayhem." He forked a hand through his thick hair. "How soon can you get here?"

"I'll be on my way within the hour. A few directions would speed me up, though."

Cade gave him detailed instructions on how to find the place, then closed by repeating, "And Stan? Don't bring Susan. It's too soon."

A pause. "Now that oughta be interesting. She's been a hound dog since she found out I knew where you were in the first place. She's not going to like being left behind, it being her missing grandson who started all these goings-on."

"Being left behind is a hell of a lot safer than being in the line of a stray bullet." And if Cade couldn't stop it, bullets were definitely in the future of Star Lake.

"You're right about that, and hell"—he laughed a bit—"if I can't shake off an itty-bitty woman, I'll have to retire my PI license."

"See you, Brenton."

" *'Itty-bitty woman'*?" Susan said from behind him, her tone dripping in honey and laced with arsenic.

Stan closed his eyes and cursed to himself, before he turned to face the music that would undoubtedly be his dirge. "Sweetie—"

"Don't even think about it, Stan. Let's pack together," she smiled and raised her brows, but the gaze under them was implacable. "And if it's guns my nephew wants, it's guns he'll get. I have a Glock in the drawer of my bedside table."

"Susan, please listen to—"

She raised a hand—the one holding the bedroom cordless telephone—and glared up at him. "If I were you, Stan Brenton, I wouldn't say another word. It will take you at least a year to atone for 'itty-bitty.' " She stomped out of the room. "I've got a call to make, then I'm packing. Then, big man, we go and find my grandson. If we hurry, we can be there in a couple of hours."

Chapter 18

Grover watched Linda Curl through the glass window in his office. She was laughing into the phone. Probably a personal call, he thought. She had lots of those. Probably had lots of friends, one of those things called a "life."

The one thing Sandra wouldn't let him have.

And the one thing he hoped to have when this thing with Bliss was finally over.

Linda got up and ambled toward his office, still smiling, and wearing some awful slack suit, the kind where the jacket looked okay, but the pants were all shiny in the ass.

Linda was no fashion plate, that was for sure, but she always had that wonderful grin, a kind of morning-after, smugly satisfied grin that made promises.

Grover watched her come toward him and again thought about those bad pants of hers and how he'd like to be in them. He stiffened slightly, and touched himself under the desk. Curl would want to be on top. He liked that.

But even if he did sort the Bliss part of his life out, there was still Sandra.

There was always Sandra. He sighed, lifted his hand from his semi-erect penis, and picked up a pen.

"Hey, Grover, I'm about to make your day." She perched on the edge of his desk and faced him.

He leaned back in his chair. "I can always take good news."

"I placed Millie Fawcett. And the home is absolutely perfect for her." She lifted a joyous hand. "And I'll even bet money she won't take off this time. I'm telling you, as foster parents go, these two are the best."

"Then it's the Johnsons."

She nodded. "Uh-huh. Like I said, perfect. Am I good or what?"

Wayne smiled. This *was* excellent news. Millie was ten, a good kid, but a troubled one. Tough, though. She reminded him of Addilene Wartenski. "That's great. I was getting worried about her." And that was the goddamned truth. Millie deserved a break and now she was getting one. If you didn't celebrate the successes in this business, you'd end up cutting your own throat. Wayne held up his hand for a high five. "Way to go, Curl."

Linda slapped his hand, her smile nearly splitting her face. "And to celebrate, I'm taking you to Holly's for a beer after work, and I—being on the winning streak that I am—will not take no for an answer. Holly's at five-thirty, earlier if we can swing it."

He started to protest, stopped suddenly. Jesus, he was a walking freak show! A fucking mental case! Yesterday he'd planned a murder, today he was afraid to go for a beer with a coworker. A tic, signaling the onslaught of yet another headache, jittered low in his skull.

His heart pounding, he said, "Done."

She gaped at him. "You're kidding me. You're actually going to have a drink with me?"

He burned and reddened, knew he'd made a terrible mistake. She'd been kidding him along, expected him to say no. She wasn't interested in him. Why would she be? Sandra was right, he wasn't a real man.

You call that excuse for manhood a cock, Wayne? More like a cocktail sausage, you ask me.

He wanted to slink away, hide, but he was frozen in place, his tongue a tangled knot in his mouth, his stomach a hard clump of organ and sinew being torn apart by metal gloves.

She stared at him so long he got uncomfortable, tugged at his collar. That's when she grinned. "Grover, baby, you've made me one very happy woman." She leaned forward. "And if you didn't have windows in this office, I'd show you how happy." She stood, straightened her jacket, and gave him an impish grin. "Hell, you start drinking with me, the possibilities are endless." She licked her lips, laughed, then turned and walked out of his office, deliberately giving her shiny-panted ass a shake before she closed the door behind her.

Grover put his head down, centered his attention on the papers on his desk, ostensibly going back to work, but mainly to hide the wash of relief. He took some deep breaths to calm down.

Then he started to sweat.

Sandra would kill him this time for sure.

If she found out . . .

His phone rang. "Grover, it's Bliss."

The voice punched at him, made his flesh contract, and he swiveled away from his office window, guiltily, stupidly—as if anyone glancing in would know instantly he was talking to a killer and parole violator on department time. "Yes," he said, and choked back the seethe of hatred that made him tremble.

"Any news on Harding yet?" Bliss sounded bad-tempered and impatient.

"No. But I've got some calls out."

"You call me, ASAP, you hear anything. Anything at all. You got that?" he growled. "My bitch is holed up in the goddamn hotel, probably won't make a move until Vanelleto gets to wherever the hell it is he's supposed to be—maybe another day or two. My guess is it's where Harding's got Wartenski. Goddamn losers must be planning some kind of fuckin' reunion."

"Don't worry, Frank," he said, hating the sound of his own soft, soothing voice, yet finding the play easier with every lie. "I'll find the Wart." He swiveled to hang up the phone, then turned back to the window.

And when the time is right, I'll tell you where she is. He had a flutter of panic at how long he could hold Bliss off, but shoved it aside. Everything was under control, and he intended to keep it that way.

How Sandra would laugh if she could see him now, making dates, plotting murders.

"Not so useless. Not such a coward now, my love," he murmured.

Still some loose ends, but so far . . .

He knew where Bliss was, where Beauty was, and thanks to Susan's excited call to him less than an hour ago, he knew the location of Harding and Wartenski. Vanelleto was still the wild card, but where Wart met the Beauty, Vanelleto wouldn't be far away. He was sure of it.

Feeling better now, less anxious, Wayne thought about what was in the glove compartment of his car—the knife, the shiny new gun—the keys to a shiny new life.

He held out his hands to the light coming in his office window. They weren't shaking. He was truly and finally ready.

Ready to kill Bliss and anyone else who threatened him.

Ready to play God.

Addy, in the office for the afternoon because Toby had a doctor's appointment, picked up the phone. "Star Lake."

"Addy?"

She slumped into the chair behind the counter. "Beauty! Where are you?"

"Seattle. The Everwood. I drove straight through. Have you heard from Gus yet?"

"No, but he'll be here, don't worry." Addy coiled the cord of the old phone around her finger until its tip went white. "Are you okay?"

"I'm fine. I think Bliss is a few hours behind me," she said, her voice flat, carrying none of the fear and emotion of her first few calls.

Addy heard her take a drink, or maybe drag on

a cigarette, she wasn't sure, but she hoped it was the latter. Booze and Beauty were too scary to think about. "Are you sure you're okay?"

"Better than okay, knowing Bliss will be six feet under when Gus gets through with him." Her voice was frigid.

"Beauty, that's not—"

"Save it, Wart, the die, as they say, is cast." Another pause, another drag or drink. "I should give you this number. Got a pen?"

"Uh-huh." Addy, her mouth dry as dust, wrote down the number, then said, "Beauty, can I ask you something?"

This time she heard the tinkle of ice in a glass. Definitely drinking. Damn! "Sure, fire away."

"That night, when Gus went downstairs and you followed him?"

"Yeah?"

"Did you see who killed Belle? Was it Frank? Or Brett?"

"You know I don't like talking about . . . what happened. Besides, you asked me that question when we first got to Star Lake."

"I know. I'm asking again."

Silence. "And I'll give you the same answer. It had to be Frank, because I'm sure I heard Brett leave before the shooting started. He yelled something to Belle about her being a whore and slammed the door—shook the damn house. Man, that family gave new meaning to the word dysfunctional."

"But you didn't actually see him do it?"

"I told you back then I didn't see anything. Why are you asking me this now anyway?"

Addy rubbed her forehead. "I don't know. I guess

I thought after all this time, you might have remembered something." She squelched her own guilty thoughts, the insecurities that had sprung up since she'd talked to Cade. She didn't understand it herself: why, after all these years, she was reliving that night, doubting her friends. What kind of a friend did that, what kind of a person? A thinking, all-grown-up kind of person, she told herself—which didn't make the shaky ground that came with the doubt any easier to stand on.

"It wasn't Gus, Addy." Beauty said, her tone low. "I know that as sure as I know Bliss is a murdering, lying, raping beast. It was him who killed Belle, then he lied and blamed it on Gus. Not only was Gus handy, Frank hated him." She took another drink. "Besides, Gus was with me. We were in Belle's room, trying to shut up the kid. I had a pillow and—"

"Dear God! You never told me that!" Addy's chest tightened, and her words came out on a gasp.

"What was to tell? I didn't do anything. I was so scared, so hyped, I wasn't thinking. The kid was fine. Really. Gus took, uh, care of it."

"Took care of what, for God's sake?"

"Forget it. You want to talk, we'll talk when I get there. This is hardly the stuff for a phone call."

"Beauty!"

"Look, I've got to go. Quit worrying, will you? And quit trying to figure things out. What happened, happened, and we can't take any of it back. All we can do is survive the best way we can." She paused, added in a softer voice. "It was such a long time ago. We were kids, Wart. Scared kids with no place to go." She let out a breath, and it came through the line guilt-laden and resigned. "Call me, will you? The second Gus arrives—the very second!" She hung up.

Addy dropped the receiver on the counter as if it were a dead rat. She couldn't take her eyes off it, couldn't make her brain stop superimposing a new and deadly image over the old—the one framed by trust, loyalty, and lost innocence.

That wild night, chaos, noise, blood, fear . . . the gunshots.

Gus and Beauty in Belle's room, both of them wounded, panicked, and angry, desperate to escape, get out of that terrible house . . . with a crying baby—and a pillow.

Had they—

No! She covered her face with her hands, her body trembling and weak. No! She would not, could not believe they'd hurt that boy. Gus was cold, self-protective, and domineering, but not inhuman, and Beauty might be rash sometimes and irresponsible, but never, never cruel.

They were her friends, the only two people in the world who'd ever cared about her, other than her mother.

She straightened away from the desk. In all these years, she'd never believed Gus or Beauty had anything to do with Belle's murder. She wouldn't start doubting them now.

That Bliss lied to protect himself, she could believe. She could also believe that Bliss . . . hurt the boy. But why? There was no reason for Frank to hurt him. At least none she could think of. Damn! The whole thing made her head ache. Just because Gus and Beauty were the last ones to see the boy didn't mean—

Startled when the bell over the office door jangled, she looked up. It was an older couple, an extremely tall man and a woman—much smaller—with silvery white hair and one of those expensive haircuts that put every hair on her head in exactly the right place. She was pretty though, and the man was smiling.

Grateful for the distraction from her miserable, disloyal thoughts, she went into work mode, and smiled back. "Hi, can I help you?"

"Sure can, little lady. If you can handle it, we'd like a cabin for a couple of days. Maybe three."

"That I can do," she said, thinking the term "little lady" would pretty much describe any woman this giant of a man ever met. She handed them a registration card. "My name is Addy Michaels, and I'm the owner of Star Lake." She stuck out a hand in the usual ritual, knowing they'd introduce themselves in return. It was her way of hearing names, rather than having to have them read to her. Names were the hardest of all.

"Stan Brenton," the big man said, his smile broadening. "And this is the love of my life, Susan."

His hand was warm, big as a shovel, and equally as firm. Addy nodded. The woman's hand was small and cool; she peered at Addy intently, as if measuring her in some way. Addy, uncomfortable under her scrutiny, said, "I can put you in Cabin Seven, Mrs. Brenton, it overlooks the lake. Will that be all right?"

"That will be fine," the woman said, momentarily shifting her gaze from Addy and nodding to-

ward the office window. "This place is a real gem—
the painted cottages are lovely." The praise was as
cool as her hand.

Addy turned to get them keys. When she turned
back, the man was picking up brochures, and his
wife was studying Addy as if she were a dissected
toad.

"Thank you," she said, vaguely uneasy. "I've been
working on the cabins for some time now."

"Well, it certainly shows." Susan took her key, but
not her eyes off of Addy.

"Let's go, love," the man said, tugging her arm.
"After all that driving, I could use a lie down."

"If you need anything, let me know," Addy
called out as they walked out the door.

"We certainly will, dear. You can count on that."
She looked back over her shoulder, gave her a
fierce look.

Addy's motel-owner smile dissolved into a frown
as she watched the twosome get back into their car
and drive the few yards to Cabin Seven. The woman
went inside, while the man went to the trunk of
the big Mercedes and unloaded two small bags.

When Cade's door opened, and he and Redge
came out, her attention switched to him. She stifled a sigh at the sight of his fit, lean body clad casually in a white muscle shirt and runner's shorts.
Such a strong body . . .

While her thoughts made an unscheduled detour into the mist of last night's lovemaking, and
her breath stumbled along her windpipe, she saw
Cade nod at the man and sort of cock his head at
the woman, who still looked annoyed about something. When Mr. Brenton set the bags by his side,

and offered his hand, Cade shook it, nodded, and the two men talked briefly before Cade and Redge headed for a run on the path circling the lake.

"New guests?" Toby asked, stepping in the door.

"Yes. Cabin Seven." She watched the man go in and close the door, then turned to Toby. "Just for a couple of nights though."

"Good thing, we're damn near empty after yesterday. Two couples leaving early and all. This keeps up and this here resort will be running on empty before the weekend."

"Motel," she corrected automatically, then blinked. "What did you say?"

"I said if we don't get anybody else checking in, we'll only have renters in Six, Eleven, and Seven come Saturday. That's only a couple of days away." He came around the counter and sat at the computer, a coffee in his hand.

God, what had she been thinking! "Leave it that way, Toby. Don't rent any more cabins, and put out the No Vacancy sign." She should have thought about this sooner. Dear God, if something did happen here in the next day or two, the last thing she wanted was a motel full of guests. Damn, if her brain weren't so full of Cade Harding, she would have thought of it sooner, and she wouldn't have checked the Brentons in.

"Are you crazy, girl? You can't afford that." Toby looked as if she'd asked him to burn the place down at midnight.

If he didn't like the first suggestion, he was going to hate her next one. "And, uh, it might be a good idea if you took a few days off, maybe go visit friends in Seattle."

He stared at her, his mouth slack. "You are crazy."

"Just do what I ask, okay?"

"You firing me?"

She went to where he sat and rested her hands on his shoulders, a gesture she'd not have made a few days ago. "Of course I'm not firing you. But there's going to be some things happening around here, and I'll need my, uh, privacy." Lame, but the best she could do.

Toby looked at her for a too-long time. "That check I did on that Cade fellow—you hear what you wanted to hear?"

"Uh-huh."

"This no-vacancy business have something to do with him?"

She hesitated, not sure what to say. "In a way."

Toby's lips curved. "All right, then. It's about time you had yourself some man fun."

"It's not that, it's . . . ." Wanting to explain, but unable to, she stopped. She'd let Toby think what he chose to think, and if everything worked out, she'd fill him in later. For now, ignorance was bliss. She'd never thought before how very true that statement was.

"I'll put that No Vacancy sign out right now, sweetums." He got up. "Anything else before I take off?"

"No, Toby . . . and thanks."

He opened the door, stood there and smiled again, his gray head bobbing. "You have a good time, hear?"

"I will." She went back to stare dully at the inde-cipherable guest register and to worry. This morn-ing, she'd trusted Cade Harding with her life and with Gus and Beauty's lives, and she'd thought of nothing else since. When she'd told him what was going on, what she wanted from him, he'd gone deathly still, and her stomach had tangled so badly she thought it would never unfurl. Then he'd said he'd think about her plan, which he was probably doing right now, while running like a big dark cat around the fringe of Star Lake.

Her throat, filled with wishes and fears, seized up tight, and she looked toward the door of her apartment; behind it were her bags, packed and ready to go.

So what will you choose, Professor? To aid and abet a woman wanted as an accomplice to murder, or will you call the cops, tell them "who's coming to dinner" at Star Lake, and go back to your upright, error-free life with a clear conscience?

Chapter 19

"Going somewhere, slut?"

The voice, a whisper from beside her, nearly made Beauty come out of her skin. Bliss!

How could she have not noticed him? She tried to keep moving, but he was too quick; his hand snaked out, shackled her wrist. And it was her own damn fault.

How could she have been so stupid! Feeling stir-crazy and edgy, she'd decided to chance the hotel dining room for an early dinner, sure it would be hours before Bliss arrived in Seattle.

"Surprised to see me, baby?" He squeezed her too-rapid pulse.

"Nope, disappointed it happened so soon." She tried to pull her wrist free.

"How about this for coincidence? I'm in the room across the hall from you." He gave a wolfish grin. "Gotta take care of my investment."

"Let me go, Bliss."

"Sit down." His voice was low and easy, a mockery of affable. "I'll buy you dinner."

She glared at him, ignored the tremors in her stomach, and said, "I don't think so. Sitting with you, there's always the chance I'll upchuck on the table—make a scene." She tugged her wrist again, but he only tightened his grasp.

"I said sit." He waved his other hand to encompass the busy dining room. "I figure we'll both be safe enough. Me from that fancy piece you're carrying and you from my—what is it women call them—unwanted advances." He snorted. "Like any woman isn't panting for it all the time."

Beauty considered making the scene she threatened him with but decided against it. Too risky. Chances were they'd both end up in jail. She wouldn't see Gus. She slid into the padded booth.

"We made our arrangement, Bliss," she said. "So what the hell do you want from me?"

Before he answered, a server came and filled her water glass, handed her a menu. She muttered her thanks.

"You mean other than to hump you?"

She picked up the water, drank to drown the nausea. "Other than that."

"I've been thinking—"

"I'm sorry, it must be hard for you." She laced her fingers together on the tabletop; her palms were fear-damp.

"Funny." He didn't laugh. "I've been thinking about the night dear old Mom . . . passed over, as they say."

"Ah, a trip down memory lane, how sweet. You always were such a doting son."

Bliss leaned over and filled her wineglass. "Shut the fuck up and listen, will you?" He growled. "Be a little friendly. I've got some questions. That's all. So relax."

She eyed the red wine he'd poured. She really shouldn't drink, not with Bliss. She'd sip. Just sip. It would calm her nerves. She picked it up, looked at him over its rim. "That sub-Neanderthal brain of yours must have nothing but questions." She took another sip, already feeling better.

He gave her a filthy look, then said. "The question is about the kid."

"What kid?" Cold washed over her, a faint damp rain of it.

"I don't know his damn name! The boy that Grover brought in the day Mom bought the farm."

She took another drink, this one more than a sip. "What about him?"

"Do you know where Vanelleto dumped him after you—"

She started to get up, and his hand shot across the table with the speed and agility of a striking cobra, forced her down. Her body was on fire as if pinned by a thousand needles. "I don't know anything about that kid."

"I think you do, Beauty."

"Well, you're wrong—as usual."

"I'm not wrong about there being some serious cash to be made if someone knows the whereabouts of that kid's body."

"There's no body!" As usual, she sounded surer than she felt.

"Yeah? If there's no goddamn body, then there's a living, breathin' kid around somewhere, which I seriously doubt." He fixed his gaze on her, his mouth a hard seam. "But I'll buy into it, babe, if you tell me where that kid might be."

She said nothing, because she had nothing to say. First Addy had asked her about the boy, and now this piece of filth. She had no answer for either of them, because she didn't know, had never known. And she'd lived with the curse of not knowing every day of her life ever since that night.

Everything happened so fast. Huddled, sick and hurting, in that bedroom, terrified the shrieking boy would attract Belle's attention, bring her and Frank into the room, she'd picked up the crying boy. He'd been left in the room for hours without being changed; his head was white hot, and he smelled like pee and vomit. She remembered thinking he must be really sick.

But all she'd wanted to do was make him stop screaming, screaming, screaming . . .

She trembled, drank some wine. The images of that night in black and white like a batch of photographs fanned so fast they became a jumble.

There'd been the . . . pillow thing, Gus's shocked curse, "Jesus, Beauty! What are you doing?"

Him yanking the bod—baby from her arms, his eyes cool and hot at the same time, his voice ragged. "Don't worry," he'd said. "I'll take care of it. Just get the hell out of this house. Wait for me by the shed. I'll find you."

He never did. It was the last time she ever saw him.

Bliss snapped his fingers in front of her face. "You with me, sweetheart?"

She blinked at him.

"I asked you if you knew where that kid ended up."

"No."

He eyed her coldly. "Maybe you don't get it, but that kid is worth some real change—dead or alive. That old lady's been looking for him for—what?— fifteen years, willing to pay big-time."

"What old lady?"

"The kid's grandma, a rich bitch on a mission, that's for sure."

The baby had a grandma . . . family.

Feeling as though she were going to be sick, Beauty downed the last of her wine, and to avoid his revolting touch, kept her hands under the table as she finally escaped the booth. "Thanks for the wine, asshole." She didn't give him a chance to answer. Turning from his handsome face, she walked quickly to the elevator.

Back in her room, she leaned against the door and panted like a dog on a hot afternoon. She used the rigid length of the door to straighten her own back, then slid to the floor and hugged her knees.

"Dear God, Addy, call me, please! Tell me Gus is here—that he'll make Bliss go away. Tell me everything is going to be all right."

After a few minutes, and a wild crying jag, she got to her feet and went to the phone.

Beauty wasn't a woman to cry in her beer, but an expensive merlot? Definitely.

She brushed the dampness from her cheeks, called room service, and though certain she wouldn't eat, ordered dinner and enough wine to swim in. Her watery gaze shifted to the security locks on her door.

Bliss. Across the hall.

She shuddered, knew she wouldn't leave this room until she'd heard from Addy and knew for sure Gus was in Seattle.

She wished she could make things right, shout to the world that neither Gus nor Addy had killed anyone.

Too bad she wasn't so sure about herself.

"I want to talk to her," Susan said—again. "I don't care what you say, Cade. I think talking one woman to another—especially when it concerns the well-being of a child—makes perfect sense. All this plotting and planning is a waste of time. Besides, do we even know for sure if the other two will show up?" She was agitated and it showed.

Stan looked at Cade, raised a brow. "She's got a point. It could work."

Cade dragged up the last of his patience. They'd been circling Susan's argument for half an hour. Time was running short, and the one thing he didn't want was for Addy to find them huddled together like some goddamn secret society. Hell, bad enough he'd brought Stan and Susan here without telling her. He intended it to be the last of his deceits.

"She does *not* have a point, Stan." Cade argued, then turned to Susan. "And Bliss and Beauty will show up. Bliss for the cash he expects to be paid, and Beauty because—according to Addy—she'd walk over hot coals to see Vanelleto again. You go barging up there, start asking questions, and not only will she bolt, there's no doubt she'll get in touch with the others. Plus—as I've told you, Susan—Addy says she does not know what happened to Josh. On that point, she's as much in the dark as all of us."

"And you believe her?"

"She asked for my help, remember? Trusted me enough to tell me about her friends, what's about to happen at Star Lake." Cade said. "So, yes, I believe her. Even if I didn't, at this point I wouldn't risk calling her a liar."

"She also said she and her 'friends' didn't kill Belle Bliss," Stan interjected, calmly. "A witness says otherwise."

"A witness with a history of violence, distorting the truth, and a thirst for revenge. Not to mention a very strong desire to cover up his own actions on that day, which included the rape of Dianna Lintz."

Stan shrugged. "That may be, but it will be interesting to hear his side of it firsthand."

Cade jumped on that. "Which we won't, if you"—he nodded at Susan, sitting on the bed with her arms crossed—"follow through with the woman-to-woman thing. Do that and Addy's long gone, taking Bliss, Vanelleto, and Beauty with her."

"You're damn sure of yourself, Cade," she grumbled.

"I'm sure of Addy, her sense of loyalty"—*however misguided.* "She asked for my help to prevent a murder, not hang her friends out to dry for a killing she says they had no part in."

"Now I'd take that to mean she thinks they're capable of killing at least," Stan said.

"We're all capable of killing, Stan, if we're

pushed far enough. You've been around long enough to know that capability and culpability don't share DNA. The thing is, she'll do anything to protect them from the law and from themselves, which right now means stopping them from killing Bliss. Those three went through hell together. She won't forget that."

Stan looked at Susan. "Now *he's* got a point."

She glared at him, got up, and walked to the window overlooking the lake, leaving her back to them.

Stan's gaze followed her, then swung back to Cade. "What do you propose?"

"That we let as much of Addy's plan play out as possible. She's convinced she can talk her friends down. Whether she can or can't, the smart thing is to sit tight until everyone is here," he said. "Vanelleto is slated to arrive first, then Beauty and Bliss—"

"Beauty and Bliss." Susan muttered from the window. "Fancy names for a prostitute and a criminal."

Cade ignored her, clung to the edges of his patience. "When Vanelleto arrives"—he took a breath—"I let Addy do her thing, talk to him." He paused, hating what was to come. "Then, regardless of the results of that conversation and before the others arrive, I tell her the truth, about you, about me, and why we're here." He stopped, his mind already reacting to the hurt and anger he'd see in her eyes. "And we confront Vanelleto, try to get some answers about Belle Bliss's murder and about Josh."

"And if we don't get the answers we want? If he refuses to cooperate?" Susan asked.

"We take him in."

"So far, so good," Stan said, nodding. "And Bliss, what about him?"

"We keep Bliss away from Vanelleto for the duration. Then we make sure he gets a one-way ticket back to where he belongs, the Smithfield prison, for parole violation." None of which would be easy. "The way I see it, our best chance of getting solid information on Josh rests with Gus or Beauty."

Cade walked to where Susan still stood by the window and rested his hands on her shoulders. "But you've got to be prepared, Susan. What we're told or not told might not be what you want to hear. If Josh is dead and either Vanelleto, Beauty, or"—God forbid!—"Addy had anything to do with it, the chances any of them come clean is nonexistent. You might be right back where you started."

Susan turned to look up at him, her jaw set with determination. "Josh is alive, Cade. I'm closer to him now than I've ever been. I can feel it."

Cade nodded, kissed her forehead. "Okay, we'll hold that thought."

"And Belle Bliss's murder? What about that?" Stan said. "We're pretty busy ignoring the fact that those kids—and that includes Addilene and Beauty—are wanted for murder." He leaned forward in the chair and met Cade's gaze straight on. "We can't let that go, Harding"—he paused, looked momentarily reluctant to go on—"no matter what your feelings are for that pretty little girl up there." He gestured with his head in the general direction of the office.

Cade went still; Brenton's words hit his dilemma dead on. Addy's name on an outstanding murder warrant and his on a criminology degree did not make for a bed of roses, ethically speaking. Add in the feelings he had for her—not yet defined, but strong enough to rattle his normally logical mind—and a man had serious trouble on his hands. But no real choice.

Stan didn't take his eyes off him, and Susan, half-sitting on the windowsill, looked at him in surprise. When he didn't immediately answer, she asked, "Is that true, Cade? You care for the girl?"

"Yes," he said, his curt answer more of an admission than he'd yet fully processed for himself. He rubbed the tension building in his neck. "But regardless of my feelings, Stan's right. We can't ignore the fact that Addy and the others are wanted by the police."

"But if we bring the police in too soon . . ." Susan chewed her lower lip. "God, this is complicated!"

"It needn't be, if we go slowly." Ever since Susan drummed him into this action, Cade had worked to separate Josh's disappearance from Belle's murder, not wanting to get more involved than he already was. Stupid thinking then, even stupider now.

Meeting Addy changed everything. But if they were to have a chance for more, she had to stop running and face those charges. And he'd have to make sure she did.

"And by 'go slowly' you mean what?" Susan asked.

Stan rose to tower over him. "What I think he means, my love, is that we play out our hand, make sure nobody kills our boy Bliss, and take it from there."

"That's about it." With Bliss dead, his damning eyewitness statement, now in the files of the Seattle PD, might as well be etched on a stone tablet.

Stan nodded, shoved his hands in his pockets. "If we believe your Addy—"

"She's not my anything yet, Brenton." Never would be if this idea of his didn't pan out. Ethics or no, turning a woman over to the cops wasn't the most seductive trick in the book, which was why Cade intended she be well in the clear before the boys in blue set foot in the door. Nothing less. And if he had things figured right, Bliss was the one to do it.

"Maybe not, but I'm guessing you'd like her to be, which puts a lot at stake. You know . . ." Stan shot Cade a wily glance, went on. "If we believe her, that Gus and Beauty were downstairs when Belle Bliss met up with those bullets, there's a chance Frank isn't the only one who saw something. We get everyone together . . ." He shrugged. "We could have ourselves some real interesting dialogue."

Cade nodded. "We'll have a couple of hours at most. After that?" He lifted a hand. "It's game over."

The next morning, a tall, dark-haired man walked out the sliding airport doors into a light rain and half the heat of the Miami he'd left that afternoon.

Seattle, just as he remembered it, green, misty, and cool.

He took a couple of deep breaths, eased the tension from his neck and shoulders, and glanced around the crowded arrivals' walkway, keeping his expression casual.

Airports, with their heightened security, weren't his favorite places these days, especially when he walked through them under a false name. But considering his current name and occupation were well past the ten-year mark, he felt reasonably safe taking the chance. From what the Wart told him, he sure as hell didn't have time for a leisurely cross-country drive.

His scanning eyes caught an interested look from a security guard having a smoke near the limo stand. The look didn't come close to scrutiny, only the usual double-take at first sight of his scar. He was careful not to look away first, nodding politely before he moved along the lineup of cabs waiting for passengers along the inside arrivals lane. He tossed his duffel onto the seat of the first one available, got in and draped his arm over the seat back.

"Where to?" the cabby asked, pushing a button to start the meter.

"You tell me. What's a good hotel in Seattle these days? It's been a while since I was here." He kept his tone even, cab-passenger friendly. Forgettable.

The cabby turned, scanned his well-worn leather jacket and jeans. "You a five-star man?"

"Hardly."

"The Hotel Philip then. Old, but the prices are good right now because of the renovations."

"Sounds good."

Gus Vanelleto, aka August Hammond, settled back in the cab, stared out the window, and went over his plan. First up, he needed a gun, and he needed it ASAP, which meant finding a local supplier. You had to have a death wish to carry a gun on a plane these days, and while Gus had death on his mind, it wasn't his own.

Contrary to popular opinion, a guy, an unconnected guy, didn't walk down the nearest seedy alley and buy himself an unregistered handgun unless he wanted to risk buying from an undercover cop. Not that he was worried. If he knew how to do anything it was be cautious—and he had a reference. Gus didn't do alleys, not anymore.

When he was set up, he'd give the Wart a call, have her get in touch with Beauty—make sure she didn't get to Star Lake before he did. No way was he letting that piece of shit have the advantage of getting there first. No, he'd be waiting for Bliss, that was a given.

Then he'd do what he'd come here to do.

Then he was gone.

He looked out the window, only dimly aware of the sights and sounds of Seattle's fifteen years' worth of growth and change—and the place where his life had blown apart in the first place. He was all kinds of fool, coming back, risking everything he'd built over the past ten years for a girl he hadn't breathed in, talked to, or touched since he was seventeen years old. Hadn't done much touching back then either, if his memories sat right. He rubbed his mouth to hide a rare smile, at once rueful and ironic. Beauty never made it easy.

So far in his life, she was the only woman who hadn't—not that he aimed high in the female department. No point.

Addy said she called herself Fallon now. Fallon West. Maybe so, but she'd always be Beauty to him.

He rested his head back, looked at the cab's scruffy roof liner. He closed his eyes and brought back the scent of her, the girl/woman who was always taking those lemony scented baths—whenever a bath was available.

She'd taken one that day . . .

The cabby hit the brakes, mumbled, "Asshole."

The shock pulled him from his thoughts. Thoughts he didn't have time for. He was here to do a job and get out. Back to his life. He sure as hell wasn't here to waste his time on a woman, any woman. Even Beauty. He'd been alone this long and he intended to keep it that way.

It was safer that way. For one thing, the less either Beauty or Wart knew about what happened to the boy, the better off they were. Being wanted for Belle's murder was enough. They didn't need to know the rest.

Gus's plan was simple—do what he had to do to ensure Bliss didn't trouble any of them ever again.

When that was done, it was back to Miami.

Chapter 20

"You've been avoiding me," Cade said from the office doorway. He'd left her to it for most of the day, but like it or not, they had some talking to do—some planning.

Addy looked at him from under the hand she put over her eyes to block out the setting sun streaming through the windows behind him. When he was close enough to provide shade, she lowered her hand, and started to shuffle papers. He would have smiled—if it were a time for smiles—watching her put one unread sheet on top of the other.

"I've got my reasons."

Cade's first thought was that she'd found out about Stan and Susan; he tensed. "Which are?" He walked around the office counter to stand face-to-face with the woman he'd made love to last night, and who'd been treating him as a stranger or, worse yet, a paying guest ever since.

She pursed her lips and her frown deepened. "I'm, uh, a little embarrassed is all. I'll get over it."

Cade's tension evaporated. This he could handle. He took a step closer, clasped her shoulders, and dipped his head to look into her eyes. "I don't want you to 'get over it.' " He lifted her chin. "And there's nothing to be 'embarrassed' about. What we did, what we had, was flat-out incredible." He refused to let her embarrassment play, but knew he'd be powerless against the ton or two of disappointment and regrets she'd have when she discovered the reason he'd come to Star Lake in the first place.

The tiniest of smiles turned up her uncolored lips. "Yeah, it was, but"—she pulled away and put a couple of feet of distance between them—"I don't want to think about that . . . stuff right now. What with everything happening or about to happen." Misery and confusion replaced the final trace of her reluctant smile. "And I sure as heck don't want to talk about us having sex. It feels too weird."

"Okay, we won't talk about it," he said, not because he wanted to avoid the subject, but because the timing was off. Way off. But he added, "Even if I haven't stopped thinking about 'that stuff' all day."

After a long pause, she said in a whisper. "Me, either."

He touched her madcap of hair. "But if it makes you feel any better, I didn't come here to make you uncomfortable, I came to ask if you know any more about your friends' ETA. But by the looks of that sober face of yours, you don't."

She folded her arms, looked aside. "I haven't heard from either of them, not Beauty, who was born with a phone in her ear and a finger on send, or Gus. I'm afraid something's gone wrong. That maybe Bliss..." Whatever she wanted to say wouldn't come out, so she resorted to chewing on her lower lip.

"They'll be fine. Let's not worry until we have to." He tipped her chin up, and the room suddenly went very quiet, very still, as did Addy when her eyes met his.

"I like that, you know," she said.

He cocked his head, raised a brow in question.

"What you said. That 'we' thing."

He ran his knuckles along her clear, smooth skin, then pulled his hand away. "You asked me to help, and I will. Nothing's going to happen at Star Lake."

"You really think my plan will work?"

No, he didn't, but he wasn't about to tell her he'd brought in reinforcements—and a loaded revolver. "We'll have to be careful—and smart," he said, noncommittally. "The trick will be to get your friends alone so you can talk to them." From then on, her scheme relied on heavy doses of wishes and dreams.

Addy planned to make Vanelleto and Beauty see reason, talk sense into them. Cade's role was to help in that process—and be "threatening" as a potential witness to what they planned to do. It hadn't occurred to her that her friends might decide to simply eliminate the witness and go about their deadly business. All she wanted to do, she said, was give them a chance to run, while holding Bliss—another of Cade's jobs—long enough to give them a head start. Naive in the extreme.

Her plan might work on Beauty, but Bliss was a

vicious bastard, a man with a mile-long sheet that included assault, rape, and manslaughter. Chances were he'd be dangerously pissed off at being duped out of the money promised him, dangerous being the operative word.

And Vanelleto? Who the hell knew what to expect from him? He'd almost killed Bliss once; there was no reason to believe he wouldn't decide to finish the job, in spite of Addy's earnest, well-meaning pleas.

"Yes, we'll have to be careful, but it will work, Cade. I'm sure it will. Gus and Beauty aren't murderers. They're not!" She shook her head firmly, and it wasn't the first time he wondered if her vehement defense of their innocence was more for her sake than his. "That whole night," she shook her head, "was a horrible mistake. They didn't do anything. If Bliss hadn't lied . . ."

Not knowing whether Bliss had lied or not, Cade interrupted. "They could go to the police. Maybe clear the whole mess up. Maybe you could talk them into it." *In your dreams, Harding.*

"No! No police," she shot back. "They wouldn't have believed us then, and they won't now."

"You don't know that for sure unless you try."

Her whole face tightened, and she looked at him with a trace of the old wariness in her eyes. Her voice low and steely, she said, "Is that your idea of help? Call the police?" She waited.

"It's an option. One you should think about."

"I have thought about it, and I'm telling you it is not an 'option.' " She eyed him, her face now a mask of concern and distrust. "Are you going to help me do this my way, or not?"

"I said I'd help and I will." He hesitated. "But if we find out one of your old friends is a killer, or a kidnapper, all bets are off. Fair enough?"

Silence fell between them, and he sensed her fast-track, survivor mind going at warp speed.

"They're not either of those things." She set her jaw. "All I want is to give Gus and Beauty a chance to get away, start over, somewhere Bliss will never find them. I don't want them to . . . do anything stupid."

"By stupid you mean killing Bliss." He didn't miss the fact that she hadn't answered his question. He let it go.

She nodded.

"And you? What about you? You think Frank Bliss is going to leave you living happily ever after at Star Lake?" He shook his head. "It isn't going to happen."

She looked at him, her expression stern, filled with resolve. "If he decides to cause me trouble, let him. I've got my own plan."

"Does that plan involve a suitcase and a road map?"

She eyed him mulishly, said nothing.

She didn't have to. Cade's gut churned. The idea of never seeing Addy again, never loving her again refused to gel. "I don't think your running away will—"

The phone rang.

Addy picked up immediately. "Star Lake," she said, her voice not as bright with hospitality as it normally was, then she seemed to cave inward.

"Gus! Thank God." Her gaze, bright with relief, shot to meet Cade's, and she nodded. He saw her grip tighten on the phone when she turned back to it. "Where are you? . . . uh-huh . . . Good. . . . No, that's a bad idea . . ." She shook her head, listened. "I said no, Gus, I won't tell you where she is. You have to come here. That's the way it is." The phone pressed tight to her ear, she massaged her forehead. "Yup, that's me, stubborn as ever. . . . Yes, Bliss is still with her." She listened for a while, continuing to rub her forehead. "Tomorrow early? Okay. . . . That would be Cabin Twelve." She looked at Cade again, let out a breath. "Okay. Fine. I'll see you then." She clicked off.

Before turning back to face Cade, she dialed another number. Waited.

"Beauty, it's Wart. Gus is in Seattle . . . No, he didn't say where. What he said was he'll be here tomorrow, but that you're not to get here before nine o'clock. . . . Yes, in the morning. He'll be in Twelve, and he wants you to go directly there. He'll be waiting for you, he said—you and Bliss." She frowned. "Uh-huh, it will be great to see him again."

She put down the phone, her face paper pale, and somewhat dazed. "They're coming tomorrow."

Her crystal eyes were bleak when she raised them to meet his, and she hugged herself as if chilled to the core. "I swear, all Beauty can think about is seeing Gus again—and she's not about to let a little murder plan get in the way. Amazing." She tightened her mouth. "All I can think about is blood at Star Lake." She raised her eyes to his. "We can't let anyone die here. We have to stop it."

Cade walked up to her and took her in his arms.

She was stiff and fiercely controlled. Even within his embrace, she kept her arms locked across her breasts.

"No one's going to die." He stroked her hair, nuzzled its softness. "Everything's going to be all right."

She pulled back from him abruptly, as if an idea had sprung loose. "Will you do something for me?"

He didn't answer, cocked his head in question.

"Gus says he'll be here in the morning. But in case he arrives earlier—"

"You think he will?"

"I think he might do the . . . unexpected. He'll go to Twelve, right across from you." She stopped. "It has a good view of most of the cabins and the road in, which is what he asked for, so he can see Bliss and Beauty arrive. He said he'd let me know when he gets here, but in case he . . . in case something goes wrong, will you watch for him?" Her grip tightened on his biceps. "Let me know the second he arrives."

"You think he'll kill Bliss on sight."

"No, it's just that I . . ." She didn't seem to know where to go from there. Either that, or she was second-guessing her plan, particularly the part involving Vanelleto.

"You're not sure what he'll do." He finished for her.

"I don't think you can be 'sure' about Gus. He generally does things his way, and everything depends on me talking to him before he does anything."

Which, the way Cade saw it, wasn't much of a

chance to begin with. He pulled her back into his arms. "I'll watch for him." Although what he'd do when he saw him wouldn't be what she had in mind.

Grover got home late. Very late. And he didn't damn well care. He'd been infused, reborn, transported . . .

He was also drunk—on alcohol and the best sex he'd had in years.

Sandra waited for him, her face contorted with rage, her tone arctic-cold. "Do you know what time it is?"

He wobbled slightly, put down his briefcase, had to pick it up when it fell over, then forced himself to stand tall enough to put them at eye level. "It's"— he looked at his watch, the face seemed to bleed across his wrist—"six minutes after ten o'clock."

"Yes, it is," she said. "And that makes you . . . what?"

He blinked, looked into the eyes of his personal hell. His stomach tried to knot, but the booze wouldn't let it. "That makes me late, Sandra. And tired. I'm going to bed." He turned his back on her and moved to the stairs. She trailed behind him like an black wraith. He didn't care.

Straight sex. He'd always known that's what he liked, somewhere down deep, under the beatings and lashes. Sandra and Belle hid it from him, hid it behind their own cruelty and need for domination. And he'd let them, feckless, cowardly asshole that he was. But no more. Now he had Linda Curl. Any way and any time he wanted her. Or so she said. And damn, the woman wore a garter belt. He'd only seen those in magazines. He took the first step.

Sandra's voice came from behind him, low and lethal. "Come back here. You'll go to bed when I say so, Wayne Grover. You know how things work. You're late, and I don't tolerate lateness. My dinner got cold, my calls to your cell phone weren't answered. Did you think you'd get away with that—without being punished?"

He turned back to look at her, scrunched his eyes to focus, and took in her blazing eyes, her compressed lips, her mean and scrawny body.

"But that's what you want, isn't it?" she spit at him. "You sick, stupid, cowardly man. To be punished. It's what you always want."

He didn't think, he moved—and it changed his universe.

He took her jaw in his hand, squeezed it hard, then lifted her contorted face to his. The stair step he stood on made him taller, stronger in some way. His grip twisted her thin lips to a sneer, pushed her cheeks up and under her slitted eyes. It was so easy. Why hadn't he done this years ago?

"Know where I was tonight, my darling. I was having sex with another woman." He bucked his hips. "Straight sex. In, out, in, out." He grinned into her widened eyes. "And I loved every damn minute of it, so much so that we did it twice. In and out, in and out. You get what that means, Sandra. It means my answer is no. I don't want to be 'punished'—ever again. I hated it when my mother did it, beating on me with her fat, cruel hands, no matter how many hugs and kisses she used afterward to make me 'all better.' And I hate your white bony hands even more."

He had to close his eyes a moment, work to blot out the sound of the whip, the sound of his disgrace, his mother's raging, venom-filled voice. When he could safely open his eyes again, he looked into the eyes of his wife and squeezed her face tighter, tighter yet. She tried to pull away, but he wouldn't let her, held on, squeezed until she winced and snorted like an animal under his digging fingers.

He soaked up the power of giving pain. His new fuel.

"And Belle Bliss? She was an error in judgment. Had I known she was a prostitute . . ." He couldn't finish, because looking back in the mist of his mind, he didn't know whether it would have made a difference. He'd been so lonely then, needy and unwell. And in the beginning—like Sandra—Belle was kind to him, said she loved him. "But I'll say this for Belle, at least she smiled when it was over. But not you, you bitch, never you. All you've ever done is . . . assault me." He stopped, blearily considered his opportunity. "It's time I did some assaulting of my own." Yes! Brilliant, he was brilliant.

His heart jumped in his chest, bright with anticipation, and he brought his face to hers, so close he felt the intake of her breath. "So why don't *you* go upstairs and take out those toys of yours. We'll play a few games, and I'll show you what you've been missing all these years." He let her go, backhanded her, and she stumbled back, hitting the wall before she crumpled to the floor.

Her face raised to his was ashen, and blood oozed brightly from her lip. She blinked rapidly, her eyes black pools of terror. Grover wanted to drown in them, drain them, watch her eyeballs roll to white. "It's what you wanted," she screamed. "What's the matter with you? You're acting crazy—"

He studied her, cowering against the wall, and his throat thickened with loathing. "I hate you, Sandra." He said the words quietly, politely. "I hate all the years you made me so sick and afraid." He shook his head, feeling empty and terribly sad. "And now you just . . . sicken me."

With that statement came clarity, reason, certainty—and blood-coursing desire. And the power to make that desire his reality right now, here, in his own house of pain.

Grover didn't want to play any more games with Sandra.

There would be no prayers tonight.

What he wanted, finally, and with absolute conviction, was to make her dead.

Redge got to his feet with a growl. Fully alert, he barked and went out the open bedroom door.

Cade's head came up, and he peered through his open bedroom door into the darkness of the cabin's living room. When Redge growled again, he flicked off the reading light beside his bed and rested his hand on the bedside drawer where he'd put Susan's Glock.

He was certain he'd locked his door.

"Shush, you silly dog, it's me," a voice whispered urgently. Redge shut up instantly, and a shadow appeared at Cade's bedroom door. The rain, which had started in earnest an hour ago, made for a dark night, but he had no problem recognizing the silhouette cast by the light of the fire he'd banked in the fireplace earlier.

"Addy?" He pulled his hand back to the bed.

"You asleep?"

Given the answer to her question was obvious, Cade glanced at the numbers on his clock. Nearly eleven. "What are you doing here?"

"Looking for company." She walked over to the bed, shucked off her shoes, pulled the covers back, and crawled in beside him, jeans, T-shirt, and all. "I'm not here to have sex with you, if that's what you're thinking."

He smiled into the dark, thought about the new box of condoms sitting beside the Glock in his bedside table drawer. "Of course you're not."

"I don't want you to think—"

"Shut up and get over here." He pulled her to him and nestled her head close to his shoulder. Her hair brushed under his chin.

After a minute, she said, "You smell good. Like Star Lake does after a good rain." She ran the hand she'd placed on his chest across his stomach and down, veering off and over his thigh. "You're naked," she whispered against his throat.

Another obvious statement that didn't need a reply.

"Do you always sleep naked?"

"Uh-huh." And if she didn't stop with the wandering hand, he'd be naked . . . plus.

She drew the hand back up to his chest and made circles in his chest hair. "I don't. Sleep naked, I mean."

When her hand wandered again, he clasped it

in his and gritted his teeth. "What do you sleep in?" She wanted to talk, he'd talk—if it damn well killed him.

"A big, ugly old tee, usually. Not very sexy, am I?"

"Hm-mm," he murmured, thinking Addy in a tee—without panties—sounded damn good to him. He slipped his hand under her shirt, squeezed the narrow valley where hip met waist. "Sexy enough. But then, I'd want you if you were wearing chain mail. So I'm not the guy to ask."

"Really?"

"So this tells me." He shifted his lower body against her thigh, offering hard proof of his statement.

Through the darkness and silence, he heard her draw in a breath. A split second later, she was out of the bed. She stripped off her shirt, shimmied out of her jeans, and took off her panties.

When she crawled into bed beside him, he stroked a bare thigh, took in the coolness of her skin, and said, "Can I take this to mean you've moved beyond the 'looking for company' stage?"

She ran her hand boldly down to his erection, stroked it from stem to tip. "You can," she murmured from somewhere near his chest. "You definitely can."

Chapter 21

Cade's muscles bunched under his skin, making it feel like a too-tight rubber glove. He let his head fall back to the pillow. Jesus, this woman could do him by looking at him.

She stroked him again, squeezed, as if she were testing his limits, measuring him, fascinated with a part of his anatomy he took for granted.

"I like this part of you," she murmured, then lifted her head to look into his eyes. Eyes he had trouble keeping open. "When you think about it, it's a pretty amazing . . . thing." She wrapped her hand around him, used her thumb to press and play at his tip.

He groaned. "I'd rather not think right now, if it's okay with you." He took her face in his hands. "Because right now the only amazing thing in this bed is you."

Addy wanted him so badly, she couldn't think. She wanted him over her, under her, all around her, wanted to have what she couldn't have the last time—Cade inside her, deep inside her.

After pacing away the last two hours, worrying about what might happen tomorrow—the nightmare she'd created with her insane plan—her thoughts turned to Cade, and when they did, all her smarts and common sense couldn't stop her from going to him.

What began as a walk to clear her head and unlock Cabin Twelve for Gus, like he'd asked her to, had within seconds taken her rain-damp sneakers and firmly planted them outside Cade's door.

And here, now, in bed with him, she had no regrets.

Because if things didn't work out tomorrow, she might never see him again, and the pain of it staggered her.

She'd burned for him all day. Every time she caught a glimpse of him, she thought about him, the feel of his skin and silky chest hair under the tips of her fingers, his expert hands, his mouth on her body where a mouth had never been before.

He really was . . . *amazing* right down to the slick velvet tip of him.

Cade stopped her hand, and his breath riffled through her hair. "Why in hell didn't you say you wanted me when you walked in here?"

Good question, but she was pleased when he let go of her hand, let her go back to exploring his silky length. "I was too embarrassed, I guess."

He pulled her to him, and even though she couldn't see his expression clearly in the dark, she knew it was serious and unsmiling. "Don't be embarrassed with me. Ever. Okay?"

"Okay." Easy promise to make in a pitch-black room when you're naked. "But I can't—"

The words flew into the darkness of the room when his tongue slowly circled a nipple, lapped at it.

"There are no buts and no can'ts."

Her breath stopped when he drew the nipple he'd been toying with deep into his mouth. He groaned at her breast, suckled with strong, deep pulls, before lifting his head to give the same service to the other.

"I love your breasts," he muttered against their flesh. "I can't get enough of them . . . of you."

He raised himself and she felt the cool evening air tease her moistened nipples. He braced himself above her, his face close enough for her to feel the rush of his breathing. "What's happening between us, Addy, I want you to know it's . . . valuable, and when this thing is over we need to talk, figure out where to go from here."

"Cade, don't." She scrunched her eyelids against an unexpected wash of tears, because if there was one thing she knew for sure, there was nowhere to go from here. This was all there was, sex and stupid hope.

He brushed some hair off her forehead, kissed her eyelids. "But not now. We won't talk now. Tonight, we make love. I want you to come for me, over and over." He took her mouth in a full, deep kiss that left her gasping, aching for more, then ran his hand down to the damp curls between her legs. "Do you want that?"

She nodded and mumbled a "Yes."

"You're already wet for me," he whispered against

her hair. He ran a finger along her slick seam, opened her, and probed deeply, one finger, two, then pulled out to play with her hardened nub, circling it with a deft finger until it stood away from her milky flesh, distinct and exposed. He touched it with a sure and gentle finger, then left it to cool, to wait . . .

A new rush of moisture pooled and heated at her opening.

She gasped, rolled her head back, and grasped the sheet on either side of her with trembling hands, clutching the bunched linen as if it were a life raft in a storm.

Cade played with her body, toyed with it, his hard length only a promise at the juncture of her thighs.

He kissed her throat, down, over her breasts and stomach, and thrust his fingers into her heat, each motion different than the last, slow now, then faster, then gone.

Replaced by a mouth that took her hard, fast, and relentlessly.

She screamed, convulsed, and came in a blinding, seething rush, a wild thing, her mouth dry with breath and fire, her heart a deafening sound in her chest.

"Oh, my God . . ." She clutched at him, pulled him to her, wanting him in, wanting him deep.

There was movement above her, then he entered her in a long, potent plunge. In deep, he raised himself again, and she could see the strain, the tautness in his neck at the effort to still himself. "You feel so damn good. Like tight satin." He flexed, went deeper, pulled back, then drove into her, to her limits, his hard, demanding length pinning her to the bed.

Man into woman . . . totally, intensely, gloriously.

She shuddered, desperate to pull him in deeper, deeper still. Her inner walls closed around him, and every nerve and sinew in her body melded to his, urged him on. A climax of her own hovered, first a flutter, then a demand, and she sank her nails into the taut muscles of his shoulders, hung on so . . . she could let go.

She bucked, panted to get her breath, tore at his back, his shoulders, his buttocks. Crazed. She was crazed.

Cade groaned, lifted her hips, dug his fingers into the plump flesh of her bottom to hold her high, and released into her in one last powerful plunge, his body a thrust of pure steel under her grasping hands, the contractions of her inner walls.

Exhausted, they clung to each other, sated, their bodies slick from heat and sex.

When she found her voice, Addy said, "You bought condoms."

"I'm a quick study," he said. Shifting his weight to her side, he stroked his knuckles along her cheek. She sensed his smile when he leaned to brush his lips across her mouth. "I wanted to be ready in case I was caught in my bed with my pants off."

She kissed his tempting lips. "Is that the male ego I hear?"

"Loud and clear." He lifted his head. "And speaking of condoms." He got up, went to the bathroom, and was back in double time.

"Now, where were we?"

"I'm not sure. The last thing I remember was me saying I didn't come to you for sex." She tapped his chin. "After that, I think you hit me on the head with a club and took advantage of me."

He laughed. "I think we started"—he pulled her to his side, put her head on his shoulder—"about here."

She rested there, calm and quiet, breathed in the scent of the man in the bed with her, and let the darkness and silence of the cabin close around her like a cozy blanket. "Cade?" she finally said, sleep curling the edges of her mind.

"Uh-huh?"

"Thank you."

"For what?"

Sleep closed in, shutting her eyes and hazing her brain, and she yawned into a soft spot near his shoulder. "For the orgasms and for . . . loving me a little bit."

She drifted away, dimly aware Cade's hand had stopped its idle stroking of her hair, that his chest, where she'd rested her open palm, no longer heaved and ebbed with the rhythm of his breathing.

Sleep, deeper now, became a wall against his whispered words, "More than a little, Addy. Much, much more."

Shortly after midnight, Grover parked his Honda across the street from the Everwood Hotel. Rivers of rain, shimmering under the street lamps, coursed across his windshield.

His head roared with pain, a blur of shooting images. Jumbled, disconnected thoughts elbowed each other in his aching head, each one ready to explode, force him to action. The painkillers he'd taken hadn't helped, had only colored the violence in his mind and given him shaking hands.

He had to calm down, had to control the fear and wildness in him—the immensity of his power.

His next thought was about food. He was hungry. A hungry lion, he told himself, ready to feed after a good kill. The headache jumped and banged around inside his skull like an electrical storm crossed with a jungle drum. He wanted to laugh. He wanted to cry. He wanted to shout his victory into the wet night sky, but the emotions fired through him too fast, chaotic and impotent, never still long enough to grasp.

His hands were sticky, and he lifted them, turned his palms up toward the streetlight to better see the blood. He couldn't get enough of it.

Sandra's blood.

In the darkened car, it deepened to black, warming him and giving him strength to stay the path he'd set for himself. In death lay glory, the ultimate power. He'd forgotten . . . No matter.

He had begun . . .

He would not turn back. Ever again. One murder. Two murders. A dozen murders . . . It didn't matter.

Grover pressed his bloodied palms hard to his temples and ordered the headache away; it obeyed, ebbing to a dull, rhythmic throb at the base of his skull.

His body was his now, from his soft belly to the

aching need in his genitals. Never again would he allow it to be violated, degraded, abused, kicked aside as if it were a bad piece of meat left in the noonday sun. As if he weren't in it. Sandra said he was nothing, no one. Not like Belle. Belle said she loved him every time, after every session.

A rush of tears blinded him, then he laughed, leaving the dampness to cool on his cheeks.

He thought of Sandra, lying on their bed, a marble figure, supine on his altar of suffering. Less than a minute. After all the pain, the endless years, it had taken less than a minute to rid himself of her forever.

She'd be angry if she knew how easy it was.

At the thought of Sandra's rage, a bolt of pure terror coursed through him . . . a remembered reflex.

Sandra was dead, bloodied, twisted, and dead. And dead was forever.

He calmed himself, his brief wave of fear beaten back by a wild, heart-stopping thrill at what he'd done. He closed his eyes, savored it, and replayed the finale. So simple really. His hands, strong and capable, wrapped around her spindly throat.

Snap!

Maybe he shouldn't have cut her first, but it had seemed right, slashing with the blade where she'd so often lashed him with her vicious tongue or the rawhide crop she kept in her bottom drawer. He might have used his new gun if he'd remembered to bring it in the house. No, the knife was a good choice for Sandra. Bullets were too impersonal.

He again rotated his bloodstained hands. In the light of the windshield, they looked mottled and greasy like the hands of the mechanic who changed the oil in his car. Dirty.

He reached into the glove compartment, shoved the gun aside, and took out the antiseptic wipes Sandra insisted he use regularly. He wiped his hands and face carefully before picking up his cell and placing his call.

It was time to set things in motion. Finish his old life and begin his new one with Linda Curl. She'd be so proud of him when she knew what he'd done for her, for them.

He gave the room number to the front desk operator and waited for Bliss to pick up, his hand stroking the bloodied knife on the seat next to him.

"Yeah?" The voice was gruff, edged with sleep.

"Frank?" he said, his voice and mind now filled with a lucid calm. "Grover here, I have some news about Vanelleto." Thanks to his dear friend Susan Moore. She'd promised to keep him informed and she had. He'd always liked Susan. It really was too bad about her grandson. Such a pretty little boy with that mop of curly hair, that smile—

"What news?"

The abrupt question pulled him back from his reverie. "He's meeting Addilene in the morning. He intends to be there before you and Beauty arrive." He ran the index finger of his right hand along the knife blade, so soothing.

"Son of a bitch means to take me out!" He followed the statement with a string of curses. "And where the hell are they meeting?"

Grover smiled. "A place called Star Lake Resort, about a two, maybe three-hour drive northeast of

Seattle. No doubt the front desk can give you specific directions. Probably best you move quickly."

"Yeah." He hung up.

Grover clicked off, peered through the rain at the brightly lit hotel entry, then rested his head on the car's headrest. His plan was flawless.

Bliss would take care of Vanelleto, then Grover would take care of . . . everyone else.

It was past time to be free of them all.

Beauty woke with her hand clutching an empty wine bottle, trying to make sense of the thumping on her door. When she sat up, the bottle rolled to the floor.

Thump. Thump.

She tried to clear her head, make sense of it, stared dumbly at the door to her suite.

"Beauty," he said, his voice a harsh, commanding whisper against the door. "Get the hell up. We're out of here."

Bliss!

She took her head in her hands, made a vise to enclose the ache.

"I've been phoning you for half an hour," he went on, his voice irritated and low. "You die in there?"

"Go away." She got out of bed, then sat on its edge, her heart beating wildly, driven by the fear blowing in with Bliss's voice.

"I am going away, baby, to a place called Star Lake. Ever heard of it?"

Every nerve in her stilled, then spiked as she digested his words.

He couldn't know, he couldn't.

She stumbled toward the door, pressed her ear against it, then said, "How do you know about Star Lake?"

"I know everything I need to know, whore." His voice dropped, grew even colder. "Like how you've been running me around, setting me up for Vanelleto."

"I wasn't—"

"Shut the fuck up," he hissed. "And get out here. We're hitting the road. No way is Vanelleto getting there before me."

She didn't move, didn't speak, concentrated on clearing her head, getting a grip. Only one thought was clear, she could not let Bliss reach Star Lake before Gus.

"Open the door."

She'd die in the damn room before she opened a bedroom door to Bliss in the middle of the night. Being a hooker didn't make her stupid. "No. I don't think so." Her mind whirled, settled on her one chance. "Besides, if you know where you're going, you sure as hell don't need me." She'd let Bliss go—which she had no doubt he'd do if it meant getting the better of Gus—and when the coast was clear, she'd head for Star Lake on her own. She'd use the old road, beat him there, no problem.

"Now that's where you're wrong, Beauty, I do need you. You're going to be my star, play a big part in some entertainment I've got planned for your boyfriend—a little live sex show where I fuck you stupid before I cut his damn balls off."

Beauty's bones turned to rubber, and her mouth went so dry she couldn't speak.

"And think about this, bitch. If you don't get your butt out here now, there's a better than even chance I'll call the boys in blue, tell them there's a street slut working out of the hotel, maybe give them a heads up about a certain unsolved murder sittin' on their books." He paused. "Then again, maybe I'd call a buddy of mine in San Fran, have him look up your friend Lisa. You remember Lisa, don't you?" He rapped twice on the door. Rhythmically. Softly. "Your choice," he whispered.

Her heart dropped like a stone. "You're a sick pig, Bliss."

"Ain't I just. Now move that fancy ass of yours."

"The lobby"—she rubbed her forehead, managed to keep her voice level—"fifteen minutes."

"Make it ten. And leave that toy gun of yours under the mattress. I picked up one of my own, and—trust me—it's a whole lot bigger than yours."

When she heard him cross the hall, close his door, she went immediately to the phone beside her bed and dialed.

It rang, and rang . . . and rang.

"Be there, be there!" she chanted. She had to warn Addy, tell her to get to Gus, tell him about Bliss.

Beauty looked up at the ceiling. "Answer the phone, Addy. Please. Please." She waited, rocking herself on the edge of the bed, her head pounding, her flesh snow-cold. "Answer the goddamn phone! It's the middle of the night. Where the hell are you?"

She slammed the receiver down, worked to ease some air into her constricted lungs. Her voice was weak when she murmured, this time in a plaintive whisper, "Dear God, where are you, Wart? I need you. I need Gus."

She didn't want to think about a three-hour drive with Bliss in the middle of the night, especially now. Now that he knew where Gus was, he didn't need her. Could do what he liked with her . . .

After two more fruitless tries to reach Addy, she went to the bathroom, splashed water on her ashen face and pulled herself together as best she could. She'd have to handle this on her own.

Staring at her image in the mirror, she said, "You're back to Plan A, Beauty girl, which means somewhere along the road to Star Lake, you have to kill Bliss."

Chapter 22

Grover didn't have to wait long. Less than twenty minutes after his call, Bliss and the girl came out of the hotel. The parking valet, dozing in a chair inside the double glass doors of the hotel, snapped to attention, and Dianna—he really must remember to call her Beauty—fumbled in her purse, then gave him what he assumed was her parking pass.

The boy was back in double time, held the driver's side door open, and held out the keys to Beauty, but it was Bliss who took them from his hand.

When Beauty tried to snatch back the keys, she stumbled and almost fell. Bliss opened the passenger door and forced her in, smiling and shaking his head at the valet as he did so.

They drove off as the boy watched, shaking his head.

Good. They were on their way.

Grover settled in behind them, his innocuous

gray Honda a trail of smoke behind the brilliant red Lexus.

Cade woke to rain and darkness outside his window, Addy's head on his biceps, and his arm dead asleep. She groaned when he shifted his position, then her eyes flew open as if he'd prodded her with a hot poker.

"What time is it?" she demanded, looking as if she still didn't have her bearings but intended to get them—fast. She answered her own question. "It's almost two." She leaped from the bed, wondrously naked, and scrounged the floor for her clothes.

He reached out, grabbed her wrist, and pulled her, tumbling, across him. "What's the hurry?" He nuzzled her neck, tried to ignore an erection that was looking for a whole lot more than a neck nuzzle. He pressed it to her naked thigh.

She blinked when he let her go. "You want more sex?" She sounded stunned, but not negative. "You're . . . what's that word? Insays . . . something."

"Insatiable. Describes my condition exactly." She didn't look as if the idea displeased her. Actually, she looked damn smug. "But it's not only 'more sex' I want." He smoothed the uneven shafts of her brown hair off her forehead.

She relaxed against him, ran a curious index finger along the morning stubble on his chin. "What do you want?"

"More you. A lot more you."

"Like in what way?" She gave him a curious look, leery but fascinated.

"Like in forever." The word hovering in his mind for the past few days claimed the room, filled it with quiet.

She tensed, but didn't push away. "You don't know what you're saying. You're just drunk on easy sex."

He let the easy part go. There was nothing easy about Addy. "If that's how you see it, I've got my work cut out for me to prove otherwise."

She didn't answer, and when she pushed to get up, he let her, but instead of getting to her feet, she sat on the edge of his bed. He could hear the waves of her breath in the night-quiet room.

The room was chilly, so he lifted the quilt to cover her naked back. "Cade," she said. "You don't have to say words like 'forever.' It makes me nervous. Besides, there is no forever. Not for me anyway."

"I think there is, and I'm going to add another word that will make you even more nervous." He braced himself on an elbow, shifted his position so he could see her face. "I love you." He paused. "I need to say that now, because there may come a time when you doubt it. I don't want that."

She slanted him a look he could only describe as pained and got to her feet. "I've got to go."

"Did you hear me?"

"I heard you." She pulled on her jeans and shirt, slipped barefoot into her sneakers, and picked up her socks and panties. She stood there a long time, looking down at him, then—and he was sure her eyes were moist—said, "I'm not the one for you. Never can be. Even if things work out with Gus and Beauty, you're too smart, too . . . upstanding.

You're just"—she paused, frowned—"too much."
She brushed at her eyes and her jaw firmed. "Me?
I'm a street kid, no family, no past that I can talk
about. Not to mention being on the cops' A list."
She shook her head. "That's a lot of baggage—
empty baggage. I'm trouble, Cade, and my kind of
trouble, a man like you doesn't need." She turned
toward the door.

"Don't, Addy. Don't walk away from this." His
gut clenched.

She stopped, her hand on the latch, but didn't
turn to look at him. "I'm not walking away, but
when this mess is over, there's a good chance I'll
either be in jail or hitchhiking along I-5. I'm pretty
sure that's not your idea of forever."

She opened the door and walked out into the
rain.

Beauty stared out the passenger-side window of
her car, growing more desperate with every passing mile. They were getting close to Star Lake. She
had to do something, and she had to do it now.

Her mind a muddle of alcohol, incoherent
thoughts, and paralyzing fear, she stared at the dark
blur of trees the expensive car purred past on its
way to . . . Gus and Addy.

Addy would have a plan by now. Addy always
had a plan. And Gus? She closed her eyes. Gus
wouldn't have let Bliss get this far. But they weren't
here. She was, and she was as brain-dead as ever.
There was no use praying for an idea, because
there wasn't anyone up there who gave a damn,
and for the first time in her life, her face and her

E.C. Sheedy

sex were no help at all. All she had were her scrambled thoughts and a lack of time.

Bliss maneuvered her Lexus up a hill and around a bend in the road.

Then she remembered!

Just ahead was a lake, sitting low in a valley surrounded by tall hemlock and cedar. To bypass it, the road they were on curved up and arced around it. At the top there was a viewpoint stop consisting of a few parking spots and public washrooms. The drop was at least eighty feet, maybe more.

Enough.

It had to be enough, because from that point on, the road's descent took them into the lower hills that formed the frame for Star Lake. After that, her only option would be to grab the steering wheel and drive them both into the path of an oncoming semi.

When they neared the top of the curve, she put her hand to her mouth and tugged on Bliss's leather jacket. "I'm not feeling well. Pull over."

"Not surprised, you smell like a goddamn winery." He glanced at her, scowled. "I'm not stopping. I don't give a shit how sick you are."

"Yeah? In that case I'll make sure to throw up on those shiny new shoes of yours and not mine." She clutched her stomach.

"Shit!" He looked out the window at the narrow curving road for a place to pull over.

"There's a rest stop at the top of the hill," she said quickly, swallowing hard. "I can hold it 'til then." She bent over and again put her hand over her mouth.

"You fuckin' well better."

A minute or two later, he made a left and drove through the trees that shielded the viewpoint area from the road. The parking lot was empty.

"Get out and get done with it." His eyes darted around the dark lot, stopped on the run-down washrooms lit by a single bulb over the door. "While you're at it, I'll take a leak. You sure as hell aren't going anywhere from here." He jangled her car keys in her face, then closed his fist around them.

Beauty opened her door at the same time Bliss did, and while he hiked his collar up against the rain and strode off toward the men's room, she walked the few steps to the low guardrail installed to protect careless tourists from the steep cliff beyond it. She clambered over the railing; there were maybe three or four feet of solid ground before the drop. She took a step toward the edge and craned her neck to peer over; her movement sent a clatter of stones into the darkness below. It was like looking into a tar pit.

With no moonlight, and a sky dulled by heavy clouds, she couldn't see the lake, but a spatter of lights far below from the handful of cabins surrounding it confirmed she was in the right place. In the years since she'd been here, the trees had grown to new heights, further obscuring the view, and a tangle of brush and thorns had grown in patches on the cliff's side.

Despite the rough growth, the drop was steep and deep—and as chances went, it was all she had. Dizzy now, she stepped closer to the edge. The rain made the ground slippery and treacherous, and when she almost lost her footing, she gasped and steadied herself.

In position, she shoved some wet tendrils of hair behind her ear, pressed her hand against the too-rapid beat of her heart, and waited for Bliss to come out of the men's room.

One good push and he'd be gone. Out of my life. Out of all our lives. Forever. I can do this. I can!

When a door banged inside the restroom, she glanced back to see Bliss exiting the men's room, doing up his zipper.

He hadn't wasted any time, nor would she. She leaned over as if vomiting, and dry retched, careful to keep herself at an angle where she could see Bliss out of the corner of her eye. He stopped on the other side of the guardrail. Exactly where she wanted him.

He cursed, let out a noisy breath. "What the hell are you doing out there? Get back over the rail. You stupid or something?"

She ignored him, stayed bent over, feigned a stumble that almost took her over the edge.

"Jesus," he said, before stepping over the rail. "What the hell's the matter with you?"

She fell back toward the guardrail, and he stood in front of her, his back to the cliff. A shadow, he was only a shadow against the gray sky.

Her heart pounded and her throat tightened. She had him where she wanted him, an arm's length away. All she had to do was give him a shove—one quick shove.

Why couldn't she move?

Do it, Beauty! Do it!

The voice screeched in her head, urging, demanding, and she wanted to obey, to move . . . anything.

Her fingers fused to the metal guardrail behind her, she stared at Bliss, frozen in place. She saw his eyes widen, then narrow. He knew! Animal that he was, his instincts were sharper than hers.

He laughed, a sharp, mean bark of a laugh. "Lost your nerve, slut?" He shook his head. "No surprise. You never did have anything more goin' for you than big tits and a pretty face." He didn't move, set his gaze to crawl over her, slowly, sickeningly. His tone lower, harder, he added, "Trying to get rid of me wasn't one of your better ideas. But to show you what kind of guy I am, I'm goin' to let you make it up to me. How about you and me rehearsing that little show I'm plannin' for Vanelleto? Kind of a dry run."

When he reached for her, she brought both hands from behind her and shoved at his chest. Too little, too late. Bliss caught her arm, swung her around, putting her back to the cliff. Using one hand, he imprisoned her, his grip a vise, his fingers digging into the flesh of her upper arm like sharp, savage teeth.

"You bitch." He hit her in the face with his free hand, and she staggered backward. Still holding her, he closed his fist, hit her again, again, hammering at her jaw, her temple. Her head bucked, loosened on her shoulders, as her neck swiveled and jerked with every merciless blow. Blood coursed from her nose. She couldn't get a breath.

Her consciousness was reduced to flashing lights and wild shooting pains. She clawed at his face, gouged at his flesh, heard him curse before he hit her again. She tasted her own blood, felt a stone in her mouth—a tooth.

He grabbed the front of her cotton shirt, and she heard it tear, but it held together long enough for him to pull her flush to his body. Seizing a handful of her hair, he yanked her head back and thrust his hand between them, tore at her bra, closed a hand painfully around her naked breast, his hot breath against her neck now the hard rasping pant of an animal.

Beauty's world faded from gray to black, the void behind her blacker still. She didn't care. Years of hurt, rage, and powerlessness exploded, filled her, fueled her—freed her—and all of it went core deep into the rigid bone and taut muscles of the knee she rammed, with the strength of a mad woman, a doomed woman, into his miserable hardening cock.

"Fuck . . ." Stunned, he let her go. She kneed him again before he doubled over.

"You rotten, low-life bastard. You'll never touch me again. You got that? Never!" she screamed. "And there's no money; there never was. Gus is going to kill you, you fucking freak, and I'm going to cheer him on." Her punished head spinning, insane with colliding images, she clenched her eyes closed against the pain, blinded in one eye by a curtain of blood, the other refusing to stay open.

She was aware of rain on her face, coldness on her naked breasts. The smell of wet earth, or was it blood?

But where was Bliss? She needed to see. Had to see. She brushed the blood from her eye, forced it open to look down, her mind reeling from Bliss's savage blows to her face and head.

He was crawling . . .

No!

His powerful hand snapped closed around her ankle.

"Stupid, dumb whore!" he shouted.

As if she were a rag doll, or a bag of garbage, he flipped her into the abyss.

Addy went directly to the shower, but instead of her usual splash and dash, she braced her hands on the wall, and let a stream of hot water course over her tight muscles and fevered brain. She made the water hot enough to burn, intending it to outpace the heat in her aroused body, the turmoil in her mind.

She closed her eyes and lifted her face.

You up there, you got nothing better to do than mess up my life? You could have sent Harding to some nice librarian somewhere, or better yet, one of the lady professors at that school of his. Why me? A woman who thinks synonym is something you'd find in a pie recipe—if I could read the damn recipe! And why now, when my life is a shambles, my friends are plotting murder, and someone is probably changing the sheets in my jail cell as we speak? It's not fair, you hear me. It's just not fair!

Her rant over, she thumped her head on the shower wall, punched the shower control to off, and shoved open the cubicle door, no closer to feeling better than when she went in. She felt edgy, dangerously exposed, as if her nutshell-sized world was under threat from a ball hammer.

The sky outside her glazed bathroom window was dark with rain and offered no hint of morning. She toweled her hair roughly and let out a

harried, impatient breath when she counted the
hours she had to wait before Gus arrived, then
Beauty. Hours to think about the stunning idea of
spending "forever" with the man she'd left behind
in Cabin Six. Her thoughts made her heart ache,
and her stomach cramped painfully, longingly.

She draped the towel around her neck, and
holding both ends, stared unseeingly at the mirror
in the medicine cabinet over her sink and said the
word aloud, softly—"Forever, forever . . . and ever
and ever." Putting her index finger on the steamy
bathroom mirror, she laboriously printed the word.

FEREVAR.

Studying the letters she'd etched on the glass as
upright and evenly spaced as the bamboo stakes
she'd put in the back flower garden, she suddenly
glared, erased them with an angry sweep of her
hand.

If she couldn't spell the word, not much point
in considering the reality of it with a man like Cade
Harding. Impossible. Like she'd told him. No point
kidding herself. She'd never been a dreamer and
now wasn't the time to start.

After drying herself roughly, she donned clean
jeans and a red shirt—no way was she going to sleep
tonight—and combed her shag of hair straight back
from her forehead. It would mess itself up in its own
good time.

She paced for a bit, then went to her makeshift
drafting table, pulled out a couple of design magazines, and started to slowly turn the pages, attempt
to lose herself, as she usually did, in the beautiful
pictures, ideas for Star Lake.

Too bad she couldn't stop her head from lifting,

her eyes from their constant checking, first the open door between her apartment and the office, then out the night-dark window, looking for any sign of the coming day.

After a time, she glanced at the clock and sighed. Barely fifteen minutes had passed.

It was going to be a long, long night.

From his vantage point hidden behind the trees, Grover watched Bliss pull out of the viewpoint parking area. When the red car was out of sight, he pulled into the parking lot and turned his car motor off.

The rain was coming in earnest now, and it was too black to see anything, but his curiosity drew him to the guardrail. Clumsily, he climbed over it, took a couple of tentative steps toward the edge.

Listened.

All he heard was rain beating on the leaves of the dwarf trees and scrub that clung to the side of the cliff and a few leaves rustling when wind gusted up from below.

But he had to be sure. This one hadn't known much of anything, far too concerned with herself to be even dimly aware of what was going on around her. But she'd belonged to Gus, and who knew what he'd filled her head with.

He looked around; the place was as deserted as a tomb.

"Beauty," he called down, "are you all right? Can I help you?"

He cocked an ear, shivered when the breeze carried the chill of night and rain through his light coat.

"Beauty?" he said again. "Are you there?" He

shifted position, and the toe of his shoe sent a stone tumbling over the edge.

Still nothing. Not a sound.

Grover stepped back. Smiled. "Good," he muttered. "Very good."

It occurred to him that his whole life had changed since he'd got rid of Sandra, and had sex with Linda Curl. Before those blessed events, he'd had nothing but bad luck. Now everything fell into place.

Bliss getting rid of Beauty was yet another stroke of good fortune. He'd seen it all, of course—the stupid girl's effort to push Bliss off the cliff, Bliss's inept attempt at rape. For a moment, he'd thought of killing them both, but that would have left him alone to deal with Vanelleto.

The idea settled badly in his stomach.

No. Vanelleto was Bliss's job. So he'd let him live. The vain, selfish idiot had work to do.

He climbed back over the guardrail, and headed for his car, light-headed with relief. Beauty had not survived the fall.

One down, three to go.

Bliss drove down what looked to be a deserted road, about a quarter mile past the sign at the entrance to Star Lake, and pulled the car into a bushy area that he hoped would hide the car until he could get back to it.

He turned the ignition off, and rested his head back. Damn! His balls were sore, and his face hurt like hell, wouldn't stop bleeding. She'd gouged him good. Probably infected him with some kind of disease. Stupid bitch.

He suddenly trembled as if he were cold, which he wasn't, and his gut rolled. Beauty . . .

Jesus! Why in hell hadn't she done what he told her to?

His chest was tight, and he felt sick to his stomach, like he was going to throw up.

You killed her, you stupid fuck! Why in hell did you do that?

The rant in his head, equal parts red-hot rage and frustrated regret, made him close his eyes.

He put his head back, tried to catch his breath. Didn't know what the hell to do with the split in his brain, the thickness in his chest. He reminded himself she was nothing but a dime hooker, not the angel in a devil's body she was when he was a kid, not the girl who made him ache in places he'd never ached before.

He pounded his fists on the steering wheel, then forked his fingers roughly through his hair.

He wondered how many times Vanelleto had had her, and he couldn't stop the roar that poured from his throat.

All his fault. All of it. Him and that dumb-ass Wart. If she hadn't told Vanelleto about him and Beauty in the barn, Beauty would have come around. Things would have been different. He'd fucked her good that day; she was his!

Now she was dead.

And Wart and Vanelleto were still alive. It goddamn well wasn't right.

He rubbed his crotch, tried to ease the painful throb in his balls, and rolled down the window. Maybe some cold air would clear his mind.

He figured he'd walk through the trees and undergrowth straight to Star Lake without anyone being the wiser.

But now that Beauty was gone, he needed an ace in the hole, and for that, Wart would do fine. He smiled for the first time in hours.

Yeah . . . by the time Vanelleto arrived, he'd have little Wart trussed up like a goddamn Thanksgiving turkey.

Vanelleto didn't come through? He'd slice her up the same way.

Chapter 23

Cade gave up on the idea of sleep. If it weren't so miserable outside, he'd run, but in the mess called weather out there, it'd be a one-way ticket to pneumonia. He tried to read, then tried to write, but nothing worked, so he poked the fire for the hundredth time and paced the cabin.

His time with Addy left him edgy, unable to focus. Saying what he'd said, when he said it, was a big mistake. He should have waited until the threat posed by her friends coming to Star Lake was over, until he'd proven her as innocent as he believed her to be. If ever there was a classic case of someone being in the wrong place at the wrong time, Addy being in the Bliss home that night was it.

He also had to find Josh Moore. He owed that to Susan, and as he'd finally come to admit, he owed it to the boy—and himself.

For the third time in as many minutes, he

pushed the curtain back and looked outside in the hope Mother Nature had done an about-face. No luck. He glanced toward the resort office. The soft light over Addy's drafting table—situated by the living room window—was on, making the shadow of her head and shoulders, lowered as she flipped the pages of a magazine, only a grayish outline through the sheets of rain.

Obviously, she was no more inclined to sleep than he was. Small damn comfort.

"Shit." He went to the door and grabbed his windbreaker from the hook on the right. If not a run, a walk would have to do. He needed to get out of here before he exploded.

He shrugged into his jacket and went outside.

Standing on the top step under the cover of the porch doing up his zipper, Cade scanned the deserted resort. Through the blackness of the rain, it looked desolate and bleak. The property was poorly lit at night. There was only a light on the toolshed and another where the driveway turned around a stand of trees, going from there to the main road maybe two hundred yards or so. Neither light was high on the wattage scale. He knew there was a couple in the far cabin at the end of the property, but their lights were out, as were Stan and Susan's. The rest of the cabins sat empty and unlit.

Walk a few feet in any direction and you'd be traveling blind.

Resigned to a short, dark, and very wet stroll, he was about to take the first step, then stopped abruptly.

Something moved on the road leading to the resort, and Cade's breath hitched. Addy? Maybe in the same tense state as himself, out for a walk? He glanced toward the office, where her silhouette was still visible on the blind.

Not Addy.

Cade inched back, deeper into the shadow of the porch overhang. For a second, there was only the sound of the downpour on the cedar shake roof, the hiss of wind through the willow on the lake.

Then a snap—a crunch on the gravel.

Unable to see clearly through the rain, he gauged the noise as coming from the cabin across from his. Cabin Twelve.

Narrowing his eyes, he peered through the gloom in time to see a shadowy figure take the two steps leading to the cabin's door and enter without a sound. Cade waited a minute or two, but no lights were turned on.

Had to be Vanelleto, determined to keep a low profile.

Cade went back into his cabin, retrieved the Glock from his bedside drawer, and stuffed it in his pocket.

He'd been looking for a diversion, and now he had one, a chance to meet and greet the mysterious Gus Vanelleto.

Seeing no reason not to take the shortest distance between two points, he went across the gravel and grass separating his cabin from Twelve, the element of surprise squarely in his corner.

He guessed Vanelleto wouldn't bother to lock his door, and he was right. He opened the door and stepped into the room.

In the cabin, there was barely enough light for shapes and outlines.

"Who the hell are you?" The voice was low, cold, and completely calm. Cade knew the cabins were all pretty much the same, a bedroom and bath, and a living room with the cooking area separated by a counter. The voice coming through the dark told him Vanelleto was behind the kitchen counter.

"The name's Harding. Cade Harding."

"You lost?"

"No. I'm a friend of Addilene Wartenski."

Vanelleto greeted that announcement with silence, then Cade heard movement and water running from the kitchen tap. His eyes more accustomed to the light now, he saw Vanelleto take a drink of water, then turn and put the glass in the sink, obviously in no hurry to resume their conversation.

Leaning casually against the counter, he said, "Must be some kind of friend if you know that name."

"Good enough to not want to see her get hurt."

Vanelleto crossed his arms. He had a predator's stillness about him, and if he had any nerves, none were in evidence. "How long has this friendship been going on?"

"When I think that's your business, I'll tell you."

"Which means not very long. And that means you know more than it's healthy for you to know."

"I'm healthy enough." Cade reached under the shade of the lamp he knew sat beside the chair inside the door, found the switch, and turned it on.

Vanelleto eyed him impassively.

"Seems to me it's your—and Beauty's—health we need to worry about," Cade said, straightening away from the lamp. If he expected a response to his use of Beauty's name, he didn't get one.

In the dim light from the lamp, the two men faced each other, assessed each other. Vanelleto, in black jeans and a black shirt—expensive black shirt, Cade noted—eyed him with the fixated absorption of a cobra.

The scar on Vanelleto's face cut a jagged swath from the front of his earlobe to under his jaw. Rough and uneven, as though the skin had been torn wide open and never stitched, the scar marked a lean, dark-skinned face that without it, and the square jawline it accented, might have been labeled pretty. In height and weight, the two were evenly matched, Cade noted, but Vanelleto's body, more tightly wired than his own, emanated a promise, or threat, of speed and lethal agility.

Cade gestured at the scar. "Belle's handiwork?"

Vanelleto's eyes, black from where Cade stood a few feet away in the dimly lit room, centered on his, more curious than alarmed. "The Wart has been busy. You sleeping with her?"

Cade let his question slide off, recognized the technique, a question for a question. "She told me part of her story, not all," he said, studying Vanelleto's hard jaw and say-nothing eyes. He'd met his share of men like Vanelleto in his time, sat in the cold gray confines of an interrogation room with them, where the game of self-protection played out for the highest possible stakes—freedom. It

was a game Cade was an expert at. "I was hoping
you'd fill in the blanks," he added easily.

"Can't think why I'd do that."

"Addy says you're innocent. All of you. She
thinks Bliss killed his mother."

"And you believe her."

"Shouldn't I?"

Vanelleto snorted, raised an eyebrow, then shook
his head slowly. "Jesus! You're a goddamn cop." The
idea didn't seem to bother him; it seemed to amuse
him.

"Was a cop."

"When it comes to cops, I don't believe in the
past tense."

Cade left a shaft of silence in the room. "You don't
have a choice, Vanelleto." Cade lifted his hands.
"Here I am. And considering you're not going anywhere until Bliss and Beauty get here, it's as good a
time to talk as any."

"Yeah? And what would we have to talk about?"
Vanelleto's tone shifted lower and his expression
flattened.

Cade didn't like it. He met his cold, assessing
gaze, and asked the question that most needed to
be asked. "Josh Moore. Where is he?"

"Never heard of him." He pushed himself away
from the counter, moved toward Cade. "Now if
you'll get the hell out of here—"

"You've heard of him, all right. Josh is the boy
who disappeared the night Belle Bliss was murdered. His grandmother hired me to find him."

His remark was rewarded with the barest flicker
of an eyelash.

* * *

"This place got cable?"

Addy, startled, spun to see a tall, muscular man standing in her doorway, looking at her as if she were roadkill.

"Can I help—" Her heart slammed against her chest, and she shot to her feet, stumbled backward until her shoulder banged into the wall.

The man scanned her from her sock-clad feet to her still-damp hair. "You grew up good, Wart. Who'd have thought it?"

Jesus, it was Frank Bliss. She was so stunned she couldn't find her voice.

His face was bloody, and he touched one side of it carefully. When he pulled his hand away and looked at the blood on his fingers, a dark, angry look claimed his handsome face. A face Wart would never forget. A face that brought the past back with such a rush her knees buckled.

"Shit!" He held out his bloodied hands to look at them, his brow furrowed in frustration. It was as though the sight of his own blood negated her presence in the room.

One cheek had four long gouges in it; some of the blood was dry, more oozed from the slashes to seep down and drip from his chin. Pushing some of his long blond hair back behind his ear, he said, "Where's your bathroom?" He barked. "I need to clean up."

If he thought Addy cared, he was wrong. "Where's Beauty?" she demanded.

His mouth turned down. "I guess you could say her and I had a little misunderstandin'." Again, he touched his bleeding face. "I dropped her off"—his lips turned up in a parody of a smile—"a few miles back. Now, where the hell's the bathroom?" He pushed away from the door and headed toward her.

"What do you mean you dropped her off?" If her stomach muscles got any tighter, they'd snap. She had the wild urge to run and never stop. Instead, she pushed herself away from the wall and faced him.

He walked past her, looked around the room. When he spotted her bedroom door, still open, and the bathroom beyond it, he headed toward it.

Addy grabbed his leather-clad arm, gripped it tight. "Answer me! Where's Beauty?"

He glared down at her, pulled her hand from his arm, then squeezed her fingers until she thought they'd break. "My guess? She's as dead as she tried to make me. And you know what? I don't give a shit." He twisted her wrist, nearly took her to her knees, then pushed her aside and headed for the bathroom only a few feet away. "Stay where you are. You and me have some talkin' to do." He stared at her, his blue eyes hard, then he gestured at the phone. "I can either tear that sucker from the wall, or you can be smart enough to not even think of making any calls. 'Cause if you do, I'll come back in here and wring your skinny neck." He pulled a gun from his jacket pocket. "Or use this." He walked into the bathroom dangling it from his hand.

She couldn't have moved if she wanted to.

Dead! Beauty was dead. No. She couldn't be. Beauty couldn't die. Couldn't be . . . gone forever.

Addy slumped back against the wall, numb, paralyzed.

For years, she'd wondered what happened to her friend, and angry and hurt as she was when she'd taken off, she'd missed her, worried about her, and somehow always believed she'd see her again. Alive. And with all the recent phone calls, the sound of her voice across the line, the connection between them had reestablished, grown strong again. Beauty was right; they'd been sisters, and nothing could change that. Thinking of her as dead, it was as though a part of her had been ripped out. And it was all her fault.

If it hadn't been for my stupid scheming . . .

Tears muddied her vision, and she brushed them away, tried to think. Her plan in ruins, another thought forged through: when Gus found out Bliss had killed Beauty, nothing under the sun would stop him from killing Bliss.

"My guess . . . " Bliss's words poked up in her brain, and her breathing stilled in her chest.

He'd said "guess." Which meant he wasn't sure! Which meant there was a chance Beauty was alive.

Addy pressed a hand to her chest, told herself to calm down. She brushed away the moisture on her cheeks, sniffed to clear her nose, and squared her shoulders. This was no time for tears. She would not cry for her friend until hope was dead.

If she could reach Cade . . . she glanced at the phone, then at the open bathroom door, a few feet away.

Too dangerous. Bliss would kill him on sight.

No. Finding out about Beauty, keeping Bliss occupied until Gus got here was her job. And she wouldn't let Bliss—or her own fear—get the better of her. If he smelled her weakness, she'd be useless.

Adrenaline replaced pain, and she hurried back to her drafting table, rifling the surface papers for anything she could use as a weapon. Her hand touched the six-inch scissors she used to cut out pictures from her magazines, and she shoved them hastily into the back pocket of her jeans and tugged her long-tailed shirt down to cover it. As protection they weren't much, but they'd have to do.

Bliss came out of her bedroom, holding a towel to his ravaged face. He went to the sofa and slumped into it as though he were exhausted. He even rested his head back for a second or two; obviously, he didn't consider Addy a threat.

It didn't surprise her. He'd always ignored her, even back then, always focused on Beauty. And after what he'd done to her, Addy had counted herself lucky. Being ignored, or better yet underestimated, had its value.

She took a deep breath, her mind going at the speed of light. She wanted information, and she wanted it now. "Beauty do that?" She pointed at his ravaged cheek.

He grunted.

"Why? What did you do to her, Frank?" She kept her voice flat, deliberately used his first name.

He scrunched his eyes together before opening them and, exhaling a long noisy breath, said, "I didn't do nothing. She asked for it." Her question appeared to rattle him, and his response sounded oddly defensive.

"Asked for what?" Addy took a step closer, stood over him. Her skin felt like a blanket of fire over her flesh.

Bliss surged to his feet, towered over her, his face dark with rage. "Quit with the fuckin' questions or I'll fuckin' show you what I did to her." He shoved her aside, ran his hands through his hair. "When's Vanelleto coming?"

Addy crossed her arms. "You don't answer my questions, I don't answer yours." She met his gaze, her heart a fear-tightened knot in her chest.

He backhanded her, the blow so sweeping and powerful that the bones in his knuckles cracked. She tumbled backward, her ear slamming against the metal edge of her drafting table, sending a sharp, intense pain deep into her head, before she crumpled to the floor.

Addy panted a second or two, got her bearings, then surged to her feet, the action more reflexive than courageous. If that was the back of Bliss's hand, she didn't look forward to meeting the front.

She leaned against her table, took another couple of breaths, and clutching the back of her chair, she rolled it between them. The side of her face pulsed from his blow, and blood ran warm and thick down the side of her neck.

"I said where's Beauty?" she repeated, clinging to the paltry protection of the old office chair.

"Jesus, bitch, you want more of the same?" He frowned.

"No, although I'm sure you'll be happy to provide it. You always did like beating up women . . . among other things." She paused, told herself to shut up, not to goad him too far. But, dear God, she'd forgotten what a beast he was! She tightened her grip on the chair. "Now, let's talk about Beauty."

He took a couple of steps toward her, then stopped in front of the chair separating them. He smiled, his lips twisting cruelly. "You really want to know?"

"You really want your money and for Gus to let you live long enough to spend it?"

He gaped at her.

"Talk, Bliss," she ordered, and kept up her pretense of courage, even though it seeped steadily into the floor beneath her like oil from a leaky tanker—like the blood from her torn ear.

He studied her face, his own a ravaged carcass. "Let me see if I remember now. Oh, yeah . . . Beauty made me stop at this real nice motel—said she couldn't wait to get in my pants, ya know." His smile was malicious, his voice low. "Said she never forgot what I gave her at Ma's house. That nobody afterward measured up." He rubbed his crotch boldly and narrowed his gaze on Addy. "How about you, you want some, Wart? Plenty to go around."

Addy dug her nails so deeply into the cheap vinyl on the chair back that her knuckles hurt. "I'm interested in Beauty, Bliss. Not the tinker toy in your pants."

"You got a smart mouth. Always did have."

"And you've got a hearing problem. Always did have." To keep him at a distance, she pushed the chair forward until he stopped it with his foot.

"You want to know about Beauty? I'll tell you

about Beauty." He put his knee on the chair seat, anchored it, and leaned over until his face was inches from hers. "After I fucked her blind, I tossed her over a cliff a few miles back."

"What cliff?"

He paused, but didn't seem to hear her. "She died one happy hooker. Did her a favor really, because after you've had true Bliss"—he grinned, a cold twisted grin, and rolled his hips suggestively—"heaven's the only place higher. You be a good girl and maybe I'll do you a favor, too." He chucked her under the chin.

Somehow she managed not to move back, continued to stare into the threatening face inches from her own, but her breath shortened to a series of gusts and backed up in her throat. Her face was hot. Jesus, even her eyes were hot, but she refused to take them off Bliss. "What cliff?" she repeated.

"Jesus!" he looked angry, but amused now. "Aren't you a goddamn dog with a bone!" He studied her from under lowered lids. She saw his mind chugging at a snail's pace, then he took his knee off the chair and a step back. "About a half hour or so before here, near that long skinny lake," he said. "Maybe a sixty, eighty-foot drop, I'd guess." He made a diving gesture with his hand, watched her. "Long way down."

Addy loosened her grip on the chair, her brain worked to place the cliff he was talking about. Sixty, eighty-foot drop? Mentally tracing the roads leading to Star Lake, she blinked.

She shouldn't have.

*   *   *

Grover finished the last of his hamburger, his second one, and wiped the drippings from his mouth. He folded the dirty napkin, crushed the empty paper cup that held his cola, and put everything back in the serving bag.

He reached into the glove compartment and pulled out a flashlight, which he'd been smart enough to get new batteries for at the last gas station. He got out of his Honda, pulled his raincoat over his head, and walked through the wet grass and low bush to the Lexus, where he let the air out of all four tires.

He trained the flashlight on his handiwork and stood back to admire it. Instead, he found himself admiring the car, allowing the focus of light to play over the silver grill, the brilliant red hood.

Red. The color of power. The color of blood.

He plodded back to his car, got in, and wriggled himself out of his damp coat. When he'd reclined the seat as far as it would go, he rested his head back.

No need to hurry.

He'd give Bliss enough time to either kill or be killed, then he'd go in and clean up whoever was left.

He closed his eyes. It was good to be in charge, good to have a plan.

About the time Cade figured Vanelleto was never going to speak again, Gus said, "This grandmother. Why did she let the state take her grandson?"

"She didn't know they had." Cade ran through

Susan's story quickly, no embellishment, ending
with, "By the time they found her, put two and two
together, Belle Bliss had been dead for two weeks,
and the boy was gone. She's been looking for him
ever since."

"Enter ex-cop Harding to save the day," he said
flatly. "And maybe pick up a few bucks along the
way."

"Ex-cop—and family, Vanelleto. A nonprofit
enterprise."

He didn't reply. As smart as he was cautious,
Vanelleto obviously intended to stay one step ahead
of the conversation. Hell, Cade knew less about him
now than he had when he walked into this room a
half hour ago.

"You know I'm the one they say killed Belle,"
Vanelleto went on.

"So I'm told. Did you?" Cade asked.

"I thought you said you weren't interested in
the murder, that your only concern was the missing kid."

"It started out that way, but . . . things changed."
I met Addy. He looked toward the cabin's night-
darkened window, heard the rain running off the
cedar-roofed porch, and rubbed his chin. His feelings for Addy weren't up for discussion, nor was
showing vulnerability to a man like Vanelleto.
"Turns out one is pretty much linked to the
other."

"Which puts you and me in a real interesting
place, doesn't it? You, the bloodhound all primed
to sniff out a murderer. Me, by all accounts, the
guilty party." He lifted his brows, looked faintly
amused. "Complicated."

"Only if you are guilty."

Vanelleto eyed him for a long time. "And if I'm not?"

Cade took the few steps to the counter, flattened both hands on it. "If you're not, you've been spending a lot of years running from something you didn't do and wasting a hell of a lot of time pretending to be somebody you're not." He stopped, added, "If you're not, I'd like to help you, Addy, and Beauty set the record straight." Cade was certain Vanelleto knew more about that night than he was letting on. He'd also noticed he talked easier about the murder than he did the missing boy, so he went there. "You may not know anything about the boy, but I think you know who killed Belle Bliss."

Silence.

Cade fired his last salvo. "And I know you've come here to kill her son." He smiled at him for the first time. "A pretty bad plan, by the way."

Vanelleto's head came up, and his eyes narrowed dangerously. "Our little chat has been swell, Harding." With the barest shift of his chin, he gestured toward the door. "You know the way out."

Cade stared at the hard-edged man in front of him. Talking to him was like whispering into a black vortex that sucked everything in and gave nothing back. Pushing any harder—right now—was nothing but a waste of Cade's time.

He headed for the door, opened it a crack. A slice of wet night air sliced into the cold cabin. "I'll tell Addy you're here." He shot a glance over his shoulder. "We'll be talking again, Vanelleto. If not about Belle, about the boy." Opening the door fully, he looked out at the black, mist-shrouded night. His eyes immediately shifted their focus to the light in Addy's window.

His blood pooled in his veins.

"Jesus! No!" He took off in a full-out run.

Chapter 24

"What was that?" Susan shot to an upright position in bed, looked blearily at the bedside clock. A little after three.

"Hm-m." Stan frowned in his sleep, but didn't open his eyes.

"I heard a shout, I'm sure of it." Susan got out of bed and padded toward the window, but other than blackness and driving rain, she saw nothing.

Awake now, she was reluctant to return to the bed, even though the cabin was refrigerator-cold, the last of the fire having died out hours ago. She rubbed her shivery upper arms, wrapped them tight around herself, and continued to stare out the window into the bleakness.

The last few days had been unsettling, and more than ever her lost grandson haunted her. For unfathomable reasons, she felt closer to him than ever—and it frightened her, made her afraid that if she found him, she wouldn't be what he needed, that he'd find her wanting. Perhaps even hate her for not being there for him—or his mother.

"Mariah," she whispered. "I'll find him. I promise." *And I'll never, never let him down, like I did you.*

"My darling," Stan stood behind her, tall as an oak and equally as comforting. "It's cold. You should be under the covers."

"I'm all right," she said, resting her head back against his chest. She was a lucky woman, finding this kind of love in the latter part of her life, and she celebrated it every day as a blessing she didn't deserve. "I was thinking about Josh."

"I know." He held her close.

"We have to find him, Stan . . . for Mariah."

"And for you." He kissed the top of her head.

"Yes, and for me." She closed her eyes against the useless tears. So little, and so very, very late. Tears wouldn't bring back her daughter, and they wouldn't wash away her failure to be the mother she should have been. Nothing would do that, but when she found Josh—and she would find him—she hoped her daughter's sad and troubled soul would rest easier. Mariah's choices had ruined her, left her sick and addicted—and desolate—until finally they killed her. But Susan knew to the depths of her soul that Mariah would have loved her son, hopelessly and helplessly, as she had loved Mariah.

"Come to bed, love," Stan said. "It's cold as a winter creek in here."

"I should have tried harder with Mariah. Maybe if I'd—"

Stan turned her to face him. "Don't." He shook his big head. "All the maybes and should-haves on planet Earth won't change the way things turned out. You know that. And whatever happens here at Star Lake, you'll have done all you can for your daughter and her son."

"But I—"

He put a finger on her lips. "Shush now." He led her back to the bed and settled her in. "If your thoughts must go bump in the night, love, tilt them toward the wishes and dreams department, and away from the trouble and woe." He got into bed beside her, and pulled her close. "It helps."

"You help," she said, cuddling closer. "I should have found you years ago."

She felt his smile in the dark. "Now there you go with the should-haves again. We're together now. That's all that matters."

"Yes . . . that's what matters." *That and finding my grandson.*

Cade, his heart pounding, slammed his way through Addy's door. Right behind him was Gus Vanelleto. Cade's senses went into overload.

Words registered darkly, soured his brain.

"I said back off, Bliss!"

"Gonna fuck you good, Wart . . ."

A scene played out, a second, a lifetime.

Addy had her back against the far wall, her face was bloodied, and her shirt was torn half off her body, exposing a shoulder and one bare breast. She was wielding a tiny pair of scissors as if they were a machete, the slim blades her only defense against a muscular blond man who loomed over her, his face a boil of rage . . . and enjoyment.

The explosion in Cade's mind was violent, fierce and red.

He dimly heard Vanelleto spit out the words, "Son of a bitch. Bliss!" before he lunged.

Vanelleto was fast, but Cade was faster.

Neither of them was fast enough.

Bliss spun to face them, his face flat with shock, a gun raised but wobbling in a shaking hand.

Addy screamed, "Stop, Cade. Don't! He'll kill you."

Jesus, don't what? Kill the bastard?

"If you're smart, you'll listen to the bitch." Bliss steadied the gun, now shifted it smoothly between him and Vanelleto.

Cade took another step, bloodlust overriding rationality. Vanelleto gripped his arm. "Ease up, Harding," he said, his tone diamond hard, calm as glass. "You won't do the Wart any good if you're dead."

A big, buffoonish grin split Bliss's face, and he shifted the gun an inch or two in Vanelleto's direction. It was a missile in his grip now, stabilized and dead straight. "Hey, Gus, old man. It's been a while."

"Not long enough," the still, dark Vanelleto said.

Bliss laughed and his gaze shot to Cade, did a quick assessment. "This your main man, Wart?" he said, turning his head, but not his gaze, briefly toward Addy who was slightly behind and to his side.

Addy, with Bliss's attention on Gus, had sidled a step or two away. To keep it that way, Cade answered for her. "I'm the man telling you to back off, Bliss." From the corner of his eye, he saw Addy garner another few inches of safety. "Let her go."

He took a step forward to get Bliss's full attention and keep the gun trained on him. Addy froze where she stood.

"Harding, right? I heard about you," Bliss said. "You're looking for the kid for that old lady."

How the hell did he know that? "I said let her go."

Bliss's expression chilled. "I'm not much for taking orders, Harding, so I'll be doing whatever the hell I feel like doing." He lowered the gun, aimed it at Cade's kneecap. "But you? You move again, and you'll need a set of rollers. You got that?"

Cade's blood still coursed wildly along his veins, his heart still hammered in his chest, but his brain had kicked in, telling him there was a better than even chance he and Vanelleto could take Bliss, given the opportunity. By his estimate, they were less than six feet away. Addy started to move again.

A few more inches . . .

"I see you're the same piece of scum you always were, Bliss. Waving guns, beating up women . . . killing others." Vanelleto spoke softly, his gaze lethally cold, his words clipped and direct. "That last woman in Pittsburgh? You really did a number on her, didn't you? Must be proud of that. Kept her for five days, they said." He scratched his jaw, idly, slowly. "Seven years wasn't long enough. Should have stuck a needle in you, finished you off for good." He paused. "The Smithfield pen, wasn't it?"

Bliss transferred his full attention to Vanelleto, and a look of unadulterated loathing tore between the two men. The room writhed with it, a soul-deep hatred only a death could cure. "You keeping track of me?" Bliss hissed.

"Always," Vanelleto said.

His curt response seemed to make Bliss nervous. "If I were you, Vanelleto, I'd shut the fuck up." He jerked the gun. "I'm the one in charge now."

"I don't think so." Vanelleto ignored the gun, took a step toward him. "I think a half-million dollars is in charge. A half-million you'll never see if you fire that piece."

Bliss narrowed his gaze, his brutish mind distracted by his own greed, embroiled in murky reasoning and self-interest.

It was enough.

Addy shot to Cade's side. Bliss—alarmed—refocused; he swung the gun wildly in her direction. Cade enveloped her, spun her away, and dropped them both to the floor—giving his back to Bliss.

He fired.

In Cabin Seven, Stan and Susan shot to wakefulness.

"What was that?" Susan said, her hand flying to her chest.

Stan flicked on the bedside light, and already had his legs in his pants, when he said, "That was a gunshot." He grabbed his shirt. "And my guess is it came from up the office way."

Susan's eyes widened. "Oh, no. The girl." She threw the covers back, got out of bed, and made for the door.

"Susan, get back here. I'll see to it."

She turned on him. "Don't even think about that 'little woman' bit."

He sighed. "Damn! Better you with me than

running around on your own. Get your coat then, and put something on your feet," he instructed. "And *you* don't even think of barging in there until I take a look around. You hear me?"

His tone didn't leave room for argument, so she nodded. "I wish I hadn't given Cade my gun."

"Dear God, all we need is you roaring around with a pistol." He took her hand. "Come with me, then, and stay close."

The bullet tore along the back of Cade's shoulder, a white hot sear of pain that took his breath away. Only Addy's scream hurt him more.

He faded out . . .

He didn't see the knife that appeared like smoke in Vanelleto's hand, coming from somewhere at the back of his neck.

He didn't see its lethal edge pierce Bliss's muscled arm, cut through sinew to bone, as if it had been shot from a precision bow.

And he didn't see Bliss sink to his knees, or Vanelleto lean over him and slowly pull the blade out.

Addy slid out from under Cade, desperate to hear a moan, an intake of breath.

"Cade, Cade!" She moved her hands over him, weak with fear, barely able to see for the blood caking her eyelids. Terrified to touch him, terrified not to, she said his name again and again. His soft irritated moan was a gift. He was alive!

He rolled over, winced in pain. "You okay?" he asked.

"I'm okay." She touched his shoulder. "Can't say the same for you. God, he almost killed you."

"He's all right," Vanelleto interrupted, sounding irritated. "The bullet didn't hit anything major. Get some towels before the man ruins your carpet."

Addy helped Cade to his feet, her heart still thrumming from Bliss's attack, the bullet's near miss.

She ran to her bathroom, grabbed some towels, and quickly replaced her torn shirt.

Handing a towel to Cade, she did an inventory. Gus was right. Addy was no nurse, but from where she sat, the bullet—the bullet meant for her—had grazed his upper back and torn a two-inch strip of flesh from the top of his shoulder.

Thank God, he'd be okay.

Unfortunately, so would Bliss, the trash slumped against the sofa. Blood oozed from a wound in the soft flesh where arm joined shoulder. Too high to have hit an artery, but either shock or anger had dazed him to a state of semiconsciousness.

Cade slanted a gaze toward Gus, who was sliding the knife into a sheath hidden down the back of his shirt. "You didn't kill him," he said, seeming surprised.

His answer was a shrug.

Addy studied her friend, then slowly shook her head as understanding dawned. She spoke to Cade, but her eyes were on Gus. "He didn't kill him because Bliss is the only one who knows what really happened that night. It would be dumb to kill him. And Gus isn't dumb. Am I right?"

"Close enough."

Aching with relief, she walked over to Vanelleto and wrapped her arms around him. "I should have thought of that sooner. I'm sorry, Gus. Sorry to have dragged you into this mess. Me and my stupid plan."

She hugged him fiercely and, without relaxing a muscle into her embrace, he let her hold him a moment before he pushed her away and kissed her on the forehead. "Good to see you, Wart."

"You won't think so when I tell you—" She didn't know how to say it aloud, afraid the spoken word would make it real. "I think Bliss hurt Beauty, Gus." The words shot out of her, and she gave the bleeding man a look of pure loathing.

Gus went stone still. "Hurt? What do you mean 'hurt'? "

She couldn't tell him everything Bliss said. Even Gus's self-control had a breaking point. "He told me he pushed her off a cliff on the way here. And there's only one place it could be." She stopped. "He left her for dead, Gus. Like she was nothing."

"Show me," he ordered. "Now."

Addy looked at Cade, hesitated, unable to ignore the blood running down his arm, knew the pain he was in. "First we call a doctor," she said, trying not to think of all the questions a doctor would ask before calling the police. She headed for the phone.

"No." With his good arm, Cade pulled a gun from his pocket. "Forget the doctor. That'll mean I have to explain asshole over there"—he gestured with the gun at Bliss—"and use time we don't have."

"Get me some rope, twine, something," Vanelleto said to Addy.

"I've got fishing line, will that work?"

"You're dead meat, Vanelleto. Big mistake leaving me alive." Bliss spit on the carpet, grimaced. "You'll be watching your back the rest of your fuckin' life."

"Get the line, Wart, and some duct tape," Gus ordered, not bothering to acknowledge Bliss's threat.

While Vanelleto trussed up the now conscious and growingly belligerent Bliss and taped his mouth, Addy splashed cold water over her face in the kitchen sink. Her face would be one giant bruise for days, but at least she could open her eyes.

Cade handed her a towel. "On your way, stop at Cabin Seven," he said. "Tell Stan Brenton I sent you. You'll need another pair of hands, and he won't ask questions—"

"For now." Stan stepped into the room, followed by Susan. "We'll take your truck," he said. "Better suited. We'll need flashlights, some rope—"

"I've got rope," Addy said, staring at Stan, then Cade. "You know these people?" she asked, thoroughly confused.

Cade ignored her. "There's a couple of flashlights in the truck. If you need more, you'd better get them," he said. "And you'd better move fast."

Stan nodded. "And maybe some blankets." He turned to Susan. "See what you can do for Cade, love, then take a look at that one." He gestured at Bliss.

"How long have you been out there?" Cade asked.

"Long enough to get the hang of things, and avoid the bullets."

"Smart."

"Didn't live this long being stupid." Stan raised a brow.

"I don't understand." Addy looked at the tall man and the woman she'd thought was his wife, who was now fussing around Cade, the woman whose perfect hair was sleep-ragged and who was now wearing sneakers with no socks and a raincoat over her nightgown.

"Explanations can wait," Susan said, relieving Cade of the bloody towel he held to his shoulder with his gun hand. "Go," she insisted. "Find your friend."

After one last twist of the fishing line, making the duct-taped Bliss jerk and wince, Gus stood. "You're the grandmother," he stated, studying the woman, his eyes level and assessing.

Susan's head came up, and when their gazes met and held, a wariness curled between them— or instant dislike? Addy couldn't make sense of any of it.

Her curiosity and confusion didn't matter. What mattered, now that Cade was okay, was finding Beauty. "Gus, let's go."

A half hour later, Addy, Gus, and Stan were at the viewpoint. The rain was a sheet of frigid water, nonstop and blinding, as the three of them ran to the guardrail.

"Spread out," Gus ordered and moved out of her sight to her left. Stan stepped briskly in the opposite direction.

Time was not on their side.

Addy took the center, peered into the black hole below them. Her skin prickled with panic. It was like looking down a coal shaft.

"Beauty," she screamed, "can you hear me?"

My, God, even if we find you, how will we get to you? So black . . .

Still calling out, she moved closer to the edge of the steep gorge, or what she thought was the edge, too damn dark to be sure. She took another step, focused her light as best she could, then tested the stability ahead by pushing the toe of her sneaker into the tangle of growth framing the rim.

It was mud, thistle, and wild grass. The grass stalks, once tall and broad, had flattened under the relentless rain, creating a slippery slope to the cliff—and over.

As close as she could go now, she arced her light into the murk of the chasm below, and yelled until her lungs threatened to burst.

Nothing came back, not even the echo of her own voice.

"Beauty . . ." She heard the name being called from both sides of her, saw the flashlights fanning into the darkness beneath them. Useless, their arc too wide.

Dear God, it was hopeless. They didn't have a chance of finding her in this rain and blackness from this angle. They needed to see farther down, get the light on the side of the cliff.

She went down on her hands and knees. Then, flat on her stomach, inched closer to the lip of the gorge.

"Beauty!" she screamed, shining her light over

the cliff and sweeping its brush and thistle-laden side. "Beauty, answer me!"

Only the maddening rain and silence. Addy shifted farther along the rim. "Beaut—"

"Gus!" she shrieked. "I've found her. Over here!"

Both flashlights swung toward her, then moved fast in her direction, disembodied as if attached to invisible high-speed bikes.

Addy immediately swung her own light back into the abyss, trained it on her friend—her sister. Relief washed through her, and her heart, its ceaseless pound a constant since Bliss arrived, slowed a notch.

Beauty was maybe twenty, thirty feet down; she couldn't be sure. "We're here, Beauty," she yelled. "Hold on." She scanned the area around her with the light. It looked as though her fall had been stopped by a rock shelf and a coarse growth of salal. Her body lay precariously close to the edge, one hand hanging over, the other hidden in the bush, the position awkward . . . and as still as the rock she lay on.

Addy's heart started to pound again.

Gus slid along the mud and grass next to her, followed the beam of her light. "Jesus!"

Stan took one look and said, "We can't risk moving her. If she is alive, God knows what's broken."

Gus's hesitation was less than a second. "You're right. Call 911, and get me the rope. I'm going down there."

Addy didn't move, couldn't take her eyes off the deathly stillness that was her friend.

"Be alive, Beauty," she whispered. "Please, please be alive."

*   *   *

Grover slithered along the wall of the toolshed and tried the door.

Unlocked. Thank God.

He was cold and wet, his very bones frozen.

Inside, the shed smelled like wet grass and gasoline. It wasn't much warmer than outside, but it cut the wind, and he was out of the rain at last.

He shoved a lawn mower aside, found a toolbox to sit on, sighed and rested his head back on a shelf loaded with paint cans, brushes, and garden tools.

It had taken him close to an hour to trudge through the trees and underbrush to get to Star Lake. Other than sex with Linda, he hadn't had this much exercise in years. The thought of her, the life he planned for them, would have made him smile, if he weren't so cold and angry.

If his spirits weren't flagging.

Grover wanted to go home, to his own warm bed, but of course that was out of the question. Sandra would kill him for getting so dirty, being so late.

No. That was wrong. Sandra was dead. Sandra wasn't a threat. It was the others. The ones in that office/house on the hill. If only they'd all stayed there, in one place, this tiresome business would be over by now!

He'd heard the shot, saw the truck roar out of the driveway with Vanelleto at the wheel. And, from the instructions Vanelleto shouted to Addilene and Stan, he knew where they were going. To find Beauty.

Now they were all split apart, and that wasn't

supposed to happen. He wasn't sure what to do, and on some level it troubled him that Susan was up there. The thought of her made his stomach drop, ache painfully. She was his friend.

He didn't want to kill a friend.

He had so few . . .

But obviously Bliss, the stupid bungler, had failed to kill Vanelleto or the Wart. Now it was up to him—and there was no room for error.

When he spotted the moving blanket folded over the handle of the lawn mower, he pulled it over his cold, quaking shoulders. It was damp and stunk of motor oil, but he huddled into it gratefully. He patted the gun in his pocket, settled back.

There was nothing to do but wait for the right moment. When it came, he'd know it.

Chapter 25

Glock in hand, Cade prowled Addy's living room, wishing to hell the phone would ring or the door would open. He moved his shoulder. As far as bullet wounds went, his was a skimmer. Other than the piece of flesh torn off the top of his shoulder—which hurt like hell—it was more like a superficial burn. He looked at his watch: after 3 A.M.

Bliss, now duct-taped to silence, sat upright on the sofa. Earlier, Susan had raided Addy's medicine cabinet, found what she needed to patch him up—even given him a couple of Tylenols, which was more than the bastard deserved. He looked too goddamned comfortable to Cade, but he was also valuable, because behind that duct tape over his mouth lay the truth about what happened that night. And that truth would, he was sure, clear Addy of all charges connected to Belle Bliss's murder.

Now if the search party would come back with—

As if in direct response to his frustrated thoughts, the door opened, and Gus and Addy came in, both looking as if they'd spent the last hour in a mud-wrestling pit.

Vanelleto's expression was fierce, crazed. Without a word he walked over to Bliss, pulled him to his feet, and hammered a blow at his face, pulled his fist back to deliver the second in what Cade knew he intended to be a series.

"Gus!" Addy yelled, her face white. "Stop it!"

Cade pulled his arm from the sling Susan had insisted he wear, leaped across the room, and with his good arm, grabbed Vanelleto's shoulder and spun him around, which earned him the punch intended for Bliss. It landed hard on his jaw.

At that, Vanelleto pulled back, snarled, "Stay out of this, Harding."

"I'll stay out of it when you tell me what the hell is going on," he said, rubbing his jaw.

"That sick bastard deserves to die."

"Maybe so, but how about we leave that to the guys with badges."

"Yeah, right." Vanelleto sneered at him. "Like we did fifteen years ago." He looked at the now-moaning Bliss. "You're not getting away with this, Bliss. Count on it." He turned away suddenly. "I'm going to change. We need to get back to the hospital." With that, he walked out.

"You found her," Cade said to Addy, almost unrecognizable under the dirt and grime on her face, the puffiness and bruises below that. Bliss had done a hell of a job on her.

"We found her, but—" Addy started. "They took

her to St. Joseph's in Bellingham." She fell into silence.

"Are you all right?" Cade said, putting a hand on her shoulder and pulling her closer.

"Yes, I'm fine, but Beauty . . ." In a painfully soft whisper, she added, "She's barely alive, Cade. It was an awful fall. She's unconscious and the doctors don't know if—"

"Don't." He put a hand on her mouth. "From what you tell me, your friend is a born survivor. She'll make it, and the trauma center at St. Joseph's is state-of-the-art. She's in excellent hands."

She nodded, but not with much conviction. Cade heard the hitch in her breathing, sensed the effort she made to stay calm. "We're going back to the hospital as soon as we clean up a bit."

"And Stan?" Susan asked.

Addy turned to her, her expression now more studious than curious. "He stayed at the hospital. Gus and I wanted to, but he told us we'd best leave the first 'little chat' with the police in his hands.

"You saw how Gus is. Kind of . . . crazy. I've never seen him so out of control." She looked at Susan again, then at Cade. "She hired you, didn't she?" she asked him suddenly. "To look for the boy? You knew who I was all along." Before he could answer, she held up a hand, looked away from him, and shook her head. "No. I don't want to talk about it right now. Don't want to think about it. What it means." She rubbed her mud-caked forehead as if she had a headache, then said, "I'm going to shower. Gus will be back any second."

She walked out of the room.

Susan glanced up at Cade. "Trouble?"

His gaze resting on the door Addy had closed behind her, Cade said, "Hard to tell."

But he didn't have time to dwell on it before the outside door opened and Gus strode in—as dirty and disheveled as when he left moments ago, his austere face drawn in deep lines, all of them filled with frustrated rage.

A gun was jammed deep into his kidneys.

"What the hell?" Cade said, when a familiar face became visible behind Gus's tall wiry body.

"Wayne?" Susan said, her eyes wide in astonishment. "What are you doing here?"

Before Grover could reply, Bliss thumped his foot on the floor, and muffled sounds of demand funneled through his taped mouth. His eyes were set on Grover, angry and impatient.

Grover cast him a glance of pure loathing. "I'll get to you, Frank, don't you worry," he said. "Now, over there, all of you. We need to wait for Addilene." He shoved the gun harder in Gus's back. "You, too, Vanelleto."

When Gus's eyes met Cade's, both men gave the barest of nods, both smart enough to respect the status quo that the shiny Smith & Wesson imposed. The nod also relayed their intention to alter that status at the first opportunity.

Cade noted the gun was equipped with a silencer. Whatever Grover had in mind, it was lethal, and he intended to do it quietly.

They did what they were told and lined up against the wall separating Addy's bedroom from the living room. Cade, nearest the door, heard the shower running.

His insides boiled when he thought of Addy

coming through the door. Pulling Susan close to his side, he shielded her with his shoulder. On her other side, Gus did the same.

"Wayne, whatever are you doing?" Susan said, her tone crisp. "With that"—she pointed angrily at the gun—"that thing in your hand. What's this all about?"

For a moment, he looked chastened. "You're the only regret I have in all this, Susan. But when you told me you were coming here, who you'd found, you gave me no choice." He licked his lips. "I'm . . . sorry."

Cade had no fucking idea what he was talking about, but he got the message. This nut-job was apologizing in advance for murder.

Grover took a deep breath, appeared to straighten his shoulders, pull in his gut. He looked at Cade then. "Sorry about you, too, Harding, but you're a threat, you see. And I can't live with threat anymore. Can't allow anyone to hurt me anymore." He shook his head as if to clear it. "I'm in charge now. Only me. And I have plans. I killed my wife, you know. Tonight." A tiny smile curved his lips, slightly lush lips, moist from his licking of them, and his eyes were flat, too bright.

Bliss thumped his foot on the floor again, yelled through his sealed-off mouth. His face was red from the effort, and a vein bulged in his forehead.

Grover shifted the gun, and without bothering to aim, got off a shot in Bliss's direction. He immediately retrained the piece on Cade, Susan, and Gus. The shooting was so reflexive, so spontaneous, Grover himself looked surprised by it.

Susan screamed and covered her mouth.

Gus didn't blink.

Cade's eyes moved from Grover to Bliss.

Grover might not have aimed, but he hadn't missed; the bullet caught Bliss in the upper thigh. His tied-and-taped body jerked wildly. His muffled wail sounded like a horn coming through dense fog, before he fell back on the sofa, staring at Grover from a face now contorted by fear.

"Shut up, Frank, or I'll do it again," Grover threatened.

Gus gave Bliss and Grover a slow once-over, then said evenly, "I see you boys have kept in touch."

Grover, his pale eyes now black with rage, spit at Bliss. "If you call blackmail keeping in touch." He looked a little wild now, as if the shooting had juiced him up.

Cade knew his heart would be pounding, that his nervous system would be on overload—like his brain already was. And, damn it, there was virtually no chance Addy heard the muted burst of the shot over the shower that he heard still running on the other side of the wall. She'd walk into this mess any minute. Whatever the hell was going on in Grover's head, it was the worst kind of dangerous—volatile and unpredictable. Then there was Bliss. Cade tried to asses the damage from the gunshot. Blood oozed from the wound, but he looked okay—for now. But if he bled out, if the son-of-a-bitch died, any chance of clearing Addy went with him. He wasn't about to let that happen. He sidled cautiously toward the door.

"Blackmail, huh? Now that's damn funny," Gus said, casting a scant glance Bliss's way. "Although it's good to know you didn't get off too easy, Grover."

"Shut up!" Grover eyes darted to Susan.

Gus caught the glance. "Ah, I see. The grandmother doesn't know about you and Belle."

"I said shut up." Grover looked nervously at the door beside Cade, as if to will Addy through it. Get the killing done. "And you," he said to Cade, "stay where you are."

"What's he talking about, Wayne?" Susan demanded from beside him.

"He's talking about a social worker who was getting a little something on the side, by placing kids with Belle Bliss," Cade said, the pieces of that night dropping into usable slots.

Gus nodded, didn't take his frigid gaze from Grover. "A woman whose idea of child care was a locked room and an iron poker. A woman who let her son rape and assault girls, because she knew you'd never do a damn thing about it."

"No!" Grover shook his head, licked his lips again, looked like a rabbit on a string. "That's not true. Not one child ever got hurt. Belle was a good woman. I loved her. And I never left the kids long—"

"You left us long enough for that piece of shit over there to rape Beauty and nearly beat her to death. Long enough for that little boy to scream for hours in a house where no one cared whether he lived or died." Gus's jaw was rigid.

Grover looked confused, shook his head in a futile defense. "I only put kids with Belle temporarily until I could move them to . . . better homes," he said. "A few government checks, that was all. I would never hurt a child. Never put them in danger. Never! I've devoted my life to children—kids no one else cares about. It's all I ever wanted to do. If it weren't for me—"

Gus didn't move, but his voice seemed to, curling tight and hard around his next words. "If it weren't for you, Grover, three kids wouldn't have had to run for their goddamn lives. If it weren't for you, you yellow-bellied asshole, Belle Bliss would still be alive."

"I'm not listening to any more of your lies." He steadied the gun, the distress on his face morphing into determination.

"And if it weren't for you"—Gus gestured toward Susan who stood at his side—"this woman wouldn't have spent years looking for a boy—a goddamn baby, for Christ's sake—you put with a snake-mean women who didn't give a damn about him, a woman who ignored his screams for hours before you showed up and—"

Grover's eyes went wide. "No. No, that's not true, Susan. You mustn't believe him. I would never hurt Josh. Never. I love my kids. I take care of them." Now holding the gun in both hands, he aimed at Gus's chest. "Why are you telling all these lies?" His voice rose to shrill.

Cade maneuvered himself between the bedroom door and Grover, who, wild-eyed, toggled the gun uncertainly between him and Gus. "We can talk about this, Grover. Make things right." Cade saw the sheen of moisture on his lips, left by his perpetually licking tongue. He reached out a hand, palm up. "Give me the gun."

"Get back!"

"Stop now, Grover, and no one gets hurt."

"No. You'll hurt me. I know you will. And

there's Linda, you see." His eyes widened, seemed to whirl in his skull. Then it was as if some new idea had entered his brain and sucked up his fear and confusion—and any remorse. Cade could see him force himself to a calmer state.

"The gun, Grover. Give me the gun."

He raised the gun to Cade's face, and a slippery, amused smile filtered over his mouth. "I think I'll give you what's in the gun instead."

Addy burst through the door at his side, slamming it so hard against the wall it damn near came off its hinges.

As a distraction, it worked. Cade didn't waste it.

He dove for Grover's knees. He heard a shot whistle past his ear in the second before the bastard hit the floor, his back hitting it with a bone-cracking thud, his lungs expelling their air in a rough, noisy gush.

Vanelleto's sneaker-clad foot stomped on Grover's wrist, ground it into the carpet. "You won't be needing this anymore," he said, taking the gun from his hand and dangling it at his side. He sneered down at him. "You really are a pathetic bag of crap." When he took his foot off his arm, Grover curled into a ball.

Cade got to his feet, ignored the sear of pain across his shoulder. "Is everyone all right? No one hit?"

"Just my ceiling." Addy pointed a shaking hand up to where a crumble of plaster surrounded a dark hole.

He nodded at her, relief choking his chest.

"You always did come through, Wart," Gus said, shifting the gun into his other hand, then looking at Cade. "That was gutsy, Harding," he said, then handed him the gun. "Look after this garbage, would you?" He made for the door.

"Where are you going?" Addy called out.

His eyes were bleak and angry. "To Beauty. Where else?" At the door, he stared long and hard at Bliss and Grover. "I suspect these two, given the chance, will talk your head off." He stopped and seemed to consider his next words. "But because most of it will be lies, it'd be better if you save the wear and tear on your ears until I get back. That way, you'll get the whole story." He paused, and for a second looked weary. "And for what it's worth, the true story."

It crossed Cade's mind Vanelleto might take off; now that Bliss was immobilized there was no reason for him to stay.

The two men's gazes met and locked. And as if Vanelleto knew Cade's thoughts, he added. "I'll be back, Harding."

Cade studied him, nodded. "Make it quick."

Vanelleto nodded, then glanced at Susan, his expression impenetrable. "Better she hear what she has to hear from me than them."

When Vanelleto turned to go, Addy ran toward him and wrapped her arms around him. "I'm coming with you."

"No. You stay here with Harding. He needs a good pair of arms." He smoothed her shower-wet hair off her brow, kissed it. "I'll be back, Wart. I promise." He looked down at Grover, who was still curled in a fetal position at Cade's feet. "It's past time to put out the garbage." Looking again at Addy, he added almost formally, "Do you agree?"

His tone was serious, his look intense, and left no doubt Addy's answer mattered to him.

She didn't speak for a moment, then said, "Yes, Gus, I do. And I think Beauty would, too. And"— she stopped as if nervous about her next words— "we owe it . . . to that boy."

Cade heard Susan, now standing beside him, let out a noisy, nervous breath. "Yes, you do, because 'that boy' we're talking about is my only grandson, the only link I have to my daughter. And his name is Josh, damn it! Josh Moore," she added firmly, as if the name gave him substance and life—and credence to her claim.

Vanelleto ignored Susan's outburst, but his expression darkened. "I never wanted you to know, Wart . . ." His voice was flat, when he went on. "I made a mistake back then. Beauty and me."

"We all did, Gus. We shouldn't have left him. We shouldn't have run."

Vanelleto started to speak, seemed to think better of it. "I'll be back," he said, and with that terse promise, he went out the door.

Addy stared at the closed door for a long moment, then turned her battered face toward Cade. A cut over her eye seeped red. For the first time since he'd walked onto her property, she looked small and tired—as if she didn't have any spirit left to draw upon.

He wanted to pull her close, tell her everything would be okay, but that would mean soothing with wishes and lies, and there'd been too many of both already. The room heaved under them—and under the threat of what nightmares lurked in the truth promised by Vanelleto. Cade drew in a breath. For that, they had to wait, which made keeping her and Susan busy his only option.

"Would you do what you can for Bliss's leg?" he said to Susan.

She took a breath, pulled her gaze from the door, then rolled her eyes. "Aren't I the lucky one?" She left the room to get some fresh towels.

Cade looked at Addy, who continued to stare at him with a vacant expression. "How about your giving me a hand with Grover? Some more duct tape would help. It's on the counter by the fridge."

She blinked, then nodded. "I'll get it."

When they had the trembling, mumbling Grover secured and sitting in a chair opposite a murderously glaring Bliss, Addy touched his hand. "Is your arm okay?"

"Fine. But it might be a good idea to change the bandage." He unbuttoned his shirt, caught Susan's surprised look as she arrived back in the room—a look to remind him she'd changed it minutes before Addy got home. Thankfully, she said nothing, and got started cleaning and bandaging Bliss's leg the best she could.

Silently, Addy changed the dressing on Cade's wound. When she spoke it was softly, so Susan couldn't hear. "You lied to me." She didn't lift her eyes from her task. "I don't much like liars."

"I don't much like women wanted for murder either, but I'm in love with one."

She took her hands from his shoulder and sat back in the straight wooden chair she'd pulled up close to his so she could work on him. Her face somber, eyes the color of rain, she said, "You know what I think?"

He tilted his head, raised a brow, and waited.

"I think we should leave all this . . . love stuff until Gus comes back and says what needs to be said."

He shrugged into his shirt. "I think you're right."

So you'd better get the hell back here on the double, Vanelleto.

Beauty wondered when it got so dark, why there was so much weight on her eyes. She tried to force them open, but they resisted. And the sounds— she couldn't place them. Beeps, whirrs, and something like music seeped into her space from far away.

I'm falling! Falling, falling . . .

Panic grew, a thickness in her chest, rolling and heaving. She raised a hand to grab something, anything, but there was only air and fear. She couldn't breathe, couldn't see.

"Shush, easy now, baby." A strong hand gripped hers, and she clasped it. Hung on.

Dreams now. Old voices . . .

"Take it easy. You'll be okay."

Still too dark. *Not okay.* She wanted to tear open her eyes, see the voice, see who was lying to her. Couldn't. A hand on her hair now, smoothing it, tucking strands behind her ear.

A kiss on her forehead, light as down. Familiar.

It had to be . . .

She willed her eyes open. One of them offered a sliver of vision, and she looked into the dark eyes of the man she'd thought she'd never see again.

"Gus?" Saying his name took effort, left only enough strength to curl her hand in his. A hand she didn't intend on letting go. Ever.

"In the flesh." The barest of smiles lifted his lips, and he brought her hand to his mouth, kissed it, and said, "We were worried about you, Beauty." He stroked her forehead, toyed with her hair.

Her eyes drifted closed again, this time against the pain, coming first in slow-moving waves, then sharp, hard stabs through her back, her chest. She gasped, and the hand holding hers tightened its grip.

"You'll be okay in a minute or two. The nurse gave you something. Breathe for a bit. Try to relax."

She did what she was told. Gus was right. Gus was always right.

"Bliss?" she said, and the gnaw of panic rushed to join the pain.

"Taken care of."

She had to know. Had he done what she couldn't? "Did you . . ." She couldn't finish.

"He's alive."

God, what was wrong with her? She was actually relieved. "Addy?"

"Fine. You got the worst of it, baby."

"If it got you here"—she swallowed—"it's worth it."

He didn't answer that, and she turned her head to use what vision she had to look more closely at him. So dark and . . . beautiful. Her pain faded, its edge numbed by the drugs, and she managed a deeper breath.

"We need to talk," he said abruptly. "You up for it?"

She nodded. She'd talk forever if that's what he wanted, but her mind drifted, floated in a way she couldn't control. She had the urge to let it go, but she hung on. Gus was here; she couldn't go.

"First, you should know I never intended to kill Bliss. I intended to give him the money he wanted and make sure he never threatened either you or Addy again." He lapsed into silence.

"And?" She said the word and coughed. Pain roared through her battered body.

"Turns out there's more to it than that. Other lives to . . . think about." He stood suddenly and looked down at her. "We know we didn't kill Belle Bliss. It's past time everyone else did, too. That leaves a problem."

The loss of his hand in hers was like an amputation, the words he spoke, "other lives," chilled her heart. She ran her tongue over her lips to moisten them, but it was too dry for the job. Even in her drugged state, she knew the problem he was talking about. She'd had nightmares about it for years. "You mean"—she swallowed hard and the ache of it touched her lungs—"the . . . boy?"

He nodded. "There's something you don't know about that night, Beauty. Something I never told you—or Addy."

No!

She wanted to clap her hands over her ears, didn't want to hear her darkest fear made fact, but her arms were useless, her hands too burdensome to lift. "I killed him . . . didn't I? I killed that baby." Her words hit the air, terrible and slow, a spill of acid into fog. She looked at Gus, but his face blurred, and she couldn't get back her focus.

"My God, is that what you've been thinking all these years?"

"The pillow. I held it . . . too long?" she whispered, the words sick and ragged.

"No! You didn't hurt him. He was okay. I said I'd take care of him, and I did."

"I thought that meant"—tears trickled from the corner of her eyes and ran into her hair—"you'd . . . buried him."

"Jesus!"

"You went away. I never . . . heard from you." The last words came out slurred, halting, and she entered a slow drifting. Suddenly cold. Too cold.

Gus sat down, and again took her hand in his, holding it between both of his. "Beauty, listen to me. I loved you. I didn't want you or Addy involved more than you were already. I figured . . . hell, I don't know what I figured."

Loved you.

Her eyes closed. Dark blue behind them. Like a midnight sky. His hand on her forehead, stroking softly.

Her eyes so heavy now, limbs loose like rubber, breath like a steady wind. No dreams. No nightmare. No pillow.

Thank God, no pillow . . .

"The boy . . ." she said, the words coming in a new wash of pain, pushed from her raw throat by her desperate need to know. To be sure. "Tell me . . ."

"He's alive, Beauty. Alive. You did nothing wrong. Nothing. Do you hear me?" His hands gripped her arm and his voice was rough. Scared? No, Gus was never scared. "You hang on. You hear me? You hang on."

"Alive." She repeated.

Gus said something more in a low, urgent voice. Something about "making things right." She couldn't make sense of it, couldn't pull more words with her into her sea of calm. Only four.

Loved you . . .

He's alive . . .

She smiled with paper-dry lips and tightened her fingers around Gus's big hand.

Chapter 26

When Gus returned to Star Lake, night had begun its exit, and a gray light lay spread across the waters of Star Lake like a clean, ironed sheet. The rain, thank God, had finally stopped, leaving the lake willow sagging and the tall hemlock beside the office dripping sullenly on Addy's cedar shake roof.

Addy watched him walk toward her door, a coffee steaming in her hand as it did every morning when she took her first look at her lake. But this morning, her heart was a stone in her chest, and her head was so stuffed with questions and confusions that she couldn't think straight.

She met him at the door. "How is she?"

His whole face went mask tight. The room deadened to silence.

Cade pushed his chair back from the table and stood.

"Gus?" she pressed, "what is it?" After over an

hour in a room with a silent Cade and two men subdued by duct tape, she was desperate for news of Beauty. She'd called the hospital of course, but they doled out information as if each word were a security leak. "Did you talk to the doctor? What did he say?" She watched him take a deep breath.

"Where's Stan?" Susan asked, her face pale and nervous. "Why isn't he with you?"

Gus looked at both women, and to Addy's irritation chose to answer Susan's question first. "He's right behind me. Be here any second."

"Gus," Addy said, not caring where Stan was. "Tell me about Beauty."

"Beauty's dead, Addy."

Addy's throat closed, her stomach retracted, as if hit by a low, direct blow to its most vulnerable part. She clasped a hand over her mouth and closed her eyes. "Oh, my God."

Cade came to her side, put his arm around her shoulder.

"I can't believe . . . I thought she'd be okay," she said.

"More internal damage than they figured." Gus rubbed his face, his expression tired and stricken.

Addy left Cade's protective arm to embrace him. "Oh, Gus . . ."

He pulled away from her, ran a hand through his dark hair, and she saw him straighten, slant a lethal glance in the direction of Bliss. "And that makes this son-of-a-bitch a murderer."

Cade moved in front of Bliss.

Gus shook his head. "Don't worry, Harding, there's been enough killing for one night. I'm not going to touch that piece of shit—as long as he ends up where he fuckin' belongs. Behind a fence, for the rest of his life."

He looked at Grover then, walked to him, and ripped the tape from his mouth. "You want to start or should I?"

Grover, who'd clenched his eyes closed when the tape came off, opened them to Cade's calm, questioning gaze, and Gus's menacing one. He started to cry.

"Jesus!" Gus shook his head, turned his back on him, and nodded toward Addy's kitchen table. "Might as well sit down. This might take a while."

Cade again placed his hand on her shoulder. "Are you okay? Can you handle this?" he asked quietly.

She hadn't intended to, but she put her hand on his, held it a moment. Then she thought of Beauty . . . dead, of what Gus might say, and tears filled her eyes.

"Save the tears, Wart. We've got work to do—for Beauty." It was a Gus-style order, but gently said.

She nodded, brushed the moisture from her cheeks, but she couldn't stop her nerves from sparking like power lines in a storm, or her stomach from curling into itself. She wanted to run, escape this room and all the cruel secrets bearing down on it. The deadly truths.

Addy again touched Cade's hand. "I'll be fine."

Stan came in just as they'd all taken seats at the table.

"I miss anything?" he said to Gus, taking a stool at the kitchen counter.

Gus's response was a head shake, then he turned and glanced around the table. "Grover killed Belle," he said. "I know it and Bliss knows it."

Addy's eyes shot to his. "You saw him? Grover killing Belle?" She'd thought he and Beauty were in Belle's room trying to quiet the baby.

Gus nodded curtly, added, "I didn't tell you, because the way things went down, I didn't see the point. And before you ask, no, Beauty didn't see anything. She was taking care of the boy."

When it looked as though Susan would speak, Stan shook his head.

"That's not the way Bliss tells it," Cade said, his policeman eyes fixed on Gus like those beams from a movie spaceship.

"No shit." Gus said, heavy with scorn.

"Right now I don't care who killed Belle Bliss or why. I want to know what happened to my grandson," Susan demanded, "or I'll call the police right now."

Gus shot her an ominous look, dark and frustrated.

Cade touched her hand, squeezed it. "We need the whole story, Susan." He paused. "There are two people in this room wanted for a murder they say they didn't commit, another lying dead in the hospital. We need to know everything, for their sakes—and to find out about Josh."

"I don't—" she started.

"Please." Cade said in that soft way he had.

"Cade's right, Susie. Be patient," Stan said. He got up from his stool and stood behind her, his hands on her shoulders.

It took a moment, but Susan finally nodded, then turned her frowning attention back to Gus. "Get on with it then."

Gus looked back at Cade. "You know most of it,

I think, from Addy. Grover brought the baby sometime in the afternoon. Belle put him in her bedroom, which was at the bottom of the stairs, just off
the living room. He was screaming when she put
him in there and he never stopped. Addy here"—
he glanced her way—"wanted to go down there.
Do something to help. I told her not to. It was too
dangerous. They were drinking, Belle and her
boys, and when they got into the booze, anything
could happen."

Addy interrupted. "And Gus was bleeding all
over the place from where Belle hit him with the
poker."

Susan looked at the scar on Gus's face. "Why did
she do that?"

"She didn't like what he did to Frank."

Susan frowned again.

Addy stared at her, wanting her to understand,
but knew she didn't get it. How could she? She'd
never lived in a cesspool, never been forced to witness things from the downside up. She'd have to
say it again, flat out. "You know Frank raped Beauty,
but he did more than that . . . awful things. He kept
her in that shed for hours, raped her over and
over again, then beat her something terrible." She
paused, looked toward Gus. "When Gus found out,
he went after him. Did some beating of his own.
Belle caught him—with a poker in her hand."

Susan's face paled. "I see."

Gus went on. "Because of Beauty, Addy, all of it,
I wanted to take off that night." He stopped.
"Lousy plan with lousy timing.

"Addy patched us up, and I went down to see if I
could figure a way to get out of the house without

being seen. My plan was to get the car keys, whatever cash was lying around and get the hell out of there full throttle." His glance swept the table of rapt listeners, and he shrugged. "I never said I was an angel." After a pause he added, "Beauty followed me down. When we got to the bottom of the stairs, we had to duck into Belle's room—where the boy was—to avoid Frank, who was heading to the back door about the same time. He took the damn car, went to get more booze, which meant Beauty and I were in for a wait. Anyway, when the boy—"

"Josh—for God's sake call him by his name," Susan demanded, looking as though she was about to either cry or explode. Addy's heart scrunched, knowing how painful this must be for her.

"Josh," Gus corrected, his voice surprisingly soft. "When . . . Josh saw us, he screamed louder. Put his arms up, the way kids do. Beauty picked him up, tried to calm him down the best she could. She said he was hot, maybe sick, and nothing she did made him stop howling." An odd smile played across his mouth, then it tightened again. "I was checking the door, had opened it a crack to see what was going on in the living room. That's when Grover arrived."

Addy saw Grover straighten in his chair, try to wipe the tears off his cheeks with his shoulder. He was utterly silent, totally focused on Gus. Bliss shook his head wildly from side to side.

Cade got up, walked over to Bliss, and tore the duct tape off his mouth. "You have something to say?" he asked.

"Fucking lies. Every word. Vanelleto killed my mother. I saw him do it."

"Either you shut the fuck up, Bliss, or I do it for you," Gus said, his voice icy, a muscle ticking fast and rhythmically in his jaw.

He turned his attention back to the group sitting at the table. "Grover started screaming about Belle being 'unfaithful' to him, about Frank talking to his wife, ruining his career. Went on about all the money he sent her way. How he'd trusted her. Next thing, he was whining about how much he loved her, how he'd thought she loved him—real Romeo and Juliet stuff. Belle was sloppy drunk, and when Belle drank, she got vicious. She hit him square in the face with her fist, shoved her face in his, and laughed at him."

"She laughed." Grover echoed from the corner, his words barely a whisper, tears again streaming down his face.

"Shut up, you dumb fuck!" Bliss spit at Grover.

This time Gus ignored him. "I guess that cackle of hers did the trick, because Grover pulled out a gun and shot her in the face—more than once, as I recall." He shrugged. "Had to be dead before she hit the floor."

"And then?" Cade said.

"He stood over her for a while—looked like he was in some kind of trance—then he dropped the gun and took off like a bat out of hell. I heard his car spit gravel on the window."

"He dropped the gun," Cade repeated, then frowned and looked at Stan. The two men exchanged glances, but neither spoke.

Gus nodded. "I knew we had to get out of there fast. I told Beauty to go, but she wouldn't leave"— he hesitated again, looked at Susan—"your grandson. I put the kid on Belle's bed and practically threw Beauty out the bedroom window, told her to run, wait for Addy and me behind the shed."

Susan stared at him, her eyes full of hope and fear. Stan continued to knead her shoulders.

Addy wished someone would knead her brain, make some shape of it. She'd been so certain it was Bliss who killed Belle. But Grover? A killer? It had never occurred to her. And the truth was, despite his sorry ethics and fixation on Belle, he'd always been decent enough to her. She remembered them talking about her mom one day, him telling her she'd have to work extra hard to make a life because she had no one to help her. And he always told Beauty how "pretty" she was, that he'd see her in the movies one day. Addy swallowed, forced her attention back to the present.

Cade, quiet as a tomb, watched Gus with intense interest as if he were recording every word spoken, every change in tone.

Addy leaned forward, put her elbows on the table and her hands together so they wouldn't shake. "I guess that's about the time I showed up. I heard the shots and ran downstairs and saw Belle. Gus pulled me into the bedroom. Beauty was gone, and Gus . . ." She glanced at Gus, half-smiled. "He threw me out the window, too. I met Beauty at the shed, and we waited for him, but he never came." Feeling numb, she rubbed her sore face gingerly and stopped talking for a few seconds. It was as if her brain lacked the energy to form more words. When she found some, she went on. "I knew we had to get away from there, but Beauty wouldn't leave without Gus. I told her to put a note on the shed, that he'd find us. All we had was some tissue, so she used that." She took some breaths. "Then we ran."

"What did the note say?" Cade asked.

"Two words. Star Lake." She looked at Gus.

"I never saw the note," he said, "because I never went to the shed. I intended to, but . . ."

Silence settled like lead into the tension-filled room. "What did you do, Vanelleto?" Cade asked.

"Truth? I didn't know what the hell to do. I knew I couldn't leave the kid, so I grabbed a blanket and wrapped him up. Had some dim idea about dropping him off at a hospital or something. I was heading out when"—he gestured to Bliss on the sofa—"that piece of slime showed up. He looked at me, looked at Belle, and came at me. I was holding the kid, but that didn't stop him. He tackled me, and both Josh and I went down hard." Again he looked at Susan. "The boy wasn't hurt, other than a small cut over the eye. I took care of Bliss, and I was gone. End of story."

"You hit me with a fuckin' wine bottle!" Bliss shouted. "You killed my ma and you damn near killed me."

Addy saw the effort it took for Gus to ignore him, but he did, forming his mouth into a tight, narrow seam.

"You went out through the kitchen," Stan said. "Not the living room."

Gus frowned, as if he couldn't remember, then, "Yeah, that's right, I did. I got some stuff from the fridge."

"What stuff?" Cade asked.

Gus looked away, and for a few seconds stared

out the window. Addy was sure he wasn't admiring the scenery; he was delaying. Finally, he turned back. "Milk. Whatever I could find for . . . Josh."

Everyone in the room looked at him, their expressions ranging from shock to confusion. Except for Cade's. He looked as if everything had clicked into place.

Addy, her own breath pooling in her lungs, knew the silence in the room was as close to one of those pregnant pauses as she'd ever come. She couldn't stand it. "Where is he?" she asked. "Where did you leave him?"

Gus looked away, hesitated.

Susan stared at him with frigid intensity, looking as if she could make him finish his story by the sheer force of her will—or she was frozen in fear of what he was about to say.

"I didn't leave him anywhere. I planned to, but . . ." Gus shrugged, looked suddenly weary. "I didn't. Couldn't."

He centered his gaze on Susan. "I call him Sam. He's a great kid. Graduated high school a year early, top of his class, and he's a hell of a baseball player."

"You took my grandson and you . . . kept him? Raised him?" If he'd told Susan he'd fed him to a pack of wolves, she couldn't have looked more stunned.

Gus nodded. "Took some doing in the first few years, until I got settled. But we made out all right."

"And he thinks you're what? His father?" Susan asked.

"Brother. It didn't feel right doing the dad thing."

He reached into his back pocket, pulled out his wallet, and extracted a school photograph. He handed it to Susan.

After studying the photo with greedy eyes, Susan slumped back, overwhelmed. "My God!"

Cade took the picture, looked at it, then passed it to Addy. The smiling teenager in the photo was as dark as Gus, but with blue rather than brown eyes, and a more open face, Addy thought. A happier face.

Cade said, "He looks like his mother."

Susan nodded and started to cry. "I always believed he was alive, but knowing . . ." She gripped Stan's hands, still on her shoulders, and he leaned down to kiss her head.

Cade walked a couple of steps away. "This might seem like the wrong time, but you mentioned a gun, Vanelleto. You said Grover dropped it. The police never found a weapon."

Gus shot Bliss a deadly look. "It was there when I left, along with a note I put beside it. Brief and to the point. 'Check gun. Grover did it.' Obviously that didn't suit Bliss as well as naming me—and the girls—as murderers and keeping Grover around to blackmail." He looked at Bliss's sneering face. "That about cover it?"

"Your story, Vanelleto, not mine."

Gus got up, walked across the room to where Bliss sat bound at the edge of the sofa, and stood over him. A flick of his wrist placed a thin, wicked-looking knife in his hand.

"Gus!" Addy yelled. "Don't."

Gus juggled the knife between his hands, smiled. "Don't worry, Wart. I'm not going to kill him, just mark up his pretty face until the bastard tells the truth." He touched the tip of the knife to Bliss's cheek, close to his ear. "Let's see . . . if I cut here, we'll have matching scars." He turned his head so Bliss could clearly see the streak of misshapen flesh that ran from his ear to his jawline. He shifted the knife to the side of Bliss's nose. "Then again, a nice straight cut starting about here would add character, make you real attractive to the ladies." A trickle of blood ran from the tip of the knife to Bliss's lower lip.

Addy could see his chest heave in horror and loathing.

"You son of a bitch," he sputtered, his eyes fear-wide.

Another trickle of blood, this one thicker.

Addy's heart was in her mouth.

"The gun, Bliss," Gus demanded. "What did you do with the gun?" The knife continued to draw drops of blood.

Addy saw the blade twist slightly, felt Cade, now standing beside her, tense.

Frozen in terror, Bliss looked up and into the implacable black eyes of Gus Vanelleto. "I kept it." Another twist. "It's in a safety deposit box."

Gus raised a questioning brow.

"Seattle First . . . near Pike," Bliss finished when Gus shifted the blade to under his left eye. "The note, too."

The knife disappeared as swiftly as it had appeared, and Gus shot a glance at Cade. "He's all yours," he said, and headed for the door.

Susan's voice rang out. "You're not going anywhere, young man. You and I have some talking to do."

The man who seconds before had threatened to slice a man's face in two parts halted abruptly. He turned back to Susan, studied her a moment. "You're just like him, you know." He paused. "Except I think he's got a better sense of humor." He took another step toward the door, stopped and waited. "Come on then. You want to talk, we'll talk. But we'll have to make it fast. I'm going back to the hospital." He paused, drew in a breath. "See to things." Before Addy could say anything, he raised his palm toward her and shook his head. "There's nothing you can do, Wart. I'll take care of her. You can see her when . . . she's beautiful again. That's how she'd like it." Then he gave Cade a level gaze, and without looking, jerked his head back to indicate Bliss. "You'll take care of him?"

"Count on it. And, Vanelleto?"

"Yeah?"

"I have Beauty's mother's address. She'll want to know."

Gus nodded, raised an impatient brow in Susan's direction, and said, "Coming?"

Susan opened her mouth, closed it again, then set it into a stubborn line and followed him outside.

Stan rubbed his temple. "Now that ought to be an interesting conversation."

"They both care about Josh," Cade said. "They'll work it out."

Addy watched them go, and for a moment closed her eyes. She thought there should be some kind of euphoria, a lightness where the weight of guilt and fear had lain so heavy for so many years. But Beauty's dying didn't allow for lightness. Instead, she felt as if her insides were all knotted and frayed.

She wanted to cry, but there were no tears.

She wanted to laugh, but her throat wouldn't let laughter through.

She looked at Cade.

She wanted to love, but her heart was too riled and hurting.

Cade, his warm glance sliding over her as if it had nowhere else to go, said nothing and went directly to the phone. He called the police; she heard him say they'd need paramedics. When he hung up from that call, he phoned some lawyer he knew and began the process of mopping up fifteen years' worth of fear and lies.

He was doing his job, she thought, the job that brought him to Star Lake in the first place. The job that included sugaring her up so he could dig around in her secrets to find Susan Moore's grandson.

She put a hand on her stomach and rubbed at the logjam of wounded, oddly resentful feelings there—for no logical reason she could think of. Because, damn it, she'd have done exactly what Cade did if it were her family, but somehow being the "doee" instead of the "doer" made it all seriously confusing.

And the love thing. When exactly did that sneak into the situation? Did it come in with the Chinese food, when they were all over each other in bed, when she ogled him in his running gear tearing up the path around her lake, or when he was sitting in the back of a rowboat reading to her? If she had more experience in such things, she'd know.

She felt like a plucked daisy after a bad count, he loves me, he loves me not, he loves me . . .

Cade spoke quietly into the phone, nodded, then reached for a pen. He bent over her patched-together desk, jotted something on one of her pads, focused on whatever was being said by the other person on the line. She liked that about him, the way he listened, the way his eyes seemed to soak up her words as if they were honey, the way they looked when he made love, as if she were the center of his universe.

She liked a lot of things about Cade. The only thing that bothered her was his timing—and maybe his reasons for looking at her the way he did, saying the things he did.

Her stomach tensed.

Maybe he'd got carried away doing his job, maybe he'd have all kinds of regrets about . . . everything.

She touched the lines forming across her forehead, and made up her mind.

She needed quiet time, and she needed to talk to someone who'd understand, and she knew exactly where to find both. At the door, she put on her yellow rain jacket.

Thanks to Gus, Cade's truck was right outside, keys in the ignition. Should she? Her hesitation was brief, then gone totally in the seconds it took for Redge to rouse himself from his sleep on the porch, come up beside her, and lick her hand.

She opened the driver's side door and looked at the friendly dog. "Get in, Redgie boy, there's someone I want you to meet."

With Redge sitting alertly beside her, she glanced

across the calm waters of Star Lake, revved the Cherokee, and headed to Seattle.

Cade found her four hours later, sitting on damp grass, running a hand over Redge's soft fur.

The rain had started again. This time it was light, misty, and joined by gentle gusts of wind that made it swirl and dance over her cool face. Kisses from heaven.

"Why'd you run away?" he asked.

Redge deserted her immediately and went to say hello.

She looked up at Cade, surprised he was here, and even more surprised to see he was angry. She couldn't remember seeing him angry before, at least not with her, and because she couldn't answer his question, she asked one of her own. "How did you find me?"

"Not hard. You've only been in two places in the last fifteen years, Star Lake and here." He waved a hand around the deserted graveyard.

"Ah, yes, the brilliant ex-cop, the *el supremo* profiler. I should have guessed." Redge, having paid his respects, came back to lie beside her, and she went back to stroking his back and staring at her mother's headstone. "I guess my next question is why? You've done your job, you don't need me anymore." She cursed herself for sounding like a needy, pouty little girl looking for assurances.

"You don't believe that and you know it."

"Not sure what I believe. That's the problem."

"Then don't believe anything—for now." He paused. "You're a free woman, Addilene Wartenski. You can go where you want, do what you want, and choose who the hell you want to do it with." He focused those intense eyes of his on her until her bones, cold from the autumn-damp grass, began to thaw and heat like freshly torched kindling.

She stood to face him, met him as eye-to-eye as their differing heights allowed. "The trouble is, whatever it is I want to do, I want to do it with you, Cade Harding. And I don't know how I feel about that, because you're a person of . . . false pretenses. You pretended to be someone you weren't and you suckered me." Which, of course, was the least of the problems between her and Cade, because there was something else that rankled her a whole lot more.

He thought a moment, then touched her cheek. "Let's go back a bit, shall we? When I drove into Star Lake Resort that day, I sure as hell didn't expect to find Addilene Wartenski—and I did not arrive with some nefarious plot to seduce you. I was looking for a lead, any lead, to Susan's grandson."

He took a step away. "But to be honest, I wouldn't have done anything different." He paused and his eyes, always so keen and sharply intelligent, softened, took on the grayness of the mist swirling around them. "Then it was all about finding Josh, Addy—a boy who'd been missing for fifteen years. It wasn't about us." He came back to her, took her face in his hands, and lifted it until their gazes met. "Now? It's all about us—if you want it to be. And we can take it fast or slow. Your call."

Her heart tumbled around in her chest like a

bunch of play-crazed puppies on spiked milk. And for a woman who'd lived in the shadows for over half her life, looking over her shoulder, and planning her days around a wheelbarrow and a dozen needy cabins on a lake, the possibilities in the word "us" were too many to process. She didn't know what to say, and she sure as hell didn't plan on blurting out, "But I can't even read."

Cade's eyebrows shot up, and he went as still as one of the headstones in the graveyard. "You think I care about that? You think I'd love you less for that?"

"I may not be able to read, but I'm not stupid. You've spent a thousand years getting educated. Teaching other people. You're a professor! You'd end up . . . ashamed of me." She stopped. "I couldn't stand that. I wouldn't stand that!" She shook her head to punctuate.

He took her by the shoulders, tipped his head to look deep into her eyes. "Addy, I love you and everything you are. When I look at you, what you've done, I'm so proud of you it goddamn hurts."

There went her heart again, thumping and banging in her chest. She wrapped her arms around his waist and muttered into his shoulder, "Well, you'd better stay proud, then, because I'm thinking I'll take you up on that 'us' thing you're so set on."

He kissed her then, and soft hearts and melting bones were forgotten in the wonder of it. "Thank God," he whispered finally, his breath hot against her forehead.

She pulled back, took a breath for courage, and said flat out, "I love you, Cade. And I owe you."

He frowned.

"You've given me back my life." And she'd never forget that. Nor would she forget the tears she'd cried when she'd arrived at her mother's grave hours before, first tears of grief for Beauty, what might have been, then tears of relief, of gratitude for what now might be.

She wasn't sure how to put it into words, but she knew she had to try. "Today was the first time I've sat on the grass beside my mother's grave. Before, I was always too afraid I'd be seen. Thank you for that. And thank you for coming after me." She smiled then.

He kissed her again and smiled back. "You're welcome. And as for my coming after you? I didn't have a choice. You stole my dog."

Epilogue

Three months later

Susan went to the window. By Cade's count, it was at least the fifteenth time in as many minutes.

"Relax, Susan. He'll get here when he gets here," he said. "You know the traffic on I-5."

Addy came in with a tray of sandwiches, the tower that was Stan a few steps behind. "Is he here yet?" Addy asked, her eyes wide with curiosity.

Addy had a lot of curiosity—and dedication, as Cade had discovered in the past three months. She was already reading at high school level, and she'd surprised him yesterday by telling him she'd signed up for some online courses and had Toby helping her on the side. When he'd told her not to be so impatient, she'd calmly advised him that her "learning" was taking up too much of his writing time, and she planned to speed things up so she could start taking college courses next year.

Cade got up from the chair he was sitting in and took the tray from her. "No," he said, "he's not here yet. Now will everyone relax? You sound like a bunch of kids in the back of a van heading to Disneyland."

"I second that," Stan said, adding, "Susie, sit down, you're giving me an ulcer. You've waited this long to see him, you can be patient another ten minutes."

She sat, but didn't look happy about it. "I'm not patient. And if it weren't for that Gus person insisting he send Josh to me—in his own good time, I might add—I'd already have seen him ten times over. Now the boy has to find his way here alone. What if he gets lost?"

"He's seventeen," Cade reminded her gently. "He can make telephone calls and hail a cab."

Susan wasn't to be placated. "And that Gus fellow," she went on. "Arrogant, that's what he is. With far too many secrets if you ask me. In the private security business, he says. Humph! He might be smart enough for that, but he doesn't seem to have grasped the fact that he kidnapped my grandson."

"He did not kidnap him!" Addy rose to Gus's defense, as Cade knew she would. "First off, Gus didn't know Josh had family, Susan. He thought he was . . . like him. That he was alone, had no one. All he wanted to do was take care of him, like he did Beauty and me."

"He should have—" Susan started.

"Leave the should-haves, love. Let it go," Stan said firmly. "Or, at the very least, reserve judgment until you meet Josh. From all reports, Vanelleto did a hell of a job raising him. If, after you meet the boy, you think otherwise, you can have the man hanged, drawn, and quartered. But the way I read it, Vanelleto and the boy are tight. Family. You mess with that and you risk alienating that boy, maybe never seeing him again, no matter what the law says."

She glared at him, unable to argue, but every bit the petulant have-everything-her-way woman Cade had come to love and respect. She might be mad as hell, deeply regretful she'd missed seeing her grandson grow up, but Cade had no doubt her every instinct was to do right by him, even if it cost her.

"I hear a car," Addy said and jumped to her feet. In four steps, she was at the window. "It's him. He's here, Susan. He's here! In a limo!"

The reality of Josh's arrival froze Susan where she sat.

The doorbell rang, and when she still didn't move, Cade walked over, took her arm, and led her to the door.

On the second ring, she opened it, and the smile that bloomed in her eyes rivaled a summer sunrise.

The boy, wearing jeans and sporting a blue backpack, was thin and nearly as tall as Cade. He stood nervously looking down at the white-haired woman in front of him.

When she didn't speak, he coughed and awkwardly stuck out his hand.

"Grandmother? I'm . . . Josh."

About the Author

E.C. Sheedy is the author of ten works of romantic fiction and two business books on organization and entrepreneurship. She lives and works in an oceanfront community just a short ferry ride from the beautiful port cities of Vancouver, BC and Seattle, Washington. Both a past winner and finalist in the Coeur du Bois, Heart of Romance Reader's Choice Award, critics call her work fast paced, gripping, and intense.

Readers can visit E.C. Sheedy at her website: *www.ecsheedy.com.*